AFTER LIFE

MICHELE BAUMANN

After Life

This is a work of fiction. Names, characters, businesses, events, incidents and towns are the products of the author's imagination. Any resemblance to actual persons, living, dead or undead, or actual events is purely coincidental.

All rights reserved. No part of this publication may be reproduced, distributed, or transmitted in any form or by any means, including photocopying, recording, or other electronic or mechanical methods, without the prior written permission of the publisher, except in the case of brief quotations embodied in critical reviews and certain other noncommercial uses permitted by copyright law.

Copyright © 2021 Michele Baumann

All rights reserved.

ISBN: 978-1-7373233-1-0

For Debbie,

*the best #1 fan a writer could ask for.
Thanks for always being honest and loving my characters maybe even more than I do (if that's possible)*

PROLOGUE

1391
Deanna Cullen

The bucket was heavy as Deanna Cullen pulled it from the stream filled with cool water. It was her fourth trip to refill the bath basin, and each time she could feel the bubbles rising in the bucket as she carried it. The heat of the day was getting to her, and she took to dragging the wooden bucket in the dirt rather than carrying it.

It was getting easier the more trips she made. A deep groove was scarring the muddy ground from the creek to the house. Sweat poured down her blood-stained face. If she waited any longer, her sweat would wash away most of the offensive blood that covered her body.

She wondered almost casually what was in store for her. What was to be her punishment? It couldn't be any worse than what had been done to Devin. But somehow Deanna knew that it would be. There was a promise of getting even, consequences for their actions. So many words and threats had been thrown around that she couldn't even remember what was said. She could only remember Devin and the blood.

Deanna Cullen was a twenty-three-year-old widow with no children. Her mousy brown hair hung lifeless even in the best of times but now more so than any other day. Since the day she was born, her hair had a damp appearance that made it difficult to style in anything other than a tight bun, giving her the perfect old spinster air even if she was nowhere close to being old or a spinster.

She felt relief as she poured the water into the already half-full basin. She ran her hand through the cool water and splashed it over her face and sticky blood-soaked hair. Several large bubbles floated to the surface of the basin as she ran her hand through the water like there was a natural spring in the bathtub. She splashed them away, hoping it would put an end to the phenomenon; she knew it would not, hearing her mother's voice in her head: *The water is emotion. Flow with it. Flow into it. The Great Mother will direct you.*

Deanna scoffed at the thought. Flowing with her emotions is what got her into this mess, and where was the Great Mother when Devin was dying? She blew out a burst of breath and shook off her anger. Even as she walked away, she could see the bubbles simmering on the surface of the bathwater.

One more trip should do it, she thought. Pouring a handful of water over her face again, she tried to block out the constant screaming that echoed in her head. It was Devin's cries that she couldn't shake. Every time the knife plunged through his chest, a guttural cry escaped him that she knew was involuntary.

And when it was done, when Devin was grasping to his last precious breaths, Deanna fell to her knees beside him. She held his head, crying as the blood filled his lungs and leaked from the corners of his mouth. His breaths sounded like walking through the marsh lands: labored and sodden. "Please, God," she pleaded, "don't take him like this." Tears poured out of her large hazel eyes, and Devin's blood covered her face as she bent to kiss him one last time.

"Crying won't save you." Jacenta's voice was unforgiving and emotionally detached as she bent close to Deanna's ear and whispered. Deanna refused to look her in the eye but instead kept her head bent as she continued. "You've sowed in the fields of the flesh and so you shall reap your just rewards." She could see the knife dangling in her thin hand as it still dripped with Devin's blood. Deanna was sure she saw it tremble ever so slightly.

"Have you even thought about what this will do to your children?" she asked, feeling the first trickle of rain as it fell from the sky.

"They will know that their father is dead and not about the filthy whore he was with."

"What of their murderous mother? Will you tell them this fairy tale at bedtime tonight?" Deanna was getting angry. Her hazel eyes were completely green, a phenomenon that had been with her since birth. With strong emotion came the green eyes and then the rain, and now it was coming down harder. She tried to shield Devin's face and whispered, "I'm sorry. I can't stop it."

He groaned, and she wasn't sure if he was feeling the rain or losing consciousness.

A sharp pain pierced Deanna's shoulder as she sat bent and weeping on the ground. Reaching blindly for her shoulder, not wanting to miss the moment Devin breathed his last breath, her hand was covered in blood when she looked at it.

"You won't be able to do it." Even in her distress, she found the strength to taunt her former best friend. "Not on your own. You are too weak and always have been."

There was no answer, nor had Deanna expected there to be. If Jacenta was anything, it was calculating. Fighting with Deanna was not part of her plan. Her plan was to curse her adulterous husband's dying soul. Fighting would only confuse her into making a mistake.

Devin wheezed, trying to grasp air as it escaped the gaping wound in his chest. Deanna felt his hand touch her arm and slip away gently. He was gone. "No, no, no, no. Please, God, no!" She rocked him, holding his head. Jacenta dropped the knife beside Devin's dead body and walked away without a word. Deanna watched her go through water-filled eyes, feeling pain and anger with every step she took away from her.

Now as the water filled the bucket for the fifth and final time, she felt the heartache in her chest as it burned. She didn't think it was possible to feel your heart breaking, but it was. Not breaking but collapsing, deflating, disintegrating. Deanna's hurt was burning a hole in her chest, an empty cavity beneath her ribs where love used to be only hours ago.

She pushed the bucket aside and ran her hand through the cool water of the stream. The bubbles started again this time, causing the current in the swelling stream. She ignored it, thinking of the times her husband, Sean, dead almost five years, would throw her into the stream. It wasn't deep but deep enough for her to submerge. She would act angry and he would laugh. They would laugh together. Looking around her meager home, the land and barn, Deanna was happy Sean had not lived to see what she had become.

The gash on her shoulder stung as she reached into the water. It wasn't deep. Deep enough to bleed. That was all she needed. *My blood and his blood.* She reached into her pocket and pulled out a tiny glass bottle filled with red liquid. *Devin's blood.* Deanna watched as the liquid flowed back and forth in the bottle. It was hypnotizing as it languidly sloshed. Whatever Jacenta had in store for Devin, Deanna was prepared. His blood was needed to break any curse she could throw at him.

Blood for blood.

The bucket sat beside her, waiting to be dragged to the waiting basin. No, she decided. She wouldn't wash off Devin's blood, wouldn't wash away the pain or the guilt. Jacenta was right. She had caused it all. She had chosen the behavior and now she would choose the consequence. Fantasizing about death as the water bubbled angrily, Deanna wanted to see Sean again and her parents. Heaven.

She pulled herself to her knees and dug a small hole beside the riverbed. The red liquid in the glass bottle sloshed around as she dropped it into the shallow grave and pushed dirt over the hole, closing it.

The clouds were darkening again as she got to her feet and stepped gingerly but deliberately into the cold running water of the river. The rocks were hard and painful on her bare feet. The icy water was numbing as it flowed around her calves. The current was strong and threatened numerous times to pull her off her feet. Almost did. It was just beginning to rain again as she walked into the deepest part of the water, and she forced herself to her knees. As it rushed past her, she fought to keep her head above the waterline.

The water was to her clavicle, lapping at her face as it splashed around her. Her thoughts were oddly on Jacenta and her fatherless children as she forced her arms out and allowed the current to take her. As her lungs filled with water and her exhausted muscles fought the rising waters for the final time, Deanna felt calm.

1907
Elizabeth Andrews-Staton

Cleaning was her least favorite thing to do in the restaurant. The scrubbing of the floors and the windows, banging out the rugs, wiping down every shelf and then carefully replacing each bottle and glass exactly where it had originally been. Elizabeth Staton wiped her brow with her hand, leaving a long gray smudge of ash on her forehead. Removing cigar and cigarette ash from every flat surface was what infuriated her, daily.

The tables were unusually difficult this morning. The buildup of wax. The tables were holding on to the dirt like it needed it to stay together. Elizabeth dumped her brush into the bucket of sudsy water and scrubbed harder.

A commotion was erupting in the upstairs rooms. She ignored it. A door slammed and a young girl's scream. "Stop! Let me in!" A boy's laughter. Running. "Duggas! I wanna play too."

Elizabeth Staton laughed to herself. *Duggas.* Alice never could pronounce his name – especially when she was upset.

"He said I could play too." Alice's voice sounded both distressed and demanding. *Good for you,* Elizabeth thought, *fight those boys.* That daughter of hers was a spitfire and Elizabeth loved every bit of her.

Another door slammed and the running continued. She wasn't sure the second floor could take the six of them living there for another moment. The rooms above the restaurant had been for rent only a week ago but now were being used to house her own family. She, her husband, and four children had taken up residence above Lizzy's Restaurant and Hotel since their house had burned only one week ago today.

Elizabeth didn't want to think about the fire. The heat, the screaming, the seemingly endless searching when they couldn't find Alice. She could still hear the windows as they blew out with the flames. All her books, clothes, pictures, all her memories – gone. Why did it bother her so much? She'd lost countless memories over the last five hundred years – but this was different.

She brushed a tear from her cheek. "Stop fussing now and bring those sheets down here," she yelled. Her voice was crisp and clear with no trace of an accent. "I need to get them in the wash before the dinner service."

There was a quiet *yes ma'am* heard from upstairs and Elizabeth continued to scrub. Her dark, almost black, brown hair, kept up in a messy bun with pins, was falling in her small piercing hazel eyes. She pushed it back for the umpteenth time, wishing she had tied it back with a rag.

"Kitchen is swept, ma'am, and everything is prepped for dinner tonight. We are low on the fish so the special will need to be changed. Unless you want to keep it as the special, but it won't last long. Get it while it's hot kind of special." A young man dressed in a white jacket over a white shirt and white pants stood before her. His double-breasted chef's jacket was open, showing a stained white shirt beneath it. His face was hard, but his eyes were kind with a wisp of curly blond hair held in place with grease. The tension in his jaw assured her that he was not a man to be trifled with, and she appreciated it.

"Whatever you think, I'm sure will be fine, Joseph. Just let Helen know what you decide so there's no confusion." Joseph was a new hire that Elizabeth had felt very strongly about. He was right out of culinary school but had learned most of what he knew from his grandfather who had owned a restaurant in Italy. He was good with the children and patient with the bizarre occurrences around the restaurant.

He reminded Elizabeth of herself. He had learned most of what he knew from hard work and determination. Unlike their last chef who was schooled in complaining and trying to dominate the restaurant. Working for a woman was not what he was accustomed to, so when hiring Joseph, Elizabeth made it clear who was the mistress of the establishment.

A small girl carefully stepped down the stairs with a load of sheets in her arms.

"Thank you, baby."

Alice smiled. Her cheeks still flushed from running and yelling. Keeping up with her brothers was no easy task, but she did it admirably well.

Joseph walked to her and grabbed the washing. "Too big of a bundle for such a little one. Where are your brothers?"

"Hiding. They are playing hide and go seek." The five-year-old smiled a big grin, showing that two of her teeth were missing.

"They are *all* hiding? Who's seeking?" Elizabeth wiped her hands on her damp apron and placed her scrub brush into her bucket for its final wash. A few bubbles circled the brush in the bucket.

"Devin."

Elizabeth nodded and wiped down the table with a towel.

"Devin? Who is that? One of their friends?" Joseph laughed.

"Alice, go upstairs and tell your brothers to stop their foolishness and start cleaning their room," Elizabeth demanded before the little girl could explain who she was talking about. Alice just nodded and walked back upstairs without another word.

"I'll take those, Joseph." Elizabeth held her arms out for the sheets. "Just update the board when you decide about the specials." She pointed to the chalk board above the bar.

"Yes, ma'am." The look in his eyes told her that he noticed her apprehension at the mention of the name, Devin. He was just too polite to mention it. She had seen that look in his eyes before and wondered just how long he could keep his feelings to himself.

"Devin, leave the boys alone. They have chores to do." She thought deeply and focused on the rooms directly above her head. It took only a moment for an answer to come.

"Are you jealous that they can sense me, Mouse?"

"Don't call me that. And jealous of what? They've been doing it for years."

Elizabeth hated this form of communication. Especially now when she wanted to scream at Devin and strangle his non-existent neck. He had burned down her house last week. Her father's house. The house where she had grown up. Gone. Burnt to cinders before her eyes. She was thankful that they had gotten the children out in time. Thankful that Alice was found.

She was found after an interminable thirty minutes of searching and calling her name. Elizabeth was frantic with fear threatening to go back in the house to find her. It took Bryon and two of their sons to hold her down. It was not until her youngest son, BJ, came running from the back of the house that their fears were allayed. "She's by the apple tree, Mama. She's with Devin by the apple tree."

There Alice sat talking with Devin. Her face smudged with black smoke, streaked with dried tears. Her dark blonde curls drooped with the weight of the fire's heat and the morning's dampness. To anyone else, she was talking to herself, but Elizabeth knew that Devin was hovering nearby, whispering so only Alice could hear. The child ran to Elizabeth when she saw her, fresh tears moistening her face. "I was in my room and Devin got me out. He helped me off the roof." She pointed to the house, now completely engulfed in flames, and cried.

This was all part of Devin's little game.

Devin loved to play games. It had been going on for far too long. Almost six hundred years by her count, and the games were getting old. Who did he think was the winner this time? Not Elizabeth; she was seething with anger. Surely, he didn't believe he had won? The mere mention of Devin's name or the sound of his voice in Elizabeth's head infuriated her.

How was that a victory?

The damnable curse that they were entrenched in together since 1391 had kept her alive by reincarnating her countless times since her first death as Deanna Cullen and had kept Devin tethered to her side – a disembodied spirit that she neither could get rid of nor control. She was tired of his games and was ready for it all to end.

But still he played them. His favorite being this:

First, pick a fight. It was a doozy this time. He had been gone for over two weeks and Elizabeth had merely questioned it when he returned. The children missed him. In truth, she sometimes missed him. Was it so bad to question his disappearances? Why the secrecy? These departures weren't as frequent now that he had the children to occupy his time, but in the past when she was a different person with a different name, living a different life, he would disappear for month-long stretches. Returning as if nothing had ever happened. As if no time had passed.

Second, retaliate when Elizabeth refuses to speak to him. Usually the retaliation would come in the form of throwing furniture or slamming doors except this time, it got out of hand. Perhaps out of his control.

Third, apologize with an act of contrition. Save Alice. Or would he have done that anyway? Devin would never hurt the children. In a fit of anger, she had doubts about her own safety and Bryon's (of course, her husband was never safe) but never the children's safety.

The game's final play would belong to Elizabeth.

This had to end soon. She couldn't continue to expose her children or even her husband to Devin's frenzied outbursts. Her husband, Bryon, had been patient for the past ten years. He had endured furniture moving, pictures falling off the walls, even disruptions when making love to his wife. But lately Devin was getting dangerous. He had burned Bryon's arm when he thought he was going to slap Elizabeth. And most recently in a fit of rage, Devin burned down their home with them in it.

Bryon knew what Devin was from the start but only began believing it after the children were born. In the beginning of their marriage, the disturbances were easily explained away. Earthquake, storms, creaky floorboards, uneven foundations, anything other than a supernatural being. After their oldest sons, Douglas and Charles, were born, it became evident that the children were responding to something other than their own imaginations.

They would talk, giggle, and even play with Devin.

Elizabeth had explained what Devin was – a cursed spirit that followed her around. A spirit that she could not rid herself of even after death. Her connection, however, was something from which she had spared Bryon. Her connection as a person just as cursed as Devin but in an entirely different way. He would never understand how she could possibly be in her seventh or eighth lifetime. Frankly, she couldn't quite remember how long it had been. Devin remembered it all. He never forgot over the years.

Devin remembered each time she was born and watched her die. He remembered each time she was reborn into another person. In her heart, she would always be Deanna Cullen, the young Irish girl who betrayed her best friend and paid an awful price. It didn't hurt that her best friend had a terrible temper and proclivity for revenge and a fleeting interest in witchcraft.

Grabbing her bucket bubbling profusely now that her temper was flaring up, Elizabeth walked toward the kitchen with the sheets on her hip. Without touching it, the door swung easily away from her as she passed through it. *"Thank you."* The slop sink was in the darkest part of the basement, and each old creaky step screamed as she placed her foot on it. She placed the sheets in the basin of the washer and dumped the filthy water into the sink. She stood there watching as it circled into the drain. If she concentrated, she could make it swirl the opposite way, but she would have to really concentrate and with Devin hovering, she knew that wouldn't be possible.

"Do it. I know you love to play when no one is watching."

"Go away, Devin. I don't . . . just go away."

She could feel his pain as he hung over her. It felt as if he had his large hands around her shoulders, pressing into her flesh. She could almost hear him breathing deeply into the back of her neck. Fighting the urge to cry, Elizabeth pulled away from his unseen embrace.

"Joseph said you were down here." Her husband, Bryon Staton, came bounding down the stairs. "Helen sent word that she will be late tonight. Some kind of family thing. I don't know. But you better be ready to serve tonight." He kissed her cheek. The bristle of his beard scraped her cheek as he pulled away.

His dark blond hair was drooping onto his forehead, and he looked a bit flush. The stains on his shirt told her he had been working in the kitchen. His beard and mustache were speckled with frost, and she was sure he had been filling the bins with ice for tonight's dinner service. The reddish-brown hairs on his face were mussed and unkempt, reminding Elizabeth of the rugged sexy man she married ten years ago. "I need a bath. Care to join me?" He grabbed her behind playfully.

She pushed him away and tried to brush a tear away before Bryon noticed. She was not quick enough. "Are you crying?"

She shook her head but didn't look at her husband. "I'm fine."

"Liz, you're not fine. Need I ask what's going on?" He wrapped his arms around her as she turned towards him. Bryon was a big man, standing over her petite five-foot frame by over a foot. His arms were muscular as they encompassed her.

"I can't take it anymore. I don't want to live in those rooms for another second. We're losing money by not renting them. I want my home back." Tears poured from her eyes and she pressed her face into his massive chest.

"Is he here?" he whispered, afraid someone upstairs might hear or perhaps trying to pretend that Devin himself could not hear.

She nodded with her face still pressed against him. "Always."

She felt Bryon's lips against her head and his arms wrapping tightly, if not desperately, around her. He was just as much afraid of Devin as he hated him. How could you fight something you couldn't see? The tighter Bryon hugged her, the more aware she was of Devin. He was surrounding them without touching and she wondered if Bryon could feel him too.

"Momma, is Devin with you?" Their youngest son, Bryon Jr., was at the top of the basement stairs. "We need to finish our game."

"Devin?" Alice was there too. She sang his name.

"Is he there?" Charles.

"He's with Mom now. We'll play without him." Ah, Douglas. Even at ten, he took after his father with his calm and empathetic thinking. Elizabeth could hear the disappointed comments and whining, mostly from BJ and Alice.

An audible shudder came from Elizabeth and she felt one from Bryon's chest as well. She didn't know why her children could hear Devin when no one else could. Somewhere deep inside, she knew it was because of their connection to her that they could hear him. *Blood of my blood.* Wasn't that part of the spell that started it all? Something about the blood. Elizabeth could never remember it. Too many years of trying to forget and now she just couldn't remember.

She felt the press from Devin once more and then he moved away. Probably to follow the children upstairs. She waited a moment, listening to her children's footsteps as they tapped lightly on the hardwood floor in the restaurant. Then she heard Alice's laughter and the pounding of the children's feet as they bounded up the stairs to their temporary rooms. Devin was with them. She knew it in Alice's giggle and the excited patter of their shoe leather on the stairs.

"He's upstairs." She breathed deeply. "Did you find anything out today?"

Bryon gave her one last squeeze before walking past her into the deepest part of the basement. "They can do it. The structure is already here so they would just need to reinforce the walls and the door." He patted the wall at the far end of the cellar. "Keeping him in there will be the problem."

Elizabeth nodded. "I have an idea, but I don't know if we should attempt it. If it doesn't work, we will be in serious trouble."

Bryon bowed his head slightly in agreement.

"It requires you to be open-minded and I'm not sure you can do that." She walked to him and smiled. "Witchcraft is the only thing that will keep him in there. And I think I met someone who can help us." She lied, not wishing to have the awkward *I'm a witch* conversation at that moment.

Her husband breathed deeply and fought not to roll his eyes in frustration. "Fighting the unbelievable with the impossible. What could possibly go wrong?"

"Open-minded." She listened again to make sure Devin was still entertaining her children. Quickly, she allowed herself to remember how Devin played with his own children. Four. Aidan, Caelin, Liam, and Brina. He was so proud of those children. *Four, just like her. Three boys and a girl.* She had never thought about it, but her children mirrored his children. Especially Alice, who was a picture of Brina. Right down to the curly hair and dimples.

Elizabeth shook the thoughts from her head. She could feel the jealousy creeping up into her chest and burning a hole where her heart should be.

"He can't know what's going on; so, clear your mind whenever you think he's around you. The work down here can be easily explained as extra storage space. We'll have to lie to the children until it's done. Alice *will* tell him. It'll be for the best."

Months passed as the construction on the basement progressed. There were questions from the patrons, from the staff, and from the children. Extra storage space. That was the answer to all who asked.

"Remember I told you I had met a woman that may be able to help us?" she said to Bryon one night. The construction on the basement room was almost finished, and time was running out to find a way to keep Devin securely within the walls of that room. "Her name is Juno or at least that's what she calls herself," she whispered. This time it wasn't a lie. She'd met a woman named Juno in a dive downtown but instead of enlisting her help, Elizabeth was using her to rekindle her own magic.

The water magic never seemed to disappear over the years. She knew, because it was part of her soul, that she was an elemental witch, as was her mother (just a different element – her mother had a way with making things grow), but the spells and energy connections had to be relearned . . . quickly. Juno may have been a charlatan, but she possessed books and crystals that Elizabeth was able to use.

It was nearing midnight as she and Bryon lay in bed together. The new house was not far from Lizzy's Restaurant and Hotel. It wasn't home yet, and Elizabeth still felt uncomfortable with her surroundings. The sunlight was wrong in the morning; the house faced east, and the sun was distracting in the morning. Better to have the sun in the back of the house in the morning; it warmed the kitchen. And her view of the lake was gone. There was no lake in town. No lake, no expansive views of the mountains, no rolling grassy hills that reminded her of Ireland. They didn't sell her family's land and could visit as often as she liked, but it wasn't the same as waking up to that view.

She thought of what her mother would have thought of the new house. The thought caught her off guard. Elizabeth hadn't thought of her mother in years, not since Alice was born. She had secretly wished her mother could see her beautiful baby girl. As quickly as she had thought of it, she pushed the thoughts to the back of her mind. Why would her mother care about anything in her life? She abandoned her children.

Now Elizabeth could hear Alice giggling in her room; Devin was distracted for the time being. She knew she should tell her daughter to go to sleep, but this may be her only opportunity to tell Bryon of her plan.

"She is helping me with a barrier spell." Elizabeth wasn't specific with this Juno person. She wasn't sure what to tell her. In the end, she made up a story about her family being plagued by strange occurrences. "It should contain him. Apparently, we will need to write the spell on the walls of the room before getting Devin in there. When he's in, the spell should keep him there."

"For how long?" Bryon looked worried.

"Until it's broken—I guess."

"How do we get him in there?"

"I've been thinking about that too. The only one he completely trusts is Alice. We may need to use her. Not that I want to, but I'm afraid that it may be necessary. She'll be in no danger. He would never harm Alice. He loves her." She smiled sadly.

"Still sure you want to do this?"

Bryon, ever the supportive husband. Bless his heart.

Elizabeth thought of her family's house, now cinders. All her memories, diaries, and family heirlooms were lost because of Devin. Yes, she was sure. She was never so sure of anything in her entire life. Without another word, she pushed back the covers and went to Alice's room. She was the only child with her own room. The boys shared a room down the hall. It was the largest room in the house and in any other family it would have served as the master bedroom.

Alice's room was the perfect little girl's room. Ruffles, lace, and a large window with a window seat that overlooked the back yard. The yard, although not large, did have a treehouse that Bryon had built for the boys. Alice would sit in the window and watch the boys play. Always seemingly content, Elizabeth was sure Devin entertained her when her brothers would not.

He was doing it now. Alice's giggling was secretive, and Elizabeth could hear whispering as well. "Tell me again. Please," Alice was saying.

"Baby, time to go to sleep. No more stories tonight," Elizabeth whispered.

"Oh, please. Devin was telling me about when you were a little girl," the child whined.

"Another time. It's late." She tucked the blankets in tight around her daughter. "Besides, I've told you about Grandma and

Grandpa Andrews hundreds of times. Grandma Gail went on a grand adventure when I was just about BJ's age." *Grand adventure, child abandonment. Same thing.*

"This is different. He said you rode a horse and lived in a castle. You weren't a princess. He said you were a . . . scull - scullery maid. Is that right, Devin? Did I say it right?"

"Perfectly, Angel." His voice was so soothing, like a warm hug. That was the voice he always used when Elizabeth was a child. How she remembered his voice from years ago. Now Alice was being lulled to sleep by that same voice, that warm hug wrapping around her as she fell into her own dreamland.

"You know these are just stories, right? Fairy tales like Cinderella and Rapunzel."

Alice smiled so sweetly. Her big blue eyes twinkled in the moonlight from the window.

"Now straight to sleep. I love you, baby. Goodnight." After the door was closed, Elizabeth felt for Devin. *"Stop telling those stories. It will confuse her,"* she said silently.

"She loves them, Mouse. Loves to hear how her Mam grew up."

"I never lived in a castle."

"I may have embellished for her. But you were the daughter of a maid and then a maid yourself. You cannot deny that. Besides, she's too young to wonder why you were in so many places with so many stories. She just loves the adventure. As do the boys, but they are outgrowing my bedtime stories."

"Just stop. We have enough to deal with, without you filling their heads with nonsense."

"It's not nonsense. It's our history. Your history. You must never forget, or we'll lose everything. She'll have won."

Elizabeth stopped short of opening her bedroom door. *She'll have won.* That phrase stole the breath from her lungs. Jacenta. That damn game again. *"Are you still thinking of this as a win or lose situation? Win or lose, my children are not pawns in your game. Stop trying to win this war with Jacenta through my children. We've lost the war. Get used to it."*

"She won the moment I walked into that water and I was reincarnated for the first time. She won when you drew your final breath. She's already won the whole kit and caboodle, darling. She should be very proud of herself as she watches us from her special place in Hell."

She heard Devin snicker slightly. *"Special place in Hell,"* he repeated. It was a phrase his wife, Jacenta, used frequently when meaning to damn someone that had wronged her.

Elizabeth bid him a good night and slipped into her bedroom, closing the door behind her. "We need to do this soon," she murmured into Bryon's ear as she kissed him goodnight. As she wrapped her arms around him, she could hear Alice's voice again – soft and secretive. Devin never listened.

The next week, structurally the room was finally completed, and all the parts of the spell were coming together. The spell, in Latin, was written across the walls and the doors. For extra protection, the Lord's Prayer was also written, although Elizabeth knew that would do no good. Devin was not a malevolent spirit nor was he religious, but Bryon had insisted.

Bryon had sprinkled sea salt on the floor with dried rose petals. Juno had told her that would confine Devin to the room long enough to get out and close the door. The plan was in place. Alice would lure him in with a game of hide and seek. She enjoyed going in the room anyway, so allowing her access was not unusual. Once he was trapped, they would get her out and close the door.

"The sooner they are out of our lives, the better," Bryon said as he sprinkled the salt on the floor of the room.

"They?" Elizabeth was washing the table linens and listening for Devin. He had not materialized in days and she was getting worried that when it came time to lock him up, he would not play along.

"Him and that crackpot you got us involved with. I think she will be more difficult to get rid of than him." He closed the door as he finished. "You know this is not going to work, right?"

"Yes, it will. Trust me, I know a thing or two about spells." She hung the linens from a rope strung across the basement and fastened them with wooden pins. "I stopped listening to that crackpot when she told me to reinforce the spell, we'd need some gems."

"Gems? Like we have a diamond mine? Let me guess, she wanted rubies and emeralds."

"Onyx. She called them protection stones. It's ridiculous, I know. She was probably thinking she could con the rubes and take us for all we're worth." She laughed. "Don't worry, I've learned everything I need to know. You won't see Madam Juno around here anymore."

Pinning the last napkin to the rope and pulling it taut, Elizabeth thought of the onyx protection stones. She knew where to get onyx if she really needed it. Her sister's cameo had a black onyx background, but she couldn't take that. The last and only family heirloom that Devin had not destroyed. The cameo was a gift from their mother and a symbol of the gifted girl child in their bloodline.

Elizabeth remembered seeing it around her mother's neck. She was only seven when her mother disappeared, or rather when she had abandoned her children. She could still remember the night her father died. Elizabeth sat on her mother's lap as she cried. Her mother's hair was loose around her shoulders. It was rarely free from the bun she wore; but on this fateful night, she had not bothered to pin it up. She was so beautiful, and she smelled of flowers. Drawing in a breath, Elizabeth loved the florid scent.

Losing her father was especially hard on Elizabeth. *Daddy's little girl.* As she nuzzled closer to her mother, they cried together. She saw the cameo as it hung between her mother's breasts. A striking white female torso surrounded in black. Elizabeth touched it gently with her small fingers. Her mother had smiled and said, "This will one day be Isabella's because she has the gift."

The gift. In her family, the gift was telepathy. A talent passed down to the women in the family. Her mother had it, her mother before her, and of course, her sister Isabella was the gifted one. She was heir to the cameo and all their mother's love and attention. Neither had bothered to notice that Elizabeth had a protective spirit that was always with her, and her brother Bartholomew was also somewhat clairvoyant. It had eventually driven him insane. He was now locked away in an institution mumbling to himself – cursing the thoughts and voices in his head.

Elizabeth smiled to herself. Her children had inherited some form of *the gift*, hadn't they? Otherwise, how could they hear Devin? *Blood of my blood*. She made a mental note to speak to them about it, if only to save them from Bart's unfortunate fate.

Days passed with no sign of Devin. "We should be happy, right?" she said to Bryon as she counted the money box behind the bar. The restaurant was full. She had scolded the children several times for running in the dining room, but she wanted them close by. If Devin was going to show his face tonight, it would be to the children first.

"Maybe he got wind of what we're trying and left . . . for good." Bryon sounded hopeful as he whispered, leaning across the bar. "Are you sure you want to do this tonight? I don't want to force you into something that you are not ready for."

"If not tonight, then when? You have endured more than any man should. I am fine and completely committed to this plan. Now let me go check on the children before Joseph kills them." She laughed and pushed the swinging door with her hip, money box in hand. "Where are the children?" Elizabeth asked Joseph.

"Downstairs. Keep them out of here. We're too busy tonight." Chef Joseph was short and harried.

"Sorry." She really was sorry; she just had no intention of keeping the children out of her sight. There was a light coming from the open basement door and Elizabeth could hear the children talking. Before her foot hit the first step, she heard "Devin, come play with me." Alice spoke the fateful words.

Feeling slightly lightheaded, Elizabeth grasped the door to steady herself.
    She turned to call for Bryon. This was it.

CHAPTER ONE

"Is there anything else I can bring you, ma'am?" *Please say no; I'd like to go on my break.*

Gail smiled, looking up to the young, almost pre-pubescent waitress above her tinted glasses. She shook her head demurely and placed her gloved hands around the hot cup of coffee that steamed before her. "Nothing, thank you," she said, smiling again, reading the girl's thoughts. *You may go on your break now.* Not that the waitress could hear her, but she thought it anyway. The young girl had short blonde hair that was tied up in a half-bun, half-ponytail that bobbed as she hurried away behind the counter and through the swinging door to the back room.

Gail Andrews, seated in the far corner of the café, was dressed comfortably in jeans and a lacy white sweater under a black silk jacket. Her amber tinted glasses hid the slight iridescence in her gray eyes, but her long black hair didn't do much to disguise the pallor of her skin. She listened to the conversations from the people around her. Not their spoken conversations but their inner thoughts and feelings regarding their surroundings. She enjoyed being around people. Her gift of telepathy passed down from her mother and many generations of women in her family became vibrant in a setting such as she had surrounded herself with tonight.

The dates, the friendships, the laughter. She enjoyed feeling that she was still a part of the human community. In truth, it had been over one hundred and thirty years since she was human in any sense of the word. Her human life had ended while vacationing years ago in England. Her temporary escape from her human problems became a permanent escape from them. She was what Hollywood would call a vampire. She preferred immortal. Vampire seemed so unimaginative.

This café was her favorite place in recent weeks. She was seated where she could see the front door; comings and goings of the patrons was important to her. She could see the busy coffee and pastry counter, the flustered cashier barking orders to the baristas making drinks and plating pastries. The cashier was cursing in his mind, thoughts only he and Gail could hear. *Get it fucking right this time! How many god damn times do I have to say iced! Go back to your fucking desk, Bob! Move your fat ass, Bob.* Gail laughed. Bob was obviously the morbidly obese white shirted bumbling man standing between the cashier and other baristas. He stood at least five inches taller than the angry cashier beside him and a foot wider. His name tag read: *Robert Collins Assistant Manager.*

This place wasn't a Starbucks and for that Gail was thankful. She couldn't get into this coffee generation. The need to fill your body with thirty ounces of caffeine hourly was confounding to her. *Sips and Sweets;* a horrible name, Gail thought. There were no pretentious sizing charts; venti, Grande, Trenta. Just small, medium, large and for the practicing insomniac, extra-large. She liked it here. The counter was long and black with a glass case filled with cupcakes, scones, doughnuts, and six different kinds of Danish. The lights in the glass case were too bright, and the grease-stained doilies beneath each pastry should have been changed hours ago but Gail liked what they were going for.

The cozy hometown bakery-slash-coffee shop. Breakfast was most certainly their busy time but looking around now at just after ten in the p.m., they weren't suffering on business with the dessert crowd either. Just down the street the small multiplex theatre still showed old, dated films for the nostalgic movie-goer. Some art films from the local college students were screened there as well. It was clear that most of the café patrons had come for a post-movie nightcap.

She could hear names like Scorsese and Coppola. From the looks of the crowd it was probably a documentary on filmmaking. The couple next to the door, Gail enjoyed watching. They were on a first date from what she could surmise. They both looked to be of college age, early twenties, dressed nice but not dressy. "The Godfather was his best film," the young man said, keeping his opinions on Scorsese to himself because it was obvious that his date loved his work and he had hopes of getting laid. "I had no idea he directed Alice Doesn't Live Here Anymore," his date said with thoughts of *Jaws* and *Taxi Driver* filling her head. She was stirring her tea slowly, humming the notes from *Close Encounter of the Third Kind*'s ending sequence. Gail knew there was going to be no sex in his future tonight if he didn't start loving Martin Scorsese and fast. She laughed to herself.

The décor in the shop was dated. The signs that hung above the counter were handwritten. She had once thought this town was too small for a Starbucks but walking to the café from her car, she had seen a sign in an abandoned shop window reading: Coming Soon. Under the words, the now famous green circle with enigmatic mermaid creature ensured that the town would become another cog in the ever-growing coffee fad that was devouring the nation, and *Sips and Sweets* would be a distant memory in a few years.

This town, though small, had served her well over the years. She raised a family ten miles from the point where Main Street and Maple bisected; the land she called Mount Orion. She lost her husband to a sudden heart attack in Mercy Hospital five miles from the town lines. And almost one hundred and thirty years ago, she had taken the coward's road and run away from her home and family when it all had gotten too difficult to handle. Then it was this town and that land that she had returned to years later as an immortal, hoping to settle in the place she loved best.

"How could you even say that? Scorsese, DePalma, even Lucas have produced better movies."

Gail looked up to her favorite couple again just in time to see the young college girl grabbing her purse and walking towards the door. *Nope, no sex for you tonight, my friend. Should have kept your mouth shut.* She laughed.

She swept the room with her eyes watching the many patrons as they came and went. Through her amber tinted glasses, it all looked very sepia and like an old, faded photograph. Some took a seat and shared stories of their day. Some just took their paper cups and sugary pastries and left.

The cup before her offered comfort and warmth for her cold hands, and that was all. It would offer her no nourishment or fulfillment with its caffeinated goodness. She raised her cup to her face and inhaled deeply. She could understand the attraction; she remembered coffee. Just not the need for it; that's what perplexed her the most. But the coffee houses were wonderful. Gail sat back and absorbed what little atmosphere there was to absorb. She pulled off her gloves and threw them on the table. Now wrapping her hands around the warm coffee mug felt like heaven. The warmth permeated her cool fingertips and crawled up her arms into her chest. It was like she was enveloped in a woolen blanket, soft and warm. Pure heaven.

"Courtesy of the gentleman." The blonde waitress appeared beside her with a plate containing a strawberry Danish with whipped topping and a strawberry drizzle. Gail looked up to her and the girl met her eyes, raising the corner of her lip in disgust. *Sorry,* she heard from the girl's mind.

Gail's eyes found the man that sent the pastry. It was easy. He was the only man that was devouring her with his eyes. A man probably in his mid-forties, a sport jacket hiding a paunch that Gail read as recently divorced and a man-bun. Her mind immediately flew to an image of a samurai and she suppressed a giggle. *Do you even know what you're in for, mister?* she thought. The idea to read his thoughts crossed her mind but it was obvious what he had on his mind. Just as the man-bun pulled out his chair, the door to Sips and Sweets opened and Jordan entered. *Oh, thank heavens,* she thought.

Jordan. He was dressed in black pants with an avocado-colored sweater. He drew a few stares from the patrons as he breezed to the rear of the café; if he sensed them, he gave no indication of it. His blond hair hung loose to his shoulders. Her thoughts returned to the first time she saw him as they always did when Jordan entered the room.

His hair was loose as it was now, and she assumed that's why she loved it in that fashion. He stood over her, waiting for her to comprehend her surroundings and her fate. The fear was something that he would remind her of later and something she never really truly remembered on her own. The only emotion she could clearly remember was attraction. The magnetizing pull she felt in her chest as she looked at him one hundred and thirty years ago. Later she would learn that pull was his immortality that was drawing her to him. Something in his being attracting her and allowing him to dominate her mind and body. It was a vampiric attribute that helped when hunting humans.

There was still a pull she felt when she looked at him. Not as intense but still present. She associated this pull with her love for him rather than her inherent need to be near him.

Behind Jordan, the door swung open again and Eric entered, almost knocking man-bun back into his seat. Eric, the polar opposite of Jordan, was generous, funny, and caring. He was dressed in a button-down metal gray silk shirt and jeans. He raised his hand to Gail as he entered and smiled. That smile is what sat man-bun down for good, dashing any hopes he may have had of a romantic encounter. Anyone else would recognize that smile as an *I love you* smile. But Gail saw it as so much more. He was quickly becoming one of her best friends. She kissed Jordan as he fell into the chair beside her and she hugged Eric, playfully running her hands through his dark brown hair as he took the seat opposite her at the small bistro table.

"Hungry?" Jordan pushed the plate with the strawberry Danish farther away from him.

"I have an admirer. But I think you two blew it for me." She laughed and gently motioned to man-bun with her head and eyes. A giggle rose in her throat as she noticed someone was missing. "Where's Abby? Isn't she coming?"

"Right behind us. You know how she is with these types of places." Eric swirled his hand in the air, motioning to the lights and the people. "She'll be in when she's ready."

Gail nodded, knowing Abby better than either Eric or Jordan. Abby was Gail's second blood child; making her immortal was a pleasure and having her by her side for over sixty years was a blessing. Just as she thought of Abby, it was as if her feelings materialized. The door to Sips and Sweets opened again and a tall brunette breezed in, looking like she stepped out of the 1960s.

Her long straight hair was caught in the breeze, making her look like she was a fashion model in a shampoo magazine ad, and her clothing, although completely in style, was what the kids today would call vintage. She smiled at Gail from behind her large round rose-colored sunglasses. The smile was beaming and instantly made Gail sure she was in the right place, doing the right thing.

At the sight of Abby, man-bun got up from his seat. He walked toward her. And Abby being Abby simply smiled at him and rolled her eyes toward Gail. *Really?* her mind said, knowing Gail would read it. Gail laughed, feeling strangely jealous that she had been so quickly forgotten for Abby. Strike two. He left dejected and in a bit of a huff.

"Why do I attract weirdos? Why?" Abby pulled a chair to the table between Eric and Gail. She kissed Gail hard on the cheek. "Hungry?" she echoed Jordan's comment, making him chuckle under his breath. Gail narrowed her eyes at him.

"I thought we were going down the street? Why are you here?" Eric stuck the fork into the Danish and made it bleed strawberry blood.

"I didn't want to wait all by myself. It's a dangerous neighborhood," Gail said lightheartedly.

"Please." Jordan's tone was short and annoyed. "Could you have picked a brighter place?"

"Seriously. Brighter and with more people? How about Walmart next time?" Abby, who rarely spoke to Jordan, shared a laugh with him.

"I love it here and I didn't want to go alone. I asked you to come with me because I'm, I don't know, nervous. I guess." She shook her head, clearing it. "Maybe we could sit a while before we go." Gail could see Jordan was anxious to leave. He hated restaurants, nightclubs, any place that humans gathered in large groups. So did Abby.

"So how is Sari?" She ignored Jordan for a moment and spoke to Eric. His newest interest was a young human girl that he had met a few weeks ago. Gail was dying to meet her and had been badgering Eric to bring her to the cabin since they met.

"She's coming along." He smiled, scanning the room with his eyes.

"Have you told her yet?" she asked, already knowing the answer.

"About my *situation*? No." He shook his head quickly. "It's too soon. Don't you think?"

"Hey, don't ask me. I once waited eighteen years to bring someone into our life." Gail laughed and looked to Jordan. "Then again, I changed Abby almost immediately. Who's to say what's too soon?" She shrugged, placing a hand on Abby's cheek.

"Do it soon. Sooner rather than later. Dragging her along will only piss her off in the long run," Abby offered.

Jordan spoke up. "How so?"

Gail could see how uncomfortable Abby was speaking to Jordan. She could see her take a long swallow and watched as her eyes scanned the café before she found the words to answer. Gail didn't know if it was his age, his authoritarian attitude, or that she didn't know him well, but whatever it was, Abby kept her distance from him most of the time.

"Well, speaking for myself, if Gail had strung me along and lied to me for months, I would have been pissed. Did Trevor string you along?" The look on her face told Gail that she regretted asking the question the moment it left her lips. But it was out; let's see if Jordan answered it.

"No," he said simply. His piercing black eyes were like daggers aimed at Abby. He didn't like talking about the past, so Gail changed the subject before Jordan could suggest leaving.

"You know how I hate those drapes in the living room? Well, I was thinking that I should call a decorator. Redo the whole first floor. During the day, what do you think?" Gail stared off into space for a moment. "We had such lovely drapes in the cottage. Remember the ones with the roses?" She spoke to Abby.

"Yep. When Nadia . . . um, when *we* redecorated. That was like forty years ago. I doubt they still make them." Abby corrected herself as if she'd said a bad word in front of her parents.

Gail tried to ignore it and continued. "Maybe we could find something similar."

"You have something similar. They're right up on the hill. Not a two-minute walk from the cabin." Jordan's tone was cross and hurtful.

"Oh, I'm so anxious to have this conversation again." Gail rolled her eyes.

The cottage versus the cabin was a debate that was a constant underlying theme in their arguments. Gail had built the cottage when she returned to America in the late nineteen forties. It was the place she loved most in the entire world. It was built on the foundation of the burnt remains of her family home. The home that had burned to the ground in her absence.

After decades of heartache and pain in that cottage, she left and wished never to return. When her wanderlust finally dissipated again, she built the cabin so she could remain on her land; her home.

"Those drapes are probably rotted away by now. I can't imagine they held up under the dust and God knows what else," Abby said, but no one was listening.

"Eric, where have you been for the past few days?" Jordan relaxed slightly, changing the subject. "Need a rest from Gail's get-togethers? Or should I say, Gail's feeble attempt to create a new life for herself." He laughed.

Eric smirked. "Something like that." He continued to stab at the Danish with the fork.

"Thanks a lot." Gail kicked Eric under the table. "I don't see you missing any of my feeble parties, darling." And the jabs and argument continued.

"I didn't say they were feeble parties, just a poor excuse for a new life." Jordan's snide tone was cloaked with a laugh.

"Hey," Eric interrupted, knowing that an argument was about to erupt. "They've finally finished the investigation on your restaurant. Did you see it in the paper yesterday?"

Gail nodded.

"Seems they ruled it a gas leak after all. I heard there was some question about arson," he said matter-of-factly. "Looks like they're going to tear it down. It's structurally unsound."

"Speaking of," Jordan jumped in. "Shouldn't we be going before it collapses?"

"Are they going to rebuild?" she asked hopefully, ignoring Jordan again.

Eric looked up from the destroyed pastry. He knew Gail already knew the answer to that question. "Gail . . ." he started.

"I know, I know. I just thought, I don't know. I guess I was just making conversation."

"Better see it before they bulldoze it. What many mysteries of the past can we uncover by walking through a burnt-out old restaurant? It's like we're archeologists of the undead." Jordan laughed sarcastically.

Abby snickered and covered her mouth to hide it. Eric quietly watched as the two stared each other down.

Gail's eyes were piercing and cold as she looked to Jordan. Eric and Abby knew an entire conversation must be going on without a word being said. Jordan, like Gail, was highly clairvoyant, and the two could argue for hours without a word being spoken.

The one connection that held Jordan and Gail closer than anyone was their telepathy. The ability to read minds was a gift not given to them by immortality but only decorated their preternatural gifts. After so many years, the gift was like a pair of earrings or a necklace. It wasn't necessary to make them stand out, but it sure helped.

And right on cue, Jordan finished a thought aloud that was started mentally. "What difference does it make whether they rebuild or not? You haven't been there in years. Many years, in fact." Jordan's tone was harsh.

"Hey, have a little compassion. I would have thought you would understand or at least . . ."

"No, Eric, let it go. Something else is going on here." Gail looked to Jordan. "What's on your mind? First, you're making fun of me, now you're angry . . . This attitude is not like you. What is it?" Actually, it was exactly like him, recently.

Jordan sat silently looking at her for a moment. His jaw clenched in anger and his brow ruffled a bit. "Why does something have to be wrong? I'm fine. Perhaps it's you projecting your frustration on to me."

"You saw Martino this evening, didn't you?" She looked to Eric for conformation. Jordan remained silent. "Last night, perhaps? He's the only reason you could be this put out. No one else usually gets you this angry." She leaned closer to him, whispering the last words close to his ear.

"Martino's been with his friends, I think," Abby said with a slight shrug. "He hasn't been around lately."

Jordan shook his head, glanced to Eric, Abby, and then back to Gail. "He was your little blunder, not mine. Why would I be *put out* by him?" Jordan rose quickly from the table. Eric could see in his face that he wanted to say more but fought to hold it in, not wanting to start an argument. "I'm more put out by your attachment to your past and this unceasing preoccupation with this restaurant. It's gone. Accept it. Possessions from our past go away. Some things can't last forever." With that, he walked to the door and slammed it behind him. Several customers watched as he stormed out the door.

Looking to the floor, Gail smiled. "He's right. I know he is. I haven't thought of that place in years. Hell, I didn't like it that much when Virgil bought it." She laughed. "And Lizzy's! I can't believe that horrid name stayed all these years. Elizabeth was my daughter's name. Not Lizzy. I hated that nickname." She shook her head as if to clear a thought. "But when it was destroyed, I don't know. It all came rushing back. Like something I needed to finish. Something I'd left behind."

Abby looked to Eric. Neither was sure what to say. Eric reached across the table and squeezed Gail's hand. "We had better go . . . before you change your mind."

CHAPTER TWO

Deanna's eyes were glued to her computer screen. She couldn't believe what she was seeing. There was debris everywhere. Glass, bricks, cement pieces and wood were as far as a block away. Large sections of the street were blown out, leaving pieces of cement and tar everywhere.

She had first heard about the explosion as a quick little news story on AOL. **Building Explodes in NYS Leaving 10 Hurt.** If she hadn't clicked on it by accident, she would have missed it completely.

The pictures were minimal initially in the news. The story was a relatively small one. Nothing on the news channels in New Jersey and nothing on the national news either. Who cared if a restaurant burned to the ground? No one was killed and there were no terrorist organizations taking credit for it. It was small potatoes in comparison to the terrorist bombings or the shootings in schools and churches. One old building didn't matter.

Except to her.

Deanna Belamy never stepped foot in that building. She had no apparent connection to the small tavern and restaurant in upstate New York. Not now. But she did, years ago. Years ago, one hundred and eight to be exact, she had made the biggest decision of her life in that building. She had locked away the fear and memories of a curse that had been haunting her for more than six hundred years. As Elizabeth Staton, she locked Devin in the basement room and walked away for good.

It was difficult to find out any information. At first, even on the local news in New York they had stopped talking about it quickly. But as soon as the rumors started about the blast coming from an old, abandoned room in the basement, a room that had words written in Latin on the walls, then the ghost hunters and the paranormal crazies started paying attention. The bizarro websites all had tapped into this seemingly uninteresting story about a restaurant that exploded in upstate New York.

That's when Deanna was able to see the photos. The restaurant, Lizzy's, had a large hole where the front window used to be, the walk was gutted, and the street was partially gone. What was left of the inner walls was blackened and dripping with water. It appeared that some of the sites had gotten hold of police photos that were not printed in the paper or on national news websites.

The story she got from the town website was simple and direct.

At 6:55 p.m. on September 26, the local restaurant and tavern, Lizzy's, experienced an explosion in the basement. The explosion caused damaged to the building's exterior sidewalk and front window. A fire started in the dining room shortly following the explosion; started by unknown source. The owner, Mr. Francis Wilder, had no comment when asked what had caused the explosion.

The local news thought it was a good human-interest story and took the opportunity to do a piece on television during the eleven o'clock news. Mr. Wilder found that he did indeed have a comment for the news and the nation. "Their investigation is a joke." The interview seemed to start in the middle of Mr. Wilder's rant to anyone that would listen. He was standing outside his restaurant on the night of the explosion. "They think they can blame me for this? It's the gas company's fault!" He was an older man with what looked to Deanna to be gray hair but most of it was covered in either blood, dust, or dirt. There was a large gash on the man's head that he held a white cloth against; the cloth was steadily getting redder as the blood poured from the wound.

She could see the police barricades in the background. A woman lying outside the building had both her legs broken when she was thrown. A man was blinded by shards of glass as he walked past. A child was pinned beneath a large piece of cement.

They drew most of the rescuer's attention in the background of the news story.

"There was a constant banging in the past few weeks from that room!" Wilder gasped as he considered the hole in the sidewalk. "Banging day and night. There was no way through that wall. We tried knocking it down years ago to expand the storage space, but all the contactors said that it would probably take the building down with it. I guess they were right." He looked dejected.

Deanna knew there was no way to take the walls down. She made sure of it. But apparently, she had underestimated the power within those walls.

It was that interview that sparked the rumors of ghosts, poltergeists, and entities. Thankfully it had, or Deanna would never have learned as much as she did about the fate of the restaurant. Apparently, within days there were flocks of people trying to feel something. Blogs about Lizzy's were the first items that Deanna started to see, the history, the architecture. There were supernatural events in the building dating back to the early 1900s.

Of course there were, Deanna thought to herself. That was when he was put in there. *I dare them to find something before then.*

And naturally, they had. Facebook pages dedicated to touring the haunted site advertised hauntings as far back as the nineteenth century. "Come see the Countess as she haunts the halls of the famous landmark. *Countess? What Countess? The building was built in 1880 and has only had two or three owners. None of them were royalty; it's upstate New York, for God's sake!*

One story quoted an interview from a local book about haunted buildings in the Adirondacks. An eighty-five-year-old man that claimed to have worked at Lizzy's spoke of the basement room and the spirit that was locked up there.

Joseph Mueller.

Deanna stopped reading. Chef Joseph? He knew all along about the construction and sealing the room off and he never questioned anything. Because he knew. How could she have been so naïve?

Deanna slammed down her laptop cover. Trying to find out what happened was one thing but filtering out all the lies and deception was quite another. She took a deep breath and realized that the internet was not her problem. There would always be someone ready to cash in on some fantastic happening. In this case, the mysterious explosion in a restaurant basement.

Again, she took a deep breath. What did she know? One – Lizzy's was destroyed. The restaurant once owned by her father, Virgil Andrews, once owned by her and her husband, was gone. Two – he was free. There was no doubt about that; Devin was no longer a prisoner in the basement of Lizzy's Restaurant and Hotel.

Devin Brodie.

She shuddered slightly, thinking that name. Thinking of the curse that followed them was worse, much worse. He was a spirit, dead at age twenty-seven. Killed by his wife. *Slaughtered was more like it*, Deanna thought. She could still remember the blood. Jacenta was covered in blood. There was no telling how many times she had stabbed him.

Deanna could only remember screaming and screaming. For hours, it seemed, she screamed. Railed at Jacenta, God, and the walls in her lonely house. She, at the time, Deanna Cullen, and Devin were lovers. Deanna Cullen and Jacenta Brodie were best friends. There was no forgiveness, just cold-blooded murder. With Jacenta it never ended that easily. With Jacenta it had ended with the curse.

Till death do you part.

Devin was dead. She was sure Jacenta wasn't strong enough in her craft to complete a simple spell, let alone a massive blood spell. But she was wrong.

Deanna Cullen couldn't take the guilt of what she had caused. She had destroyed a family; Devin and Jacenta's family was gone. Destroyed a life; Devin was dead. And she had destroyed a friendship, a bond of sisterhood. She and Jacenta could never mend the broken bonds, never.

Taking her own life was both a victory for Jacenta and what Deanna had always believed to be the beginning of the end. The curse was fulfilled when her lungs could no longer draw breath and she was reincarnated for the first time. A baby with full consciousness of her surroundings. A new life, new parents, a new world. And Devin.

Devin had returned to her in a spirit form that she could not see but only hear. A spirit form that succeeded in driving her to the brink of madness until she decided to rid herself of him in a small restaurant and pub in a small town in New York.

Slowly trying not to think about too much too quickly, Deanna Belamy opened her laptop again. This time she searched Lizzy's to see what smaller sites had picked up on the phenomenon. Too many was what she found. There were some that had pictures of the building from the 1940s.

After she sold it.

It was beautiful. Even in black and white, she could appreciate the red awning above the front door. She could see the small bistro tables lining the front window outside on the sidewalk. What a great place to sit on a summer evening, she thought. The sign out front in the dated picture advertised live music and half-priced drinks for the ladies on Mondays and soldiers on Thursdays. Ah, the end of prohibition. Deanna could remember the trouble they had getting something to stock the bar (even if it was very weak and mostly watered down).

There were rooms over the restaurant; the tenants in the early part of the century were mostly musicians and artists. Now as she watched them being evacuated, in an online news piece, they didn't look like musicians anymore. They were mostly students that attended the nearby community college.

The bar. She couldn't see it in any of the photographs. All the interior shots were of the basement and that damn room. But the bar was what she would have loved to see; the large oak bar that her father so loved. She remembered working behind that bar before and after her father had died. She oiled the wood every night just to keep the shine. The stairs to the offices, the kitchen, everything had a hint of her father to it.

He named it Lizzy's for her in the late 19th century shortly before he died, and her mother abandoned her and her siblings.

That was when she was Elizabeth Staton.

And in 1907, a young, married mother of four, a restaurateur with a body that housed a six-hundred-year-old soul. A soul that was exhausted and frightened for her family. Something needed to be done about Devin.

Surprisingly, the apartments were not damaged, partially due to the heavy walls and ceiling in the basement room. The firemen were guessing it was reinforced pretty well. Mr. Wilder had no idea why when he was asked – no one knew. *Except Deanna.*

"They were strange people. The ones I bought it from. They probably used it for some sort of weird rituals," Mr. Wilder offered in yet another online interview.

It was reinforced to help save Deanna's life; to help keep her sanity and better yet to help her to forget the past. It was times like these when the memories would flood back that she realized that she was truly cursed. The memories were the curse. Devin was part of that curse and if she didn't find him soon . . . he would surely find her. Giving Devin the upper hand was never a good idea. And he was sure to be angry now that he was free.

Two days later, it was raining – again. Walking home, arms full of grocery bags, Deanna's mind was not on where she was or where she was going. Her thoughts were in a ruined upstate New York restaurant and the being that was no longer captive beneath it.

It had been raining for days now and it wasn't helping Deanna's mood; in fact, she knew her mood was the very reason the rain had not let up yet. Since spending days reading and researching the explosion, she had decided to take a trip to her former hometown and look for herself what devastation Devin had caused.

The rain was stopping her. The rain was her excuse. When it stopped raining, she kept telling herself, when it stopped raining, she would take the four-hour drive to visit what was left of Lizzy's Restaurant and Hotel. Deanna needed to go soon because the last update she had found regarding the restaurant said that it was going to be torn down. It was structurally unsound.

As the days dragged on, she was having dreams – nightmares. She had the normal chase dreams at first. Monsters chased her, people chased her, but her most frightening dream was where the Devil chased her. There was no escape in this dream. She ran with force and speed but no matter what she did or where she went, he was there. His face, handsome, silky dark hair like delicate feathers and eyes the shape of almonds and the color of emeralds.

Now she had to wait. Wait for him to arrive.

When she got home, Deanna had a frightening feeling in the pit of her stomach. A heavy sensation weighed down inside her and she was afraid she'd throw up. The water was running in the other room. This lifetime's poor excuse for a boyfriend, Max Brewer, was in the shower. She didn't love him. She didn't hate him. He didn't understand her. She didn't really expect him to. He never really understood anything that involved her feelings.

Max understood few things: football, beer, sometimes school – depending on the class – and his friends. The guys. The guys were John Stone and Bobby Belamy. Deanna liked John; she'd known him for years. They went to school together and he was dating one of her best friends. Bobby was her twin brother, Robert Belamy Jr. and she adored him. They were inseparable since birth; she was three minutes older than him and never let him forget it.

Her mother always said she felt twins at the moment of conception. Blair Belamy was highly intuitive, or at least that's what she claimed. Each of her children's names were chosen by a spiritualist reading her tarot or reading Blair's energy after conception. Her cosmic freak, as Bobby called her, hit the nail

After Life

right on the head with Deanna. Maybe she wasn't such a freak after all.

The football game was on in twenty minutes, meaning John and Bobby would be arriving any second. That was the last thing Deanna needed – the smell of cigarettes or worse, cigars mixed with beer, fast food, and knowing her brother Bobby, there would be pot.

Deanna started straightening up. Getting her mind off the pain, that was the plan. Newspapers were scattered all over the apartment. Max had some current events thing he was doing for his government class and he never cleaned up after himself. Deanna rolled her eyes as she pieced together the newspaper sections.

"Hey, babe?" Max was suddenly next to her, wrapped in a towel and still dripping. "You see my jersey?"

"In the wash," she murmured. "Tee shirt's in your drawer."

He kissed her cheek. "Feeling any better?"

She started throwing the papers into a pile on the floor.

"Babe? What are you doing? Feeling any better?"

"Not much." She finished with the papers and started collecting Max's school books. "Can we tape the game and watch it tomorrow?"

"Tape football?" He playfully held his heart. "We don't tape Giants games, you know that. I should be at that game if your brother didn't fuck up the deal we had. He still owes me money. I gave him a lot of fucking money for those tickets and he still has it." Max pulled his Giants tee shirt over his head when his phone signaled a new text. "John's here."

"Where'd you get that?" She pointed out a large bruise on Max's shoulder blade as he pulled on his shirt.

"What?"

"A huge bruise on your back." She pulled his shirt up to get a better look. "What did you guys do, get in a fight at the bar?"

Max shrugged and pulled his shirt down. "Doesn't hurt," he said nonchalantly.

Deanna shook her head and started searching for the laptop. Not tonight, she kept saying to herself, not tonight. Somehow, she knew it would be completely out of her control when Devin decided to show his face, so to speak. In the past, she had been able to control him, but something told her it would be different this time. She had locked him up and used witchcraft against him. That was the worst part, she assumed for him, the betrayal and use of witchcraft.

She had to; there was no other way. He was getting out of control.

She put her hand to her stomach as it tightened. It felt like menstrual cramps except more toward her stomach rather than her uterus.

"Game's on." Max pushed passed Deanna with a bag of chips and six pack of beer that he slammed on the table. He checked his phone as it rang for a new text. "Open the door, babe."

"Maxwell, we have arrived." John Stone burst into the apartment as Deanna turned the deadbolt. Bobby was trailing not too far behind. With him were Maggie and Connie, each carrying a large paper bag. Deanna groaned to herself. She could possibly have hidden in the bedroom as the guys watched the game but now there was no way she was getting any rest.

"Guess what we got?" Maggie sat on the floor beside the coffee table. From the bag, she pulled out several small bottles of liquor. "Thanks to my dad." She laughed. In her other hand, she held two half gallons of ice cream. "You up for some of my special shakes?"

Deanna groaned again.

"You OK?" Connie asked.

"Just a little queasy," Deanna explained. "What's in the other bag?" She had to change the subject. These were two of her closest friends in the whole world. She was dying to tell them the truth. It was impossible. They would never understand. Sari might, but Sari wasn't there.

"Sari coming tonight?" she whispered, knowing that Max couldn't stand her and if she spoke any louder, her stomach would erupt. Not to mention the smell of the tacos that were being passed around didn't exactly have a stomach-settling aroma.

"Eric kept her waiting – again. She said they'd stop by later." Maggie took a bite of her taco.

Eric. Now he was another story. Deanna knew there was something off about him. Her gut told her he was vampire. It was obvious, not only from her past experiences. Deanna knew of what she spoke. She knew vampires. Two lifetimes ago, she was free of Devin (having successfully locked him up) and travelling Italy. Meeting a vampire wasn't like in the movies. There were no hypnotizing stares, no mind reading, no helpless fainting spells. It was just a guy lying about who he was until he came out of the immortal closet and sank his teeth into you.

To be fair, Deanna admitted that she was lying to him too. She had described her predicament as *everlasting reincarnation*. But lying about not dying was not the same as lying about being a murderer. Or at least that's how she argued about it then.

So, she knew vampires. Detested them for their dishonesty and unwillingness to listen and . . . oh, come on, Sari, just look at Eric. The way he looked, spoke, reacted, everything. The pull, Deanna remembered it well, it had to be the pull that was blinding her to his obvious differences. That feeling deep in your gut that is impossible to deny. That feeling, that need, to be with them. Pull or no pull, it infuriated Deanna to watch them together, knowing what he wanted and how he would stop at nothing to get it.

"Pass the food, lady." Bobby poked Maggie.

"Can we get you anything, Deanna? Some aspirin or something stronger? Good for what ails ya." Connie waved a joint in the air.

"I'm fine." She grimaced.

As the game went on, the tacos and nachos disappeared, as did the beer and a joint or two. Everyone was drunk except

Deanna and she was hating every bit of it. The beer was replaced by Maggie's special shakes. Deanna knew they were delicious and highly potent.

There was a knock at the door and Deanna jumped. *As if what she was waiting for would knock.*

"That's got to be Sari," Maggie said as she filled her glass with what appeared to be a harmless chocolate shake.

Sari took two steps into the apartment when she realized everyone was already drunk. "You guys have only been here for two hours." Her hair was the color of tangerines and had a sparkle to it that could have only been achieved with cheap Halloween glitter hair spray. She pulled the newspapers off the loveseat and dropped down into it. "What's wrong with you?" she said to Deanna. "Too much ice cream in the shakes?"

"She's got cramps." Connie whispered cramps as if it were a great embarrassing secret.

"Just an upset stomach," Deanna corrected her. "You want a drink?"

"I'll have a shake, if there's any left," Sari said and took a hit of the joint Bobby offered to her.

"No Eric?" Maggie carried a large glass of chocolate alcoholic shake to Sari and sat beside her.

"Never showed. Traffic from the city is a bear at this time of night, so I'll give him a pass on this one," she said simply. Tilting her head back, she downed half the shake in a single swallow. For the first time in a week, Deanna laughed. She loved Sari and didn't want to see her get hurt by a man that was so clearly lying to her.

The Giants beat the Bills and Max was happy. At least, that's the way it appeared. Drunk, high, and standing on the coffee table yelling that Buffalo could suck his dick. Deanna assumed that meant happy in his current state.

As another game consumed everyone's attention, Deanna's health was slowly deteriorating.

A soft knock on the door caused Deanna to shudder. "I'll get it." Sari squeezed Deanna's hand gently. "You look like death, Dee, seriously."

A high-pitched squeal told Deanna that Eric had finally arrived. Without thinking about it, she glanced at the clock over the television and the window behind her. Nine o'clock, well past sunset. Eric looked uncomfortable as he accepted Sari's invitation into the apartment. "Let's just stay a few minutes and then we'll go," she whispered in his ear.

"Deanna, you look ill." Eric handed her a napkin to wipe her forehead. "You should lay down." Polite and considerate. Two things going for him. Eric seemed to be studying Deanna's sickening progression into hell. For a moment, she wondered how anyone could accept him into their group. He was clearly different. Of course, this group was almost always high or drunk and couldn't tell the difference between a vampire and a hole in the wall.

As she watched Eric pretending to fit in, she could see he was growing eager to leave. Then a strange feeling came over Deanna. The pain in her stomach had risen slightly and intensified. Cold sweat poured from her skin and she began to salivate fiercely. She was going to hurl. Running to the bathroom was no easy task. She dodged bottles, glasses, food wrappers, sofa cushions, and bodies.

Moments later after emptying what little was housed in her stomach, she took her head from the porcelain bowl. "Damn you, Devin," she whispered aloud.

"Miss me, darling?" he spoke into her ear, it seemed, although she alone could hear him.

She quickly and without knowing why looked around, frightened of what she might see. Of course, she saw nothing.

Devin came close to her face. She felt him brushing through her hair and tickle her ear. A warm feeling of recollection tingled her heart. He was back. For better or worse . . . But those weren't their vows; those vows belonged to the one that did this to them.

"Why such a violent return?" She wiped her mouth and rinsed with water. Several bubbles rose in the cup as she lifted it to her mouth.

"Serves you right for locking me up. And your curse was rubbish; it didn't work. Lucky for you, I'd say. We play dirty, you and me. Don't you agree? It's what draws us together." His voice was just as she remembered it. Deep and masculine. Smooth and hypnotic.

She remembered how he used to put her to sleep many times as a child. His lullabies were ancient stories of their lives together. It was Devin who kept her memory sharp, remembering every detail. She now remembered the true reason she locked him away.

She could blame it on her husband, Bryon Stanton. He was jealous and scared. She could say it was because of Devin's growing strength and anger. She could even say that she feared for her children's safety because it was all true. But the real reason was that she no longer wanted to remember.

"So, that was the reason. I often wondered as I fought for my freedom." Devin easily read her thoughts. *"You didn't want to remember? Remembering is the key, my darling."*

"Remembering is the curse," she said inside her head. Sadly, she also remembered he could read her thoughts.

"How?"

"Just forget it. We're together now and there's no avoiding the memories we remind each other of," she said, disheartened and aloud. Deanna took a deep breath and opened the bathroom door. Sari was sitting on the bed waiting for her.

"Are you OK?" Sari asked.

"Yeah, much better now. Thanks." She looked to Eric lying comfortably on her bed. There was something alluring about him in that position and she was sure he knew it. His dark hair bent in a gentle wave over his forehead, just touching his eyebrows, and his brown eyes were full of concern. The whiteness of his skin was lessened by the dim lighting in the room, and she thought he looked almost angelic as he looked up to her.

Deanna felt Devin close to her. He was encompassing her with his energy as if he were suddenly afraid. Eric sat up on the bed with a panicky look in his eye and his fist pressed hard into his stomach. It wasn't just panic but a supreme *holy shit* expression. He whispered her name as if just meeting her and yet confirming something at the same time.

Deanna shook Devin off and smirked slightly at Eric. "What's with you two?"

"Why do all your friends, no matter what lifetime, look and act the same?"

She was sure he was being evasive and ignored him.

"Sure you're OK?" Sari handed her a glass of water. "We heard you talking to yourself."

Deanna looked her straight in the eye; she felt a lump rise in her throat. In that brief moment, she wanted to bare her soul to Sari. To expose Devin and her whole life experience. As she stared at her friend, bubbles began to rise in the glass of water. Deanna grabbed it from her and drank it so she wouldn't notice.

As if Sari could feel her uneasiness, she said, "Why don't we go out for a while. Just us. We'll get some air, away from this crowd." She grabbed Deanna's hand. "And if you want to talk, we're here for you." It was as if she knew there was something more than just stomach pain behind Deanna's eyes. As if she knew Devin was hovering beside her, ready to confront the twenty-first century with full force.

Deanna knew things were worse than she realized when she didn't care if Eric put his hand on her shoulder for comfort. She could swear she saw Eric look up as Devin circled him. Eric guided her out the door, and she could literally feel Devin's jealousy in the pit of her stomach. She told him to relax but still his fury mounted and quaked her innards.

CHAPTER THREE

She was walking quickly. Passing people as if they didn't exist. They were a blur to her as she sped past them. She could smell their fresh warm skin and the blood that pumped just below the surface. All of them were deliciously distracting, but Jacenta needed to get back to Haven. The others were waiting for her there.

She sped past the lights on the beach and the music in the air. Haven awaited her, and she was called to return immediately. A call had come not an hour ago. A call on the small silver box that was still clutched in her right hand. Modern technology frightened her but was necessary if she was to keep in contact with the multitude of safe houses that she created.

The silver box sang again. Britney Spears sang that she did it again. Piper had programed the song to sing whenever Haven called. She found it funny and ironic. Jacenta was beginning to hate the song. She pressed the green phone button on the screen to shut Britney up. "Hello?" She held the box to her ear uncomfortably.

"J, are you on your way? She's kind of freaking out." It was Piper.

"Almost there. Just a few more blocks." Jacenta impatiently hit the red END button on the screen.

She's freaking out? You're freaking out, she thought. After thirty years, Jacenta would have thought Piper would know what to do with a newbie. Newbies were young or just turned immortals that were improperly or violently brought into their world and abandoned by the piece of trash that turned them. Jacenta dreamed of the special place in Hell for those pieces of trash, but they would never see Hell. You had to die to go to Hell. She didn't believe in Hell anyway.

"Of course, there's a Hell," a voice rang in her head. *"It's where you left me."*

"Not now, Devin," she said in her thoughts. *"I'm busy."*

His voice was deep and smooth; the definition of sexy. *"You can't run from me forever, Jacenta. You can't hide. You know that."*

"I'm not trying to hide. I have bigger problems than you tonight."

She had reached the doorway to Haven or at least the doorway that led to the actual doorway. She liked to keep it hidden from those that might accidentally stumble upon it. No good to have a curious tourist poking around rooms that housed sometimes twenty sleeping vampires during the day.

Haven was a place that offered security and sanctuary for those immortals that were travelling or needed shelter. Sometimes protection. Jacenta had been running some form of Haven since the seventeenth century. It began as a hut that would welcome those seeking protection from the Wars, then a cave for those wanting to hide after the war ended. After years, it was simply a sanctuary for immortals that hadn't found their place in the world and needed guidance.

The structure was inconsequential. A hut, cave, tavern, apartment, or row house. It didn't matter. As long as she was able to provide the protection and caring that the others needed from her. Haven moved periodically in the early days to guard against the Council's wrath and punishment. Today there were over a dozen Havens across the globe.

Brazil was, by far, Jacenta's favorite Haven and the one that she most frequently called home. Salvador was the most beautiful coastal city and she loved walking the bay shores at night. She painted, read, and even practiced yoga on the balcony of her rental overlooking the bay.

Tonight, however, the beautiful shores did not entice her.

"Oh, thank goodness," Piper attacked her as she closed and locked the door. "She's over there. This newbie is ca-ray-zee. Apparently from what we could get out of her so far, she was jumped while on vacation with her family. Why he or she turned her, I do not know. That place in Hell you always talk about, well, I think this guy has got a room reserved. Nut case, let me tell you.

"Hunter got her calmed down now, but she could blow at any moment. She was throwing things and cursing us out. I thought we were gonna hafta erase the problem. If you know what I mean. In this case, I say we'd be doin' her and us a huge favor."

Jacenta stared at Piper as she explained. She was very animated in her description of the problem, her thin hands showing a bomb exploding around her head when she said *she could blow* and one thin finger swiping against her throat as she said, *if you know what I mean.*

Piper was a tall thin girl with long light brown hair. Her hair was pulled up in two ponytails and her hazel eyes were hidden by the long bangs that hung over her brow. The ponytails danced playfully as Piper spoke. Jacenta placed a hand on Piper's shoulder to calm her down.

"Has she fed?" Piper's hair bounced as she nodded yes and motioned to the small flask sitting on the table. "You and Hunter can go," she said plainly and assertively.

"You sure? She's not stable, J. Seriously." Piper followed Jacenta as she walked toward the sofa in the center of the room.

"Just go. But before you do, please pick up those chairs and tidy the room up a bit. I would have expected you to be able to handle this without making such a mess." Her tone was annoyed and impatient. More impatient than she meant to be, but with Devin around, the anger was always boiling just below the surface. Jacenta pulled her long red hair over her shoulder and motioned for Hunter to vacate his seat.

"Sorry, J. We did our best."

Jacenta had stopped listening to Piper and Hunter. She was fixated on the small mousy girl that had apparently bested two of her top counselors. She sat beside the girl. Trying to smile a friendly smile and not clench her jaw impatiently, she said, "I'm

Jacenta, and welcome to Haven." This was the textbook stuff that she hated but knew always worked. "What's your name?"

The girl's tear-filled eyes rose from the floor and locked on Jacenta's. A tremble in her chin developed into a complete body quake as the tears rolled down her cheeks and a sob escaped her throat. From the corner of her eye, Jacenta could see Piper and Hunter stop their work. They waited, expecting another outburst and when none came, they returned to their work.

"That's OK, you don't need to tell me your real name. You probably don't even feel like that person anymore. One day maybe you will again but for today . . . let's see, where were you born?" She acted as if she hadn't used this technique a million times.

A lock of blonde hair fell into the young girl's boyish face and Jacenta brushed it away delicately. Again, her eyes locked on Jacenta's and her mouth opened slightly before a sound came forth. "A-A-America. California," a small whisper escaped her semi-parted lips.

"Excellent. May I call you California for now?" It was a trick she used on many newbies. They felt connected to something, and she had a name to put to the face. There was most recently Sydney; in the past she'd met and named Brooklyn, Austin, Paris, Jackson, and even Chelsea, who was one of her first newbies in England. Jacenta took a small forward quiver as a yes and continued her conversation. "Now, California, do you know where you are?"

Again, another quivering nod of confirmation.

"Ask her if she knows she's dead." Devin had joined the conversation.

"Do you understand what's happened to you?" She ignored Devin.

"Ask her if she knows she's dead. Bet she doesn't." He laughed.

California looked around the room, bewildered. *Not a clue.*

"You need to know that you're safe. I'm going to take you to a room where you can rest. The sun will be rising in a few hours and you will remain there until tomorrow night. You will be safe there. Do you understand?" Jacenta placed a hand on California's hand. "I will stay with you until sunset. Is that alright with you? You may not leave your room until sunset. The sun will kill you. Do you understand?"

Again, California looked dazed but rose when Jacenta did and followed her. The room kept especially for the newbies was in the basement. It had no windows. Nothing for them to break and no way to escape. There was one large bed in the center of the room but no other furniture. The walls were simple and neutral with no decoration at all. The lighting was electric with a dimmer switch to keep the brightness from hurting their sensitive eyes.

"Thank you," California whispered. It sounded more like a question than a feeling of appreciation. She stood in the room beside the bed, holding tight to the bedpost. Her body was trembling as Jacenta placed a hand on her arm.

"You are most welcome. Tomorrow when you wake, we'll talk more, and we'll hunt." Jacenta closed and locked the door behind her. Walking down the hall, she could feel Devin hovering over her. She shook slightly, hoping to jar him from her side. "Piper, Hunter?" She found them in the common room still picking up the mess caused by Hurricane California.

"She's in her room. I'll be staying with her tonight. Tomorrow she needs something more than week-old stores. She needs to hunt." She ran her hands through her hair. "How many do we have tonight?"

"So far, just us and her, California . . . oh, and Sydney should be back by daybreak." Hunter picked up the empty flask, ran his finger over the opening, and licked it. He was handsome and young when he was changed over three hundred years ago. His chestnut brown hair was cut short in the back and kept long in the front like she had seen in so many fashion magazines. He was the perfect picture of a GQ model or possibly a Calvin Klein underwear model. It humored her to think that when she first met him, he was covered in the blood of about ten Council soldiers he had killed single-handedly. "This was the last of the O negative. Not that it matters, but it was older than a week. Just saying." He flashed her his brightest toothy smile.

Jacenta nodded and collapsed in the armchair near the fireplace. She hadn't fed tonight, and it was taking its toll on her. She looked around the room. The effect of Hurricane California was now mostly picked up and looked as if it never happened.

"You look exhausted." Piper ran her hand down Jacenta's face. "You want me to get you some of the good stuff?"

Ah, the *good stuff.* The good stuff was blood from their private store of blood. Clean, young, healthy blood. No hunting tonight; the blood would come to her. Jacenta smiled and raised a single brow playfully. "The good stuff," she whispered.

Piper was gone. Happy to make Jacenta happy.

And she was happy. It was good to be right where she sat. Warm, soon to be placated with the good stuff and with friends.

"Friends? What friends?" Devin reminded her of unhappy times. *"What of your best friend? Do you miss her?"*

"Be quiet."

"Do you ever regret what you've done to her?" he pushed.

"You reap what you sow," she said plainly in her mind. "Thank you, Piper." Jacenta took the wine glass Piper had filled with the good stuff. She sniffed it, letting its aroma fill her senses before the taste hit her palate.

As the blood warmed her, Jacenta felt her strength returning. Strength to mentally fight Devin. She didn't want to give in to his emotional and psychological torture. But she felt at times he was winning the battle. Since he had returned to her, she could feel how much stronger he was. He hadn't told her where he'd gone for the past century, but she imagined it to be a gym for spirits. *A phantom gym.* She laughed to herself and sipped her blood wine.

"Being strong is something I learned so I could escape prison. A prison that was designed by you and built by your monster."

"Monster? Is the honeymoon finally over? You haven't called her a monster since. . . I don't know. . . Emily, or was it

Aggie?" The blood was helping. Her humor was returning and her ability to keep Devin out of her head was stronger. *"Agatha was almost completely blind, and she still got the best of you."* She laughed.

It felt good to take shots at Devin. He'd been driving her nuts, making her work overtime to keep him out of her head. She'd been failing miserably at keeping him out for over a week now. She was unaccustomed to having to protect her thoughts or explain her actions to anyone. Not in a century. Now that Devin was back, he was with her constantly, playing with her emotions, reminding her of unwanted memories and distracting her from her work. She had hoped when he found Deanna, she would get a reprieve. That was too much to hope for.

"She used witchcraft on me, your monster. Did you know that?" he whined.

Jacenta took another sip and smiled to herself. *"Did she? She must have learned to fight fire with fire. What did you do to her to make her resort to her old ways?"* Deanna was an elemental witch since birth but had never used her gifts until Jacenta was dabbling in what she liked to refer to now as her witchcraft phase. There were spells that Deanna was able to perform that Jacenta could not. Jacenta never considered herself a witch. She was just a curiosity seeker that stumbled upon a hidden talent. Deanna, on the other hand, had witchcraft in her blood. Her mother was able to make plants grow. Deanna could make it rain.

The one real spell that worked for Jacenta was the one she regretted the most. And unfortunately, Deanna unknowingly had helped her with that one too. *"Does she do it often? Spells? Or was it a one-time thing?"* Jacenta found herself genuinely curious.

"Apparently, I frighten her. Ah, she's a monster!"

"Oh, stop calling her that. You know damn well that you'll be back in her arms by sunrise." She took a deep inhaling breath, enjoying the aroma of the blood in her cup.

"Is that so? Well, wait till you see her now. She's a real stunner. Quite beautiful, even by your standards." She could

almost hear him smiling as his tone changed from angry to conniving.

"I'm so pleased that her beauty is helping you to forgive her for the grave injustice she has perpetrated on you. God help her if she was ugly." Jacenta laughed and licked blood from the rim of her cup.

"Why do I frighten her? Do I frighten you?" He was getting angry again. Jacenta could hear it in his tone and she could feel it bubbling in her belly and the shaking sconces on the walls.

"That may be part of it." She pointed to the teetering glass on the table. *"I'm sure it was just the circumstances of that lifetime. Husband, children, the restaurant . . ."*

"How did you know about her life?" His voice had gone from angry to jealous.

She waved his comments away and sipped her drink. *"She got used to being without you now. Be patient with her. I don't think you frighten her as much as she needs to learn how to fit you back into her life. Believe me, I sympathize with her on that one."*

She could still feel Devin's anger and fought herself not to bait him.

"What is this place that you've created? Why help the damned?" She could hear the acid in his tone. He meant to hurt her with his words. But not tonight. The blood was relaxing her completely. She could feel it in her veins. Running through each tiny capillary and pumping into her muscles and arteries.

"You remember the Wars. And why I started Haven. It's just a little different now." She smiled, proud of herself and her accomplishments.

"Absurd then and it's still absurd to protect these reprehensible creatures."

"Goodnight, Devin," she said aloud to the empty room. "Go back to Deanna. It appears she needs you more than I." The dawn was coming within minutes. Jacenta checked the locks on the doors and windows. The others were now safely hidden in the rooms below and had been for at least an hour. She wished she could just go home to her rental and sink into her soft down comforter that felt like a hug when she fell into it.

There was her newest ward to think of. California would be waiting for her when she woke. The days that followed would consist of trying to get this girl to talk about what happened to her in the Brazilian streets. Jacenta needed to also figure out how far her understanding of what happened to her stretched.

California's face would be on the local and national news. There would be posters and flyers – a media frenzy. What else could she expect for a beautiful, young, and defenseless American girl that disappeared while vacationing with her family? The internet would eat it up. Facebook pages dedicated to finding her. Search parties and local police dragging the bay for her body. There would be interviews on TV and the computer with her family that Jacenta would have to shield her from; it was too soon to see them.

The best thing to do was to send her to another Haven. Possibly one far away. *Which one to send her to?* Jacenta was having a hard time thinking as fatigue was consuming her body. Which Haven would be the safest and at which Haven did Jacenta wish to spend her next six months?

Six months was her typical time that she would give a newbie to come around and accept their new life. After that it was up to them to flourish or accept the flames when they came. Some didn't survive after the six months, and Jacenta had to come to terms with such losses.

There were others, like Piper or Hunter, Jacenta kept after the six months. Both for assistance with the houses and for companionship. There were others in the other sanctuaries that she had rescued and refused to let go of. The *lucky ones* is how she thought of them.

In truth, she was the lucky one and was well aware of it every time one of them fixed her when she was down. When she couldn't get past a loss of a newbie, that was always a hard time, and Piper was always there for her. In the early days when the

Council would destroy a Haven, that was Hunter's best time. He always kept her together when she wanted to give up.

Now with Devin's return, she needed to talk to someone. *Sabina.*

Her creator, her sire, was one of the only ones that knew the entire truth about Devin and Deanna. Sabina would understand. Jacenta had heard rumors that Sabina was in America. Her connections with the three Haven houses in America alone helped her keep track of where some of her loved ones were travelling or settling. Knowing Sabina, she would be near a big city. There was a Haven in Portland, Oregon, one near Dallas, Texas, and the third in some small town in Connecticut that Jacenta could never remember the name.

Tomorrow she would use that hellish little calling device again to contact the homes to see if Sabina had checked in recently. She had to understand or at least just listen. Sabina and Eric were the only ones to truly know the whole story. But Jacenta had no idea where Eric was these days. With all the Havens around the world and not one whisper about him. Nothing.

Almost two hundred years and nothing.

She missed him; he was her first. The first man since Devin that she had truly loved, and she turned him to have him forever. Now she missed him desperately. Thinking of Eric was exhausting her.

Jacenta walked quietly to the newbie's room and turned the knob. She was not surprised to find the lights were still lit. California was unconscious on the bed and looked as if someone dropped her that way. Jacenta smiled sadly. She ran her hands over California's curly ashen hair. Secretly she wondered if saving this girl was the right thing to do.

Would she survive this brutal world for more than a month or even a week?

Jacenta crawled into the bed, exhausted from fighting Devin all day and from dredging up the past, fighting his intrusion in her life. Wrapping her arms around California, Jacenta could feel her trembling in her sleep. Jacenta hugged her tighter, letting the warmth of her blood-filled body calm the sleeping girl. She fell into unconsciousness after mulling over the day's matters. Her sleep was restless and plagued with nightmares. Just as she predicted, Devin was gone when she awoke, but she had him to thank for infecting her dreams with his special brand of twisted humor all day long.

CHAPTER FOUR

Devin was resting when the buzzer sounded. A bright, shrill sound that didn't annoy anyone, it seemed, except him. Deanna strolled calmly to the small white box perched on the wall beside the door. The voice of her friend sang through the speaker, "It's us," and Deanna pressed the button for several seconds, sending another maddening deadpan sound through the room.

Slowly he began to move through the spacious home Deanna Belamy had built for herself. *Deanna Belamy.* Devin wasn't sure if he liked her yet. She was different. Not in looks. In looks, she was beautiful, as she always seemed to be. Her eyes remained hazel in each lifetime. It was the one purely Deanna attribute that he could hold on to. Those eyes were hazel until she got angry or emotional and then they would turn earthy green and it would rain or snow or a pipe would burst, or the tides would change. Something would happen that was completely out of her control, and the severity of it would depend on the severity of her emotion.

Deanna Belamy had those lovely hazel eyes surrounded by porcelain skin with a scant bit of freckles on the bridge of her nose. Her hair was dark brown and wavy. So different from the stringy brown hair pulled tight in a bun when he first laid eyes on her.

It wasn't only her hair that was different. All the lifetimes had added their knowledge to what he saw before him. She was different than Elizabeth, different than Aggie, completely different from Sophie. How he loved Sophie. So innocent and trusting. She was one of the first. When she still allowed him to help her and remind her. Every lifetime she changed. Every lifetime she learned, and slowly she moved away from him. Elizabeth was the worst. She had fallen in love. Real love. There were children and a husband, a home, a life – without Devin.

It had been three lifetimes since Elizabeth locked him away – he wasn't absolutely sure how many he'd missed – Deanna told him about Margaret Cooper. The young college student that had fallen for the wrong man and died young. He knew she was keeping information from him about that one. It was in her eyes; it was in her heart – those secrets ran deep.

She had told him about Chynna. Beautiful little Chynna Gavin. Seven years old, dead at seven from leukemia. For a reason he could not explain, Devin's soul ached for this little Chynna Gavin that he never knew. And then there was a gap of time, twenty years unaccounted for. Twenty years between Chynna Gavin and Deanna Belamy. She had only shrugged, as confused about it as he was, when asked for an explanation. In true Deanna form, she refused to allow him into her heart. That he blamed on Elizabeth.

"Grab me a beer, will ya?" Max yelled, slumped on the sofa surrounded with textbooks, notebooks, and his laptop open beside him. Deanna groaned and tossed a can from across the room. Devin laughed.

"I'm so glad you find this funny." Her tone was short and bothered.

She had been rushing around since they came home from the food fair. It was the 200th anniversary of this little hamlet of Torry that Deanna called home. The festivities were all weekend but tonight it started with Deanna's favorite part: the food fair. She had always loved food. Cooking it, preparing it, creating it. There were food trucks, tents, cooking demos. They closed two blocks in the center of town to set up the food fiesta.

Deanna had worked all day at Nicodemus, New York with Devin at her side. She was a hair stylist and colorist. All morning on her feet and the long commute home from New York had wiped her out. Now getting ready for her friends to show up to drink the night away – she was completely zonked. He could feel it in her tone, and in her mind.

Her morning began with a rushed breakfast of eggs and waffles eaten at a tiny table littered with books and papers. The one she shared her life with – Max Brewer, she called him – was asleep on the sofa as she scarfed down her breakfast. He had been studying all night with Devin keeping a watchful eye over him. Devin couldn't understand what she saw in this one.

"Max, will you please get your ass off the couch? The girls are on their way up," Deanna complained as she poured a bag of potato chips into a large bowl. She had the chips, pretzels, and some organic celery and carrots with some kale chips for Sari. *"Sari may look punk but her eating habits are very hipster. She would have loved all the food trucks tonight."* Deanna laughed to herself and to Devin. "I need you to set up the card table for the game."

Devin watched curiously as Max ignored Deanna and continued reading.

"Should I help you, Mouse?"

"If only you could," she huffed audibly. "Max, hello. Enough studying. Get up!" Max made a sound of approval, but his eyes didn't leave his text.

When he didn't move, Devin went to him. His first thought was subtle and non-threatening. The pages of Max's government textbook rippled and turned in his hands. Several newspapers flew off the coffee table. "Is the window open?" Max brushed the pages down with his hand and kept reading.

Deanna laughed under her breath. *"Nice try."*

Devin's next move was less subtle and more jarring. He slammed into Max's shoulder with as much energy as he could muster. A small electrostatic charge in the air raised the hair on Deanna's neck, and small electrically charged crackles emanated from her socks as she walked across the room.

"What . . ." The only words from Max's mouth were stopped as his book flew from his lap and his body pitched forward toward the coffee table. His head stopped only inches away from slamming into the hard, unforgiving reclaimed wood of Deanna's favorite piece of furniture.

"Devin!" Deanna scolded, too late, and then fought to stifle a laugh.

"What the hell was that? What did you say?" Max got to his feet like he was drunk. "I got pushed."

"Oh, you tripped, clumsy-pants!" She laughed aloud, happy to release it.

Devin laughed again. *"Maybe now the lazy son of a bitch will help you."* His energy was low at the end of this exhaustingly boring day with Deanna and her sad dull life. At the salon and on the path train, he was full of energy. There were so many people that he was able to consume vast amounts of energy from them. But here Deanna was drained, and Max was — well, Max was Max. His energy was unusually low for a young man and most of it was spent drinking or studying. Devin was losing his oomph.

Obtaining the energy was the easy part. Most creatures on the Earth had an aura surrounding them that contained energy that protects their life-force. Devin was able to feed off this energy and grow stronger. With this abounding strength, he found he could move objects, start fires, and most recently he found that when his energy was at its peak, he could breach a creature's aura and attach himself to their life-force.

Although the feeling was temporary, Devin was able to walk in another creature's skin. To look out of their eyes, feel their beating heart in their chest and touch — anything.

Animals were easy for him, although he couldn't maintain a hold on them for long — he didn't know why. Humans were more difficult. Max had proven to be the easiest human to breach so far. Perhaps because he was so often exhausted or inebriated that his aura was weakened and stood as no defense to intruders.

It wasn't easy to accomplish — this breach. At first, Devin would bounce off and lose all his energy in the process. The bounce caused bruises on Max whether Devin breached or not. Once inside Max, the bruises would disappear. Energy heals. Although if he couldn't successfully breach, then Max was covered in unexplainable bruises. These bruises were upsetting Deanna recently. She didn't understand them and at the same time, she was frightened by Devin's growing powers.

Devin would never admit it to Deanna, but his powers frightened him as well. It frightened him when he got angry – sometimes he couldn't control it.

The front door burst open just as Max finally shook off Devin's love tap and pulled the soft topped card table from the closet. "Hey, hey." Connie opened the apartment door without knocking. "You guys ready for us yet?" She was already a little drunk.

"Hey, the cooler's still down in the car if you could go get it, Max." Sari was holding the door open, hoping Max would get the hint. Maggie slipped by her carrying a bag with chips and dip. "Need some help?" Sari let the door close with a gentle yet annoyed shake of her head. It was clear Max had no intention of going downstairs.

Devin liked Sari. She loved Deanna and that was enough for him. He didn't think Deanna had a true friend since his wife, Jacenta, and that did not end well. He admired Sari for her independent thinking and individuality. Her choice in boyfriends left something to be desired, but Devin could work around that one problem.

Eric – Devin didn't even want to think about that mess.

"You OK? You look a little flushed." Deanna studied Sari's face.

"I was almost killed by these two huge dogs."

"Where? Are you hurt?"

"OMG, D, they were on top her like that!" Maggie snapped her fingers.

Sari shook her head. "Here. Downstairs. We were waiting for you to buzz us in, and boom, they were on top of me. The guy was like 'oh, sorry' and just left. Frickin' dick." Sari took a deep breath, still visibly shaking.

Deanna walked to the window but saw nothing unusual. "This neighborhood is going to the dogs." She laughed at her pun, but Sari and Maggie only stared at her.

Devin circled the apartment building looking for the dogs. He could see Maggie's truck with the door open and the cooler sitting in the front seat. Around the corner under a street lamp, two shady characters stood flanked by two enormous dogs. He went in for a closer look when the dogs sensed his presence. The barking was frantic and unrelenting. Devin withdrew quickly but not before he got wind of the two trying to hush the dogs. Vampires.

As he pulled away, a third approached. A beautiful brunette who embraced the others firmly, not wanting to let go. A happy chatter accompanied her arrival and the dogs slowly relaxed as Devin pulled farther away.

Deanna and Sari were still talking when he returned. "Is Eric coming?" Deanna tried not to make it obvious that she was forcing herself to be interested in Sari's love life. He knew Deanna didn't trust Eric and was quite overjoyed that he had gone to New York to visit his mysterious friend.

Devin was with her on that one.

"No . . ." Sari trailed off. "Come on, Max. The beer's not going to just walk up here, and I'm not going back down there." She shook her head and began collecting the newspapers from the table to help Deanna straighten up. They were all out-of-town papers, all dated over two weeks ago. Each paper had stories circled around a small restaurant that had burnt down in upstate New York. "How was your food thingy? Any good?" she asked Deanna.

"Delish. I wish you had come. Max is not exactly a food connoisseur. I really miss you. We never hang out anymore." She laughed uncomfortably.

"I know. But you work and then with me going back and forth between here and the city. It's kind of rough. I could stop by the salon next week and we could have lunch?"

"Yeah, I'd like that." She looked to Sari in such a genuine way that Devin knew her feelings without telling him. Her eyes misted slightly, and she changed the subject. "Everything go all right with the ID?" To buy beer for the party, Sari had obtained a fake ID, and tonight was the first time using it.

Sari rolled her eyes. "I was a wreck. I thought I'd have a heart attack. I'm never doing that again." She laughed and sat on the floor with a newspaper in hand.

Deanna cracked up laughing.

"You left the truck open, Mags." Bobby stormed into the apartment carrying the cooler with John in tow. "Maxwell."

"Robert." Max flipped on the TV. "Let's watch the game."

"What game?" He stared at the TV.

"No game. No TV. We're playing a board game tonight!" Deanna yelled from the kitchen.

"Whatever's on. We've got like ten sports channels now. Sit down. Have a beer." He patted the seat beside Connie, ignoring Deanna. "Dee, get your brother a beer."

Deanna just looked at him but said nothing.

"That's OK, I'll get it myself." Bobby laughed and flipped open the cooler beside him. "Now this is service. Want one?" He threw a beer to John.

Connie plopped on the floor beside Sari. "What are you reading?"

"They don't say what caused the explosion," Sari commented, running her fingers through her pink hair and taking a sip of Connie's beer. "There's a bunch of articles about this restaurant that blew up a couple of weeks ago. They don't say how the explosion started. A friend of mine posted something on Facebook. She lives up there now. But I didn't really read the article." Sari shrugged.

Connie pushed a pillow under herself for comfort.

"Don't bother. The newspaper doesn't say what caused it. I saw online that they think it was a gas leak." Deanna began picking up the papers and neatly stacking them.

"*It was me. Remember?*" Devin snickered in Deanna's ear.

Sari and Connie stared curiously at Deanna. "By the look of these papers, it looks like someone's obsessed." Sari smiled and nudged Connie.

"Who reads newspapers anymore?" Connie sipped her beer.

"Not obsessed just interested. I got most of my info online. Max needed the papers for his government class, and I started reading them too." Deanna shrugged, trying to sound convincing.

"Sounds like obsession to me," Sari teased.

"Me too."

"Like you were obsessed with the Vampire Killer when you were a kid?" Connie laughed. "You told me that as soon as you read that book about the case, you collected every article online and newspaper clipping the library had on record. And you slept with your lights on for weeks." She laughed again.

"So, I know what I'm talking about." Sari laughed, kind of embarrassed. "They never caught him – the Vampire Killer. The FBI profiler said he was probably a glory hound. You know some nobody looking for a little bit of the spotlight. They assumed he just slunk back into the shadows of his boring life. Last two girls were butchered. And then there was a rash of copycats." She saw a sparkle of interest in Deanna's eye. "Here's the kicker. The last few people killed by the actual Vampire Killer, not a copycat, were all related or knew some girl named Nadia Bishop. She was from right here in Torry. Spooky."

"She's probably the killer." Deanna nibbled on a cracker. "Some crazy jealous chick that went nuts and started massacring people. They never suspect a woman can be a serial killer. Lucky for her."

"You thought he was a real vampire, didn't you?" Connie chortled. "You did. I know it. And that girl that disappeared is now a vampire, right? Weirdo. You have this sick romantic desire to be with someone mysterious. Explains your fascination with Eric."

"She's off to a good start," Devin commented. Deanna silently agreed.

Devin thought of the group of vampires assembling outside. Quite a coincidence that Eric was a vampire and crushing on Sari. And now three vampires were gathering on the street below Deanna's window. Not to mention the two dogs that treated Sari like hamburger meat only a short while ago. Interesting.

Looking back at Sari, he saw her smile trying not to look in Deanna's direction.

"He is cute, though. Yum-mee! Have you two *you know* – yet?" Connie raised her eyebrows in a teasing manner. She was just able take a sip off her beer before Sari belted her with a pillow.

Deanna shook her head.

"*It won't be long before she's in his bed,*" Devin said.

"*I'm surprised it hasn't happened already. It's not for a lack of trying on his part, I'm sure.*" Deanna rolled her eyes and shook off the thought of losing Sari to Eric's life.

"So, what are we playing?" Maggie shuffled through the board games Deanna had piled on the kitchen counter.

The night went on with more drinking and Monopoly – the drinking was winning out. Sari had received a few texts from Eric and retreated to the sofa going back and forth with him on her phone. Maggie and Bobby accepted their bankruptcy and retired from the game. Leaving John, Connie, and Max to fight over property and several pirated *Get Out of Jail Free* cards.

Sitting on her window sill as the game spiraled into a screaming match, Deanna watched as the townspeople left the center of town. Food trucks passed her building on the street down below, followed by the last of the foodies hoping for end of the night freebies. Parents were tending to their children. The children were wired from all the candy and soda they had consumed during the evening. It was really only the teenagers and young adults that enjoyed the gaiety of the night. Music blared from down below and she could hear firecrackers exploding several streets away.

Devin loved watching her when she didn't know he was doing it. Her long dark hair was pulled back out of her face. She was beautiful as Deanna Belamy. She was always beautiful. He guessed beauty really did come from within and emanated outward. Each woman she had been – each little girl he adored – was beautiful.

Again, he thought of Chynna Gavin and Margaret Cooper. The two he had never known. He wondered what they looked like – were they beautiful as well?

Below Devin saw the vampires still standing outside, now just below the window. There was one more now. Two with the dogs, the beautiful brunette and now a tall slim dark-haired man with large soulful eyes. He was clearly looking at Deanna as she sat oblivious to him in her window.

"Turn around," he whispered in her ear.

Breaking out of her spell, she nearly fell off the sill, startled.

"What do you want?" she asked mentally.

"Someone's watching you." She could hear the smile in his words. Devin watched her eyes as she searched for who he was talking about. *"There, beneath the street lamp. With the dark-haired beauty. You know what they are, don't you?"*

Deanna flinched at Devin's last comment and looked away from the window.

"Do you think it is death that makes them so beautiful or were they like that before, do you think?" He knew it was maddening to her for him to appreciate another woman. *"You know him, don't you, Mouse? I can see it in your eyes. How do you know him?"*

Deanna said nothing for a while and stared at the bottle in her hands.

The vampires below were arguing, discussing, and doing whatever vampires did. Devin found them interesting and kept wondering why they were here. The new one to join the group kept staring at Deanna in her window. Like Rapunzel in her tower. He knew her too. Just as she knew him.

"Margaret."

He didn't respond and waited for Deanna to continue. If he didn't say anything, perhaps she would reveal the secret that she'd been hiding regarding Margaret Cooper. *"I saw him last week at OCI. I thought he was macking on Sari but then he was staring at me. I can't figure out how he thinks he knows me. I don't think he knows either."* She looked back over her shoulder at him and quickly looked away.

It was her eyes, Devin thought. It was always her eyes. Deanna's eyes never changed. It was like the new faces were a mask that she had slipped on. The eyes were always hazel and always truly Deanna. As a baby, he could see the hurt in those eyes, the frustration when she was unable to accomplish something as simple as tying her shoes. As a young adult, his heart ached for her when she was heartbroken by a crush. It was all in her eyes.

The day she nearly died while giving birth to Alice. It was her eyes that cried out to him to stay with her. It was her eyes that sparkled when the fever broke, and the pains subsided. It was all in her eyes.

"How did he find you – here?" Devin could feel the jealousy rising and tried to suppress it. *"Do you think Eric is involved?"*

"No," she said with a false air of confidence. *"That has to be a coincidence."*

There was a silence between them as they both stewed on their own truths or version of the truth. And then Deanna shrugged. *"Martino,"* she said finally. *"That's his name. I met him in Boulder at CU. God, I don't even know when . . . early sixties, maybe. I haven't fallen for someone like that since Bryon. Martino was something."*

Ignoring her during her romantic flashback, Devin saw a silver Lexus drive up and park in front of the building. "Dee, I'm going. Eric's here." Sari was glowing. "Talk to you tomorrow. Sunday we're doing the fair and fireworks, right?" She quickly kissed Deanna's cheek and ran out the door.

Devin and Deanna watched as Sari burst through the glass doors on to the street, forgetting completely about her earlier encounter with the dogs. Eric got out of the car, kissed her briskly, and walked her to the passenger side. His attire was vampire casual. Dressy and in-style yet somehow vintage in its charm.

Before dropping into the car seat, Sari looked up to the window where Deanna sat. A bright, beaming smile and a wagging of her fingers to Deanna and she disappeared into the vampire's mobile lair.

"Did you notice that your friend has disappeared? As soon as the other arrived, he vanished. Maybe not so much of a coincidence after all." Devin heard Deanna's breathing stop and her brow crumpled in a frown. She knew he was right and refused to admit it.

CHAPTER FIVE

Standing around the corner, watching for Eric's Lexus to drive away, Martino didn't want to be here any longer, staring at her. She was beautiful and most definitely who he thought she was – even if she would never admit it to him. Or speak to him. And apparently, she was having a hard time just looking at him.

He wished to be out of the city. Away from all the lights. It was the first thought he had when he woke after sunset. No, the second thought. His first thought was much more immediate and kind of wet and slobbery. Richard's dogs were licking his face when Martino opened his eyes. Licking his face and jumping on him impatiently. "Aah, off! Now!" He pushed at them. "Did you not feed them yet?"

"They are always excited to see you. They're just extra pumped tonight." Richard crossed his arms across his chest. "Must have been that girl. Eric's pink-haired friend. Must have been his scent on her. I can't think of another reason for them to attack her."

Thor and Attila were Richard's dogs. They were everywhere he was – no exceptions. He loved nothing more than those two large German Shepherds. Martino had known Richard for more than half a century, and during that time many dogs had filled his life. Usually large, usually work or sporting dogs, but these two were special, somehow.

"Call them off, will you?"

Richard laughed and whistled. Immediately the dogs were at his side, though their stance said they were ready to run at any moment. He stood between them staring down at Martino. His eyes were dark jade, especially in the dark room, and his cherub features made him appear much younger than he was.

"What do you mean, attack her? Is she hurt?"

Richard shook his head, already bored by the topic. "She'll live."

"Where are we?" Martino got to his feet and examined his surroundings. He was in a low-ceilinged basement of some sort. He could smell the dampness and there was a chill in the air that came with being below ground that was unpleasant. He rubbed his eyes.

"Safe. Pretty awful but safe." Richard's face twisted in a grimace as he looked around. "Come, the others are waiting and Bith is in a mood, so let's be quick."

"Bith's here?" He was excited. Tabitha hadn't been around in months.

As Martino brushed off the dirt from sleeping on the floor and the massive amounts of dog hair that clung to his clothes, he listened to the sounds around him. He heard a car door slam just outside, people laughing as they passed on the level above him, and he heard whistling. A distracting tune really. A woman. He could smell her. The scent of onions and laundry detergent were the strongest of the fragrances. Inhaling deeply, he could make out her scent under the others. Her scent. The musk of her body; the aromas that the adrenaline in her system exuded. He closed his eyes and felt his thirst building.

"Is this a laundry room?" Martino listened closer. He heard water running and the spinning of the electric dryers.

Richard nodded. "For the apartments next door, I think." He rubbed the dogs absentmindedly. "You want to go up north tonight to hunt?"

Martino nodded. That sounded very good to him right now. Going to Mount Orion where there were deer that outnumbered the humans at least three to one. Hunting was one of his favorite activities since he'd returned to America. The chase, the blood, and the flesh. He didn't eat it as much as savor it and consume every drop. Drawing every drop from the flesh before discarding it.

Life was good at Mount Orion for now at least. He enjoyed being with his sire, Gail, and sharing some time with her. It was only recently that he had reunited with Gail. Over sixty years stood between now and their last meeting. Martino didn't wish to remember all the details of his creation. They were difficult years for him. Gail's immaturity, Jordan's disapproval, and finally his estrangement. In the years that followed their separation, Martino found Richard and his friends.

Gail hadn't met his friends yet. Martino feared Jordan's continued disapproval and judgement. Jordan who was always at her side. He always disapproved of something. That was Jordan. He and Martino didn't see eye to eye on anything. It was the main reason Martino had left Gail all those years ago, but it wasn't going to stop him now.

"So, what's with Bith?" Martino plunged his hands deep into his pockets to ward off the chill that permeated the dark basement.

"Bith being Bith is all. Come, boys."

As Richard opened the door to the laundry room, up three steps and around a bend, Martino followed diligently like the dogs – although they went first. The night was dark and starless. He hated the city for this very reason. Too many lights from buildings and homes muted the stars. The moon was hidden behind a veil of clouds that gave the night an unnatural feel.

"It's about time. Why must we always wait for Tino? Have you hunted yet or are we to wait for you again?" That was Phillipe. There was never a hello; it was always *what have you done for me lately*. Martino laughed.

"Later." He looked at the young vampire before him and reminded himself that Phillipe was much older than he was. Centuries older. His hair was the color of coffee with a touch of cream and his eyes the color of storm clouds rolling over the darkening horizon. He was beautiful to look at, yet his personality was unruly and challenging at times.

As he stared at Phillipe trying to keep his humor about him, Martino felt a pair of arms wrap around his chest. "So, who is this girl?" She kissed his ear, grazing her teeth against it.

Martino turned and threw his arms around Tabitha. Her dark hair was pulled back as her chocolate brown eyes smiled at him. She stood almost as tall as him, but her thin frame made her appear taller. "Bith," he whispered, "I almost didn't believe it when Richard told me you were here. He did say you were in a mood."

"Did he?" Tabitha eyed Richard with a bit of humor and a bit of annoyance. "Never mind that now. Tell me about this girl I've been hearing about."

"Look up; she's right there." Richard was with Phillipe, leaning against a street lamp waiting for them. The dogs stood flanking him on guard as always.

They looked to the windows in the apartment building. There she was the beauty that had enticed him only weeks ago in a local pub. She was sitting in her window, staring off into the distance until she turned to look at him. She had turned as if told to do so and then turned away.

When he had first seen her two weeks ago, Martino wasn't sure what he was seeing or even feeling. They were following Sari and had been for days. Phillipe was curious why Eric was wasting so much time with a human without killing or turning her. There seemed to be no point to it. They watched her at her apartment, at Eric's New York flat, and even as she visited with her friends.

It was at a pub that Martino became entranced with Sari's dark-haired friend. He watched her from afar – as Phillipe watched Sari – and he couldn't believe what he was seeing. It was . . . Margaret – but not Margaret. The eyes were Margaret. The expression was Margaret. But still not Margaret.

Sometime during the night, Sari and this *is Margaret/is not Margaret* went to the ladies room together. Passing Martino at the bar, Sari whispered for her friend to look at him. It was then that their eyes met and he saw the recognition in them. He wasn't being foolish; she knew him just as he knew her. It was unclear if she knew from where but his *is Margaret/is not Margaret* feelings were right on target.

Now looking at her sitting in her window, her profile was as gorgeous as he remembered it. Her slim delicate chin and nose poked out from behind her hair that was falling loose from the confines of a ponytail. Then she looked at him again. His heart leapt. Her hazel eyes darkened and studied him, looking almost frightened. She looked away and then back again.

"Is she what you remembered her to be, Tino?" Tabitha placed her hand on his shoulder.

"Does she look frightened to you?" He could not take his eyes off the young girl. "She looks frightened. Surely not of me."

"Trouble, guys." Phillipe grabbed Tino's arm. "Lexus pulling up."

"Shit," Martino whispered under his breath. He pulled Bith along as they quickly rounded the corner.

Eric's silver Lexus pulled up and stopped in front of the building's large glass entry doors. The glass doors swung open as Eric pulled himself out of the car. Looking behind him, Eric sensed others around him but felt no immediate danger.

As Sari exited the building, Martino watched her as he stood hidden from their view. He couldn't figure out what Eric found so enticing about this girl at first glance. Her hair was cut short and very choppy as if she did it herself and it was sticking up in several directions. And it was pink. Not just pink, it was pink with blonde tips and her dark roots were showing through. But the worst part was her eyes. They were hidden behind a mask of black makeup. He couldn't even make out the color of them.

Eric ushered Sari into the car with gentlemanly grace, again looking around to the festival's few stragglers. And just as Sari got into the car, she looked up to the girl in her window above and she smiled. It was a simple, eye-catchingly brilliant smile that he was unprepared for. It was natural and almost alluring in its ease. He saw her appeal in that instant and suddenly it seemed inappropriate to be following her and potentially sabotaging this relationship for Eric.

The car door slammed shut and they drove away without looking back.

"That was close." Phillipe laughed. "I'm pretty sure he would have been super pissed if he knew we were here."

Bith's eyes rolled back in an exhausted huff. "He did, genius. Use the sense that God gave you, please."

"God?" Richard snickered.

"The sense that I gave you, then. Why can't you ever read the emotions of others? Or sense their defensiveness or protective instincts? He knew we were here. All of us. Probably mostly you and Tino and of course those damn dogs." She sneered at them, and only Richard smiled. "He could smell them and you two never hide yourselves very well. I expect it from Tino because he's so young but, Phillipe, you constantly disappoint me."

Phillipe appeared to be ignoring Bith, but Tino knew she had hurt him. Richard did say she was in a mood tonight. It looked as if he was right.

Finally coming out from behind the clouds, the moon was high in the night sky as they walked slowly away from the apartment building. The streets were near deserted of the food truck enthusiasts. The nauseating smell of cooked meat that had permeated every inch of this small hamlet since he awoke was finally dissipating.

Martino walked silently with Richard. Richard was Martino's best friend and had been for almost six decades. He was a beautiful young boy with dark, dark hair and the greenest eyes Martino had ever seen. The paleness of his skin only added to his irrepressible beauty with a bright grin that only slightly exposed his perfect fangs.

Looking at Richard now, Martino wondered how old he really was. Maybe five hundred years? Maybe older? He looked no older than a teenager as he stood there under the street light. Richard didn't like to talk about his age. Martino knew Bith had brought Richard into this life and he knew that he was older than Chelsea, but exactly he couldn't say.

"Martino, look." Richard smiled without ever turning towards him. A pet store at the end of the street was pulling in their sidewalk signs advertising an adoption day.

"You and those dogs. You'd figure after four centuries you'd tire of looking at them," Martino said, hoping that he had guessed his age correctly.

Richard quietly laughed. "Not even close." His eyes stayed glued to a Siberian Husky in the window that couldn't have been more than a few months old. He loved dogs. It was the only living thing that remained constant and loyal. He trusted nothing as much as his dogs. "One more. What do you think, boys?" He rubbed the German shepherds beside him. "Need a friend?" Thor and Attila circled his legs playfully.

Phillipe was talking endlessly about some young man he had met earlier. This young man was clearly no longer walking the Earth from the particulars of Phillipe's story. The screams, Phillipe described in detail, the man's screams were the best part. And Phillipe laughed and laughed. Martino shook his head. That was Phillipe; no matter that he was well over six hundred years old, he would forever have the heart of a seventeen-year-old boy.

That was Bith's responsibility. She freely admitted that she should have waited to turn Phillipe until he was older. She just couldn't bear to be without him.

Martino looked to Bith now as she stood a few feet away, smiling patiently as Phillipe told his tale. Her mood was brightening a bit; he could see it in her eyes. She looked beautiful tonight. Her hair was pulled back from her face and she wore what any other twenty-something would be wearing. Black jeans and a plaid button-down shirt. Her brown hair was tinted naturally with highlights the color of an autumn sunset, and her brown eyes danced with flecks of amber. She was so natural and yet so frighteningly out of time. She caught his eye and smiled. Momentarily the years faded away and she was a fresh young girl looking for a good time.

Martino shook his head. Any other night he would be entertained by the tall tales that Phillipe spun, but tonight he had no interest. He was too overwhelmed by the idea of that girl. Briefly, he closed his eyes and saw her profile again. The way she played with the bottle in her hands and gently pushed her hair behind her ear.

"Hi," a voice sang behind them. It was Chelsea. A beautiful blonde taken directly out of a fashion magazine. Her hair, the color of sunshine, framed her face, falling in perfect waves down her back. Her eyes were grayish blue that danced when she smiled. Her beauty was perfection in Martino's eyes. He was constantly amazed at how well the iridescence of her skin brightened her eyes and made her smile that much more dazzling. She threw her arms around him as if knowing his thoughts. Loving his adoration.

"So, where have you been for the last two months?" Bith grabbed Chelsea's sweater sleeve.

Chelsea laughed and hugged Martino again. She didn't feel that she needed to explain herself and he loved her for it. Compared to Bith who had seen a thousand years pass, Chelsea was an infant of a mere three hundred years, but they behaved many times like they were sisters with not more than a year between them.

"I sent for you a month ago," Bith continued. A car roared passed with its radio at peak volume and yet her voice was barely above a whisper.

"Sent for her?" Phillipe mocked Bith.

"Exactly. It was so lovely to be summoned as I was." Chelsea rolled her eyes. "By the way, I hope you weren't too attached to that messenger." There was a small lisp hidden beneath her British accent. Not a *she-sells-sea shells* lisp, just a hint lilting on some words that Martino found endearing.

Martino shook his head and winced. "Dead?"

She nodded. "You expected that, right? That's why you didn't send one of these guys?"

"I didn't send them because I knew I'd never see any of you for another year if I did." Bith half-laughed and rubbed her eyes as if they hurt. The group walked farther down the street towards the cemetery. Chelsea clung to Martino as they walked, and he enjoyed the adoration for as long as she was willing to give it.

"So, what'd you want?" Chelsea's demeanor was so relaxed that Tino felt calm when she was around.

"Just to see you." Bith hugged her from behind and continued walking.

"Someone died so you could see her?" Phillipe tone was like acid. He was still angry and hurt by Bith's comments earlier.

"We do what we need to do." Bith laughed and rubbed Phillipe's back playfully.

"Oh, not the cemetery again." Richard groaned. He made a small motion with his hand to keep the dogs by his side.

"Just for a while," Martino promised Richard as they walked through the rusted iron gates. As they passed the threshold of the cemetery, Martino ran his hands over the gates. The rusted, peeling metal was adorn with intricate patterns and the words *Torry Cemetery* spun into the detailed archway.

An old cemetery! His favorite kind.

Comments were minimal from the group. Bith hated cemeteries; cautiously she looked to each marker with a clenched jaw. Chelsea and Phillipe were bored and feeling mischievous. The cemetery walls blocked out any noise from the street and Martino was thankful for the silence. Phillipe pointed out a star, Vega, and continued to talk about something mind-numbing to Richard. The temporary silence was gone.

Then Chelsea giggled, breaking free from Martino's arms, and Phillipe laughed. Their unspoken mischief for the evening had begun. They ran ahead of the group, disappearing into the darkness, followed closely by Thor and Attila.

"Should we follow them?" Richard groaned, not wanting to.

Martino shrugged and Bith seemed uncaring. They walked farther into the cemetery, hoping whatever trouble Phillipe and Chelsea had found would not involve them. Martino grabbed Bith's hand as she looked cautiously around the graveyard. He knew that she had always hated the idea of immortalizing the dead under a monument of stone or marble. *Why would you want to visit the rotting corpse of your beloved grandmother?* she would always ask him.

She smiled weakly and squeezed his hand. "Have you gotten your fill of this garden of corpses?"

Martino laughed aloud as images of zombies filled his head. Richard only smirked and shook his head. The night was becoming cooler. The darkness was absolute and somewhat oppressive. Far ahead, Martino could see a light, but it was flickering and confined to the stones surrounding it.

"Come here," a voice called. "Come on." It was Chelsea. She and Phillipe were hunched behind a large tombstone. "Look."

Chelsea grabbed Martino's hand, dragging him to her side. There was some laughing and singing a few feet ahead of them. It was the lighted area that was drawing everyone's attention. The drunken singing was from some teenagers that had trickled into the cemetery from the street.

"Shall we join in?" Phillipe pressed his hand into the small of Martino's back. "They look like they need us." He laughed. With mixed emotion, Martino followed, knowing that these teenagers would be dead within the hour.

With perfect estimation, an hour later, the group emerged from the cemetery.

"Tino, are you all right?" Bith touched his back. "Did we scare you back there?"

Martino half-smiled and shook his head.

"Oh, we were just having a bit of fun." Chelsea threw her arms around him. "Just because we don't need the blood as much anymore doesn't mean we don't still crave it." Her bottom lip twisted as her words formed around her lisp.

"I know," he muttered, still a little overwhelmed by the spectacle of the past hour's feasting frenzy. Although he knew the bodies were safely hidden in a random tomb that they had broken into, there was an underlying fear of being discovered. A small piece of what his sire, Gail, had taught him clung to his subconscious. *Never leave evidence of our existence.* Her words kept reverberating in his head.

"Why were you so apprehensive about joining us?" Richard was almost innocent in his question. "I know you have been craving this since you woke. I would have thought you'd have been the first one to dive in."

Martino didn't answer for a long while and then finally said, "Sometimes you all make me feel so young and inexperienced. And in the back of my mind I keep thinking of that girl. Who she is or where she's from?"

"How human of you," Phillipe mocked.

"That's it. I do sometimes act so human and I know it has a lot to do with Gail, but then I think that maybe it doesn't." He paused. "I feed just as you do. I enjoy it, just as you do. So why does it make me feel dirty or – I don't know – guilty to watch you enjoying it?" He turned to Bith, the eldest of the group, the only one he could trust for an explanation.

Bith shrugged and said, "Tino, we are solitary creatures. Do you know how strange it is that we have become pack hunters? Most of our kind are repulsed by what we are or do. Hunting as we do is almost completely unheard of. Not to mention that it's not exactly a safe practice to adopt."

Martino was confused.

"There's more of a risk of exposure in packs. Vampires prefer solitary lives in an attempt to blend into normal, human society. We don't blend in very well at all." She laughed at the muddled look on Martino's face. "If you see one white face in a crowd or spy the iridescent eyes of one stranger, most people wouldn't think twice about it, but you see the four of us walking down the street . . . well, you're going to cross over to the opposite side."

He nodded, accepting that explanation for now but knew there had to be more to it than that. Every vampire he knew had someone. Someone to live with, to hunt with, to love. If they were meant to be solitary, then why did they retain any emotions concerning love or devotion?

Chelsea wrapped her arms around him as they walked. "My truck is just down here." She pointed down the street. The warmth of her body was calming as usual. He let her tranquility soak into him as they walked. The blood he had consumed filled him and he was feeling drowsy as they reached Chelsea's F150.

"You better wipe that blood off those paws before they get in," Chelsea warned Richard without looking at him.

He pulled down the tailgate for Attila and Thor to jump in the back. The seats were cool as Martino slid into the back seat.

"What's our heading, captain?" Bith's mood had lifted again. The power of human blood on immortal emotions was pure magic.

"Tino wanted to return to Mount Orion tonight," Richard offered.

"I'd love to see Gail again. It's been years." Phillipe sounded drowsy. "But Jordan will be there as well. My dear Tabitha will love that." Not too drowsy to take a cheap shot at Bith.

She shrugged as if it were no big deal, but Martino saw her exchange a look with Chelsea and mouth the word *fuck* as she rolled her eyes. Chelsea laughed and put the truck in drive. With Richard on one side of him and Phillipe on the other, Martino laid his head back and closed his eyes. Images of the girl flooded his thoughts, pushing away all his insecurities and worries as they drove toward Mount Orion.

It was time to introduce Gail to the gang.

CHAPTER SIX

The fireworks were starting within the hour. Deanna had finally convinced Max to put down his books and turn off the computer. He had spent all day Saturday and a good part of Sunday trying to finish his Civics paper. She could see he was spent and needed a night out with his friends.

Deanna had spent the day with Sari at the fair and flea market. She was free of Devin and without Eric to distract her, Deanna was glad to have Sari all to herself. They bought weird, useless trinkets from local vendors. They got temporary tattoos. Sari bought baubles for her ears and fingers and a small dragon claw necklace for Eric. "He's been going on about dragons lately. He's weird." Sari tittered.

They also ate – a lot! Zeppoles, sausage and peppers, candied apples. And what Deanna loved most of all was how they talked and laughed. Easily and without worry of judgement. She had never had a friend like Sari – not since Jacenta.

"*Don't get too close. You know how this will end,*" Devin warned her.

"*Not necessarily.*" Who was she kidding? Sari was head over heels for Eric, and his intentions were abundantly clear. She was going to lose Sari, sooner or later.

After running home to coerce Max to leave behind the more respectable part of his life, Deanna noticed that the fair was winding down and everyone found a seat to watch the fireworks. The music was still pretty loud, and the lights surrounding Main Street were bright and glittering. There were blankets and lawn chairs on front lawns and completely covering the park.

The cemetery was the only area not consumed by people. Deanna's friends were the only ones pouring over the cemetery wall. Deanna, clad in white jeans and a tee shirt, danced merrily on the wall. The fluffs of her brown hair fell in perfect waves down her back. Her pallor was white and thin; her angular body swayed back and forth with the music. As she laughed and danced with her friends, she was not aware that she was being watched.

"Mouse, someone's watching you again," Devin whispered in her ear.

She nearly fell off the wall, startled by his presence. *"What do you want? Where have you been?"* she asked mentally.

"Someone's watching you. Look," he said. His voice was silky and clean. She imagined the Irish accent but in reality, it was hardly part of his voice after all these years.

"Leave me alone tonight, Devin. Do what you want to him. I don't care?" Devin wasn't invited to be a part of the celebration with her friends. He was intruding and Deanna wanted him to know it. Martino wasn't invited either, but here they both were.

She felt Devin leave her side and suddenly she felt sorry for what she said and how she said it. Casually, she swung around, still dancing to the music. It took only moments for her eyes to find Martino deep in the crowd. Again, he stood with the same girl as the other night. Deanna felt a wave of jealousy as the beautiful girl put her arm around him.

They were not alone. Deanna could see a group of them. White faces, somehow strangely out of place, yet no one noticed them in the crowd. How did they blend so well to others yet stand out so blatantly to her? For only a single moment, he smiled at her. A chill ran through her and struck her heart. That smile caused a pain that stopped her breath.

The dogs were back as well. She could hear them howl as Devin circled the unnatural group.

"He needs to leave us alone." Devin was back at her side and getting jealous again.

"Let it go. Trouble is something we don't need. Especially from you." She turned her back to Martino and his friends. Showing any interest in them would only instigate Devin's jealousy. And when Devin felt jealous, he got defensive. And that was dangerous! There was no need to protect Martino. He was

immortal. But Devin had powers that she didn't fully understand and didn't want to expose Martino to that kind of power.

"They need to start this show. This is getting fucking boring, man." Max wrapped his arms around Deanna.

"Let's hit the cemetery." John jumped off the wall. "Little music, little grass, little fun." He ran his hands over Connie's hips. "Creepy cemetery makes Connie horny."

"Shut up." She laughed.

They crept into the cemetery, keeping an eye out for police that were stationed randomly throughout the crowd. It was dark and silent as if the outside world did not exist. The tombs and markers sat on their grassy plain, shielding their owners from the torment of changing weather and constant tread of passers-by. Near a large tomb, a small clearing proved to be an adequate spot to set up camp. The same spot, ironically, where Martino and his friends had encountered another group of teenagers only two nights before.

John and Connie dropped to the ground wrapped around one another. It was quick and his theory proved to be accurate; the creepy cemetery did make Connie horny. Bobby started a small fire in the preexisting fire pit with some leaves and sticks while Max brought up Pandora on his phone. Sari leaned against a tree, tapping away on her phone.

"Eric coming?" Deanna pressed her chin into Sari's shoulder, eyeing her text messages.

"Nope." She quickly hit the power button and the device went black.

"Still got us." Deanna gave her a quick hug. Max called to her. She left Sari sulking against the tree. "Come sit with us," she said to Sari as Max pulled her to the ground. He was kissing her neck as she giggled. "Stop. I don't want to make Sari feel left out." Max didn't seem to care as his hands continued to travel the line of her body.

"Forget about Sari for one minute, okay?"

"Sorry." She kissed him hard on the mouth, wanting to let him know that she missed his touch. And she did. With work,

Devin's return, Eric's presence in Sari's life, Deanna found her mind was on everything besides Max. It wasn't fair to him and it wasn't fair to her. Her teeth nibbled his ear as her hands slowly moved toward his crotch.

Max winced as she touched his thigh. Another bruise on his leg. Deanna was getting angry just thinking about Devin putting his nonexistent hands on Max. She tried harder to block him out as she allowed Max to unclasp her bra.

She could hear Devin in a muffled way. *Don't. Care. Love.* Those were the words that she could make out as she started to unzip Max's jeans. She assumed he was saying something like "Don't you care that I love you." Or "I don't care if you love him." And then a clearer, more accurate thought occurred to her: "Don't you care if I kill him, my love?" The last thought struck her brain hard and she jumped up, her hand still stuck in Max's pants.

"Sorry, gotta pee." She darted into the darkness. "What is your problem?" she said aloud to the air around her, trying desperately to reattach her bra.

"Quiet, darling, you don't want them to hear you."

"I don't care if they hear me. You're killing my buzz."

"Your what?"

"My buzz. I need this every once in a while. I want to have fun with my friends. So beat it. Scram, Devin!" She caught herself before she yelled. And to ensure his departure, she said, "There are some things you can't do for me anymore. Things that Max can."

Walking back to the group, Deanna started to hear voices over the music. "Did you hear that? D, is that you? Something's moving out there, man. Don't you hear it?" It was Max. He always got paranoid when he was high.

"No! Shut the fuck up! You're shitfaced, Max." Bobby yelled at him. "It's just D. Don't make us pull you out of the brush bare-assed!" He laughed.

It's not me, she thought as she stood several feet away, still shrouded in darkness just outside of the fire's glow. She stood quietly and waited for whatever it was they were hearing to happen again. In the distance, she could hear the high school band playing something patriotic. Not a few feet away, Deanna definitely heard footsteps and muffled voices. More kids that had gotten the same idea as her friends did, or maybe it was the cops checking for teenagers getting drunk in the cemetery.

She heard Sari and Bobby laugh, but then Connie said she heard it too. Ah, Connie, ever the irrational one. The one friend that could be counted on to see ghosts and find conspiracies where there weren't any. "It's because you're in a cemetery. Your mind is playing tricks on you. Just relax," Sari said. And Sari, Deanna knew she heard the voices. She could hear the uneasiness in Sari's voice. But she knew that Sari was trying to be cool. "Max is just trying to scare us."

The sound became louder and everyone heard it that time. Deanna took a few steps back behind a tombstone and watched. "There it is. What is it?" Max was panicky. "Like a slow whistle. Listen."

"Maybe the fireworks are starting."

"Just sounds like talking. Why are you so jumpy? Relax, man!" There was more muffled talking, and it was coming closer. "Max, why don't you go get Deanna and we'll get the hell out of here." John jumped to his feet.

Good idea, John, Deanna thought but Max didn't move.

There was a silence suddenly and everyone was becoming really nervous. Sari and Connie came closer and clasped hands. "D? Where are you?" Sari whispered. "God, I wish Eric was here."

"Who do you think it is? Do you think it is Deanna having some fun with us?" Connie whispered. Sari didn't answer.

From the shadows, Deanna heard screams from two directions. First, John screamed and ran past her, being chased by something. The speed he was moving, any normal person would have thought it was a bear. Max panicked. "What's going on? John?" Someone or something was after John and stopped when Max bellowed his pathetic, drunken outburst.

The second scream came from Sari as two huge dogs burst into the fire's light and picked her to play with. They were yelping and fighting to lick her face.

Deanna watched as several people approached from the shadows. Two girls and a few guys. It was Martino and his friends. Seeing them in the light, she guessed they were around her age, maybe a few years older to anyone that didn't know they were immortal. The girls, one a blonde and the pretty darker haired one she'd seen twice already, scared her more than the guys. They looked like they were looking for trouble. They were laughing.

A whistle came from the distance and the dogs disappeared in the blackness.

"What the fuck?" she heard Connie say as she dropped a beer bottle. "What the hell are you guys doing?" She walked to Sari to make sure she was all right.

"Those are the same dogs from the other night." Sari was shaking. "Are they following us?" she whispered.

The new group laughed and continued to stare at Sari and the others. John walked back to the fireside, brushing off his jeans and looking incredibly frightened. Behind him a young vampire was laughing, enjoying this game they were playing. Deanna could only wonder why he hadn't killed John when he had the chance.

Max cursed something and started gathering their things. "Let's get the fuck out of here. These fuckers are crazy!" He was visibly shaken. "D?"

The two girls separated from the others in their group and came up behind Max. They still said nothing but just their presence scared him. He was dropping the bottles and his voice was shaking terribly as he shouted at them to stay away from him.

Deanna waited for the pull to kick in and for her friends to surrender to the game. With all the movement, she figured it didn't have a chance to take hold – yet.

There were at least three guys in this new group but only one seemed interested in this little game they were playing. The one that had chased John was loving his role in the game. Martino was standing back with another young boy with dark hair and soulful eyes. The boy was flanked by the two very large dogs that had taken a liking to Sari, twice now. He and Martino had no stomach for what was unfolding before them. The one that was playing the game followed the girls' lead and circled Deanna's group. Again, they said nothing but laughed.

It was time to join her friends. Deanna took a deep breath and felt for Devin. She could feel him near her but not being interactive at all. *"Are you there?"* she asked silently. No answer. *"Just don't do anything rash. Please. Let's see how this unfolds first."* Her voice sounded timid even in her own head. Pleading with Devin was never fun, but sometimes it was very necessary.

"Sorry guys, private party." Deanna took a step out of the shadows. "You've got the whole cemetery to party in." Suddenly, the laughing stopped. She tried to be cool and easygoing. "Leave us be."

The blonde began to laugh again. As she approached Deanna, she pushed her long blonde hair behind her shoulder and tried to become quite serious. Slowly she raised her hand to smooth Deanna's hair back, but Deanna pulled away before the girl's hand could make contact with her head.

Deanna raised an eyebrow and frowned. She could feel the pull and she stepped away, trying to avoid being taken in by it. The blonde girl smiled again. She was good at manipulation, damn good.

Except the manipulation was lost on Deanna, who stood her ground. "What are you doing here?" Her stare didn't waver. She could feel that damn pull weakening her resolve and she fought it.

"We saw your fire and heard your music." When she finally spoke, Deanna was surprised at the soothing, almost relaxing, tone she used.

Deanna smiled briefly and her glance fell toward Martino, who stood the farthest from the group. "I know what you want." She looked away from him. "You're not wanted. Go away!"

"Come now, you can't mean that." The blonde didn't back down. "We haven't even begun to have any fun." She smiled, her

British accent making her words sound welcoming rather than manipulating. "Just allow us to stay for a moment longer. May we all share in the fire and music?"

Deanna glared at her. *Why aren't they killing us?* It couldn't be because of her; why hide their way of life from her? She already knew what they were, and she was sure they knew that she knew. Deanna looked to each of them.

She looked to Martino and his young companion. She looked to the dogs. The girls were talking to each other, almost losing interest in this game. The young vampire that had chased John was clearly bored now and was leaning against a tombstone twirling a glow stick that he found neglected on the ground.

"D, you coming?" Sari called from a few feet away. She nervously eyed the dogs as they turned toward her, tails wagging impatiently. Her group had successfully gathered their bottles and were making their way away from this scene. The fireworks were beginning. "Let's find somewhere else to watch the show."

The two vampire girls stopped talking to each other and watched Sari as she followed her friends out of the cemetery. The look in their eyes was one of curiosity and interest. When Sari turned away, they resumed their conversation, completely ignoring Deanna now.

That's when it occurred to Deanna. *Sari.* It was Sari that was stopping them from killing her friends. It had to be. They knew Eric. Devin was right; it wasn't just a coincidence that they were here. Deanna watched them as they watched Sari. She knew she was right.

"Deanna, let's go," Sari called again, completely oblivious to her power here.

As Deanna stared the blonde girl down for another minute and then turned to join her friends, Martino's young companion spoke up. "Deanna? Is that your name?"

"Why?" she replied defensively.

"Just being friendly." The dogs stood up; their tails were tense and straight.

"You don't need to be. We're not friends." She started to walk away to join Sari, who had been the only one to wait for her.

"Why are you speaking to them?" Devin was beside her. *"They only mean to harm you."*

"Not with you around they won't." Deanna laughed to herself.

"But you know him, don't you?" This time it was the girl with the brownish hair that spoke, motioning to Martino when she finished. "Look at her, Tino. She stares you down like a jilted lover. Doesn't she?" She looked to the others for confirmation.

Jilted lover? I do not! Deanna thought and turned to face this woman. It was the pretty one that kept putting her hands on Martino. Jealousy started to build again, and Deanna laughed out loud this time.

"This is funny to you?" The young man that chased John approached from the other side of her. The game was getting a little more interesting now. Deanna was starting to feel surrounded. What had she gotten herself into? And that damn pull kept pulling her into it, stopping her from leaving.

Deanna shook her head. *"I'm feeling a bit trapped."*

No answer from Devin but she could feel him circling her. The young *friendly* boy beside Martino flinched slightly and took a step back and his dogs started to bark. Deanna could see a trepidation growing in him and he hushed the dogs.

"Do you know her, Tino?" the brown-haired girl asked.

Tino. Deanna liked the nickname.

Martino just stared at Deanna.

She suddenly felt a hand on her arm. It was Sari urging her to follow the others out of the cemetery. "What are you doing? Let's go." Deanna shook her off.

Martino's friends were watching the exchange between Deanna and Sari cautiously.

"Yes," Martino finally answered. "I do know her."

Damn. He admitted it. Damage control. Play dumb and control Devin. She couldn't do anything better than that. Control Devin and leave quickly.

"You must be mistaking me for someone else." She saw the smiles on the girls' faces. Deanna wanted to smack the smiles off their smug faces. *What kind of game is this?* "Just stay away from me." With that, Deanna walked toward the exit. *"Be calm. Don't worry about anything. They're just playing right now. They don't know anything."* She kept repeating these useless phrases to Devin, hoping that he would listen; really hoping that he would not.

Sari followed her. She was trembling both from fear and the chill in the air.

"Do me a favor." Deanna turned and rubbed Sari's bare arms to warm her and calm her down. Fear was not an emotion she wanted these vampires to smell on them. "Call Eric."

"What? Why?"

"Just call him. Don't text, call. Make sure it's loud enough for them to hear. Tell him anything. You just missed the sound of his voice. Anything. Just make sure they know who you are talking to."

Sari warily pressed a face in her contacts. The three smug bastards that were getting in Deanna's face watched attentively. "Hi," Sari's conversation started. Her hands were shaking as she dragged her fingers through her short sparkly hair. "I just wanted to say hello. I miss you."

"Say his name. Say his name," Deanna kept saying under her breath.

"Do you really think he matters to these predators? They've caught the scent of her fear and your adrenaline, darling. You'll be mincemeat by morning." Devin snickered at his alliteration.

"That's what I'm afraid of," she said silently to Devin. "Who are you talking to, Sari?" she called out.

"You told me to call Eric," Sari yelled back. "What, nothing. Just Deanna. Do I? I guess I'm a little nervous. Some weirdos are harassing us in the cemetery." She listened for a moment. "You'd do that? No, it's not worth the trip. I'll be fine. No, really."

Deanna came up beside Sari. "What did Eric say?" She put a great deal of emphasis on Eric's name.

"OK, I love you. Bye." She pressed the end button. "He said he'd come if I needed him. Do we need him? I told him we'd be alright." Sari took a deep breath, still glowing after talking to Eric. Deanna was sure the smell of fear on her was being replaced with the smell of desire.

Deanna looked to the group. They were really losing interest now. Her look was smug and knowing. Martino's expression was a perceptive smile. It was small and secretive and Deanna was sure that it was meant just for her. The smile on Martino's face made her want to smile. He knew what she had done, and she had done it well.

Without warning, the young vampire with the dogs started flinching as if he were caught in a swarm of mosquitos. The dogs went mad. They were barking and growling wildly. Deanna knew he could feel Devin – somehow. No one else seemed to feel him. Just that one young vampire. His eyes looked terrified.

"What are you doing?"

"*Playing along.*" Devin tried to sound innocent.

"You OK?" Sari commented to Martino's friend and looked to the dogs.

The boy nodded to her politely. "Let's get the hell out of here, Tino." The others in his group had already started to make their way out of the cemetery in the opposite direction of Deanna and Sari. Sure didn't take long for vampires to become bored with their games.

Deanna smiled. *"Playing along? So that's the best you could do?"*

"What did you expect?"

"Well, a little more than circling his head. I was hoping for some levitation or maybe smacking that one girl that was in my face." She was annoyed.

"You told me to be calm. Besides, slapping is more your department, not mine."

"I knew you wouldn't listen. You never listen. I was counting on you to scare them as much as they scared my friends. I can't do that." She started walking with Sari. *"What's the point of you having all this power if you can't use it when I need you to?"*

Devin was quiet for a moment. *"So, you want me to perform at your whims. Is that right?"*

"Not my whims, necessarily. But when I need you, yes."

Again, Devin was silent.

Sari stopped under the wrought iron gate. "Everything all right?"

Deanna nodded and smiled.

"Why'd you have me call Eric, anyway?" Sari linked her arm through Deanna's.

Deanna shrugged and lied her butt off. "I don't know. But it worked."

"I should have told him to come. I wish he was here."

"Me too," Deanna whispered and meant it.

The fireworks were in full swing over their heads but neither of them looked up to them.

It was hours after the fireworks and Deanna was still amped up from seeing Martino and feeling threatened by his friends. *Friends*, Deanna scoffed to herself. *Why did they find it funny to scare us?* But still, they didn't want to cross Eric. If only Sari knew the power she held; if only she knew what Eric truly was.

Now lying in bed, Deanna was thinking of Martino and truthfully Eric slipped into her subconscious a little too. But mostly Martino, not his friends, not the fear they were trying to instigate, just Martino. She pictured his calm, loving face with his big brown eyes that glistened when he smiled. They glistened when he lied too, she remembered. That sparkle in his eye and a crooked twist of his mouth told her he was lying every time.

She thought of his skin. It had gotten so pale since she had last seen him decades ago. Maybe that was her fading memory or that it was just too many years ago, but it definitely looked whiter even in the failing light of the campfire.

Deanna smiled as she thought of him. He remembered her. He knew it was her even without being or looking like Margaret. Somehow, she was still showing through no matter who was on the outside. Deanna Cullen shined through every lifetime.

There was a scuffling noise in the living room. Deanna pushed back the blankets and pulled her legs free. She heard something fall to the floor with a crash. Deanna shook her head. Max was so drained from the drugs and drinking he had consumed since leaving the cemetery that he collapsed on the couch as soon as they got home. Deanna had taken off his puke-stained shirt and covered him with a blanket.

She couldn't help but notice two large bruises on his arm and shoulder. They were blue and purple. Another bruise was on his chest, but this one looked like it was in the process of healing. Deanna reached out to touch them lightly, but even in his sleep Max flinched and pulled away. Gently, she had kissed his forehead and headed to the bedroom to sort out the myriad of emotions evoked by the night's events.

Now, she pulled the blankets up and lay back down. He probably woke up not knowing where he was and was stumbling around the living room, she thought. As she resumed contemplating what to do about Martino, Max stumbled into the room. He held fast to the furniture and the walls so as not to fall. His eyes were half closed like he was sleepwalking. He shuffled as he found his way to the opposite side of the bed.

Deanna heard his foot slam into the chest at the foot of the bed and winced for him, fully expecting to hear a long string of profanity, as usual, but none came. *He's still asleep,* she laughed to herself. *That will hurt tomorrow.*

As Max roughly and clumsily pulled back the covers and fell into bed, Deanna noticed something odd about his naked torso. It was free of bruises. The two large purple welts that she had examined not two hours ago were all but gone. The one on his chest was completely gone with no marks whatsoever. She frowned and touched Max's chest as he rolled toward her. Without words, his hands quickly found her legs and were creeping up her thighs.

"Max, stop, you're drunk." She pushed him away playfully.

He inched closer to her and awkwardly fell on her bare midriff. Kissing her stomach hungrily, his hands played uneasily with her pajama bottoms. "Max, come on, stop." Her tone was pleading yet stern.

Max pulled himself up on his arms, gaining better control of himself and looked Deanna in the eyes. His eyes, though vacant and eerily distant, held a disturbing glimmer that stopped Deanna's heart. "Max?" she whispered, knowing deep down inside it wasn't him staring back at her.

It was Devin. She had no idea Devin could possess a person. "Maxie, look at me."

There was no response and his hands were more focused; their purpose was clear as he removed her clothes hastily and climbed on top of Deanna. As he kissed her mouth and nibbled her neck, she fought the desire to surrender herself. The feeling in the pit of her stomach said that this was wrong.

"No, stop. I can't." It was wrong to use Max's body to make love to Devin. It was wrong; she kept telling herself. It was wrong. But as he held her in his arms and entered her, Deanna closed her eyes and saw Devin. His shaggy, unkempt hair hanging in his eyes as he looked down at her, thrusting roughly into her. She saw his crystal blue eyes sparkle as she cried out again and again. And it was his sun-freckled skin she kissed as he held her afterwards.

Sweating, out of breath and completely satisfied, Deanna watched as the glimmer of Devin faded from Max's eyes. Max's body slumped in the bed and she could hear him quietly snoring beside her.

"Devin?" she whispered into the darkened room.

"I love you, Mouse. Don't ever forget that," he whispered close to her face.

She wanted to respond but knew that Devin was gone. What she didn't know was that he had used up all his energy to possess Max; he had gone to recharge.

As she slowly fell asleep, Deanna thought of Max's bruises again. It had to be Devin's energy that sped the healing process. Devin caused the bruises and Devin took them away. Perhaps he could do good things sometimes. Her final thoughts were of Devin as she fell into a deep sleep.

CHAPTER SEVEN

Deanna. That was her name now.

Hours later, Martino slowly trailed his friends, thinking of Deanna. She knew him, he was sure of it. The sparkle in her eyes, the tremble in her hands, and even the acid in her tone told him so. He remembered that defensiveness in Margaret. She never wanted him to get too close. Still she couldn't stay away from him.

This new Margaret did seem agitated. Of course, she was surrounded by the undead. Bith and Chelsea frightened Martino when they got intense. And he was immortal. Being human, knowing what they were and feeling trapped – Martino could not imagine it.

Ahead of him, Phillipe was still talking about new Margaret's red-headed friend. He remembered her from the pub a few weeks ago. He found her *delicious.* His word, *delicious*, made Martino cringe. Just a little more time and new Margaret and her companions would have been dead. That was what *delicious* meant to Martino.

The night was clear. New Margaret could not be far away. Was she thinking of him as he was thinking of her? Martino grinned uncontrollably. He could see her imagining them years ago. The long walks they used to take were always his favorite. Colorado. He remembered the snow. So much snow that winter. The starry nights trudging through the snow to her home. No car could make it in the ice, and the hill was so steep. There was never a worry. Martino would make it in any weather.

"Drop it, Fleep!" Bith burst out.

The outburst tore Martino from his fantasy.

"Just stop. You'll get over it." She was sick of hearing Phillipe blaming Richard for his fruitless evening. "You were never going to have that girl. Do you realize how enraged Eric would have been if we compromised what he's trying to accomplish with that pink-haired girl?"

Phillipe didn't look at her.

"And Tino didn't want to upset his girlfriend," Chelsea teased. He ignored her.

Bith turned to Martino. "How do you know her? She certainly knew you." She touched the small of his back. Martino half-smiled but said nothing. "It was fun to bug her. Oh, come on, Tino. You were never going to talk to her on your own. That was clear." Bith grabbed Martino's hand. As much as he wanted to pull away, he knew it would do no good. Pushing Bith away would only result in more Bith. She would never leave him be.

Attila trotted to his right as he allowed Bith to wrap herself around his left arm. Her skin was like ice and he could feel it through his jacket. He knew she hadn't fed since the other night at Mount Orion when Martino introduced his friends to Gail. The tension between Jordan and Tabitha was palpable, and her only recourse to avoid a fight was to escape into the woods. Later that night when he went to look for her, Bith had told Martino that the hunting was spectacular on the grounds.

"Sorry," she whispered. "I just thought this way you broke the ice and we had a little fun in the process. Win-win, don't you think?"

"No, I don't think," Richard blurted out. Thor winced at the outburst, putting his ears down and thrusting his tail securely between his hind legs. "There was something definitely strange about that girl. It doesn't help you poking fun at it."

"What was with this?" Chelsea swung her arms around her head as Richard had moments ago in the cemetery. Her movements were much more dramatic and pronounced but he got the picture. "I thought you were having a fit or something. I was ready to tie you down and cut out your frontal lobe." She laughed.

"Just drop it," he whispered, stroking Thor's head.

"Yes, this kind of talk isn't helping anyone," Martino spoke up.

"You have to tell us how you know her," Bith pressed, playfully biting at his jacket sleeve. "She knew us. I nearly lost it when her friend called Eric. That was too much. How did she know what we are, Tino?"

Martino looked at his friends. They would never understand how he knew this girl was Margaret. They would never understand his feelings.

"She's bad news, to use a colloquialism," Richard spoke up finally. "I'm sorry, Tino, but she is. I felt something surrounding that girl. Something angry. They felt it too," Richard whispered, motioning to the dogs. He knew only Bith and Tino would believe him.

Martino looked to each of his companions. He knew Bith and Richard were listening, but Chelsea and Phillipe had already begun another conversation. They were walking ahead of them, laughing about something ridiculous, Martino was sure. The anger that was building between them was passing as they walked farther away from the cemetery and new Margaret.

"This Deanna, she's not who she appears to be. I knew her as . . ." He took a deep breath. "A girl named Margaret. I think."

"You think?" Bith was still attached to his left arm and Richard stood to his right. "Aren't you sure who she is?" Bith said.

"I told you she's not who she appears to be. I knew her as Margaret over fifty years ago."

"Fifty years? Is she immortal? I've read about creatures that live forever as we do but they use the sun to regenerate. Is she one of these creatures? Or perhaps another type of monster?" Richard looked frightened.

"Is she a werewolf? If she is, stay away from her." Bith was serious.

"Why?" Martino got off point.

"Their blood is poison to us. Take it from someone who knows. Just stay away from her."

Martino shook his head, no. "She's not a werewolf or any kind of monster. She's cursed. Maybe. That's what she told me.

Her soul moves on after death to another body. Everlasting reincarnation, she called it once."

Bith and Richard were silent for a while as they walked, and Martino was grateful. He didn't know if this young girl was really Margaret. In reality he knew she definitely wasn't Margaret. He knew where Margaret was, flesh and bone. Margaret was locked in a basement in Colorado. This girl was some new incarnation of Margaret and even of that he was unsure.

His friends wanted some kind of answers. He didn't have them yet. Speaking with new Margaret was his next step. More than a few words, away from his friends and hers.

"What's this feeling Richard keeps getting?" Chelsea turned and asked. She and Phillipe had silently been listening to the others as they discussed this girl. Martino shrugged.

"Maybe it's the curse. Perhaps it's designed to keep beings, like us, away from her." Phillipe joined the dialogue.

"If it is, then it's not working very well. We'd all feel it if that were true. Not just Richard. That can't be it because unfortunately Margaret is already one of us." Martino kept looking straight ahead when that brought the entire group to a sudden halt – the dogs too.

"What?" Chelsea was the first to shout it, but the others followed closely with similar exclamations of astonishment.

"I was in love with this woman about fifty years ago. She was young, maybe twenty. She was gorgeous, brown hair, hazel eyes. A figure . . ." He stopped his recollection. "You get it. Well, she said she had some sort of curse against her. She told me her body was not her own. That her soul was constantly reincarnated. I didn't understand what she was telling me about her situation. I thought I'd help her live forever. I just couldn't lose her. I found out she was telling me the truth all along. I also realized, too late, that making her a vampire killed her and freed her soul again.

"Apparently I forgot the part where we're technically dead. Margaret became an immortal, but her soul left her dead body. This curse is real and it doesn't stop." Martino stared at the faces of his horrified friends.

"Talk about star-crossed lovers. She found you again. That's so romantic." Chelsea swooned.

"Technically, we found her. Strange that she would know Eric, right? I mean what are the chances?" Phillipe commented.

Bith looked dumbfounded. "You two have got to be kidding me. You're missing the bigger issue here. Out there – somewhere – there's a vampire with no soul? No conscience? No fear? Just unrestrained power." The others said nothing and tried to digest the question. "She is like a time bomb waiting to go off. Why haven't you killed her, Tino?"

Martino felt like he was just hit in the stomach by her words. *Killed her?* Why hadn't he killed her? It never – ever – crossed his mind. He had locked her up but the idea of ending her life was never a part of his plan. "I couldn't." The words left his mouth in a thick emotion-filled crackle that made Martino clear his throat after he said it.

"How does Eric's friend play into this?" Chelsea said.

"Unfortunate circumstances is my guess. Guilt by association," Martino responded.

"Eric must know this girl. Ask him, Tino. Ask Eric if he ever felt anything bizarre when he was around her."

It was so simple. Why hadn't he thought to ask Eric before? It was his girlfriend they were following when he found new Margaret. Eric must know her and had spent time with her. Eric was so much older than he was that Martino often kept his distance unless others were present. "Let's go to the cabin," he said simply and was surprised when no one argued.

"Sari has a friend," Martino started. They found Eric sitting comfortably in the basement living room in front of a fire. He was relaxing and listening to Gail's country music coming from the upstairs rooms. Attila and Thor had found him before Martino. They had bounded down the stairs and greeted him with slobbery kisses before retreating to the warm rug in front of the fireplace.

Eric smiled, waiting for him to continue. He was dressed simply in jeans, button down shirt, and a black velvet jacket (now covered in dog hair and large paw prints). It looked as if he had just returned home when they met him in his favorite spot. Martino knew Gail had just come home and assumed they had spent time hunting together.

Tabitha and Phillipe decided to hunt while Martino interrogated Eric, while Chelsea was upstairs enjoying time with Gail. The two, although having just met a few days ago, were becoming fast friends.

"She's got dark hair. L-long dark hair. P-pretty." Martino didn't know why he was nervous, but his voice broke a few times as he spoke.

"That could be Maggie or Deanna." He ran his hand down his mouth. "Probably Deanna. Why?"

"How well do you know her?" It was the first time Richard had spoken since he entered the cabin. He would have preferred to hunt with the others, but Martino insisted that since he had felt the weirdness that he should be there to speak with Eric.

Eric looked to Richard curiously. "Not well."

Martino didn't know if he should explain the whole story to Eric. It was Phillipe's idea to follow Sari to the pub and torment her friends at the cemetery. It was wrong what they had done, and he knew Eric would be angry if he'd known.

"Why?" Eric pushed, looking up to Martino urging him to sit.

Martino could feel the nervousness in his stomach as he tried to remain calm. He glanced to Richard, who appeared confident as he sat waiting for this to be over and he could escape outside with the dogs. Martino took a seat. "Without getting into too much detail, I know this Deanna."

Eric's brows met but he waited for Martino to continue before asking him the myriad of questions that were building.

"What do you know of her, this girl?" Richard sat on the opposite side of Eric. He said *this girl* with disdain.

"Hold on, are you the weirdos that were harassing them at the cemetery tonight?" Eric chuckled and shook his head. "My advice. Stay away from Deanna. There's so much more to her than just a pretty face." He shifted uneasily in his seat and he fiddled with the pocket of his jacket. His eyes were saying much more than his words.

Martino nodded. "So, you do know something?"

"Just what I've seen briefly. She doesn't like me or more accurately, she doesn't trust me. She knows what I am, though she'll never let on. That's the part I can't figure out. Why doesn't she tell Sari? Unless she's waiting for something to go wrong . . . I don't. But yes, there's something strange about her or that surrounds her."

"Yes. There is something that surrounds her." Richard jumped up and pointed at Eric. "I felt it. Thor and Attila did too."

"Dogs are highly intuitive. More so than we are. They sense when things are amiss," Eric said plainly. "Trust the dogs over your own instincts. I'm bringing Sari here next week. As long as you don't scare her, try talking to her. She and Deanna are like sisters. She'll know something."

"So, Eric tells me Sari's coming here?" Martino asked, trying to act as if he had very little interest in the subject, but he could feel that his true feelings were transparent.

"Next week." Gail was brushing her long black hair. "What do you think? Braid or bun?"

"Braid," he said, not really caring either way. Gail would look beautiful if she chopped her hair short. "So, how did you convince Eric to bring her here?" The subject was Eric's pink-haired friend, Sari, and if he thought too much about it, Gail would get wind of his recent stalking from his thoughts.

Gail laughed quietly. "I just simply told him that after so long, didn't he think we should meet her. I know he wants to slowly introduce her to this life, but his pace was ridiculous. I've never seen a man move so slowly."

Martino was hardly listening. He was holding Abby's tablet in his hands, reading the local news and trying to learn how to swipe the page. He tried several times to make the page disappear to the left before he got frustrated. Placing the tablet on the chair beside him, he cursed under his breath.

"Besides, Jordan is away for a few days. He thinks I'm being ridiculous about this girl and says I should keep my nose out of it," she said.

Jordan had been away more than usual recently. It didn't go unnoticed by Martino that his recent absence seemed to coincide with Tabitha's presence at the cabin. She avoided visiting with the others, although Phillipe and Chelsea loved being here, saying that she didn't feel *comfortable* around Jordan. Martino knew there was more to it but never pressed her for answers.

"He's not wrong. Why must you get involved? Let him do as he wishes with this girl. If he decides to mutilate her body tomorrow, that shouldn't concern you."

Gail rolled her eyes and continued to braid her hair. "You know how I am. I know he doesn't want to *mutilate her body,* as you so colorfully put it. He feels something for her. I can tell." She paused. "And I am never wrong about these things."

There was a long silence before Martino spoke again and he picked up the tablet. An article about a dead body found washed up on the shore caught his attention. It had been drained of blood. The authorities believed that it was possibly a drug-related crime, but Martino knew it was a vampire. The drug lords wouldn't go through the trouble of draining a person's blood. They would simply kill and dump the person off the dock – at least that's what the movies had led him to believe.

A vampire killed the man found half naked and water-logged on the beach. There was no doubt about it. He wouldn't be surprised if they didn't revive the late, great Vampire Killer from years ago.

It had been almost forty years since the Vampire Killer rumors raged. He was copied by many humans that couldn't quite match his unmistakable style. There were never any leads, and no one was ever apprehended. Of course not. The Vampire Killer was a real vampire. One of Gail's many blunders for an offspring, as Jordan would say. Martino laughed to himself.

Jordan hated all of Gail's offspring, didn't he? Martino had always taken it so personally that Jordan didn't like him. But it was any one that Gail created that he despised, especially the Late Great Vampire Killer. He laughed again. He mustn't show the article to Gail. It would upset her.

"I've already seen the article, darling. They didn't even mention him. You're the one who connected the two. It could have been anyone that killed that man. Even you." She read his mind easily. "So, everyone should be here when Sari arrives on Friday. Eric's bringing her by ten." Sitting beside Martino, she fastened her braid and drew it over her right shoulder. "You've met her. What's she like? Eric tells me nothing."

He loved to watch Gail excited. Her eyes danced and her normally white complexion reddened slightly. It was yet another reason he loved when Jordan would go away. Gail was never like this with Jordan. This playful, excitable, loveable way about her seemed to evaporate when Jordan materialized.

Martino thought for a minute. "I haven't actually spoken to her, but she'll surprise you. I'm sure she's not at all what you're expecting." He shook his head. "Too much makeup. Ghastly pink hair! Ugh, that's got to be the worst part. That hair." He laughed and swiped to another page on the tablet.

Gail studied him silently. "But there is something that you enjoyed about her. I can tell." Gail bit her lower lip in anticipation. Another habit that would only appear when they were Jordan-free.

The front door opened wide, stopping him as he tried to put her smile into words. Abby was laughing before she entered the room. Her chestnut brown hair was swept up out of her face in a large plastic clip and her complexion looked as if she had used stage makeup to disguise her pallid pallor. Behind her was Chelsea laughing just as uproariously as Abby. Since their introduction two nights ago, the two were becoming inseparable.

"Gail, you're here. Thank God. You've got to hear what happened." Abby, still laughing, grabbed Gail's shoulders and hugged her roughly.

Chelsea greeted Martino with a kiss and Gail with a gentle wave of her hand. Gail smiled in return, cringing at the roughness Abby was using on her shoulders. "You're drunk. She's drunk, isn't she?" She looked to Chelsea, who shrugged sheepishly and nodded.

"That's what I'm trying to tell you. Drinking from a drunk gets you drunk." Abby laughter burst from her mouth like a bomb sounding somewhere in between a belch and her best duck impression. She climbed over the back of the sofa and dropped beside Gail.

"Not that this is news to you. She does this and plays innocent. I hate when you're drunk. Glad to know you are spending quality time together." She raised an eyebrow to Chelsea, who only laughed. "Just stay close to the door."

"Why?" Abby pulled on her braid playfully.

"Again, as if you don't know. But I'd prefer you not expelling your exploits onto my rug." She ran her hand down Abby's face. Turning her attention away from her inebriated companion, Gail looked to Martino. "So, you were telling me what you liked about Sari?"

"Eric's girl? *Pinky Tuscadero*?" Chelsea laid her head on Martino's shoulder. "She's a trip. The other night, we were just playing around . . ." She glanced up to Martino. The smirk on his face looked as if she was speaking a foreign language but was clearly understood as *shut up*. "Sorry, go ahead, Tino."

Gail bounced a bit in her seat as she awaited his answer, and Martino was immediately transported back in time to the night of his creation. She was so eager to turn him, though he didn't know it at the time. That bounce, he hadn't thought of it in years. He could see Gail standing by that fountain in a small town in Italy biting her lip, bouncing, fiddling with his jacket. Her questions of the afterlife had frightened yet enticed him. She had changed him quickly and hated him for years because of her guilt. Seeing her bounce now brought a small tingle in his chest that felt like magic.

He stroked her face delicately. "Her smile. Absolutely brilliant and natural. You'll love her." He paused. "Is she coming alone?"

Gail thought of Sari from the brief images she had gotten from Martino's mind. "Eric's bringing her here for the party. It wouldn't be safe to bring anyone else. Don't you agree?"

He nodded, half-heartedly. *Safe?* With a house full of vampires there would be no poorer time to introduce an unsuspecting human.

"You'll be here as well?" She took his hand. She looked to Chelsea. "And your friends?"

"You bet."

Abby rocked on the sofa and Gail knew vomiting was imminent. "Oh God, take her outside now. Now!" The frenzied bumbling trying to drag Abby from the sofa continued into the front yard as she leaned into the bushes and deposited the remains of her drunken meal from an hour ago. "Better?" Abby nodded and leaned over for an encore performance. "Do you think Tabitha will come next week?" She tried to draw the attention away from Abby's guttural retching.

"Will Jordan still be away?"

"I can't promise anything. He's been very unpredictable recently."

"He likes things calm. The least bit of upheaval and he gets antsy. He's always been that way."

Gail stared at Chelsea in a distrustful way that troubled Martino, but if Chelsea noticed it, she gave no indication. She wrapped her arm around Abby's waist, supporting her as they walked back to the living room.

"Have you seen Rapunzel recently?" Chelsea teased him about Deanna. He swatted her playfully but sternly, hoping Gail would let it slide. No such luck.

"Something you want to talk about?" Gail picked up the neglected tablet and pressed a few apps clumsily.

Chelsea smiled apologetically to him and indicated that she would take Abby downstairs to rest for a while. When they were safely out of the way, he said, "Sari has a friend."

Gail's eyes darted to the side and then back to the game she had accidentally opened on the computer screen. "A pretty friend?" she asked coyly.

"Very pretty." He took the tablet from Gail's hands and resumed his newspaper article.

She sat despondent for a moment. "That's all you're going to give me? You really know how to hurt me." Playing with her braid, Martino could see the twinkle in her eyes return and knew she had returned her focus on Sari's anticipated arrival. "I should get food."

Martino switched from the local online news to world news. Another article absorbed him.

"Like what?" Gail looked to him and smacked his leg. "Are you listening to me?"

"Humph."

"Why is that stupid article about some child's death so important?"

Still he didn't answer.

"Tino, I need your help. I'm not used to this anymore. There hasn't been a human at Mount Orion in years. I don't know what to buy."

A slight warmth ran through his chest when she called him Tino. Gail had rarely used a nickname with him, and it made Martino feel distant from her. His friends used this pet name frequently, making him feel loved and respected by them. Hearing her use it now made him hopeful for their relationship.

He laid down the tablet momentarily and laughed. Even without being able to read her thoughts, Martino knew she was thinking about entertainment, filling the refrigerator, and finding a sound excuse as to why she wasn't going to be around the next morning. He knew that as soon as Sari arrived, Gail would be calm and composed. She would put on the perfect hostess persona and Sari would be captivated.

There was no way not to be captivated by Gail. She was beautiful and eloquent. And her thoughts were constantly on others. She would constantly sacrifice her own enjoyment or comfort to accommodate those around her.

"Gail . . ."

She wasn't listening. "I don't know what she likes to eat or drink."

"It's a party. If memory serves, I don't think party food has changed much. Beer, crackers, and cheese. It'll be fine." He returned to his virtual newspaper.

CHAPTER EIGHT

As she opened her eyes, Jacenta sensed something was different. Wrong. Her enormous double king size bed felt strangely empty, and as her eyes scanned the dimly lit room, she could see that the drapes were open.

A deep breath slowed down her thoughts for a moment. The dim lights from the town far below gave off a glow in the darkness outside. The relaxing sound of the tide coming in and receding helped her eyes to close once more.

With her eyes closed, although relaxed, Jacenta could hear movement in the outer rooms. Pacing. The tide was both relaxing and aromatic. The lulling sound of the water called her back to dreamland, but the gentle scratch of socks gliding across her hardwood floors kept her in the present. The pillows beside her smelled sweetly of California's expensive shampoo and the blankets had a slight hint of coconut – also California's.

She had spent the night again. Not in her own rooms but with Jacenta.

It was Callie who no doubt opened the drapes – regardless of Jacenta's strict instructions not to – and it was Callie she heard pacing in the outer rooms.

The girl was coming along. After only two weeks since coming to Haven, she was becoming better accustomed to her new life. Not a lot of press as Jacenta had first expected. She was sure in the States, stories of a girl going missing in Brazil covered the headlines for the past week, but in South America there was not much more than a few mentions on the local news and a flier that California's parents had wallpapered along the streets.

Lauren Palmer. The twenty-year-old was being mourned by Becky and Glenn Palmer, although they hadn't realized they needed to mourn just yet. They were still in searching mode. Callie, as California became known to everyone at Haven, thanks to Piper, looked at the fliers and all the news reports on TV and online. She cried and cursed and cried again. Why was this done to her? She railed at everyone. Especially poor Piper, who taken Callie under her wing. They cut her hair into a simple, fun, shaggy bob. Her hair was colored so as not to attract any attention when she did finally venture out into the streets.

The Lauren vs. Callie discussion was not a long drawn-out debate. Callie liked being Callie. Lauren was her former self and she would never be her ever again. Someone had seen to that two weeks ago outside a bar when Lauren left to catch a cab back to her hotel. She remembered feeling ill, kissing her parents goodnight, and never seeing them again. The attack and subsequently bloody details were a blur; at least that was the story Callie was trying to convince everyone to believe. Jacenta knew when she was ready, the truth would come out.

Jacenta took Callie to her parent's hotel. She watched her mother cry. She heard her father reassuring her that they weren't abandoning Lauren, but they needed to go home and rally the troops. That's the words he used, *rally the troops*. What it sounded like was that he intended to go get help from family and friends and then return to find Lauren. Jacenta knew that really it meant go home and accept the fact that they had lost their only daughter on the worst vacation of their lives.

After that, Callie was attached to Jacenta's side. Sleeping, working, hunting. There she was.

Over the last week, Piper was teaching Callie to hunt. It was a talent that was not lost on Callie. She was actually quite good. But as in every young vampire, her need for blood was overwhelming, and her patience was nonexistent. It was left up to Piper to help replace Callie's need for the blood with a need for acquiring the blood. The hunt, the chase, the desire. They made the blood much more rewarding and satisfying.

Teaching Callie to feed on animals proved difficult. The smell of fear and adrenaline was what drove most young immortals to kill. The smell wasn't as strong in animals as it was in humans. But they were larger – which meant more blood – and faster. The hunt was meant to wear Callie out by the end of the night.

Jacenta pulled herself from under the blankets. The wool blankets, although cozy and inviting, were warm and becoming somewhat oppressive. Her room was warm, too warm. When she touched her bare feet to the usually cool tile floor, even the tile seemed to be sweating. She pulled on a long silk robe and followed the sound of the tide.

"Cal?" she called as she strolled from the bedroom, her robes billowing behind her. In the hallway, the thermostat read 85 degrees. Jacenta shook her head. "Why did you put the heat up?" She pressed the button to lower the temperature several times. "It's like a sauna in here."

The feeling of talking to herself washed over her. "Cal?" She listened intently. No more pacing. She heard the heat turn off and nothing else. She saw a neglected pair of socks near the terrace door and then a pair of legs extending over the railing on the balcony.

The curtains blew in the breeze through the open terrace doors. The salty air was intoxicating as she pulled back the sheer fabric and walked out on to the deck. It was a large balcony that was mostly empty except for a few chairs. Without a word, Jacenta leaned on the railing beside Callie's feet, looking over the beach and the water. The moon was full and the few stars that were scattered winked brightly. There was music in the distance but Jacenta couldn't figure out if it was coming from the town, the beach, or the small speakers nestled throughout her rental flat.

"Something you want to talk about?" She didn't look back at the young girl seated behind her.

"Do I really have to go away?" Callie's voice was strong, but a small amount of uncertainty tinged its edges. "Especially back to America." The sound of disgust was evident.

Preliminary plans were made to transport California to Haven in Connecticut. Jacenta had spent the better part of last night on the phone with Roderick – who had been running some form of Haven for over a century – making more concrete plans. They were expected to arrive in America next week.

"Yes," Jacenta said with a coolness in her voice. "It'll be safe for you there."

"How do you know?" Her ring-clad feet wriggled with her doubt. "J, look at me, please."

Jacenta smiled and watched Callie's feet start to nervously hop on the railing. Her toes were painted teal and several toes had a ring or rhinestone attached to it. A rope was tied around her left ankle with small seashells dangling from it. Jacenta turned, still leaning on the railing. Callie was wearing bleached and worn-out jean shorts with a ripped-up sweatshirt. Her dark blonde hair was pulled back in a ponytail, accentuating her blue eyes and large dangly earrings. "I've been there. There will be others – like you – and they will help you until you're ready to go out on your own. If that's what you choose."

Callie's face darkened as her eyes turned toward the sky. Her brows knit together as a thought formed in her head, but she did not voice it. Jacenta sat down in the adjoining chair. The delicate silk of her black sleeping gown danced around her legs as she waited for Callie to continue.

She didn't continue, and a silence fell between the women. Jacenta breathed deeply, inhaling all the wonderful aromas the breeze carried with it. Her eyes were closed, and her hands absentmindedly braided her red hair. The music was louder now, and she was sure it was coming from the city and that it was live, not recorded. Any music Callie ever put on in the apartment always included Flo Rida or Rihanna or something equally painful to listen to for Jacenta. This music had a deep rhythm that made her want to move her body. She felt her waist swaying in her seat as she threw her head back and let the music flow into her.

The memories of coming to Brazil years ago flooded back as the music took hold of her. Thoughts of Eric and Sabina and the marvelous times they had spent together on the beach. Memories of the ocean covering their naked bodies as they swam and laughed and loved each other. It was almost too good to be true; almost like a dream.

Devin had been there as well, ruining the magic, extinguishing the dream. She was capable of creating magic, no matter what Deanna said. Her magic just happened to be with people and not potions; with love and not the elements. Maybe she couldn't make it rain or cause the river to swell with her tears, but she could feel true love and that was magic enough for her.

Still Devin ruined that as well. Fighting and accusations replaced the laughter and frolicking eventually between Eric, Sabina, and Jacenta. Devin was always ruining her relationships – right from the beginning.

The French doors leading on to the balcony swung shut, catching the sheers between them, ending Jacenta's memories. The women shared a startled glance. "A breeze, maybe?" Callie shrugged. Her bottom lip straightened in her confusion. She hadn't been let in on the prankster that was Devin just yet.

"From inside?" Jacenta got to her feet and pulled the handles on the doors down. The levers both moved easily but the doors wouldn't budge. *"Damn it, Devin. Let go!"* she said silently to him.

A diminutive chuckle accompanied the doors swinging open and Jacenta fell into her apartment.

Sprawled on the floor, Jacenta remained for a minute trying to compose herself. Her black gown inched its way up until her white thigh was exposed and her hair falling out of its confines covered her face. *"You are such an ass!"* She pulled herself to her knees. Devin laughed uproariously.

"Use too much strength?" Callie's hand was extended, offering assistance. She was laughing.

Waving her away angrily, Jacenta got to her feet under her own power. It infuriated her to be laughed at, especially by the two creatures that were dependent on her attention. Her gown was wrapped around her body so she looked as if she was wrapped in a black cocoon.

"I'm going to get dressed," she said, still aggravated as Callie pushed the French doors fully open again and retreated to her balcony chair.

"Hey, turn down the heat when you go past the thingy. Why'd you put it up in the first place? It's boiling in there," Callie called through the doors.

"I didn't and it's down. I thought you turned it up." Jacenta felt a growl growing in her throat. She heard Devin laughing softly. *"Why? What does it accomplish besides irritating me?"* she said to Devin silently.

"Just having a little fun. When did everyone lose their sense of humor?" He sounded dejected.

"I suppose you opened the drapes as well. And if I didn't wish to rise this evening? . . . I guess I would have taken my chances in a few hours with the sun. What are you thinking? These little things you do are not funny anymore. They're just exasperating."

She stormed into her dressing room and slammed the door. A flip of the switch and the entire room was flooded with luminescent light. Racks of clothes, dresses, jeans, leather, silk, cashmere, the finest materials in the brightest and boldest of colors. Her shoes had a wall of their own. Then drawer after drawer of undergarments: silky, lacy, and beautiful.

The black sleeping gown slipped off her body easily and piled on the floor. Jacenta went to her many drawers of undergarments and selected a pair of lacy pink panties and matching bra. Her pale naked body shimmered in the bright sparkling lights of the dressing room and she heard Devin sigh.

"So beautiful." He ran through her hair. *"There isn't another woman alive that is your equal."*

Jacenta smiled a secret smile, not wanting to enjoy the compliment but did. As she stepped into the panties, she felt a shiver run up her back and heard Devin hum in her ear. "Stop it," she said harshly and aloud. "Those days are over for us."

"They needn't be. I've discovered something since my incarceration." He waited for her to answer or show some kind of interest.

Oblivious, Jacenta searched her racks of clothes, pushing the hangers this way and that, trying to decide on a proper garment.

"J?" Callie was knocking.

"Hmm."

"Before we go to America, can we do the Amazon . . . just once? Please?" She leaned on the door frame and picked at her cuticles nervously.

"You're not being sentenced to death, you know. You're going to another country -- temporarily. We'll still be here if you want to return." Jacenta laughed but thought on the prospect of playing in the rainforest for the next few nights. Watching Callie enjoy the hunt was enticing. Big cats, monkeys, deer. "Yes, pack a few things. We'll leave in a little while."

Callie's bare feet bounced on the wood floor. "Can we stay with Rani?" A smile spread wide across her face.

"You like that old man, don't you?" Jacenta's brow raised with playful accusation. "Go and get ready." Callie tore down the hall to her own room.

"Rani? That old vampire hermit?" Devin remembered Rani from centuries ago when Jacenta was starting Haven. He was the one that gave her the confidence and protection she needed to defy the Council. He was a dark-skinned vampire that could have thrived easily amongst humans but chose to hide away and lead a solitary life. As for the *old* part, it more referred to his age as an immortal and not his age when he was reborn. It was always a joke that Jacenta called him old; Rani laughed and smiled. Patient as always.

"The one and only. He's been in the Amazon for years. He visited us last week and apparently Callie took a real liking to him. He's quite wise and charming." Jacenta, now armed with a destination to dress for, chose a simple pair of cargo pants and white tee shirt. Grabbing several items of similar comfort, she

threw them on the chair to pack for their trip. *"I'd invite you, but Rani was never really fond of you. The reason was something neither of you cared to share with me . . . so stay here or go home. Whichever."*

"Perhaps going home would be the right thing to do." Devin paused waiting for Jacenta's reaction. She had none. Her mind was on her impending trip. *"When I left Deanna, she was quite exhausted."*

Jacenta swallowed hard and took the bait. *"Why, what did you do to her?"* Her tone was apprehensive but not without her usual sarcasm.

"Not to her but rather with her. We made love."

"How!" she said aloud and louder than she intended. The thought was both ludicrous and invoked a certain amount of leftover jealousy that bubbled in her belly.

"Hidden talent, darling. Something I didn't think was possible, but I can possess people." His voice sounded boastful.

"Oh, you are so full of it. Are we starting to believe those ghost stories that the movies have made so popular? I guess if you can possess people, I should just break out my Ouija board and exorcise you." She threw a few more items into a duffle bag and zipped it quickly, shaking her head and mumbling to herself.

Devin was silent for a while and Jacenta could feel static around the base of her neck. He was upset. She rubbed her neck quickly. He hated when she refused to believe him.

"So, are you going home or not?" She shook off the tension that was building in her shoulders. *"Where is home these days?"*

"New Jersey," he said simply and without further signs of anger.

"I thought it was something like that. She felt closer this time. Last time, she had to be in Australia. I didn't check but I was getting a strong pull when I was there in the early seventies. Before then she had to be in the US but out west. It's really odd when I get that tug after she's reborn." Jacenta made a fist and shook it in front of her heart. *"I had a hard time of it for a while

and I went underground. Not for long but I wasn't able to track her at all. But I know this new incarnation was born when I woke." She unzipped her duffle and tossed two pair of boots in with her clothes. She continued talking to Devin, envisioning him leaning against the wall in his usual cavalier manner. "*It was weird. My sleep was wearing thin and I knew I wanted to rise. The thirst was killing me, and I missed my work desperately. Couldn't let emotion get in the way of my life. But then I got that old familiar tug on my heart and I knew she was still out there.*"

Jacenta's mouth twisted and her eyebrows shot up as if she just spilled something personal to a stranger and instantly regretted it.

"*Can I guess how long you were out of commission?*" Devin was up to something.

Jacenta nodded, not trusting where this was headed. She pictured him pacing with his fingers steepled to his lips.

"*Twenty years?*"

She nodded again. "*How did you know that? You were in her prison, weren't you?*"

"*That's exactly the amount of lost time between when Cheynna died and Deanna was reborn. There's been nothing. Cheynna died of cancer at seven; then Deanna has no memory until she was reborn as Deanna Belamy. That's the present lifetime. Did you do something different to her than you did to me with that curse? Something perhaps that ties her to you and not me?*"

Jacenta looked around the room. Giving Devin too much information was giving Devin too much power. She heard Callie's footsteps approach the dressing room door. "*Look, I've got to go. We'll talk about this another time.*"

"I'm ready." Callie appeared in the doorway. A backpack was slung over her shoulder and Converse shoes were on her feet, but otherwise her outfit had not changed.

"Me too." She grabbed her duffle. "*See you later, Devin.*" And without thinking, she added, "*Say hi to Deanna for me.*" As she and Callie headed for the front door, Jacenta heard the doors to her dressing room slam shut and the mirror shatter. She closed the front door gently, hoping he didn't completely destroy the apartment in his rage.

CHAPTER NINE

By Friday morning, while Sari searched her closet for something suitable to pack for her first weekend away with Eric, and Deanna argued with Devin about yet another disappearing act, Max opened his eyes to one of the worst hangovers he had ever had. The taste of stale cigarettes and beer still lingered on his tongue. With his eyes still fighting for that last bit of darkness before the light paralyzed his senses, Max searched for the bottle beside his bed. He couldn't remember exactly what it was he was drinking before he passed out, but as soon as the liquid hit his lips, it would come back. It always did.

Finally, his fingers found the neck of the bottle and wrapped themselves around it. The glass was cool and a bit clammy under his palm. His other hand reached for the tumbler on the nightstand. It was as if his hands were working by their own direction; they were so used to this ritual. And as it did every morning, his hand clumsily knocked the tumbler to the floor along with several objects on the nightstand. His car keys and the remnants of a note Deanna had left for him last night. He paid no attention to these things as the bottle met his lips.

"Damn." Max rubbed his eyes, pulling the bottle to his lips again. The burning liquid was comforting going down his throat. Whiskey. Just enough left to open his eyes and clear his sinuses. "Ahh." He sighed.

His eyes were open, and the sun was shining its brightest in three days. Through a drunken stupor, Max could remember only the sound of rain on his roof. The television was still on and blurry images of *I Love Lucy* were passing back and forth as Max blinked his eyes.

"D?" he called. He sniffed the air for the pleasing aroma of coffee or perhaps bacon and eggs. Neither of these things were in the air. "D?" he called again. Max closed his eyes and shook off the annoyed feeling.

Another swig from the bottle, and then he pulled himself into a sitting position and lit a cigarette. Something was different; something was wrong. Where was he? The room was not his bedroom. There were half-filled glasses on every flat surface in the small room. A small round table lay on its side, surrounded by food wrappers and wads of sauce-stained napkins. The stained carpet and thin aged comforter on the bed said No Tell Motel. Max ran his hand over his mouth and tried to think. No good; it was too early, or he was too drunk, or both.

He swung himself out of bed, bottle still in hand. Still a bit disoriented, he scratched his naked chest and ran his hand through his hair. His back ached terribly and felt as if he had been in a bar fight.

The sun was shining, and the rays squeaked through the drapes, making the dust visible as it flew through the stale smoky air. There were sounds of people walking past his door and the old analog clock ticked beside the bed.

"Get yourself together," he said aloud. After one more swallow from the bottle in his hand and then finishing his cigarette, Max picked up his phone. Punching in Deanna's number, it rang. And rang and rang. The annoying robotic voice: "You've reached the voice mailbox of . . ." Max hung up before he could hear Deanna's perky voice say, "Deanna Belamy."

"Where r u call me" he texted hastily.

He punched in another number, only briefly noticing several text messages that were sitting in his notifications unread. He pulled another swig of whiskey from the bottle. It rang nearly five times before the soft voice asked, "Nicodemus, New York. How may I help you?" Such a melodious voice, the woman had.

"Lydia?"

"Yes, this is she. Who is calling please?" She was so polite.

"It's Max Brewer. Is Deanna there?" He licked his lips dully. Lydia had come to one of their Super Bowl parties and had spent the night hitting on him. It was the last time D had invited any of her work friends to their parties.

The room was spinning for a moment and righted itself after he shook his head again.

"No, sweetie. She called out today. Did you want to leave a message?" She sounded distracted but tried to remain professional.

He said no and pressed END on his phone. "Where the hell is she?" *Called out.* Deanna never called out sick to work. He lit another cigarette and stared at the television. *I Love Lucy* had disappeared and was replaced by *The Beverly Hillbillies*. Max didn't even hear the inane jabbering of the Clampetts; he couldn't figure out where Deanna had gone and why she wasn't answering her phone.

Looking around, he noticed the room was a mess. Half-empty glasses, cigarettes, food wrappers and containers; they were everywhere. He rubbed his eyes with his palms. The reason he was in a hotel room, he couldn't remember. Something about an argument with D. He could see her screaming at him, though what she was saying was still a blank. It was coming back slowly, and in pieces. Deanna had walked out on him. Something ridiculous like that. Had he hit her?

The note. He remembered the note. On the floor beside the nightstand, the note lay face down. Max grabbed it and fought the dizzy spell that reaching to the floor caused. It was crumpled and ripped as if he had read and reread it again and again. But he was sure this was the first time he'd actually read it.

Maxie, I know this is not you. Please call me when you feel like yourself again. ❤ *Deanna*

What the hell did that mean?

It took some strength and the rest of the bottle to lift him from the bed. Carelessly, he tossed the note on the bed, turned off the TV, and turned on the radio. He grabbed a towel for a shower.

The radio blared as the shower beat down on his newly throbbing head. His head was clearing after a few minutes in the shower. A dull throb ached behind his eyes as he wrapped the towel around his clean naked body. As he slathered shaving cream on his cheeks, Max noticed a bruise on his shoulder. Turning in the mirror, the bruise stretched down his back to his spine and there was another smaller but much more purple bruise centered on his back. It was a mixture of purple, red, and blue with a huge laceration through the center. It was tender to the touch but not as painful as he thought it should be. It looked like it was healing a little too.

He'd woken up with bruises before, a lot lately, but this one was the worst.

His phone rang, causing a quick shudder to run through his body, and his head felt as if it would explode. "D?" Max grumbled into the phone without looking at the caller ID. Not D.

The conversation was short and not much was said. John was on his way over.

Pulling his jeans on, he thought about Deanna. She was probably with Sari. Sari was the only important thing in Deanna's life these days. She had asked him so many times to understand that she never had a best friend before. Sari was her first best friend. Max rolled his eyes. He was sick of Deanna's friends always coming first in her life. If Sari needed her, Deanna was there. If Max needed her, Deanna was nowhere to be found.

Quickly, he ran his hand through his damp hair. He was getting sick of Deanna's antics. The talking to herself, the obsessions with the restaurant in east bumble-fuck New York, and those weird-ass stories she blurted out when she was drunk. And she was always drunk recently. This was the end.

He righted the table and his back screamed in pain. Max picked up the McDonald's wrappers and examined the wadded-up napkins. A closer look and a sniff determined that it was blood and not sauce on the napkins. Dried blood. He threw them in one of the paper McDonald's bags and walked to the bed. On the sheets there was a smear of a brownish stain. Blood as well, he assumed.

Now he was even more curious to know what the hell happened to him.

"Maxwell," a voice called from the other side of the hotel door, followed by a pounding knock. John poked his head into the room. "What the fuck? You missed class this morning."

"Shit. What time is it?" Max stopped what he was doing to slap his forehead with the palm of his hand, not looking to his friend as he entered the small smoky room. "What day is it?"

"Friday. Papers were due. You just lost one letter grade, my friend. Not great. I texted you like twenty times. Your phone dead or something?"

"Fuck!" he shouted and then winced in pain. "Help me with this, will you?" Max was struggling, trying to put a cool wet towel on his back. "Holy shit! What happened to you?" Max looked up from where he was sitting on the bed to John and the shiner around his right eye.

"Shit, that didn't look good last night. Looks even worse now." John cringed a little.

"Wait, you were here last night? What did I do, fall off a balcony?" Max shook his head and handed John a wet towel for his back. "Hey, hey, go easy. I was hoping someone could fill in the gaps of my last twenty-four hours."

"You were seriously messed up and you took a swing at Bob. Then fell on the table, flipped that, and landed somehow on your back. You didn't even notice it. You were fucked up. You just kept coming."

"Hey, I can't get a hold of your sister. Where the fuck is she?" he said to Bobby as he entered the room.

"What, you think D did this to you? You were drunk and did this to yourself, man." Bobby was dumbfounded and sounded slightly offended.

"Hey, I'm just following the crumbs. Why would I take a swing at you?" He looked at Bobby and winced as John applied pressure to the swelling around the slash.

Bobby picked up a few glasses with one hand and the empty whiskey bottle with the other. "Here's your memory loss, right here. The table and the broken glass did the cuts. The bruising, I can't believe D could be violent. She more of a yeller, bitch, bitch, bitch. All my life. But she never hit anyone."

Max shrugged and made an *I have no fucking idea* sound followed by a teeth-sucking wince as John applied more pressure.

"Cut's not bad, but we should put some kind of antiseptic on it. Maybe some gauze."

"What about you? Bar fight?" Max asked John through his teeth.

"You really don't remember me telling you this story last night? Connie and her fucking Fifty Shades of Grey crap. She's out of control. Belted me, boom, and no time for a safe word either. I was down for the count. She freaked. Had I been conscious, it would have been pretty funny."

Max slapped his leg and laughed out loud. "No shit?" He turned to John to examine his eye. "Does it hurt?" Max almost touched the bruise that surrounded a large blood clot on John's half-opened eyes.

"Only when someone touches it." John pulled away.

A half hour later, Max got dressed carefully and was ready to see how far from home his stupor had taken him. Opening the door, he was blinded by the sun for a second, and he froze in place until his vision cleared. Well, at least his car was still there. Once he had awoken to find that he had lost his car in a poker game and he was at least thirty miles from home.

Expectations was the name of the hotel. What a hole. Luckily, it was only about three miles from Torry. Max rolled his eyes. A few couples passed him as he walked toward his car. One couple was two women and two others were men. Max laughed. "What the hell was I thinking?" Again, he laughed as he got into his car.

John and Bobby decided to follow Max to the diner. There was no use in Max leaving his car in a dive like this. Sitting in his car, he pulled out his phone, hoping for a new text from D. New notifications alerted him to several upsetting things. His calendar alert reminded him of the history paper that he failed to hand in at 8 a.m. and would now get no better than a B on; Facebook told him he had at least a hundred and fifty likes, comments, and reactions to the new video he shared at 2 a.m., and he had four new text messages.

The texts were from John before, during, and after class.

He opened Facebook to check out the video he made in his alcoholic stupor – always the best kind. As he clicked on the still of his face, too close up to be flattering, almost up his nose, he braced himself for the worst. What he saw dropped his jaw and gave him the first wave of nausea of the morning.

CHAPTER TEN

The morning after Eric brought her to Mount Orion to meet Gail was painful. Sari awoke with a pounding headache, acute disorientation as to her surroundings, and temporary amnesia regarding the events of the previous night. The bed she woke in was huge. King sized with a massive number of pillows and covers. The windows were covered in heavy drapery and electric room darkening shades.

Thank God, she thought. The sun was not her friend after a night of drinking. At least she thought she had been drinking. Yes, of course she was drinking. She remembered Eric refilling her glass quite often.

Sari sat up in bed slowly. The room was pretty, a little overdone, but still pretty. The wallpaper and the drapes were matching, which was the reason it was not beautiful. Sari was not an artist but still, a little contrast would have been appealing. She shook her head, wondering why she cared.

Focus. What happened last night? She closed her eyes and tried to picture it. She met Gail as soon as they walked in the front door. The most stunning thing about Gail was her black hair. It was flowing in long waves down her back, kept in place by a waterfall braid that cascaded down the right side of her head. Gail enfolded her in a hug and Sari remembered liking it and liking Gail immediately. Her eyes were piercing and gray but soft in an understanding sort of way. Her smile was the essence of warmth. Her features were small or at least appeared so under the mane of hair that encompassed them.

Sari had met Abby within two steps of Gail as if she were walking a receiving line. Abby was strange to Sari. Their greeting was simple, not as warm as Gail's, but Sari felt that if she lost eye contact with Abby, she would disappear into the crowd quickly. Abby was lovely as well. Light brown hair not styled like Gail but as simple as her greeting. Her eyes were blue – cornflower blue, and her skin was pearlescent.

The only feeling that Sari could remember having as she allowed Abby to depart and Eric to guide her through the crowd was jealousy. Not only jealousy but all its cousins too. Envy, self-consciousness, and distrust.

The party. There was a party. Yes. Now she remembered holding tight to Eric's arm as he guided her through the crowd. He handed her a drink. It was bitter and strong, but she drank it anyway.

Her head pounded behind her eyes. For a moment she put her hands to her temples and concentrated on the pain. Find its center, she told herself. Deanna had always told her that. If you can find the center of your pain, you can control it. Sari knew the center of her pain was in her brain and if she concentrated any longer, it would explode.

With hazy eyes and a brain that was still half asleep, she scanned the room. On the nightstand there was a note beside her cell phone. *In the refrigerator there is a remedy for your hangover. See you later this evening. Gail.*

Sari got out of bed carefully. There was a cure hiding somewhere in the refrigerator. Where was the refrigerator? Where was the kitchen? Where was the door to the bedroom?

"Eric?" she called. She wondered why he hadn't slept in her room last night. Somewhere deep inside she hoped he wasn't sleeping with Gail or Abby. Or anyone else from that party last night. Maybe the remedy would cure the headache enough to help her remember what happened.

"ERIC!" Her eyes went back into her head as she called his name for a second time. "Damn you, I'm hungover," she whispered into the air. "What the hell was in those drinks you gave me?" Not even Maggie's shakes ever affected her this bad.

Getting down the stairs and into the kitchen was no easy task. Every step caused her head to throb, every move her body to ache. "Eric? Abby?" She peered into the kitchen. "Hello?"

The refrigerator and the blessed remedy was right in front of her. Not much in the refrigerator besides a shot glass of thick dark liquid. Sari grabbed it and sat by the table in a small sunroom in the back of the kitchen. The room was full of plants that sorely needed to be watered.

Sari sniffed the liquid in the glass. She cringed and wrinkled her nose. She hoped for tomato juice or even something simple as aspirin would be good. She pinched her nose and took a sip. The heavy liquid coated her tongue as it passed down her throat. "Oh God." She was going to vomit. *No, thank you*, she thought and pushed the small glass away. The aftertaste in her mouth reminded her of the fruit smoothies her mother would make when she was dieting. She swore she tasted mangos or maybe kiwi, something fruity. The texture was off-putting, and she could still feel it lying on her tongue.

Strangely, that one sip was doing something. Her headache was a dull pain instantly instead of daggers in her brain, and her eyelids didn't feel as heavy. She cringed and pulled the glass back to her. Another pinch to her nose so she wouldn't taste it and she threw back the liquid into her mouth. The coating was thicker, and she felt that she would vomit again. *Water.* She ran to the kitchen sink and put her mouth under the faucet. *Better.*

Within minutes, it was as if her hangover had never happened. The room had stopped spinning and was coming into focus. There were two doors out of the back of the house. One leading to the patio in the back yard and one leading from the breakfast nook to a porch. The cabinets were all white with stainless steel appliances. The floor was her favorite part; wood. Not harsh linoleum, warm wood that gave it a very country feel. Like the décor in her bedroom, Sari didn't know why it mattered.

She sat back down and tried to see if she could remember anything yet, or was it all lost to her weary drunkard's brain?

It was difficult to remember. She could remember driving to the cabin. The nervousness was mounting, especially being without her friends. Driving into this mysterious world of Mount

Orion, Eric kept reassuring her that everything would be all right and that Gail was a very nice woman.

Still, Sari wasn't convinced. Eric never told her anything about Gail except of course that she was a close friend that had a house in Upstate New York. Now suddenly, she had to meet her and was expected to become her life-long friend.

Sari was stubborn. Why should she accept the other woman in Eric's life? Why should she share him with anyone? When they first arrived, there was a party of sorts in progress. (That part she had happily remembered earlier.) Sari took a deep breath. It was enough to meet Gail and Abby, but to meet everyone they knew at the same time was impossible.

"You didn't say anything about a party." She pulled on Eric's sleeve as he led her to the house. Sari looked down to the simple outfit she had chosen. It was leggings, a simple cami, and a sweater. Chosen more for comfort than style, she was feeling horribly underdressed and out of place.

"I wasn't sure there was going to be one," he said dismissively. "It's just a small get-together. It'll be fine. Gail and her parties. I usually escape early. They are painfully boring." Eric stopped and looked down at her. A look of concern crossed his brow and then brightened into a warm, reassuring smile. "You look beautiful." He gently took her face in his hands and kissed her lips. Sari reached up on tip toes to kiss him, reminding her that she had worn tennis shoes instead of heels. Again, she took a deep breath and allowed Eric to lead her.

The room was full. *Small get together, my ass,* she thought. As far as Sari could see there were people lining the walls, sitting on the floor, draped on the stairs and sofas. She hadn't seen a party like this since her brief flirtation with college life last summer. A sorority party that Maggie had gotten them invited to and all she remembered of that party was the smell of pot and vomit.

The music at this party was pretty loud and the lights were very dim. Very college party.

How old is Gail?

Even with all the music and people, Gail knew exactly when they arrived.

"Hi, darling. I'm so glad you could make it." Gail kissed Eric on the lips.

I'm standing right here, Sari huffed in her head. Instead of saying anything, Sari looked away as the two kissed, hating herself for not saying anything aloud.

As if right on cue, Gail turned to look at her. "Sorry. You must be Sari." Gail enveloped Sari in a hug, and she returned the hug rather openhearted. She liked Gail but didn't really know why. Not the twenty-something that someone would have expected to see throwing such a party, Sari guessed Gail's age to be somewhere in her late thirties or forty. She was so naturally pretty. Her skin was like porcelain. It was perfect and unblemished. Sari found herself wanting to reach out and touch her long black hair.

The rest of conversation was lost in the background of the music or her drunken memory. All Sari could remember was smelling Gail's flowery perfume during the hug and as she leaned in to speak in her ear. The music forbade any other communication although she could clearly see others speaking easily.

The evening was pretty uneventful after the first meeting with Gail. Sari met Abby with the same amount of struggling to understand her words over the music. Eric came and went throughout the evening, only stopping to hand Sari a drink or perhaps refill her glass.

She could remember one guy had spoken to her. He was very good looking but very touchy. He kept reaching out to touch her arm or her hair or putting his arm around her waist. His eyes were covered with blue tinted John Lennon style glasses and his blonde hair was almost glowing in the dim light. For a moment, Sari couldn't take her eyes off of him and she knew it was the alcohol impairing her judgement.

Because of the volume of the music, she had no idea what he was saying to her, and still she knew his intentions were not good. Each step she took away, he took toward her. Soon she was pressed up against the fireplace looking for a way out.

Before she could manage an escape, Eric was beside her. His arm clasped firmly around her waist, he glared at the guy. It was very medieval knight in shining armor chivalry stuff and Sari secretly loved every minute of it. The blond guy tried to stare Eric down, but it didn't work. Gail was suddenly between the men and motioned for Eric to take the high road and retreat.

By midnight, Sari was drunk. Very drunk.

She remembered stumbling outside for some quiet and some air. Three doors were in the kitchen. One was clearly a basement door that was blocked by a few people that didn't seem interested in moving for Sari to pass, and she wasn't that interested in a fight in her intoxicated state. The other two were exits. Outside. Air. Two welcoming words. She chose one.

She remembered not being alone outside. There were others that looked somewhat familiar but even now sitting in the sunroom the next day, Sari could not remember where she had seen them before. One girl started speaking to her; her voice was slow and distorted, and her words were lost in a memory. Sari's walked toward her to say hello, but her legs were suddenly jelly.

Oh my God, I fell on a stranger! Sari thought. She dropped her head to the table, mortified by the memory. Her fingers played with the empty glass in front of her. The liquid, looking very red, still clung to the side of the glass.

"Eric, darling, come put your friend to bed." She could hear Gail's voice as clear as if she was standing behind her. "I think she's had enough." That was it. End of memory. The night ended badly. No wonder no one was around this morning. They were probably hoping she would leave before they got back and would never return.

Sari started to go upstairs to gather her stuff and leave. Now that her hangover was gone, she felt like taking the steps two at a time. When she got to the top of the stairs, she stopped to think. As embarrassing as it was to pass out drunk at a stranger's party, Eric hadn't driven her home. And Gail did leave the miracle hangover remedy. What about Eric? He'd seen her drunk before. Not blind, falling on a strange girl drunk, but he wouldn't just abandon her. She decided to wait for Gail or Eric to return and gauge their reaction to her presence.

There was a bathroom attached to her room. A small but adequate bathroom. Sari looked at herself in the mirror. The black eyeliner around her eyes was smudged almost to her chin, and her hair was pulled in too many directions. With a damp cloth and soap, Sari scrubbed her face clean of all traces of makeup. It had been forever since she had left her face clean of makeup, and she quickly pulled a comb through her hair.

Again, she looked in the mirror; her pink hair was standing straight up in the back and completely flat on the right side. She needed to take a shower. *Make a better impression than last night and they'll let you stay.* In the shower, she watched as the temporary pink hair color washed from her short hair. *Better impression,* she kept reminding herself. *Better impression.*

Sari almost didn't recognize herself. Now if she could only find nail polish remover, then the look would be complete. Eric had brought home a normal girl. No, he hadn't, but they didn't need to know that. She laughed to herself.

After the shower, wrapped in a bathrobe, Sari went out to Eric's Lexus and pulled her overnight bag from the trunk. She had packed a skirt and sweater – for later—and stretch pants and a tee shirt. Pulling on the stretch pants, she laced her sneakers up and headed outside. The front yard was marred by the tire tracks of at least a dozen cars that were parked on it last night.

She took a deep breath into her lungs and couldn't believe the air was so fresh and clean. Outside of the tire tracks, the house was beautiful. The porch was uncharacteristically off the kitchen door rather than the front, but still facing the front of the house. The flower pots lining the porch were dead or dying. Sari made a mental note to water the plants when she returned.

The land was huge. Last night, she had noticed another house on the hill above the cabin, but it was too dark to see much of anything else besides the illuminated cabin. Gail must own at least fifty acres, she guessed. There was a lake down the road and from where she stood, Sari could see a small dock and some ducks playing on the surface.

The energy in her was building. The sun-filled day, the restful sleep, the crisp, clear morning air. Something attributed to it but nothing Sari could put her finger on. She felt like a run. Not that she had ever really run in her life. That was Deanna's department. Running, yoga, exercise to beat stress. Deanna was always moving. Sari was simply content to lay on the couch and watch television or read a book. Not today, though. The driveway to the main road looked pretty long to Sari, so she started there. Passing the lake would be heavenly too, she thought. As the cool air burned her untrained lungs, she could feel the muscles in her legs stretching and straining.

When she got to the end of the drive, not even winded, she turned right and continued down the road. It was a two-lane road with barely any shoulder to run in, but Sari continued. The pain in her lungs filled her chest, and she could hardly feel her face as the wind whipped against it. But still she didn't stop. It felt incredible to run, to feel as if nothing could stop her. Almost two miles from Mount Orion, she felt a vibration from her phone and slowed; still moving in a slow-motion walk, she checked her messages.

It was Deanna. "Just checking in to see how everything went last night."

Sari shut her phone off without texting back and replaced it in the tight waistband of her stretch pants. Running her fingers through her now brown and very sweaty hair, she turned back towards the cabin. As she approached the cabin, another vibration signaled another text.

"Feeling a little down today. Hope you are fitting in with Eric's friends"

Her face was dripping with sweat and her clothes were glued to her body. Another shower sounded just about right. Again, she ignored Deanna's text and tossed her phone on the bed before jumping into the shower.

The skirt and sweater was the only other outfit in the overnight bag, so Sari slipped them on her clean body. A pair of taupe tights and black loafers finished the outfit. "What to do now? Water the plants," she said aloud. She filled a pitcher with cold water from the tap and started in the sunroom slash breakfast nook. It took a lot of water before the dirt stopped drinking it in, and then she went on the porch to tend to the outside plants.

It was there that Gail found Sari hours later. The sun was just setting behind the house and Sari sat with her feet up on the porch railing reading a book. "You watered the plants?" Gail examined the regenerating fauna surrounding the porch.

"They needed it – badly. I hope you don't mind." Sari put her book beside a glass of water on the side table. "I also alphabetized your bookcase. Cleaned and organized your silver and um . . . I don't remember what else. I was kind of bored and jittery. I went for a run, but it didn't really help. Oh, I dusted the living room."

Gail stared at her with amusement in her eyes and a slight sideways smile. "It's chilly tonight. Come, we'll build a fire." She reached out her hand and reluctantly, Sari took it.

The sofa enveloped her as she watched Gail place logs on the grate and ignite them. The fire was slow at first and grew steadily throwing heat into the room. With the fire built, Gail sat beside her on the sofa, offering a blanket for extra comfort. "Are you feeling more relaxed now?" Sari was not but nodded anyway. If she had another set of clothes, she would go for run even in the dark. Gail was smiling at her in a knowing way that made Sari feel naked all of a sudden.

There was a sound of a closing door from the kitchen and Abby appeared in the doorway. Her light brown hair was pulled back in a braid, making her pale skin and large blue eyes appear otherworldly. "Room for one more?" She sat on the opposite side of Gail and stared at the fire. "Just us tonight?"

Gail hummed an affirmative sound.

"So, I heard you took a dive last night?" Abby looked to Sari.

She closed her eyes, feeling more embarrassed than she could have imagined. She could see Gail shaking her head at Abby's crassness. "I was hoping I dreamed that."

"Nope. From what I heard, Chelsea said hello and asked if you were alright and you swayed like a tree branch, her exact words, and fell on her." She mimed a tree falling with her arms and made a crashing sound. "I wish I had seen it. Sounded hilarious." Abby sat back on the sofa, laughing.

"Glad no one got a video of it. I would hate to end up on YouTube looking like an idiot." Sari looked to Gail and then looked away.

"That would have been stellar. Wish I'd thought of it. Next time." Abby sounded like she was making a mental note.

Sari crossed her legs, feeling like she was about to jump out of her skin and bounced her foot nervously. Gail gently stopped her foot with a hand to Sari's knee. "Would you like some tea to calm you?"

Before Sari could answer, Eric appeared in the kitchen doorway.

"Well, it's about time." Gail laughed. "We've been waiting for you. I was about to get Sari some tea. Would you like some?"

Eric kissed her respectfully on the cheek and smiled. He looked to Sari as she sat beside Gail on the sofa. He seemed to devour her for a moment. Sari felt self-conscious that he would not like the cleaned-up version of her. She swallowed hard.

"Well, that's enough for me. I've got dinner plans." Abby rose from the couch and grabbed her jacket, surprising Sari, who was still captivated by Eric's stare.

"You're coming back later, aren't you?" Gail asked.

"Yeah, just meeting someone and then I'll be back." She winked at Gail and laughed. "See you later."

As the door closed behind Abby, Eric walked to Sari. "Have you eaten?" His voice was firm yet loving.

"No." She nervously looked to Gail, trying not to offend her, though she seemed not to notice.

Taking her hand, Eric pulled her easily to her feet. Sari didn't argue and followed obediently behind, never letting go of his large cool hand. Once outside and out of range of Gail, Sari dared to ask, "Where are we going?"

"You haven't eaten, I would guess, all day. There's a restaurant in town that is quite good."

"Sure, I guess." She pulled on her boring brown sweater and skirt. "Maybe a diner or something would be better." She could hear the trepidation in her own voice and hated herself for it.

He turned toward her suddenly, stopping her breath as he held her face with two fingers. "You look beautiful." His finger grazed her lower lip as he pulled away and started walking again. "We're not eating there."

Eric opened the car door and held her hand as she sat in the passenger seat. He closed the door behind her and came around the front to the driver's door. He was different tonight. Different here than at home. His hair was combed back, removing most of the waves, and the brown looked almost black in the darkness. His skin was glowing in the reflective light from the headlights, and Sari reached out to touch the back of his hand. And there was a smell about him that she had never noticed before. A deep masculine musk that made her want to kiss him.

He looked at her again, almost like he knew her thoughts. Devouring her with his eyes like a wolf, making her breath trip as she tried not to hold it. A broad smile crossed his face, bright and loving, and the look of a wolf disappeared. Again, she swallowed and realized she had been holding her breath after all.

The car started easily when he pressed the start button and Sari sat back comfortably in the leather seats. "What do you mean we're not eating there?" she asked gently.

"I've arranged to have our food ready when we arrive. We'll have a picnic by the lake."

The night was chilly, but Eric had thought of everything. A warm blanket, a bottle of wine, and some of the most delicious food she had ever eaten. "You barely touched your dinner." Sari placed her plate into the basket that had been prepared for them. "Not hungry?"

Eric stared at her for a long while not answering. "Let's go back to the cabin. You must be cold."

She was freezing, if she were to admit the truth, but having such a lovely time that she didn't want to move from their spot beside the lake. Placing the basket and blankets into the trunk, Eric drove to the cabin while Sari needed to walk off the excess energy that was still burning through her.

Her senses were more alive in the darkness. The lake smelled of moss and algae. The grass was light against her legs, but she could feel the dying blades as autumn was drawing to a close in another few weeks. She could see nothing except the cabin, the moon, and the stars. And somehow, she felt that was how it was meant to be.

"Got the wine?" she commented as she met Eric waiting for her at the front door.

He raised the bottle and glasses in his hand and smiled. "Burned off all your energy yet?" Eric held the front door open and gestured for her to enter. He kissed her neck as she passed through the open door.

"Not even close." Sari giggled.

The living room was empty when they arrived. A fire was burning bright and more wine and glasses were arranged on the table with candles. Sari smiled and looked to Eric with a blush.

"Have a seat and I'll open the wine."

The room was warm from the fire, but Sari found herself trembling slightly. She wrapped the blanket around her shoulders to give her nervous hands something to do. Eric handed her a glass of wine the color of caramel. He took a small sip from his own glass and placed it on the table beside the candles.

His eyes were devouring her again and she pulled the blanket closer to her chest, almost spilling the wine. Eric took the glass and placed it beside his on the table. Without saying a word, he pulled her closer to him opening the blanket and wrapping his hands around her small waist. Sari swallowed hard, frightened by his swift movement and the anticipation of what was to happen next.

His kisses were brusque and impatient. His hands were pressing hard into her back. Sari found herself holding her breath again. "I guess I should tell you," she began, not meeting his eyes, "I've never done this before." The air around them seemed to fizzle. The electricity that was building between them had diminished and Sari was immediately sorry she had said anything. "I just thought you should know." Again, she didn't look him in the eye.

A soft buzzing in her pocket indicated a new text on her phone. A brief look told her it was Deanna again and she put the phone back in her pocket.

Eric pressed his lips against her hair and wrapped his arms around her. They stared at the fire for what seemed like an eternity to Sari. The energy in her was building again and she could feel her leg begin to jump with it. Again, she could feel Eric's lips against her head, and he stood up. "Come," he said.

Standing was better for her legs that only wanted to run, but her hands jittered with anticipation once more. "Where?"

"To burn off some energy."

The hallway to her room was interminable. The eagerness of what was to come next and the pent-up energy bubbling in her muscles, Sari wanted to run again. Up the stairs, down the hall, take laps around the bed.

Sensing her edginess, Eric lifted her into his arms and carried her the rest of the way. He passed her room and continued down the hallway to a closed door. The door opened with a creaking sound as if it was rarely used. Immediately the scents she had smelled earlier surrounded her again. This was Eric's room.

Manly and dark, books covered the shelves and there were things everywhere. Pieces of Eric. An old rotary telephone stood in pieces on the desk, beside it a reel to reel tape player with stacks of tapes beside it and on the floor. A large tool box overflowed on the floor beside the desk with wires, cables, and electrical doohickeys that Sari recognized from when her father would fix things at home.

A large hulking bed stood in the center of the room. The old-fashioned heavy-wooded bed brought images of those awful romance novels her mother would read. A woman, prize to be won, taken to bed by her victor, her oppressor. Or the knight in shining armor rescues the damsel in distress. It was nauseating and yet it was happening to her. "No, please put me down. It can't happen like this." She stopped the madness. "I want to do this. I do. Um, just not like a cheesy chick flick. I could die from the saccharine."

Eric laughed and threw her on the bed. "Better?" he teased.

He was on top of her before she could catch her breath. His kisses were urgent and overwhelming. The smell of him was overpowering and she buried her face in his neck. "I love how you smell tonight." She nibbled his ear and he pulled away.

A look of regret creased his brow and Eric sat up. "We should go slowly." His voice was low and sincere but somehow wrapped in a hidden anguish that Sari didn't entirely understand.

"I don't think it matters. My heart is beating so fast right now. I can't keep my hands off of you." She laughed, still nervous but losing patience. "I'll let you know if we need to slow down. Okay?" Her eyes travelled the circumference of his face and she bit her lip.

The remorse in his eyes softened, being replaced by the wolf. He looked up at her with a sly smirk from beneath his arched brow. His hands and lips travelled the length of her legs, tickling her as he gently touched behind her knee. Sari's breath tripped again as his lips touched her stomach and he removed her boring brown sweater.

The next morning, Sari awoke to the room black as pitch and Eric sleeping soundly beside her. Their night of lovemaking was more intense than her friends had led her to believe it would be. Eric was passionate and domineering. He was forceful yet loving. His lovemaking was desperate and unyielding and yet there were times it seemed he was holding back.

In the middle of the night she awoke to find she was alone, whispering his name in the darkness of the room. "I'm here. Still feeling a bit jittery?" he asked as he opened the bedroom door. Back in bed, he touched his lips to her shoulder and wrapped his arms around her, pressing his cool naked chest to her back. "Want to go for another run?" he said, playfully referring to how energetic she was with him in bed.

Now slipping out of bed, still feeling the electricity streaking through her muscles, Sari grabbed her clothes and Eric's keys. It was in the bathroom that she noticed the enormous hickey on her shoulder. A large blood clotted marking with a light bruise surrounding it. It was sensitive to the touch but appeared to be already healing.

By noon, the mark was gone, and she had finished her second run of the day.

Chapter Eleven

Deanna felt strange as she drove to this Mount Orion. It could possibly have been the hangover from the previous night's party; a private party. Just her and a bottle of Jack Daniels. Devin hadn't returned after disappearing on Friday night, and the next time she'd heard from him was this morning. Max was gone and Deanna was feeling scared and lonely.

She texted Sari several times yesterday with no response. The fear and worry were growing as she visualized too many bloody scenarios in her head. By ten o'clock she had texted once more just to calm her nerves, but by that point she was really drunk. "I miss you. Please text me, call me, something. I need to know you are alright."

Deanna woke up this morning face down on her apartment floor. The empty bottle of Jack was lying beside her. The cell phone on the table blinked repeatedly. She had missed several texts but only one that really mattered. It was from Sari. "Im fine but sounds like yur not. Come here. Im lonely during day Luv to have company." The second text was directions to the cabin and a plea to bring a few days' worth of extra clothes. The third and fourth were from Max telling her he was at John's and that when she was ready to talk to call him. She wasn't ready to talk or even sure what he wanted to talk about, so she didn't respond.

Instead, Deanna pulled out her overnight bag and threw some clothes in it. Devin returned as she texted Max that she was going to visit Sari in New York.

Now her head throbbed as she drove into her third hour of highway travel. The area was beautiful and nearly deserted as she got closer to her destination. Sunday morning travel was the best time to go anywhere. People were either sleeping in or going to church. After noon, they headed for the malls.

Deanna took a deep breath and a swig off her water bottle as she heard Devin begin humming – she cursed him, knowing that song was going to be stuck in her head all day. He spoke to her as if he was sitting right beside her. *"Did you see that hawk's wing span? He was a big one."*

Deanna nodded or smiled.

Devin started humming again.

"Mind if I put on the radio?" she asked softly, massaging her temples. Deanna spoke aloud to Devin because if she even tried to say words in her head, it would explode all over the dashboard.

"Not at all." She could feel him smiling, knowing it was his humming that was annoying her.

Well, she thought, I'll never be lonely. I'll always have someone to keep me company. Deanna sighed and rubbed her temple again. The pain was unbearable, and she hoped that whoever this mystery woman was, she kept a fully stocked bar.

Right on cue, Devin asked, *"Who is this woman that Sari is visiting?"*

"She didn't say. All she said was that she was lonely and wanted me to come stay with her?"

"But who is she?"

"A friend of Eric's." Deanna groaned at the mention of Eric's name. Yes, a drink was definitely what she needed. "No one is around all day, if you know what I mean."

"Vampires."

"Bingo," she said and as she said it, she wondered what Devin knew about vampires. He didn't know Martino. He hadn't been around for Margaret's short lifetime. How was he so familiar and comfortable with the existence of these creatures?

Just as she was about to question him, he belted out a song verse of the Turtles' *Happy Together*. *"Aren't you taking a big chance? What if you-know-who is there?"* he asked.

"What are the chances that he'll be there?" Again, it seemed odd that Devin was so blasé about these blood-sucking beings surrounding her.

"You know that he knows Eric. Sari went to see Eric. Seems the chances are pretty great that he will be there or will figure out we're gone and come here."

"I'm gone," she corrected him, not knowing why it mattered. "Martino doesn't really know anything about you. Or that you even exist." Deanna cringed slightly, waiting for the backlash that would cause. Her head felt as if would crack in two and she felt Devin's anger rising.

"What does that mean?" He tried to sound calm, but she could feel his rage in her teeth. They were vibrating with it.

"Well . . ." was all she could manage before he jumped all over her.

"Well, what? You mean that in all the time you were with him, you must have told him. No? You must have. Explained your situation?"

She immediately regretted telling Devin about Margaret and her connection to Martino.

"It never really came up. You were not part of my *situation* at the time and he never asked the particulars. I just told him that I was cursed. He just kind of accepted it. I mean, what was I going to tell him?" She was yelling and her head felt like it was about to burst. "I have a spirit that is my companion. Oh, well, don't worry about him, I've imprisoned him about fifty years ago," she mockingly explained to him.

"Who blindly accepts a curse as an explanation? What kind of fool is he?" He stopped ranting for a moment. *"I can't believe you didn't tell him about me!"* he burst out.

Deanna jumped and almost lost control of the car. She felt the windows shake and trembled a bit herself. "He blindly accepted the curse like you blindly accepted that he was immortal. You just did. What are you so angry about? Do you want me to expose you?" She rolled down her window. "Ghost! We have a ghost here! Come get him, boys!" she screamed out the window to the passing cars. "Feel better? Do you really want paranormal investigators all over us?

"I've lived in this century a lot longer than you have. In this century, they don't accuse of witchery. They investigate, they probe and dissect. It's not fun."

Devin wasn't listening. She could feel that he was getting angrier and angrier. He didn't appreciate that Deanna would fall in love with another man who had no knowledge of him. Even her second husband had known. It might have been this knowledge that led to Devin's imprisonment, but still Devin felt he had control.

". . . so, I'll tell him, OK?" Deanna was saying when he started to calm down. She was sure he still wasn't fully listening, but she hoped he at least understood what she was getting at. The windows stopped shaking and her teeth stopped throbbing from his rage. None of this talking made her headache any more bearable, so she tried to remain quiet.

Driving down the road, Deanna kept looking for a sign for Mount Orion. Her GPS found nothing. Sari gave her the main road's name and told her to look for a sign that said Mount Orion and turn right there. After a few miles of nothing, no houses, no stores, she saw a stone gateway. On the placard in fine etched calligraphy it read *Mount Orion*. Deanna turned the car down a seemingly unending stretch of road.

The area felt familiar to her. Certain trees brought back memories of climbing to the top and watching her brother playing in the yard. There was a lake in the distance. Not close but she could make out a small dock or wooden bridge; from the car she couldn't tell which it was.

There were two houses in the distance. The first was small but quaint. It had a full stone façade and a cherry wood front door. Deanna loved it. The driveway ended in a circle to the right of the house, right in front of an enclosed side porch.

The second house was much larger. The façade was similar, but it had a large wraparound porch instead of the side porch. The grass around the house looked unkempt and overgrown. Deanna read that sadly as abandoned.

"Ready?" She breathed deeply.

"Are you alright, Mouse?"

"I keep getting a strange feeling. Maybe it's hunger, I don't know. Just forget it."

"Trust your instincts, Deanna. They will never fail you."

Devin rarely called her by her given name. He had taken to calling her Mouse in her first reincarnated lifetime. He had told her that it was unsettling to call her Gemma and since she was so small, he took to calling her Mouse. Now using her full name was strange and immediately caused her concern.

"What? Do you know why I'm feeling strange, Devin?"

He didn't respond.

As she got out of the car, she saw Sari waiting on the porch. At least she thought it was Sari. Sari with no makeup. It was unnerving to see her friend's beautiful face, clean of the black eyeliner and heavy eyeshadow. Even her hair was tame and not in the least spiked, colored, or sparkly.

"What happened to you?" Deanna needed to hear her speak before she could make a positive identification. She came around to the back of the car and popped the trunk.

"What?"

"Look at you. Wow. These people are a good influence already. And is that running gear you're wearing?" Deanna walked up the porch steps and opened the side door, knowing no one would be around to care. "Got your clothes."

"Who were you talking to you?" Sari trailed her into the house.

Deanna pushed her hair out of her eyes. "Just singing. I can't get this damn song out of my head."

Sari showed her the room that she'd be staying in and let her get settled. It took her only moments to unpack the one bag she brought. When she was finally settled, Deanna wanted to eat. Sari ordered pizza.

"I had to give them directions. No one knows where this place is. I'm lucky I have cell service. It'll be here in about thirty minutes," she said. "That's another crazy thing: not only are these people gone all day, but there's no food! I took Eric's car this morning to find a store. It's like twenty miles from here." Sari poured Deanna some soda and handed her the glass. "So, I got some breakfast stuff: eggs, milk, soda, munchies, but I don't cook so I got a few microwavable meals."

"Where does Eric go all day?" Deanna asked, trying to sound curious instead of accusatory.

"Right now, he's upstairs completely conked out! All day. We were up late last night," she said coyly.

"You didn't?" Deanna's hands flew to her mouth.

Sari smiled, embarrassed and proud at the same time.

"Why aren't you with him now? Why call me?"

Pulling a water bottle out of the fridge, Sari paced the floor in the kitchen. "I'm a bundle of energy or nerves or something. I've been running. Like four miles a day. It's crazy. Last night was, well . . . unbelievable but did nothing to relax me." She took a drink from the bottle and continued. "Then in the middle of the night, in between – you know – "

"How many times?" Deanna was amazed.

"Three. I'd doze and then he'd wake me up again. But around, I don't know, two, maybe? I heard Eric arguing with Gail about telling me something. That's why when I got your text, I figured I could use some backup. I was freaking out. They were talking so low I couldn't hear most of it. But I definitely heard my name and something about staying here and I should know . . . something." Sari shook her thoughts clear. "Not to mention I drink way too much here. The first night I couldn't tell you what I was drinking, but last night it was wine."

"Drink? So, there is something other than soda to drink in this house?" Deanna's mood brightened a bit. Deanna started looking around the cabin. The glass of soda was in her hand. Apparently, Sari hadn't come across the secret hiding place for the hooch in her few short days yet. Although her head was still throbbing, the drink was helping, and Sari had a few aspirins in her purse.

There were pictures on nearly every wall of the cabin. Lots of expensive paintings and some photographs strategically placed for a homey feel. This vampire was good at this deception she was running. The furniture was somewhat normal; nothing antique or collectible. She had a TV and a computer. If Deanna didn't know better, she'd say this woman was human. Good job, mystery woman. Well done.

"I'm not as impressed, Mouse. There are rooms downstairs. Not as normal as up here. I guess that's what they call their 'lair.' Very creepy seeing them down there. And there aren't just two; there's more."

She stopped walking. *"How many more?"*

"At least three from what I saw. They sensed me even in their slumber. I left quickly but not before I spied a familiar face."

"Familiar face. Shit, is Martino here? We've got to get out of here." Deanna put her glass on a nearby end table and almost knocked over a framed photo. As she was righting it, she stopped to look at it. There was a woman with two younger women, one a brunette and the other a blonde.

The woman, maybe forty years old, had to be the mystery woman. She had really dark, almost black hair and those smiling eyes. Deanna stared at the woman, not wanting to know her. Not wanting to remember the pain she had caused. *I spied a familiar face,* Devin's words mocked her. She had all the tell-tale signs of a vampire, white skin, sparkling eyes, and for the picture she had conveniently smiled without showing her teeth. A vampire.

"... so, what do you think they meant by telling me or I should know. You don't think Eric's fooling around with Gail or something kinky like that, do you? Because that would really piss me off. I was convinced yesterday that they were just friends, and I just love Gail, but now I don't know." Sari came out of the kitchen with a bottle of water.

Gail? Did she say Gail? Deanna thought to herself. *It's a coincidence. There's no way that's my mother.*

"Same name, same face. Got to be a coincidence." Devin was sharp and sarcastic.

Deanna allowed Sari to show her around the cabin. She was in a daze. The upstairs rooms were just bedrooms, just boring everyday bedrooms. The only one she didn't see was Eric's and Deanna wasn't in the mood to wake a sleeping vampire. She was happy to skip it.

In every room there was at least one picture of the dark-haired woman, Gail. Deanna could only stare, close to tears, trying desperately to convince herself of what she knew to be true. *That is my mother. Elizabeth's mother.* "What's Gail's last name?"

Sari shrugged. "No idea, why?"

Deanna didn't answer. Her heart was racing.

"This is her room. Check out the closets and jewelry boxes. This chick is loaded. I can't get over it." Sari kept talking but Deanna didn't hear her anymore. She couldn't; tears were standing in her eyes, blurring the painting that stood before her. It was a wedding portrait of Gail and a very handsome man. Gail and Virgil Andrews, Deanna's father when she was Elizabeth.

"*And there he is,*" Devin said. "*Virgil Andrews, the son of a bitch that knew you were the special one and ignored his instincts. He allowed her to put you second to Isabella. She wasn't even his daughter.*"

Deanna took a deep breath. She tried so hard to convince herself that Gail was not the woman who had given birth to her in 1878, but there she was. She was also the same woman who had abandoned her seven years later after her father's untimely death.

That was it; this was all a strange coincidence and none of this was real. It had to be a false reality that she was seeing. Shadows of the past. Gail merely looked like her mother and that man was just – just the spitting image of her late father.

Her tears were burning her cheeks as she glanced at the smaller faded photos. There was one of her older sister, Isabella, sitting in a chair. There was another of four children. All were looking pretty miserable in Deanna's assessment. Three girls and one boy. Isabella, the eldest, Bartholomew, second, Elizabeth, on his lap, and then Katherine.

"*Katherine didn't live long after this photo, did she?*"

"No. She got really sick a year before Papa died." But Deanna didn't want to discuss Katherine; she was slightly frightened by the sight of her former self in the photo. *Elizabeth.* She looked at the perfect ringlets in her hair. The ringlets that Isabella had to hold her down to make so perfect. Elizabeth didn't like these new photographs; they had scared her. But there it was, proof of her past. Proof that she was Elizabeth.

The daughter her father named a restaurant after, the daughter ultimately raised and abused by her sister, the daughter whose soul was not her own.

"D? You OK?" Sari shook her shoulders. "Looks like you've been crying."

Deanna shook her head clear of all the memories. She closed her eyes. "Nothing, just dizzy. I guess I'm a bit hungover. Really hungry too."

Sari nodded but didn't completely trust the explanation. "Food should be here soon. You up for a walk in the meantime? I need to move a little. There's a really neat cottage on the hill."

The walk up the hill was daunting for Deanna, but Sari was practically running it. Deanna had yelled several times for Sari to wait up, only to be called a slow poke. Sari kept going. They circled the house for a while and after ten minutes of trying, it was clear they weren't getting in. They checked windows and doors, basement windows, anything they could. It was locked up tight.

"Whose house is this?" Deanna started to walk around to the front of the cottage.

"Gail's, I assume. Don't ask me why she doesn't live here. It's like twice the size of that cabin. Eric says this has been locked up for years. I don't know, but Gail's a little strange, you know?"

The view from the top of the hill was the clincher. This was her land. Deanna stood in front of the cottage looking down at the land before her. The cottage stood exactly where her house had stood; exactly where the cinders of her house had settled. The lake – her lake – was so beautiful from up here. Deanna inhaled deeply and closed her eyes. She and Bryon had never moved back on to the property after the house burned. They moved into town. Isabella had died several years before Elizabeth. How did Gail get her hands on this property? Deanna's blood was boiling. The property should have passed to her children following her death.

Shaking the anger away, trying to stay calm, Deanna could feel the bubbling in her stomach and was sure her eyes were close to being green. She took a deep breath and looked around the property again. If the lake was in front of her and the cottage was behind her, then to her right would have to be – the family cemetery. Deanna turned to her right and walked to the side of the cottage. There in the field under the apple tree was the Andrews family cemetery. A plot of land, now overgrown with weeds, was surrounded by stones and anchored by the apple tree; it held several small stones and one large cross. She could feel Sari following her and not saying a word.

There were seven graves. Deanna was nauseous. The earth was moving beneath her feet as she looked to her father, brother, sister, and Bryon and Elizabeth's graves. She remembered burying each of them, but seeing her own grave marker stabbed her in places she didn't know she could bleed. *Elizabeth Andrews–Staton 1878 – 1943.*

So many lifetimes, so many families. But they were still her family. Virgil was still Papa, Bart was still her big brother; no matter how many years had passed.

Her eldest sister, Isabella, was not buried here and she was thankful. She probably bought a plot beside her rich husband in some upscale cemetery. Deanna rolled her shoulders and closed her eyes. She couldn't believe she was still jealous of her older sister after a century.

"I'm sorry I wasn't there for her at the end." Devin's voice sounded pained and Deanna could hear a trace of his accent when he spoke.

"You were always with her even when you weren't. When I needed you, I'd go into the basement and just lean against the wall where your room was."

"What would you do?"

"I'd either cry or tell you that I missed you or both. I think that was one of the big reasons Bryon made me sell the place. He said it wasn't healthy for me to talk to the walls." She laughed and covered it up with a cough. *"But I knew I wasn't talking to the walls; I was talking to you. Alice started doing it too. Drove Bryon mad."*

"Serves him right."

"I'm glad you're here for me now." She wiped the tears from her eyes, hoping Sari wouldn't notice.

"Wow, those two were young." Sari pointed to two graves. The first was Elizabeth's older sister Katherine, who had died when she was just fifteen. The second was an unknown grave that was marked Renee Marjorie Jacobs, who had died at eighteen. That grave and one other were two graves Deanna didn't recognize. "Sad."

Deanna made a non-committal nothing sound, still hoping she wouldn't puke from seeing her own name on a tombstone. The more she thought about it, the more she needed a drink. "Let's go find Gail's liquor cabinet."

"My God, it's only two o'clock in the afternoon. I'd prefer that you were sober when you met Gail." Sari lagged behind as Deanna headed back down the hill to the cabin. But not for long.

Deanna continued to walk. She definitely needed a drink if she was going to face Gail. After over one hundred years, she had to see what her excuse was for abandoning her children. Blind, stinking drunk: that's the only way she could picture herself facing her long-lost mother. Doubled over, vomiting, cursing-her-name drunk.

When they got back to the cabin, the delivery man was waiting for them. Two large pepperoni pizzas and two liters of Coke. They found the hooch in the pantry where most people would keep their cereal or canned goods. Deanna mixed herself a

Captain and Coke and sat in front of the TV with Sari until sunset eating and drinking. Lather, rinse, and repeat.

"They are awake. I must go for now." And Devin was gone, leaving Deanna to panic on her own. She looked to Sari who had been watching her every move closely. "I'll be right back." She sped to the bathroom.

In the bathroom, Deanna sat on the floor wondering how she would bring herself to face Gail.

"Just do it." Devin was beside her again.

"Oh, thank God! I don't think I could have done this without you." She took a few deep breaths. *"Do you think she'll recognize me?"*

Devin laughed softly. *"By face? I don't think so, Mouse. I think you might have to tell her."*

"Maybe not. She was always kind of intuitive. I remember her always knowing things. Things she couldn't know." Deanna sat thinking. *"Isabella too. She knew things. Remember how they both sensed you but refused to acknowledge that you were more than my imaginary friend? Weird, right?"*

"D, are you all right?" Sari knocked on the bathroom door.

"Uh, yeah," Deanna replied. "What should I do?" she whispered aloud to Devin.

"About what?" Sari asked through the door.

Devin laughed again.

"Please hurry; Gail's eager to meet you."

Deanna rolled her eyes. *"What I am I gonna do, Devin? How can I face her? I don't know how I'll react. What if I suddenly hit her? What if I suddenly hug her?"*

"Deanna?" It was not Sari this time, Deanna knew it was Gail. Her eyes began to burn, and a lump rose in her throat. "Deanna, dear. Is there anything I can do?" Gail's voice was just as she remembered it, soothing and loving.

"I vont to suck your blood." Devin imitated cartoon vampires he'd seen on TV recently.

"Shut up!"

"What was that, dear?"

Had Gail just heard her thoughts? "No, nothing. I'm fine. Can you please wait for me downstairs?" Deanna's voice was shaking violently.

"Sure, honey."

Honey? When was the last time she had heard her mother call her honey? *Oh, honey, I'll only be gone a few weeks. I love you, Elizabeth.* A few weeks, then a few months, then years. She had never seen her mother again.

"Deanna, she's a vampire now. Your mother is a vampire." It sounded like a cheesy B-rated drive-in movie. *"Don't forget that. And they're waiting for us."* Devin opened the bathroom door.

Deanna jumped to her feet for fear that someone had seen the door open by itself.

"What about her telepathy? She'll figure this out, probably has already. She'll sense you without even trying. We are so screwed. I think she heard me tell you to shut up just now. Was that my imagination? We are so screwed."

Walking into the living room took a great deal of effort, more than Deanna possessed at that moment. Everything was exactly as she had left it: the pizza box was on the coffee table, empty glasses and plates with half eaten crusts were on the end tables. The television was still tuned to an HBO channel except the volume was now turned off. The only thing that was different was that her mother was now sitting in the middle of the room.

"Finally." Sari rolled her eyes.

Gail sat across from Sari, smiling patiently.

"Hi." Deanna kept her eyes down and her hair falling over her face.

There was a silence for a moment until Sari spoke. "I guess I should apologize for Deanna." She glared at her friend. "I've never known her to be so shy. Of course, she's been acting strange all day."

Devin crept beside Deanna. *"She'd be acting strange too if she just found out what you found out."* He laughed.

Deanna mentally told him to shut up again.

Gail was staring at Deanna through the entire exchange with Devin. She had heard something, Deanna was sure of it.

"I'm going to get a drink? Anyone want anything while I'm up?" Neither answered her. "Is Eric up yet?"

"You'd know better than me. Is he still in his room? Maybe you can go check on him." Gail looked to Deanna as she spoke.

It was several minutes before either Gail or Deanna broke the awkward silence that hung over them after Sari left the room. Devin had been telling her to relax, to look at Gail, and was trying to convince her not to worry. Gail didn't know anything. Just as she was starting to believe it, Gail got off her chair and sat beside her on the sofa.

"Who's Devin?" she whispered.

Deanna swallowed hard. The smell of flowers, specifically jasmine, filled her senses as Gail leaned close to her. "What? Who? What do you mean?" Her eyes were bulging from their sockets. "I don't . . . I mean . . . oh God."

"Don't be scared." Gail put her hand on Deanna's hand. "I heard the name. It doesn't matter how." Gail waved her hand dismissively. "My youngest daughter had an imaginary friend named Devin and I just thought . . . frankly I don't know what I thought. It was just strange, I guess." She stopped, studying Deanna's face.

"Your d-daughter?" Deanna stammered. "Well, I d-don't really know who D-Devin is. Maybe you *heard* wrong."

"Elizabeth. That's my daughter. She used to talk with him quietly in her room or in the garden. Anytime she thought she was alone." Gail laughed. "You know how children are. Her brother and sister were older and there were few children for her to play with."

Deanna didn't say anything but instead tried not to have a panic attack. She concentrated on her breathing and her heart rate. She was failing miserably and was afraid she would pass out. The soda in the glass on the coffee table began to bubble.

Gail made no notice of it. She was not really talking to Deanna anymore as she strolled down memory lane. "Elizabeth was so cute. I've got a picture somewhere around here. She was Daddy's girl, though. Lizzybeth."

"Lizzy," Deanna finally said through clenched teeth. "Isabella liked the nickname Lizzybeth." Her tone was groaning. She hated that nickname. Hated her older sister as well.

Gail studied her for a moment, eyeing her up and down. "Who are you?"

"Who are *you*?" Deanna was slowly gaining control of herself. She eyed the glass of soda. The bubbles were larger, and she tried to stay calm, but it wasn't working.

The sound of footsteps on the stairs brought their conversation to an abrupt end and Deanna noticed the soda had stopped bubbling as she found some comfort in the presence of others. Deanna could hear Sari talking with whom she assumed could only be Eric. The two joined Deanna and Gail in the living room only to be met with looks of sadness and confusion.

"Are we interrupting?" Eric asked Gail as he kissed her cheek.

"No, of course not. We were just getting to know one another. Deanna is a very interesting girl." Gail smiled as if nothing had passed between them.

Eric sat on the loveseat beside Sari, who sank into his arms comfortably. Deanna was frightened for Sari. She looked to her sitting blindly in the arms of certain death and that stabbing pain returned, except now it was just below her heart.

Gail sat comfortably watching Deanna as she watched her right back. The blackness of her hair that was always pinned up in a bun; the gray eyes that she remembered blazing at her when she had done something wrong. The smile that was just as warm as she remembered it. Mother. The thought burned the backs of her eyes, and tears flooded them until she could no longer see. She bowed her head so as not to draw attention to herself.

Cautiously, she looked up to see if anyone had noticed. No one but Gail; her eyes were just as steely and stormy as before. Eric and Sari were cooing at each other. Something that would have normally nauseated Deanna but flew right by her radar as she sat staring at her long-lost mother. Blair, Carolyn, Junelyn, Gail, Anne, Genevieve. . . They were all her mothers. She loved them all.

Gail shifted in her seat and her lower lip stiffened as her long, thin, pale hands clutched at her sweater. Deanna swallowed hard and wiped her nose and eyes with the back of her hand.

"D, are you feeling all right?" Sari handed her a tissue from her pocket.

"Just a little tired, I guess. The long trip is catching up to me."

"Would you like to rest?" Gail stood. "Or some tea?" She was anxious and a little too eager in her movements.

"Tea would be great. Thank you." Their eyes met again. Deanna wanted to hug her. She wanted to scream that she was Elizabeth. She wanted so many things that she couldn't express in an instant. And it seemed that Gail felt the yearning as well. That overwhelming desire to hold each other until the pain of the last hundred years disappeared.

The tea was comforting as was the fire that Eric stoked to a pretty substantial roar. Deanna nibbled on biscuits that Sari offered, and they spoke of less soul-exposing things. Sari asked Deanna about Max and what was going on with them and they spoke of a confrontation in the cemetery only a few nights ago with street toughs. Or at least that's what Sari thought they were. From Deanna's mind and a few stray thoughts from Sari's muddled brain, Gail could clearly see that those street toughs were Martino and his friends.

The picture in Deanna's mind was clearly on Martino. She had only a few stored or remembered images of the others. They didn't seem to matter as much as Martino. But from Sari's confused mind, which was very difficult for Gail to follow, let alone read, she got clearer pictures of Bith and Chelsea. And Richard, whom Sari had actually spoken to.

Sari liked them, although Gail couldn't determine why. Trying to follow Sari's thoughts was like trying to catch a hummingbird; if she intended to do it, she'd need to have her trapped into thinking of one thing. And that seemed impossible for Sari. Perhaps after Eric brought her into his life, her mind might just settle down. It made Gail dizzy trying to track her thoughts, so she centered on Deanna.

Abby appeared an hour later. "Are we still going out tonight?" she asked Gail, knowing that she hadn't hunted since Sari had come to the cabin. It was wearing her down.

Gail smiled gently. "Yes, of course. I'd almost forgotten."

"We won't be long." Abby looked to Sari. "When we come back, we can do each other's hair and paint our nails and trade stories about our first kiss just like a real sleepover." She rolled her eyes.

Sari laughed. "And tell ghost stories. I always love the ghost stories."

Gail walked to the front door with Abby. Looking back, she could see the mistrust in Deanna's eyes. She knew. For a moment, that look made Gail feel dirty about what she was about to do. An intense feeling of anger towards Deanna started to rise and she needed to push it back down inside. "We'll continue when I come back." She was looking at Deanna.

When the door closed, Sari asked, "Hey, do you know anything about that little graveyard by that house on the hill?"

"You were at the cottage?" Eric looked nervous. His face lost expression and he looked a little alarmed. "You didn't go inside, did you?"

"Couldn't. Everything is locked up. Why?" Deanna was gaining interest.

"Just don't mention that you went up there to Gail, OK?" Eric said. "She's real jumpy about that old place."

Sari smiled. "Why, what happened there? Murder? Were those tombstones victims of a horrible serial killer?"

"Oh, don't get all excited. It's not the Shining hotel. Just something deeply personal and *private* to Gail." Eric emphasized the private as he looked at Sari. "Don't bring it up again. All right?"

"But there are two graves that are more recent than the others. Are they family or something?" Deanna's eyes widened.

"Ooo, vampire secrets," Devin whispered in her ear.

Deanna flinched slightly. *"You know something, don't you?"*

"It's a feeling." He left it at that.

"Come on, you know what happened. I can see it in your eyes." Sari was teasing Eric.

"Well, you found us out. Those two graves were from the last visitors to Mount Orion. They, too, were wondering about the cottage on the hill. Now they are part of the cottage on the hill." Eric looked from Sari to Deanna. "Now we're going to have to dig more graves. I told you not to ask too many questions. I told you. Oh God! I think I hear Gail coming now!"

Deanna and Sari looked at each other and then to Eric. "Will you please stop?" Sari shook her head.

"Well, I was just trying to show you how ridiculous you're being." Eric laughed. "Listen, I don't know anything about the graves, but let's drop it now. I do hear someone coming. This subject does seem to put everyone on edge, so let's drop it. And let's not discuss it again."

Sari nodded.

"OK?" He needed an answer from both women.

Deanna nodded half-heartedly.

"But they are buried in your family cemetery. You have every right to find out why." Devin found a way to stir up trouble.

"It was hers before it was mine, remember? No use arguing about it." Deanna looked up as the front door swung open to see a very attractive, very tall vampire staring at her disparagingly. He exchanged a look with Eric, was gracious with introductions, and disappeared to the basement quickly.

CHAPTER TWELVE

The evening was unusually warm for October, but a nip was still in the breeze. The kill was quick this evening; Gail had other things on her mind. A vagrant that no one would miss. Homeless, drunk, and smelling of urine and something moldy. Abby was beside her the entire time, watching as she got her fill. When it was her turn, she seemed to barely notice the appalling scent of the man and drained him completely.

"Are you going to tell me what's on your mind or do I have to guess?" Abby slipped beside her and took her hand. They were headed back to the cabin. Walking the deserted road just off the interstate, they slipped through the trees as they came to the edge of the property. "You've been acting strangely since we left home. Is it that girl, Sari's friend, what's her name?"

"Deanna."

"Whatever. Is it her? Because that's an easy fix." Abby sucked on her long canine teeth and laughed. "It can't be Sari because she's fine. At least, I think so. Human but that's also an easy fix."

"No, not Sari." Gail shook her head, not really wanting to talk about, it but there was no one else that she could tell without judgement besides Abby. "It's Deanna. I'm getting one of my – what do you call them?"

"Bizarro feelings."

She couldn't get the image of Elizabeth waving from the parlor window out of her mind. Her little dimpled hand waving slowly as tears poured down her face when Gail's coach pulled away. Tears had saturated Gail's face that day. She knew it was best to mourn for her husband alone. No pressures, no children. She kept telling herself that repeatedly on the coach ride to the docks. Best to mourn alone. She was sure Isabella would care for her sister and brother just as well as any mother. She was sure of it.

As the boat set sail for England, Gail felt that she would never see her children again. She was right. Not six months into her vacation, Gail was attacked by a vampire. True, it wasn't just any vampire. Jordan was a god to her and soon became her entire life. Her family disappeared, and her new existence was all that mattered.

"I think she knows my family. My human family. I mean, she knows things about my daughters, and from her mind I saw images of my house . . ."

"See that's your first mistake. Stay out of people's heads. If you are eavesdropping, you are bound to hear or see things that you don't want to see or hear. What does Jordan always say, 'you control what you can control'? They don't send the messages to you. You go looking for trouble and see where it gets you."

Gail nodded, knowing she was right but hating her for throwing it in her face. "Listen, you know I carry around a lot of guilt about what I did to my children. And when Bart died, I think I was able to get past most of it. But there's something about this girl. She talks to an imaginary friend just like Elizabeth."

Abby put her hand up. "Wait, imaginary friend? She's crazy? Well, that makes this much easier. I say we wait until Eric takes Sari out and have ourselves a nice meal. No one's going to miss a nutjob that talks to the walls."

"She's not a nutjob. Elizabeth had an imaginary friend named Devin and Deanna was talking to *something* named Devin in the bathroom. I heard her tell him to shut up a few times. Maybe he wasn't so imaginary. Maybe I should have paid closer attention to Elizabeth and not as much to Isabella."

Deep down, Gail didn't want to know the suffering her children had felt when she left. She didn't want to know if Isabella abused them or if Neville beat them. What if he beat them? What if Isabella did neglect Elizabeth in favor of her own daughter, Catrina?

Hadn't Gail done the same thing? Hadn't she favored Isabella over her other children because she possessed the gift of telepathy? Hadn't Catrina favored Marjorie, and Marjorie favored Nadia, and Nadia favored Rhea? All because these daughters could read minds. All because they shared that special connection that no one could possibly understand. That's how it went, not necessarily the first-born daughter, not always a daughter, but each generation had the gifted ones.

"Forget about these people. They were a part of a different lifetime. You are a different person. You are strong and beautiful and . . ." She took Gail's face in her hands. "I love you. Jordan loves you. You made mistakes in your past? Yes, but you have been a great mentor and sire for me, Martino, Jake, and whether you want to hear it or not, to Nadia. We all love you. Your children are long dead. Let them rest. And if this girl is playing you, then let me deal with her. Agreed?"

The cabin was in sight and the cottage just beyond it was a dim shadow on the horizon. Too many memories in that cottage. Too many lives lost. She knew the moment she stepped back into that cottage she would step back into the past. A past that she should have buried years ago.

The cabin was alive with lights and the faint flutter of country music. Gail smiled, trying to push the intrusive thoughts of the past out of her head. Jordan reminded her time and time again what had happened in the past, in that cottage, was not her fault. Well, not entirely her fault. There was so much left to live for and she had the rest of eternity to forget what happened. But what had happened never did completely die, and Gail knew it would someday come back to haunt her.

She looked to Abby, who was still at her side waiting for her to figure out the encyclopedia's worth of worries she had building in her brain. "I wonder if I can shut it off?"

"What's that?"

"This gift. Not use it when I'm around Deanna. That way I won't know what she doesn't want me to know."

"But she will know that you know that she knows what you know, you know?" Abby laughed at her joke. Gail snickered, trying not to laugh, but Abby made it extremely difficult sometimes.

She thought of the gift again. Elizabeth had a gift. If what Gail guessed about Devin was true, she could talk to spirits. Why didn't Gail see it then? Why hadn't she sensed that Devin was there and not just part of her imagination? Gail had spent the better part of her life trying to turn off the spirits that intruded in her life. Devin never had a chance.

She did love Elizabeth, but she was Virgil's prize. After their fourth child died during childbirth, Gail didn't want any more children. They had three and that was enough. Virgil's constant pressures resulted in Elizabeth, and he doted on her.

So much had changed in her life since she was human. Not only the physical differences of becoming a vampire, there were also emotional changes that she carried with her and tried to let go of years ago. So many changes she let go of thanks to Nadia, but quite a few were outgrown and forgotten. She didn't fear the dark any longer. Bugs didn't frighten her. She wasn't so obsessed with the creation of a life. That was definitely because of Nadia, the last one she had brought into this life.

Gail missed Nadia more than anyone she had ever missed before. There was an empty space in her heart that hurt when she thought of Nadia. She, too, like Deanna, was a distant family member. Not so distant now. Nadia had withdrawn over twenty years ago. Jordan referred to it as hibernating. Gail thought of it as hiding from the world. Either way, Nadia wasn't coming out any time soon. Behind the rotting curtains in the cottage, beneath the dust-covered, sheeted furniture, she remained hidden away.

Perhaps that was why Gail was apprehensive of Deanna. She couldn't make another catastrophic mistake like she did with Nadia.

Gail turned back toward the cabin. The night was getting colder and her mind still wasn't made up. She wanted to run away again. She didn't want to hurt any more lives. She thought of Sari.

Sweet, innocent Sari. Eric was intent on making her immortal. Whether Sari wanted it or not. Gail could feel the grave error he was about to commit—though she couldn't tell him. He was at least two hundred years older than she. He had to know better.

"Where's your little friend?" Abby called out.

Eric and Sari were walking back from the lake. "Jordan's enthralling her with his tales of France. He just got back." Eric kissed the back of Sari's hand. "She speaks French, apparently."

"Yeah, news to me," Sari chimed in.

"Is he alone?" Abby asked.

"Were you expecting someone?"

"No, just asking." She lowered her head. "Kind of hoping Joss would show up. Guess I should go find her one of these days." Abby kicked the ground like a small impudent child.

Gail could see through the bay window Deanna and Jordan laughing. She fought herself but, in the end, it was impossible to stop; she listened to what they were saying both with physical hearing and mental. They were discussing their travels in French. Gail found her trust of this girl slipping as she listened to her speaking fluent French, speaking of things that were impossible for her as a twenty-three-year-old to know.

"Let's go inside."

The living room was warm – toasty was the word Abby used as she rubbed her hands together in front of the fire. Jordan sat facing Deanna with his arm over the back of the sofa behind her head. They were laughing until the front door opened, depositing the quartet into the entryway.

"This looks cozy," Abby teased, dropping on the chaise across from Jordan and Deanna.

Gail glared at her but said nothing.

"Where did you two disappear to? You missed the stories of Jordan's misadventures in France." Deanna laughed, looking to Jordan as if they were long-lost friends that had just reunited. "I turned around and you were gone." Eric remained quiet, but Sari couldn't keep her tongue.

"I was feeling a little left out – not being able to understand a word you were saying." The acid in Sari's tone was evident and Gail could see from Deanna's expression that she hadn't realized the position that she put her friend. "Can we keep the conversation on this continent from now on?"

"Sorry," Deanna whispered. "I guess we got carried away. I didn't realize. . ." She let the thought linger without finishing it.

"You're awfully quiet." Jordan pulled Gail into the spotlight, a place she didn't wish to be right now. "Something on your mind?"

"Nothing of consequence," she lied. If Jordan weren't so distracted by this beautiful young woman fawning over him, he would have known that Gail's mind was overflowing with questions. Thoughts, feelings, speculation about Deanna and who she really was. "Abby, please make sure Deanna has everything she needs for a comfortable stay. I'll be upstairs if anyone needs me."

Within minutes of her dropping onto her bed with a book in hand, there was a knock at the door. "What's wrong?" Jordan poked his head into the room. Waiting for her to answer the door was never his strong suit. If they were arguing, he would perhaps give her a minute to compose herself, but otherwise his knock was merely a warning that he was entering the room.

This time she was pleased to see him. Those questions that were overflowing in her mind had become a flood, and she couldn't hold back the flood gates any longer. She smiled, put down her book, and patted the bed beside her. He sat on the edge of the bed in a very gentlemanly manner that brought to mind images of a blushing bride.

She ran her fingers through his long blonde hair. It was rare that he left it loose around his shoulders. Gail always thought it made him look young, carefree, and unbelievably attractive. "How was France?"

"Lonely." His eyes were penetrating. He didn't wish to talk about his latest travels.

"I missed you." She scooted closer to him, laying her head on his shoulder.

"What's going on?"

She could feel him resisting the urge to penetrate her mind.

"When you spoke to Deanna earlier, did you speak of anything besides France?"

"Not really. She said she hadn't been in years. I guessed since she was a child. Her French is perfect. If I didn't know better, I would have thought she was born in Nice." He shrugged. His eyes scanned her face, travelling over her hair and down her body. His hand stroked her arm slowly.

Gail nodded. "But she didn't say anything about me or my family?"

"Your family? How would she know them?"

"I don't know, but she does – my daughter, Elizabeth, at least."

"The restauranteur? You are not dwelling on that damned restaurant again? I thought we agreed to drop it. It was nothing more than a hole in the ground. An unstable hole in the ground but one nonetheless."

"No, not the restaurant." She waved away his attitude. "She spoke of Elizabeth . . ." Gail stopped herself. How much did she speak of Elizabeth besides telling her about some old forgotten – inconsequential – nicknames? Had Gail filled in the blanks and come up with this tale on her own? Had she been overdramatizing and emphatically fictionalizing this whole scenario? "Damn it. Abby said she might be playing me . . ."

"Want to fill me in or should I do it the old-fashioned way?" He raised an eyebrow, knowing that she detested his intrusion in her thoughts as much as anyone else.

"Sari invites this friend of hers to stay with us. When I met her, there's something off about her . . . I'm surprised you didn't pick up on that, at least. I guess she's too pretty for you to see past it. Anyway, she mentioned something about Lizzybeth and Isabella liking that nickname. I don't know, but she also has this spirit or something named Devin that she talks to, and Elizabeth had an imaginary friend named Devin, so I . . . fabricated this whole damn thing. I hate when I do that."

Jordan stared at her, amused by her enthusiasm but confused by her tale. "Let's pretend any of that made sense to me. This is what I got out of that mess. You created a story in your head because of a nickname and an imaginary friend."

Gail nodded, embarrassed to admit the truth. "What about Devin? I didn't invent or imagine that. She did speak to him silently – I heard that. I did. Who is he? And isn't it a little too coincidental that my daughter and this girl have the same imaginary friend? I mean, Devin isn't exactly a common name."

"Depends who you ask."

"Well, I intend to ask her."

Gail opened her bedroom door, almost walking directly into Eric and Sari, who were heading back to his bedroom for the night. She apologized and bid them a good night, knowing she wouldn't see them again until the next evening.

Deanna was sitting on the sofa, flipping through a magazine. The television was on and her eyes bounced from the magazine back to the screen periodically.

"Deanna, may I ask you something personal?" She sat across from her on the chaise, reaching over to switch off the TV. Jordan remained in the doorway with his arms crossed over his chest and his legs crossed – rather sarcastically – at the ankles. "Earlier I asked you who Devin was, but you never answered me. Who is he? I heard you speaking to him earlier and just now when I came into the room."

She put down the magazine in her lap and took a deep cleansing breath as if she were about to spill government secrets to the KGB. Her mouth opened several times as if she were about to speak, only to be shut closed again, as if she had thought better of it. She swallowed hard and tried again. "He's a spirit." The words came out more like a question than a soul-exposing admission.

"Spirit?" Jordan was skeptical.

"A spirit." She was more certain this time. "I can hear him. He's always with me."

"Until you die?" Gail said it like she didn't believe Deanna realized her relationship with this spirit would end abruptly when she bit the dust.

Deanna shrugged but didn't continue.

"What aren't you saying?" Jordan's arms were no longer crossed.

"He's with me after death. He's *always* with me." She didn't look directly at anyone, keeping her eyes on the magazine in her lap.

"How do you know that?" Gail leaned forward, placing her elbows on her knees. "You'd have to die to know that."

"Believe me, I know."

"How?"

Gail could tell by his tone that Jordan was losing patience with these little half answers and half-truths she was feeding them. "You are not immortal. You are not mortal either, are you?"

Deanna's face went blank. She didn't know how to answer the question. "I am mortal. I will die. This body will die but I will come back. I used to tell Martino that it was *eternal reincarnation*. He thought that was something straight out of the horror comics he was so obsessed with." The blank expression melted into humor as she spoke of Martino.

"My Martino? What does he have to do with this?"

"Don't you get it? It's cyclical. I'm born, die, born again, die again. Over and over."

"For how long?" Jordan's tone was softening as he was gaining interest.

"About six hundred years by my count."

"And Devin has been with you all that time?"

"Not the whole time. I locked him up in the basement of Lizzy's a century ago." She chewed her lower lip, still not looking at Gail or Jordan.

"How did you get into Lizzy's?" Gail asked.

Deanna paused for a moment, obviously speaking to Devin. "He doesn't want me to tell you this. I think you have a right to know." She put her hand to her racing heart. Gail could taste her blood racing through her veins. "I was Elizabeth Staton, your daughter."

Gail stared at her, horrified by her words. Her mouth hung open. She could taste the words that lay on her tongue but could find no voice to speak them. Deanna glanced up quickly, catching Gail's eye as she stared mutely at her. There it was, the truth. It was there all along – in her eyes. Those large hazel eyes were the same clear beautiful eyes that smiled up at her when she was cooking dinner or tending to the housework. The same eyes that blazed at her defiantly when she was told to go to bed or do her chores. The same eyes that cried after her father died and the same eyes that watched as her mother drove away forever.

"Elizabeth," she whispered finally.

"I didn't know how to tell you. I wasn't sure if I should." Those soulful hazel eyes, now rimmed in an earthy green, filled with tears as she pushed the magazine to the side and put her hands over her face. "Elizabeth was a soul-defining lifetime. So much happened. I had children – I'd never been a mother before. I stood on my own for the first time. Locking Devin away was one of the hardest decisions I've ever had to make, and there were times that I didn't think I could do it without him. But I did. I missed you every day. I wanted so much for you to meet Alice and my husband, Bryon. And my boys. But you never came back. At least now I know why."

Deanna laughed, wiping the tears from her cheeks.

"Elizabeth," Gail said again. She couldn't believe what she was hearing.

"This is why you speak French so beautifully?"

"Sophie. Born in Belgium, raised just outside Paris. She was . . ." She thought on it for a moment. "Devin says she was my third lifetime. Somewhere in the neighborhood of the mid-sixteenth century. He'd remember exactly if I gave him time. He remembers it all. Every lifetime, every death, everything."

Gail wanted to touch her. "How does Martino fit into this?" she said, finally finding her voice.

"Margaret Cooper. I met him when I – she was attending CU. It was a whirlwind romance." She smiled and felt the blush touch her cheeks. "He didn't understand what was going on with me. He tried to help. He didn't. I saw him a few weeks ago at a bar with my friends and then again at the bicentennial thing in Torry. I don't know if he's figured it out yet, but he knows something. He's been following me around incessantly."

"How did he find you again?" Gail moved over to the sofa beside Deanna. The need to touch her was great, but she didn't want to frighten her.

"I don't think he was looking for me. I think, after having a few weeks to think about it, that they were following Sari. His friends seem to be 'interested in her' but won't touch her because of Eric. It's really strange."

Jordan laughed out loud. "Tabitha's spawn are troublemakers. We should make Eric aware of their intentions."

Gail didn't answer. Her mind was still reeling from all that she learned. "One more question and then I'll let you get some rest; you look exhausted." She could feel the fatigue weakening her body. Those lovely hazel eyes were getting red and weary. "Why are you like this? What happened to you and Devin?"

Deanna's eyes met Gail's and she smiled wanly. "Best explanation and the easiest is that we are cursed. Witchcraft is a dangerous mistress."

CHAPTER THIRTEEN

About the time that Jordan was doubting Deanna's credibility, Jacenta was boarding a flight to America. It was miserable as usual. Especially when she was forced to fly commercial. Jacenta hated to fly. She hated the loss of control over whether she would live or die. She hated the proximity to humans and the constant intrusion of the flight attendant.

She hated it all.

Callie, on the other hand, loved every minute of it. While Jacenta hid behind sunglasses, headphones, and a book, Callie stared at the night sky for the entire flight to JFK airport. She limited her questions to one every fifteen minutes so Jacenta wouldn't kill her. Jacenta closed her eyes and tried to ignore every irritant around her.

Their time in the Amazon was resplendent. Rani was the perfect host and Callie took to the rainforest like the true animal she had become. Worries about her family and being transferred back to America were forgotten as she basked in Rani's essence. He had that way about him. Something about him allowed the world to disappear.

The Connecticut Haven was excited for her visit. There had been at least four phone calls between Jacenta and Roderick, the house director, since she decided to transfer Callie there a week ago. Jacenta found her cell had no signal in the middle of the jungle. Rani offered her the use of his emergency satellite phone. Roderick assured her he would prepare a room for Callie. Jacenta's usual wing, which was never used except when she visited, was being made ready for her arrival.

She was patient as Roderick gushed over her impending visit. Big changes were happening at the facility and he was eager to share them with her. He assured her that Callie would be assimilated into the community at her own pace or whatever pace

Jacenta deemed appropriate. Roderick was in the process of choosing a companion for Callie; someone to show her the ropes for the first few weeks to take some of the burden off of Jacenta. It wasn't necessary for her to stay any longer than she wished, Roderick told her. Their new program was designed for every individual and a plan would be designed especially for Callie based on how she completed the testing.

Testing? Jacenta had so many questions, but it would all have to wait. She had asked Roderick if there had been any word from Sabina in the last few months. He was only too eager to please Jacenta and indicated that he would find her if necessary.

When the plane landed at midnight, there was a car waiting for them. A young immortal that Jacenta had never seen before, named Takoda, greeted them and ushered them through the terminal to the waiting limousine. Takoda had long black hair that he kept pulled back in an elastic. Jacenta eyed him carefully as he offered his hand to Callie as she climbed into the rear of the car. His skin was pale but still held its natural tanned shade. He was Native American, she surmised from his complexion and his name.

"Well, at least Roderick has style." She smiled as she climbed into the car.

"Yes, he does," a voice startled Jacenta as she took her seat beside Callie. A man sat in the seat facing hers. He was immortal. "Welcome to New York, Jacenta. I'm Gabriel. May I offer you a drink?"

Jacenta cautiously declined but Callie eagerly accepted. Gabriel removed a large thermos from a duffle bag at his feet. Grabbing a tumbler from the limo's bar, he poured the contents of the thermos into the glass. "I hope you prefer it warm. I do. Cold blood is repugnant, don't you agree?" He handed the glass to Callie, but his eyes remained fixed on Jacenta.

"I hope you don't find me rude; I am extremely tired from that ghastly flight . . . but who are you, exactly?" She was direct. "Why are you here?"

"Gabriel." Callie giggled. "He said his name was Gabriel." The blood was obviously working its magic.

Jacenta continued to stare at this man in his finely tailored charcoal gray suit with plum colored shirt and tie. His hands were folded neatly in his lap, and his legs were crossed comfortably at the ankle. His hair was wavy and a bit shaggy. His eyes were crystal blue and his face lit up when he smiled. A dusting of a beard covered his chin, completing the rugged yet sophisticated persona this immortal had carefully created for himself.

"Sorry." He smiled again and Jacenta held her breath. She was very aware that she had been visually devouring him for the last few moments. "I'm the creative consultant for the Connecticut Haven."

"Pardon?"

He laughed and sat forward. "I am in the process of reimagining our facility. I am the dreamer. Roderick is the doer."

"I see."

"I was hoping we could discuss this later to . . ."

"Well, we do have about two hours on our hands. Please enlighten me." She shifted uncomfortably in her seat.

His smile dwindled and the cocky sparkle in his eyes died. Gabriel ran his hand through his hair and for the first time, Jacenta noticed the gray at his temples. "We should wait until we're with Roderick. As I've said, I'm merely the dreamer."

"Yeah, J. Let's just relax and get to know each other." Callie pressed the button to lower the divider between the driver and passengers. "So, Takoda, how's the air up there?" Takoda laughed; he couldn't have been more than a few years older than Callie when he was changed.

"No, I'd like to hear how you are *reimagining* a system that has been in place for hundreds of years." Jacenta reached for the thermos and a glass and poured herself a drink. She was going to need it.

"Please help yourself." Gabriel unbuttoned his suit jacket impatiently. "I didn't intend for this to be an argument..."

She sipped the warm, thick liquid and it was like drinking heaven. *The good stuff.* Jacenta felt her muscles instantly relax and her jaw unclenched. She hadn't even realized it was clenched. "Look, it's been a long night and again, I apologize for my rudeness. I've got a lot on my plate right now, so you'll forgive me if I don't immediately accept your version of *my* dream. But please, do tell me how you're *improving* Haven."

Gabriel sat back in his seat, the cocky grin returning to his face, and he stared at Jacenta for a moment. "I love your accent. Irish?" he asked.

"Nice deflection." She laughed in spite of her growing frustration.

The drive was pleasant, mostly. Jacenta couldn't get Gabriel to talk about the changes he was making to Haven, but his knowledge of Haven's history and crude beginnings astounded her, keeping her interest for the entire trip. He even got her to laugh a time or two. Callie had climbed up to the front seat, and she and Takoda were forming a friendship that Jacenta didn't think was possible for the girl, especially so soon after leaving Brazil.

Arriving at Haven was like going home, always. Roderick was just as she remembered him. Tall, handsome, and dreamy. His skin was the color of deep caramel and his clothing reflected nothing short of a wizard. Thankfully, she was able to escape to her rooms with a quick "good day" before he could finish gushing about how happy he was that she had chosen his facility to house her newest recruit.

Facility? Recruit? These were words she wasn't thrilled with. They sounded like buzzwords that she had tried to avoid from the beginning. Haven was not a facility; it was home. The recruits were struggling souls that needed help. Recruit made them sound like the newest additions to a cult.

She checked on Callie briefly before returning to her private wing. Callie's room was simple but comfortable, not unlike the rooms in Salvador. The windows all had electronic covers that blocked out all the light. They were on a timer. They opened and closed with the fluctuations of the sun.

One of Gabriel's improvements, no doubt, Jacenta thought.

"Looks like you'll have a roommate." She pointed to the twin bed directly opposite the bed Callie sat upon. Callie nodded; she didn't appear thrilled with the prospect of sharing the room.

"All settled in?" Takoda appeared in the doorway dressed more comfortably than when he picked them up at the airport. His tee shirt and jeans gave him the air of a college junior. "Your bags have arrived. We'll have them up here before you wake this evening."

"Thank you, Takoda." Callie smiled. She was smitten. Jacenta echoed her sentiment and left the two alone.

Walking back to her rooms, Jacenta noticed newly painted walls, new furniture in the common room, and an entire wing of technology. Through the double doors she could see one large room with computers, game systems, tablets, and televisions. The room was devoid of people.

"You like?" Gabriel was suddenly behind her.

"Is this part of your reimagining?"

"Partly. We'll talk more tonight." He ran his finger down her cheek and Jacenta pulled away. The cocky smile was the last thing she saw as he turned on his heel and disappeared down the hall. His swagger angered her as she watched him go.

She continued her trek back to her room. It was all so different that she almost lost her direction. Jacenta passed a library on her way. Poking her head in for a minute, she felt the emptiness of the room. Like the computer room, no one was there. Everyone had retreated to the safety of their technologically sun-proofed rooms. She wasn't sure if she could get used to being surrounded by this much machinery all the time.

"Wake up, J." Callie was knocking at her door. Jacenta had been ignoring her for several minutes now, but the knocking was relentless.

"Go away," she said from under the covers.

"J, they're all waiting for you." Callie continued to knock as she spoke. "I have so much to tell you."

"Oh, for the love of Pete, stop that infernal knocking and come in!" Jacenta could sense that it was much later than she usually woke. Reaching blindly for the remote, she pressed a button. (No timer in her room.) The blinds raised and she could see that it was well after sunset. Not even a hint of light existed on the horizon. She pulled the covers back over her head without looking at Callie.

"Come on, sleepyhead. Get up." That was definitely not Callie's voice. "They're gathered in the common room waiting for you." The voice was soft yet strong; not young and immature like Callie's.

Jacenta pulled the covers down slowly and peeked her eye out. "Sabina?" she whispered.

Callie giggled.

The woman smiled. She pushed her long dark hair behind her shoulder and grabbed the comforter that Jacenta was using to hide beneath. "Get up. We will wait for you no longer."

"What are you doing here?" She reached for Sabina and pulled her playfully into her embrace.

"I'm trying to get you out of bed. There will be plenty of time for our tearful reunion, but Roderick is waiting." Sabina pulled herself gently away from the bed and headed for the closet. "The young one, what was his name? Pagoda, Katoga . . . something." She laughed at herself. "He has put all your clothes in your closet while you were hiding under your blankets."

"Takoda," Jacenta corrected her mildly. She had finally gotten out of bed and followed Sabina to the next room. "I wasn't hiding; it's called sleeping. Some of us still do it. You're just too old to remember." She laughed.

"Oh, really," Sabina called from deep in the closet. "How long are you staying? Did you bring your entire wardrobe?"

"Most of it I left here the last time I was here. Ages ago."

"Must have been decades by the looks of some of these vintage pieces." Sabina held up a gold lame pant suit.

"Ooo, that's cool. Can I try that on?" Callie appeared beside Jacenta.

Jacenta laughed in spite of herself. "It really is good to see you. I've missed you so."

Sabina smiled, kissed her quickly, and dove back into the forest of outdated garments.

Fifteen minutes later they were entering the common room together; Sabina, dressed in a tunic style dress adorned with crystals around the neckline. The sparkle set off the sparkle in her brown eyes, J mused. Callie, dressed in one of Jacenta's bellbottom polyester pants suits was on the opposite side of Jacenta, who chose a simple tee shirt and jeans combo with a brown suede jacket that suddenly made her feel underdressed. The room was full of new faces that Jacenta had never encountered before. It was becoming abundantly clear that this Haven was no longer hers. It had been decades since she was last in America, let alone Connecticut. She entered the room with a feeling of insecurity that she was unfamiliar with. Grasping both Sabina and Callie's hands at the last moment, they entered with a false air of confidence that she was sure was completely transparent.

The room was very welcoming despite her feeling of insecurity. Sofas, chairs, tables for games all surrounded a large fire pit in the center of the room. A large funnel-shaped pipe reached up into the ceiling, pulling the residual smoke from the fire through it. Each wall was painted with a mural. One looked as if the observer was looking out of a window in the Italian countryside. Another a spectacular view of the ocean. Even the ceiling had small LED lights that looked like star shine.

The attendees were overjoyed to meet her. Roderick was on his feet before anyone else and before Jacenta made it past the entry. He embraced her warmly and led her away from Sabina to make his introductions. Jacenta's air of confidence was faltering as she took a few steps from her companions.

"You know Takoda and Gabriel," he began. Gabriel was smoking a thin cigar, looking almost regal as he nodded to her. Roderick continued, "Gwendolyn, Esme, Peter." He gestured with his hand as each one nodded. Peter gently kissed her hand and intimately touched her elbow. She knew she would never remember any of the many names except maybe for Peter but continued to smile and nod as each one stood and said hello. With one hand, she reached for Sabina's just to remind herself that she was not alone in all of this. Looking into her eyes, she saw the patient, loving, non-judgmental gleam that she had been dreaming about since planning this trip.

There were more introductions and Jacenta said a few words to encourage and inspire those before her. She felt like she was lying. Looking into Gabriel's smug face sitting in the chair closest to her made her feel like a stranger and not the founder of a long string of safe houses around the world. Within minutes of her rousing words of wisdom, everyone had broken off into their smaller groups or paid their respects to her and left. She watched as Callie, Takoda, and the young woman named Gwendolyn sat on the beanbags and pillows in front of the fire pit, deep in conversation.

It gave Jacenta hope that she wouldn't have to stay here any longer than necessary.

Gabriel approached, cigar still in hand, as Jacenta and Sabina began to walk the room and enjoy the many artist-created details. There were harlequin masks hanging near the exit that were beautiful. They were studying the detail when Gabriel said, "Ladies, shall we?" The aroma of the cigar was sweet and strangely comforting to Jacenta. She thought of Devin smoking his pipe after dinner. Ghosts of another lifetime, she reminded herself.

Gabriel offered his arm to Sabina, who took it gladly. Jacenta followed, shaking her head at his fraudulent chivalry and her little girl giggly acceptance.

Roderick offered them a seat at one end of a banquet-sized table in an adjoining room. He instructed Gabriel to close the large glass doors for privacy. "I'm sure Callie told you that she has tested already. We've placed her in a program that is fairly advanced from what we got from her readings. You've done well assimilating her. Gwendolyn is her sponsor."

"Like an alcoholic?" Jacenta was skeptical.

"Yes," Roderick said simply. "Gwen will teach her how to survive in this world. To hunt, and further adapt to her surroundings. Gwen is a fine teacher. You'll see." He studied Jacenta's reaction and continued. "Now with that behind us . . . you've seen the cosmetic changes that we've been making, no doubt. The paint, the furniture, the facility has expanded. Buying the rest of the block on this street has enabled us to triple the size from what we were the last time you visited." His tone held none of the gushing fan from earlier. Jacenta preferred him like this.

She nodded.

"It's all very superficial, really. The real changes and what we're really excited about are the computers, the rule changes, and the community atmosphere." He was smiling broadly.

"Rules? Which rules will you be changing?" Jacenta looked from Gabriel to Roderick and back again.

"There are no rules," Roderick said.

"Excuse me?"

"Jacenta," Gabriel started, "the old rules were excluding. We're trying to create a community here, not just a safe house. Not everyone needs protection. Some just need a friend or a bed for the night. We strive for that sense of oneness that you shaped years ago."

Jacenta shifted in her seat and found that she really wanted to walk out her frustrations. She wasn't sure if it was the fact that they were undoing what she had spent hundreds of years working for or that it was Gabriel who had said it. Either way, she could feel a pain in her chest stabbing and hurting her.

She looked to Sabina, hoping she could find all the answers in her eyes. But all she saw was the same calm patience as usual.

"We are offering a home for wanderers. A gathering place for friends," Gabriel went on.

It was as if he was selling her a timeshare. Jacenta kept wondering at what point he would start talking about her investment.

"Why continue as Haven? Why not start your own facility?" Sabina asked. Her voice was smooth and relaxing, and reminded Jacenta of a meditation therapist.

"Branding," Gabriel had said as if it was the most obvious answer in the world. "You've done a wonderful job making Haven a household name in our circles. We just want to bring it into the twenty-first century."

Jacenta didn't respond right away. The pain in her chest was spreading and beginning to burn. She swallowed hard. It was as if her heart was breaking. The ghosts were creeping back into her mind. She remembered the pain from years ago when Devin had betrayed her; it was the same. Except now it was hundreds of years of love and hard work taken away, changed as if what she had done wasn't good enough.

It was very much the same. Being a wife and mother was her life then and when Devin cheated on her, it was the same as saying that she wasn't good enough for him; for their children. He took away her family and her best friend in one instant. But she had showed him, hadn't she? They weren't going to take Haven away from her. The pain was sharper but now it was fueled by anger.

Roderick had been watching her reaction to the news. "We've been speaking with Portland and a few others. They are on board with these changes. Texas has even begun construction on their tech wing."

"Have they?" Jacenta said. The pain exploded, expanding from shoulder to shoulder. She felt as if she might hyperventilate. She was losing it all. He was taking it. Twisting it into some sort of perverted timeshare for the undead. He was turning Haven into a hotel. It was no longer a place of safety and security; it was Club Med.

"I would love to give you a tour to show you the advances we've made." Roderick could see Jacenta was moments away from a meltdown. He watched as Sabina held her hand and gently whispered to her, trying to diffuse what could potentially be a volatile situation.

She listened to Sabina assure her that they were not trying to cut her out of the project – Haven was still hers – but Jacenta's ear was caught by another voice.

"This is your way out, darling." Devin's voice tickled her ear and she smiled a small private smile. *"Take those walking papers he's handing you and run."*

Deep down, she agreed with him. Hearing Devin's voice calmed her more than she could have imagined. She knew he was right; maybe her time at Haven was over. Maybe this was her opportunity to start living for herself and not for others. Maybe the ghosts from that other lifetime had a point. "Gentlemen," she rose from her seat, "I would love a tour."

The look of surprise on Roderick and Sabina's faces was almost comical, but to see the smug look of self-assurance drain from Gabriel's face made it all worthwhile. It was as if he was enjoying her painful reaction to losing Haven. *Not today, jerk!*

Roderick walked ahead, leading the troupe through the halls of the growing facility. From the street it was only a façade of a two-story apartment building. However, the catacombs beneath the street went deep. It was a building built on a small underground city. Generators, security systems, massive computers running the lights and temperature. The generators were solar and water powered. The facility was completely off the grid. Powered entirely by those generators.

The hum coming from what Roderick called the P&L level hurt Jacenta's head. She was trailing behind close enough to hear what he said but far enough to absorb every detail of the building and enjoy Devin's humorous commentary.

"A swimming pool? Do the undead swim? I thought the dead could only float."

She nearly laughed out loud at his comments.

"What's so amusing?" Gabriel was at her side, his face close enough to feel the unmistakable heat that comes from a well-fed immortal. "It's pleasing to see a smile on your face. Since you've arrived, I believe your smiles have been a bit . . . well, forced. Your smile is very beautiful."

"He is a pompous ass." Devin sounded jealous.

Jacenta found herself smiling again. It was an easy humor-filled smile that made the pain in her chest cease for a minute. "Are most of your inhabitants transient?" she asked.

"Some. We do have a few that call us home. Myself included." He smiled. "It's my hope that Haven will be thought of as a community for all. Not just the young, frightened, and lost."

She put her hands up to stop him. "Can we drop the act, please? Stop trying to sell this place to me. It's already mine, remember? I started it."

Roderick and Sabina stopped short in their tour. They turned tentatively to see how this would unfold.

His mouth twisted in thought. A gleam in his eye allayed their fears. "How are we to proceed?"

"Pretend I'm one of those looking for a bed for the night. Stop trying to impress me and just help me to appreciate what you're doing here."

Gabriel's brows shifted in a distrustful yet humorous manner.

She took his arm and let him lead the way.

They were passing the library and Jacenta saw it was full. So many reading and writing.

"Roderick, hold up. I believe we wish to explore the library." Gabriel placed his palm on the small of Jacenta's back. She fought a shiver that ran up her spine.

Entering the enormous room, she nodded to those that looked up from their studies. She could smell the books and hear the pages turning. A wave of contentment washed over her. She looked to Gabriel's cigar as if it were an affront to this place of learning. He noticed her looking and snuffed it out.

"I love this," she whispered to herself and, of course, to Devin.

"It's my favorite as well." Gabriel moved his hand from the bottom of her back to the center. "We have one of the most expansive libraries that I've had the pleasure of collecting." His smile was easy and unassuming. "There are books dating back to the fifteenth century." He wasn't looking at her when he said this, and she saw the first glimmer of honest pride in his face. Haven wasn't his masterpiece; the library was.

"You've done all this?" Jacenta unconsciously grasped his hand. "It's marvelous."

"It's a room of books, not the Sistine Chapel." The tone of jealousy returned to Devin's voice in her head.

The tour continued with Gabriel and Jacenta leading the way, talking of what worked and what didn't. She found herself listening to and enjoying every word he spoke. They passed the medical and research lab, which also held Gabriel's rooms and office. "The tech wing is Roderick's baby." He smiled. "Being connected to the rest of the world is important to him. Information at his fingertips."

"All right, enough." Roderick laughed from behind them. "No need to make fun."

When they had circled back to the common room, Sabina said, "Thank you for the tour, gentlemen. But I would like to steal Jacenta. We have not had the opportunity to get properly reacquainted." Sabina reached for Jacenta's hand.

Strangely, Jacenta found it difficult to leave. She enjoyed Gabriel's wit now that he wasn't trying to impress her constantly. And the more he spoke, the less Devin did. "Thank you, Roderick, Gabriel. We'll talk more tomorrow."

Back at her room, Jacenta could see that Callie had been raiding her closet for more vintage clothes. The door was left open and several outfits and shoes were left strewn on the floor of the changing room. Callie was going to fit in just fine, Jacenta thought. In fact, she hadn't seen her since she left the common room.

"So, is he here now?" Sabina closed the doors to Jacenta's bedroom.

"How did you know?"

"I've been watching you. You were obviously talking to him the whole time." She kicked off her shoes and climbed up on the enormous bed in the middle of the room. "Until the library. After that it was, *Yes, Gabriel, no, Gabriel, whatever you say, Gabriel.* It was getting so I thought you might be falling for that arrogant windbag."

Jacenta smiled and bit her lower lip ashamedly. "Just a little."

"What?" Sabina fell back into the massive pile of pillows behind her. Her arms were splayed out like she was about to be crucified on a cross.

"I know, I know . . . he's pompous and self-righteous and full of himself, but he's cute." She collapsed in the chair beside the gas fireplace. "I'm weak. I get it. Some things never change. Cute guys, right?"

"Speaking of, have you seen steamy, creamy, tall, dark and dreamy lately?" Sabina flicked her eyebrows up and down a few times. Too many times for Jacenta's taste.

Jacenta rolled her eyes. She knew she was referring to Eric. Sabina always had a soft spot for Eric and his big brown eyes. When Jacenta had first introduced the two, she was worried that there would be competition for him. She knew Eric loved her but today she was in no mood to talk about it.

She didn't want to talk about how much she missed him. Missed him until her heart ached so bad that she would have sworn death was viable had she not been immortal. She didn't want to talk about how equally angry she was that he had deserted her.

True, it was to save his own life. Devin was getting dangerously jealous.

Those were the times that she had considered ending the curse. Send Devin where he couldn't hurt anyone, be it heaven or hell. She wasn't sure where he belonged. Alive or dead, she couldn't decide if he was good or evil. Perhaps he didn't know either.

Missing Eric outweighed the anger exponentially. She was just glad that wherever he was, he was free of Devin and safe from the jealous rages that sometimes even frightened Jacenta.

"You have seen him, haven't you? It's been too long to hold a grudge." Sabina put her fist into one of the oversized fluffy pillows.

"I'm not holding a grudge anymore. I just . . ."

"What? Afraid he won't take you back? You're kidding me?" Sabina laughed satirically. "You really didn't know how much that boy loved you, did you? You're always too wrapped up in yourself and your problems to notice what's right in front of you."

Jacenta took a deep breath and exhaled audibly. "I can't FIND him, okay? He's disappeared. Off the radar. Poof." She gestured with her hands like she was doing a magic trick and she just made the bunny disappear from the hat. "I don't want to talk about him. It still hurts and we always fight when it comes to Eric. Sometimes I think he should have fallen in love with you."

A smile spread across Sabina's face as she was clearly thinking of that possibility. "No, he loved you and there was no changing that . . . try as I might." Sabina sat up and shook her head. "Forget him for a second. So, Devin is here, am I right?"

"He's been back for more than a month now. Off and on like before. He's with her and then with me."

"What do you mean *back*? Where'd he go?"

"Oh, that's right, you don't know. Well, apparently, she locked him up almost a century ago. Got fed up with him and trapped him . . . with witchcraft." She laughed, speaking as if it were a rumor and she was the middle schooler that was spreading it.

"That little minx."

"But it wasn't good enough; he escaped." Jacenta shrugged, in a *that's-the-way-it-goes* kind of way.

"Took him a hundred years, though." Sabina sounded impressed. "Have you seen *her* lately?" Sabina pulled her legs around and crossed them in front of her.

Jacenta shook her head. "Not since I last saw you." It had been over a century since Jacenta and Sabina sat together and held each other. A silence encompassed them as they both thought of their last meeting, their argument and the years in between.

"Do you know where she is?" Sabina broke the silence as she lay back on the pillows that threatened to devour the bed.

"No. Last time I saw her, she was some barmaid or something. Elizabeth or Eliza, something. Anyway, she had four little brats. Cute husband, though." Jacenta thought of Deanna with her hair pulled up in that lazy bun, apron stained and hanging askew. She was carrying a small girl that was the picture of this new incarnation of Deanna. Devin was doting on those children. Jealousy raged in her then and she could feel the bile rising in her throat now. "I guess I could ask him, but I've enjoyed not seeing her. Or following her. Or seeing them together," Jacenta said. "Brazil is my little slice of paradise."

"You should have had a little rumpus with her husband. You know, eye for an eye. End it right there." Sabina pushed herself up on her elbows and looked at Jacenta as she stared at the fire. She could see Jacenta knew what she was getting at. "Ever think of ending it?"

"Why would I do that?" Her answer was short and sharp. Too quick and angry. "They don't deserve it."

Again, Sabina stared at her. "I was thinking more for you. Freedom from the guilt, freedom from the bad memories, freedom from Devin."

"I don't even know if I remember how to end it anymore."

The closet door swung open and slammed hard.

"Hello, Devin." Sabina smiled, unafraid.

"He doesn't think much of Gabriel," Jacenta said in a quiet voice as if Devin couldn't hear her. "He kept making fun of him during the tour. What did you think? Of the changes they're making, I mean. Not of Gabriel." The fire popped and Jacenta felt Devin push up against her; it felt like he was nuzzling up to her like a lover. Oddly, she liked it. "I like the structural changes. If we had the generators and electronic gizmos in other Havens, it would be amazing. But the rules, the *community atmosphere* sounds so. . ."

"Domestic? Social? Interactive?" Sabina laughed into the pillows.

"I was going to say cult-ish." Jacenta sat forward, trying to make a point. "Remember the first Haven, before it was even called Haven? Remember those we helped? The victims of the wars, those scared and hiding. Running from the Council. Would they have run to this new Haven? Would they have felt safe here?"

Sabina thought on it for only a second. "Probably. We are hidden in the middle of society. Right under their noses. Even the Council, even Jordan himself, wouldn't find us here. It may not be what you envisioned for Haven originally, but times have changed, are changing, will continue to change, and Roderick is changing with it. He's on the right track at least."

Jacenta took a deep breath, still feeling Devin's pressure encompassing her. She walked across the room and climbed beside Sabina on the giant bed that looked like it was built for a king. "I don't want to change." She buried her face into a pillow, whining like a child.

"I know, baby, but you must. You're too old not to evolve." Her voice was maternal and tender. "Spend tomorrow with Gabriel, let him show you their grand plan. Let him immerse you in his vision, as he calls it. If you don't like it, I'll stand with you as you tell Roderick to change it all back, but not until you first give it a chance."

"So, you are giving me a direct order to spend the whole day with Gabriel? That was an order, wasn't it? I guess if I have to, I'll do it. But I refuse to enjoy it." She laughed, ignoring Devin's constant flickering of the lights.

Sabina looked to the chandelier as the electric lights flickered and the whole fixture swung like a pendulum. "He won't enjoy it. . ." She pointed into the air, specifying Devin. "But I'm sure you will."

CHAPTER FOURTEEN

Mount Orion proved to be boring and predictable. Devin needed time away from Deanna as she basked in the glow of her former delinquent mother and time away from Jacenta as she fought for the last remnants of those damn safe houses that she had built during that ridiculous war.

Immortals fighting immortals – for what? Rules or lack of rules. They were really fighting about ego and pride. They were really fighting about their rightful space in the world. Devin couldn't understand these issues, not even then. How many times did he have to pull Jacenta from a burning building or warn her about an attack that he saw coming miles away, which she could never see?

She never learned. One would burn down, and she'd rebuild. The next would be raided and all the occupants captured and killed, and she would relocate. It wasn't until the Haven in Amsterdam was destroyed that she got scared. She had been caught. Caught by the trackers. Caught by the Council.

He didn't want to think about Jacenta and her ridiculous notions. He didn't even want to think about Deanna tonight. But still Devin found himself drifting back to Deanna's apartment to see what his friend, Max, was up to. The apartment was dark when he arrived but across the street, he could see Deanna's old flame, Martino. Keeping him company tonight was the pretty brunette from the cemetery.

Tabitha.

Devin remembered her from the old days, from the wartime. She had ties to Jacenta, although he doubted she would ever make that connection on her own. But he remembered. He remembered the concern Tabitha showed as she searched the charred remains of the Amsterdam Haven. He remembered how Tabitha was the one to storm into the Council's Motherhouse and save Jacenta's life just as her head was to be removed from her body. He remembered.

He respected Tabitha.

But there they were sitting on the rooftop of the building across the street from Deanna's building. Apparently, Martino hadn't gotten the memo that she had already found her way into his lair. So, he sat and waited. They talked and waited.

"You know, Tino, I don't think there is anything as beautiful as a sunset," Tabitha said. The sky was a lovely shade of eggplant with streaks of pink and dark purple thrown in for contrast. Behind it all, the sky was still blue, but the sun was just about gone. It was beautiful even to Devin, who couldn't believe this once strong warrior was now caught up in Deanna's nonsense.

"I don't think I've ever been up this early in the evening." Martino laughed. "It's been years since I've seen a sunset. Longer since I've seen one this gorgeous."

She sat back and relaxed. Resting on her elbows, still staring at the bleeding horizon, she smiled. "This is the one thing that I missed after the Wars. I wasn't able to see the sun rise and set."

Devin came closer. He had missed the end of the wars. The wars had ended when Deanna was Virginia and he loved her. Doted on her and rarely spent time with Jacenta in almost sixty-five years. Before Virginia was Emily and Emily and Devin did not get along.

He laughed to himself. Who was he kidding? Emily was Deanna and she was fed up with him. They fought constantly until she began to openly ignore him. He found that Jacenta was a comforting shoulder to cry on during those years. It was those years that he learned of the open hostility between the immortals. It was those years he met Eric and learned to detest him.

When Deanna was reborn, and Emily was finally dead. He vowed to make a fresh start with Virginia. But during his make-up years with Virginia (otherwise known as Deanna), the war ended.

It was horrible and bloody, but it was over and Jacenta refused to speak of it. Now he moved in close as Tabitha (the Great Warrior Tabitha) was about to enlighten him of the catastrophic ending of the hundred-and-twenty-five-year war.

Martino looked away from the street where his eyes had been fixed for almost twenty minutes. "I've heard you and Chelsea talking about the wars, but no one has told me what really happened."

He sounded just as eager as Devin felt to hear about the war. As he hovered over Tabitha and Martino, he was missing Max as he walked up the street from his parking spot around the corner.

She only nodded and changed the subject. "So, why this obsession?" Bith motioned to the apartment building across the street just as Max was walking up to the door.

Who cares about the girl, you idiot? Talk about the war. Devin was getting aggravated.

"She's just a girl," he said as Max checked his phone quickly and disappeared through the large glass doors.

"She's more than that, Tino, or we wouldn't be sitting here at sunset just waiting to see her." Bith laughed. "She's lovely. But she's caused you pain, hasn't she?" She looked to Martino and continued. "Believe me, I know pain, and you want to talk to her but yet you don't. Sounds like me with Trevor. I see him but don't want to speak to him . . . and yet I do."

Martino smiled.

Trevor. There was another name that was always tossed into the salad of partial stories that Devin had been hearing since he'd been around these immortals. There was Margaret (Deanna's former self), he'd heard the name Trevor from that annoying Jordan, and we can't forget about Eric and how he fit into all of this mess. Today the war was the main ingredient in the salad, and it sounded like hurt and regret were the dressing. A little at a time it was coming out. Trevor had caused Tabitha pain. Pain like Margaret had caused Martino, so they were lovers – if he was tossing the salad together correctly.

The light went on in Deanna's apartment and Martino (and Devin) could see Max talking on the phone. He was yelling. Questions and accusations could be heard through the windows easily enough with preternatural hearing. *Sari again. I'm getting sick of this, D. Who the fuck is this Gail? Where? Where the fuck is Mt. Orion? No, don't bother.* And he hung up and threw his phone on the table.

"We should go," Martino whispered, having a hard time suppressing the smile that was filling his whole body.

"I guess she's not just a girl after all." Tabitha smiled.

Ugh, we're back to Deanna again. Why are you people so boring? Devin groaned to himself.

"If she's with Gail, it'll be easier to meet her. Right? I'm not stalking her. I'm just visiting a friend and, oh, look who's here. Sound convincing?" He knew it didn't, but it was worth a try. He jumped off the fire escape to the sidewalk and offered a hand to Bith.

"Why are you trying so hard with this girl? You've had her before. Why not just walk up and reintroduce yourself? If she's who you say she is, she'll remember you. Unless there's something you're not telling me. Is there?" She lifted his chin. "Pain or no pain. No secrets, *remember*?"

"That goes both ways, you know."

This could be interesting, Devin thought. *Just spill the details about you and Margaret and then we can get back to the war.*

Tabitha pulled her hands away. "You want to know about the wars, don't you? Why?"

"Every time it's mentioned, everyone gets quiet and almost repentant. I just want to know why. Richard seems to be the only one who feels no guilt whatsoever."

"Maybe because he's the only one without guilt." She raised an eyebrow and absorbed Martino's pleading expression. "Those are times best forgotten." She rubbed her side as if she had an itch.

Martino nodded and looked away. Devin could see he was disappointed, but in what was clearly becoming a trait to Devin, Martino didn't press for details and accepted her answer. "We should go. Where's your car?" he said finally.

Pussy.

She grasped his arm as he turned to leave. "Fine. But let me tell it with no interruptions and no questions. Understand? I don't like talking about it, so the faster it goes, the better."

They drove in the direction of Mount Orion, almost two hundred miles north of where they stood. She told him about her sire, Evie, and her affair with Trevor. "The easiest and quickest way to explain what happened is to compare it to the street gangs in that movie you like . . . *West Side Story*. The Council were like the Sharks and the Warriors were like the Jets. We didn't sing or dance but there was plenty of fighting and a lot more than two were killed."

"Jordan was a Warrior?"

Tabitha laughed. "Hell no. He was the leader of the Council. They were a group of bureaucratic vampires that determined we, as immortals, needed laws to govern us. Jordan's a lifetime member."

"That's why you hate Jordan?"

"That and . . . wow, there's so many reasons." She rubbed her side again. "Well, war raged and then, needless to say, I was caught along with a few others in the early part of the eighteenth century and we finally got our trial."

Martino (and Devin) listened intently. "How did they catch you?"

"Council was smart. A lot smarter than we were. They employed trackers. Caught us in our own hideouts. They were good." She smiled briefly. "Chelsea was a tracker."

She smiled at Martino's look of astonishment and continued. "Most of the rebels were killed by dismemberment and then their bodies were charred." Bith shivered a little. "I was fortunate, I guess. I was tortured for a few weeks and then thrown in prison without nourishment before they lost interest."

Bith paused in recollection. Her eyes welled with tears and she looked to the darkened horizon.

"How long were you in prison?" Martino asked.

"My punishment was for four hundred years. There were no windows, no doors, no light. I was thrown in some kind of root cellar like a piece of trash that they could no longer be bothered with. Buried alive for four hundred years."

Devin waited for her to continue but he feared the story was over. Her punishment meant that the Warriors had lost. *The Council won? Are you kidding me? Ask where the Council is now?* Devin was pressing into Martino, hoping by sheer force or possibly osmosis he would hear his words.

Martino coughed like he couldn't catch a breath. He straightened himself behind the steering wheel and shook away the feeling of having lead weights laying on his chest. "Wait, eighteenth century? Your sentence is not up yet? I don't know exactly, but I believe you've got another century to go on your incarceration. Am I aiding and abetting a known criminal right now?" He smiled playfully and then laughed.

"Yes, I know. It didn't quite last a hundred years. Richard busted me out of prison." She laughed to herself.

That imp with the two dogs? He busted you out of prison? Devin couldn't believe it.

"No one noticed you were gone?" Martino couldn't believe quiet, peaceable Richard had broken her out of jail either.

"I guess by that time, no one really cared. Aaron was dead. I guess they figured without him, we wouldn't fight. They were right. I remember not wanting to go anywhere, near anyone I knew. Friends were not safe. We were outlaws." Again, she laughed sadly. "We still are."

"Whatever happened between you and Trevor?"

"I haven't seen him since . . ." She looked down into her lap. "Since Lucien died. He was the leader of the Warriors. His death hit Trevor the hardest."

It was almost sunrise when they reached the cabin and Tabitha turned toward Martino before entering. "Thanks, Tino.

Thank you for listening. I haven't spoken or really even thought about some of the things I told you in years. It felt . . . good." She reached for his hand. "By the way, your little friend is definitely here."

Devin was on Martino's tail as he went around to the back of the house. The light was on, illuminating the back yard and side entryway. Martino walked down three steps to a sunken doorway that intrigued Devin. *The basement lair.* Through the door he heard the laughter of Jordan and Eric and he realized there could be much more excitement to this evening than he realized.

This weekend was filled with its hidden entertainments. First, Deanna meets her estranged mother from another lifetime. Then, Jacenta finds Haven is moving on without her. Both of these things entertained and aggravated Devin equally. Returning from Connecticut, he learned about the wars, and how they ended disappointed him greatly.

Now he not only gets to spend time in the lair of vampires while they are awake, he also gets to experience how the former leader of the Council gets along with one of the leaders of the Warriors on a day-to-day basis years later. Who would have guessed this weekend would have unfolded so rousingly?

The sense of giddy excitement was building in Devin. A little too much, too quickly. The sconce light beside the sunken door pulsated and popped.

"Damn." Martino reacted as he threw open the door.

"What's up?" Abby called from the sofa.

"Power surge or something. Light exploded in my face." He brushed glass pieces out of his hair and off his shoulders. He looked back as he entered. "Are you coming?"

Devin pulled back, feeling the negative energy coming from Tabitha. He loved the vibration that emanated from her as her stress levels spiked. He circled her, feeling the energy fill him and feeling her anxiety fuel him. She wavered on her feet and nearly lost her balance.

"Bith!" Martino was at her side, catching her in case she fell to the ground.

"Come, bring her to the sofa." Jordan was at the door. "Abby, get another cool cloth."

Devin circled the group, watching and studying them. Abby, full of life, bolted up the stairs to the kitchen for a cloth. Eric was sitting in a chair by a small table with a chess board. His face looked concerned but also slightly annoyed.

Gail lay on the sofa with a cloth of her own covering her eyes – or at least it was on her eyes before Martino rushed Tabitha to the sofa and sat her down. Gail pulled the cloth from her face, which had concern tattooed across it. "What happened?"

"I don't know." Tabitha's voice was slow and slurry. "I was going to go. I was just dropping Tino off. And after the light exploded, my legs felt like jelly. And I got lightheaded."

Abby returned holding a wet but not dripping cloth.

"Lay your head back." Jordan's voice was uncharacteristically soothing.

"I've got it." Tabitha took the cloth from his hands. "Thanks." Their eyes met and a bit of leftover old hostility bristled between them until Jordan got up and returned to his chess game. "What happened to *you*?" She looked to Gail as she replaced her own cloth and laid her head back on a pillow.

"We have guests."

"We know. That's why we're here." Tabitha lay back and placed the cloth over her eyes. "Martino has been pining for your guest." She giggled.

Devin hovered above, trying to keep his excitement in check as he surveyed the situation. If he concentrated, he could hear Deanna sleeping in the rooms above. The soft wheeze of her throat as she breathed in and out. If this got boring, he knew going to Deanna and caressing her in her sleep would be good fun, indeed.

"She's asleep upstairs. We could wake her and tell her everything. Won't that be fun?" Abby picked up a fashion magazine from the coffee table with Jennifer Aniston on the cover. Her tone was sarcastic, and Devin could tell Deanna was as unwelcome in conversation as she was in person with her.

"Hush. I don't wish to get into this tonight. I've had my fill of the past..."

"Halleluiah," Jordan grumbled as he moved his knight closer to Eric's queen.

"... for one night." She pressed on with hostility in her voice, ignoring Jordan's comment. "Tomorrow we need to talk. I'll tell you everything, baby, but *please* can we discuss something else?" Gail's tone whined.

Martino nodded and kissed Gail's forehead. "Is Sari here as well?"

"Same conversation, different person." Abby laughed. "Asleep too. She also knows nothing, but she's not as annoying about it. But next time you want to scare anyone in a cemetery, give me a call. Sounds like it was a blast."

"So much fun!" Tabitha was obviously feeling better. "Her friends were scared shitless."

"But not her?"

"No, she knows. I don't know how, but she knows what we are. She had what's her name..."

"Sari." Eric didn't look up from his chess pieces.

"Sari call *him*." She pointed to Eric. "You know, like, we need your help." She imitated a scream queen from horror movies. "So, we left it alone. She is a piece of work, though. I agree. You kind of want to hit her but you don't know why."

Devin laughed and the lights flickered. Tabitha's energy was still working its magic. Jordan's eyes searched the room and Eric tensed slightly.

"Yes. Exactly." Abby felt vindicated.

"Hey. You don't even know her." Martino sat beside the fireplace listening and silently fuming.

"Neither do you. You said you knew her years ago. This curse thing sounds a little hokey to me. She's probably not even who you think she is." Tabitha twisted the cloth in her hand.

Yes, she is.

"Yes, she is," Gail said from beneath her cloth mask. "I knew her as someone completely different than who Martino knew. And it really is her. She has some spirit that is with her."

Eric's eyes shifted.

Jordan looked to the ceiling and frowned.

Oh, shit's going to hit the fan now, as they say, Devin thought. He decided this would be a good time to make himself scarce. As he moved slowly from the room, he looked back to those around him.

"What?" Martino stood up.

"Tomorrow. I don't want to talk about it now." Gail was sounding serious.

CHAPTER FIFTEEN

The next evening, Deanna sat quietly in the kitchen, sipping her coffee and watching the ash grow on her cigarette. Just an hour stood between now and when Gail would awaken. The clock ticked and another minute passed. Another minute closer to talking with Gail about the past and reconciling.

The coffee steam billowed from her cup as she looked around the kitchen. She wondered why a house full of vampires would need a stove and a refrigerator and a dishwasher. Why would they need the coffee machine that was still dripping as she sat staring at it?

Devin wasn't with her as these thoughts came to her. He had not been around for two days and she was wondering where he was. Pushing her hair behind her ear, Deanna crushed out her cigarette and lit another. This was the first lifetime that she found any pleasure in smoking a cigarette. Looking at the thin white stick burning between her fingers, she didn't understand how any pleasure could be found in sucking smoke into her lungs. But here she was sucking on it like it was her lifeline.

Her phone rang. Sari's face smiled on the screen. Deanna looked at it disbelievingly.

"D? It's Sari."

"Where are you? At the mall or something?"

"I left this morning. Didn't you get the note I left?"

"No. I saw my car was gone. I just figured you went for a ride or to the store. I don't know. I've been kind of caught up in my own head all day."

"So I've noticed."

Deanna looked around the kitchen and there on the counter sat a white sheet of paper with Sari's cramped handwriting on it. *Need to get back home. Call you later. Sari.*

"Found it. Not very riveting." She laughed.

Sari didn't say anything at first. "I think you should come home tonight. I don't know what's going on with you and Gail, but you can't just completely forget about Max and your life here. And your mother has called here about three times today. She says your voicemail is full and Max is not being helpful. He's angry. Check your messages, will you?"

"Sure." Deanna didn't want to hear from anyone until she was sure what was going on with Gail. After finally telling Gail about the curse and seeing her interest, she was hopeful maybe Gail could break it. And if that was going to happen, the only thing she wanted to say to anyone else was goodbye.

"Do you plan to stay at the cabin forever? What about your job?"

"I quit this morning," she whispered. It was true. She spoke with Nico and Dante that morning and explained that she had some personal issues that she couldn't ignore any longer. They understood and were sad to lose her. They had also let her know that they'd hold her place for a while until she sorted everything out. If she wanted it, her job would be waiting for her. But Deanna knew that if her personal issues did sort themselves out, she'd not be around to take her job back. She'd be dead.

"You quit? What's going on, D? Have you talked to Max about all this? He's been asking about you. He even called your job to see if they had seen you." Sari sounded serious. "What about us? You're just going to stay there and forget about your friends?"

"Would you let me say something? Max and I are over. Just over. And you, well, I thought you'd be here. With Eric," Deanna said simply. "I see what's going on with you two. I just figured moving here was the next logical step." She was reaching with this line of thought, but Sari seemed to be buying it.

"I'm not sure about me and Eric but I'm talking about you and getting lost in that weird world."

Weird world? Could she suspect the truth? "I just thought with all the changes with you . . ."

"You mean the makeup? That's just it. That was part of the weird part. I woke up with a hangover and take this miracle tonic and then I feel like being what my mom would call normal. And I was in love with Mount Orion for a few days too. That's weird. The kind of weird I'm not ready for, you know."

Miracle tonic? What the hell did they do to Sari before she came to visit? Deanna was wondering why Sari didn't question their sleeping habits. "Are you back to normal now? I mean, back to being you?"

"Kind of. Hair, yes, makeup, no. I liked seeing my eyes. But my hair definitely needed the color." She laughed. "So, are you coming home or do I have to come get you?"

It was decided that Sari would come and pick her up. She had her car anyway. Deanna sat back and sipped her now tepid coffee. Max. He was a problem. She didn't love him, that was true enough, but she did care for him. How would she end this without hurting him more than she had already? Breaking ties was the worst part of this whole crappy curse.

She needed to lie her ass off. Lie like her life depended on it.

Idea #1: Sari wanted to move closer to Eric and she needed a roommate.

But why wouldn't Sari just move in with Eric?

Idea #2: Nicodemus was opening a salon near Albany and she was going to run it.

Yeah, he would pick a part time hairdresser to run his new salon. Fat chance.

Idea #3: Break up with him. Make it clean and painless. For both of them.

Yes.

An hour after her conversation with Sari and contemplating what to do about Max, Gail appeared before Deanna as if by magic. Deanna was sitting on the porch swing covered in a warm blanket, watching the light die on the horizon.

"I have a surprise for you." Gail walked to Deanna and reached out for her hand.

Her hand was cool and dry, and Deanna hung on to it like she was that long-ago seven-year-old clinging to her mother.

"Wait until you see this." Devin had returned. He had been gone since she arrived three days ago. Deanna wanted to ask him where he had been but found that this was not a good time. *"Not really a surprise as much as an ambush."* His vivacity was suspicious.

Deanna apprehensively allowed Gail to lead her into the house. Standing in the living room as they turned the corner from the kitchen was Martino. His back was to her as he looked out the picture window in the living room. Deanna swallowed hard and tried to pull away from Gail, but she kept her hand tight in her grasp.

"What am I going to do?" Deanna asked silently to Devin, trying to block Gail out as much as she could. It seemed to be working. If Gail had heard her words, she made no reaction to it.

"Talking to him is always an option." Devin was feeling playful.

"I can't do that." She shook her head. *"It's impossible. I . . . I wouldn't know what to say."*

"It's the only way you're going to stop him from stalking us. Now go."

She felt a slight shove on her shoulder and pulled her hand free from Gail's grip. So many ideas coursed through Deanna's imagination. *Hi, Martino, remember me? Or, I'm Deanna; weren't you at the fireworks last week?* It was all hopelessly dumb.

Just as she reached Martino, Deanna looked to Gail for support and she smiled. Looking patient but nervous, Martino turned to look her in the eyes and Devin pushed her full force into his arms. Martino barely flinched, almost as if he was expecting the impact.

"Thanks a lot!" Deanna said aloud. Then she realized she was still pressed against Martino with his arms around her waist. She got to her feet. "I am sooo sorry! Very clumsy of me."

Gail laughed.

"Quite all right." His eyes twinkled as he spoke and just a twinge of an Italian accent still clung to his words.

Deanna laughed uncomfortably.

"This is funny?" Martino questioned.

"No, just the situation, I guess. Very awkward." She twirled her hair in her fingers. "Sorry, not you. *I* am very awkward. I don't know what I'm saying."

Devin circled them, softly repeating, *"Tell him who you are."*

"I'm Deanna Belamy." She offered her hand. "I'm sure you know that by now." Another awkward laugh followed by more hair twirling.

He gently touched her hand to his lips, sending a chill up her spine. She caught her breath before she could exhale. "As I am sure you know, I am Martino."

Deanna hesitated. Her fingers fiddled with the hem of her jacket. "Yep," she whispered finally.

"Oh, yes, from the cemetery last week." He was being coy. "I must apologize for my friends. They were a bit . . . impossible that night."

Deanna nodded as if confirming she thought they were being more than impossible. Impossible was not the word she would have used to describe the situation. Perhaps murderous. She pushed those feelings aside. "Martino . . ." She looked at him, devouring every feature. She couldn't believe how generous the years had been to him. He was more handsome now than he was last time she saw him. "How much did you tell him?" She turned to Gail, who was quietly watching as the meeting unfolded. Gail nodded for her to continue and forget that she was there.

"We've only had moments to speak about you." He took another step closer.

Deanna huffed her frustration audibly. "I don't know how to say this."

He stepped closer to her. "You want to tell me that you are Margaret," he whispered in her ear. His lips touched her ear, and again a shiver crept up her spine. Deanna closed her eyes for a moment and remembered when he used to kiss her neck years ago. She could feel his lips as they delicately touched her skin and how it felt when he pierced her flesh with his teeth for the first time. Her breath quickened as she found herself clutching his wrist with her hand.

When she opened her eyes, Martino was staring at her. He had a look of confusion with a hint of a smile like he knew what she was thinking. "Please sit. We should talk." He was just as polite and courteous as she remembered.

Deanna took a seat on the sofa, facing him. She swallowed hard. "Martino," she whispered. "Do you remember anything Margaret told you? That I told you?"

He stroked her face with his hand. "I remember she – you spoke of a curse. I didn't believe it then. In truth, I'm still finding it hard to believe. But here you are before me, I think. I know it's you. I don't know how I do." He grasped her face with his hands and pulled her closer to him. "Your eyes. Your mannerisms. I'd know Margaret in a darkened room. I know you."

Deanna felt her heart in her throat and knew he could feel it too. She had forgotten the passion he had. The need to kiss him was defeating her. She laughed uneasily again. "I was Margaret; I have been many different people. I am now Deanna. Can you love Deanna like you loved Margaret?" Her hands were grasping his wrists as his hands held her face.

With strength that she couldn't fight, Martino pulled her to him and kissed her hard and ardently. In that kiss, she felt the hardness of his body, the intensity of his will, and the unyielding need he felt for her. Her hands pulled on his back. The muscles didn't budge as she pulled at them. His chest pressed into hers with a power that somewhat frightened her. He was different than before. He was stronger.

It had only been fifty years since she had last touched him, and he had gotten so much stronger. What would another fifty do for him? How strong could he get? The strength excited Deanna, and she slipped her hand under his jacket. The muscles were more defined under the thin piece of cotton of his shirt.

He was kissing her neck and shoulders now. She didn't want it to stop, until . . .

"Now tell him about me." Devin's voice woke Deanna from her part in the adult film they were reenacting on Gail's sofa.

"Go away. I can handle it from here."

"You are not handling anything. You are going to end up like Margaret!" Devin screamed and a vase toppled from the mantel.

Deanna pulled away from Martino, startled by Devin's outburst in her head. She smiled, trying to catch her breath and wanting so much to kiss him again and feel his lips on her body. "I have to tell you something else." She swallowed hard. She looked back to the kitchen doorway and saw that Gail had left them alone.

The look in Martino's large brown eyes was tantalizing. Deanna kissed him quickly.

"I'm not alone."

His eyes went from tantalizing and seductive to confused and unsettled. "There are others . . . like you?"

"Yes and no. Not others *like* me but others *with* me. This is the part I wish Gail had filled you in on."

Still his eyes were lost. The twinkle had dissolved into a cloud of confusion.

Deanna continued. "I have a spirit that is always with me. His name is Devin and he's part of this curse too." She spit it out so quickly that she wasn't sure if Martino had even followed what she had said. "He is here now."

"A spirit, did you say? Like a ghost?"

"Kind of. No, I don't think ghost is the correct term. He is not visible. Just energy and thought. It's hard to explain."

Martino thought for a moment and a light of recollection shown in his eyes. "Richard felt him. At the cemetery. Scared the bejesus out of him too. And the dogs. Attila and Thor, they felt him too. This spirit has a name, you said?"

"Devin."

"Margaret has never spoke of this Devin."

"He never knew Margaret. Long story." Her eyes dropped momentarily.

"He talks to you?" He was fighting to understand.

Deanna nodded.

"Will he talk to me?"

"*Never.*"

"He won't but you wouldn't hear him anyway. I have thought on this for years. I think it has to do with the blood. The curse combined our blood. Mine, Devin's, and the one that cast it. I think only she and I can hear him and since she's dead, I guess only I can." She shrugged as if it was no big deal. "I found people with a more profound grasp of their supernatural abilities can feel or at least sense him. Like Richard. Jordan too, I think. I don't think Gail can unless he's angry. Then it's easier to sense him because he uses the energy around him to gain strength."

They sat together silently for a while, each thinking on what they had learned.

"Martino, may I ask you a question?" Deanna was delicate with this one.

He nodded and stroked her cheek with his finger.

"What happened to Margaret?"

"She's still in Colorado. In your house."

CHAPTER SIXTEEN

The slow walk home was interminable. Margaret felt her legs dragging beneath her body, and the weight of her arms was a burden as well. It seemed the events of the night had drained her completely and she couldn't find the energy to drag herself back to the house.

The few streetlights that were scattered on the two-mile stretch of road were still bright, but the lights in the houses set back far from the road were extinguished. Well past midnight, she assumed. The blood covering her clothes looked almost black in the dim light of the moon and stars. It was all over her. Her hair was matted, and her clothes were so saturated that they felt sticky and heavy even in the cold breeze that was blowing in from the north.

Margaret pushed her bloody hair from her face, thankful for the late hour. What would her neighbors think of her as she dragged her tired, blood-soaked body up the street and into her house? Not that she had ever met any of her neighbors. It wasn't a small neighborhood. The houses each stood on at least two acres of land, giving her plenty of privacy and plenty of room to roam with no one seeing her. Behind her house there were acres of state sanctioned land that she would hunt, except recently when she decided to go into town.

The hunting was good around her home. The deer, rabbit, and if she was lucky, a bear once in a while. She didn't need the blood as often as she took it, but boredom breeds mischief.

Tonight, it wasn't about hunting; it was about seeking. Finding the others that she had been following for months now. The night was unusually warm for October in Colorado. A light jacket was all that was required to shield her from the crisp but not frigid wind that blew in from the north. The smell of snow was in the air or maybe that was just the scent of a wood burning fireplace from a distant neighbor. It was a memory that always accompanied that familiar scent. Perhaps from her life before when she spent her time with the family in the photos that were in her room.

The handsome man was her father. She could remember that. He would light the fire when the night became chilly. Then it would snow. So maybe it didn't smell like snow after all; maybe it only smelled like a cold night at home.

Memories of that other life would come back to her in pieces, triggered by something completely random usually. Like the smell of a wood burning fireplace or even freshly cut flowers could get her thinking of the fake, dust-covered flowers that sat on the mantel at her grandmother's house. Margaret laughed to herself as she took another deep breath. She loved that smell whether it reminded her of snow or not.

It had taken a lot of courage for Margaret to leave the house. Especially following a rare visit from Martino. She loved his visits, as rare as they were. She loved how he talked to her, surprised her with gifts, and brushed her hair. If they did leave the house, it was only to go into the woods to feed. Hunting with Martino was always a treat. He was cavalier yet dashing but always supportive and helpful with her.

Leaving the house without Martino was new for Margaret. He didn't know and she wished to keep it that way. His visits were getting fewer and further apart. By months sometimes. But when he did visit, it took Margaret a week or two to work up the nerve to leave the house again. The feeling that he might show up unexpectedly and catch her outside the house was itching its way up her spine even as she was now returning home. She would never have gotten the nerve up at all if it wasn't for that glow she kept seeing.

In the last few weeks, a glow circled around her. There were no voices like in the movies. There were no mysteries to figure out. It was just there. It hovered, growing bright at times and fading into the darkness of the shadows other times. It was that glow that had helped her find her way out of the house without Martino. It sparked her interest, gave her the courage, and more importantly, it unlocked the basement door.

Her first few visits to the world outside her door were short. Margaret circled the house following the glow, but nothing enticed her any further. She returned inside the safety of her rooms and didn't venture out for days.

It became easier to leave after the first attempt, but still Margaret felt no compulsion to leave the grounds around her home. Then the glow tempted her – not with words but she was curious and followed it – and it drew her into town. Finding herself in the center of town with people – living, breathing, mortal people – was frightening and at the same time exciting. She hadn't experienced a human that wasn't sedated and left for her to drain in decades.

Her first real human kill was empowering. She felt alive and powerful and not at all the same creature that sat night after night in a basement room waiting for a death that would never come. Then she saw them. The others. And her fear faded. Fear that Martino would catch her, fear that the world would point its bony figure in her direction and say, *you don't belong out here*.

The others were like her. They had the same white skin as her, the same sparkling eyes, and they appeared to float into the café instead of walk. Margaret had first seen them two weeks ago. Since then they were as close to an obsession as Margaret's limited grasp of her emotions would allow.

There were three of them. Two men and a woman. They liked the coffee shop, seemed to use it to hunt. When she saw them a few nights ago, she sat perfectly still, watching as they drifted to the counter. Drawing absolutely no attention to themselves, they each ordered a perfectly normal drink and sat safely facing the front door with their backs to the wall. They looked as if they were waiting for someone.

It wasn't their precautions that drew her attention; it was their vibration. The vibration was a subtle murmur that she associated only with Martino. She could tell he was in the house by three things: his smell, his heartbeat, and that vibration. It drew her to him, and she loved falling asleep listening to it hum in her ears. These three practically pulsated as they sat across the room from her. The vibration emanating from her didn't appear to draw their attention and it occurred to Margaret that they didn't hear it. So, she stayed blessedly anonymous with her hands wrapped around her undrunk cup of java.

Two weeks ago, Margaret was petrified that they would discover her intruding on their privacy. But after seeing them for the past few nights, they knew she was watching them, and she was dying to speak with them. The one that she wished to speak to most was the female.

The young woman was not more than thirty when she became whatever it was that she was. Margaret was still unclear where she fit into the grand circle of life. And seeing others like her, like Martino, she was seeing a niche opening for her unique (or not so unique) abilities. This woman was beautiful. She had small delicate features that were hard and chiseled. Her hair, which was pulled back into a tight, schoolmarm bun, was light brown with streaks of blond throughout it, making it shimmer in the harsh café lighting.

The blue in her eyes appeared periwinkle as she scanned the area. Her frame was small as well, dressed completely in taupe from the turtleneck sweater to the army boots pulled up over her cargo pants, and she looked like a Korean War soldier from an old sepia-toned photograph. Margaret loved her. Wanted to speak to her and learn why she looked so guarded at all times.

Now walking down the deserted road in the small hours of the morning, covered almost completely in James's blood, Margaret's emotions were bubbling over. First, fear from what she had done in anger. She felt irresponsible for letting strangers get too close. And finally, she felt angry that they had put her in such a position as they had tonight.

Tonight, she sat in the café waiting for them, knowing that they would be there. She studied the patrons, knowing that one or two of them would be singled out by the threesome and murdered later tonight. The glow was not with her. It hadn't been with her for days. This excursion was her own idea. She needed to see the others again.

She had felt them before she saw them. Their vibration called to her. She felt it deep within her. They walked in looking like they stepped out of a novel. The three vampires were scanning the cafe for safety, she assumed, but it also appeared that they were looking for something or someone. It was the girl who found her first. She was ahead of her friends who flanked her like some sort of security guards. Margaret doubted this petite woman needed any protection at all.

Her periwinkle-colored eyes glistened and her lightly painted lips spread easily into a smile. She glanced back at the man to her left and nodded in Margaret's direction. His eyes easily found their target and then quickly darted to the floor.

Margaret's did the same.

The third, taller man, to the woman's right, laughed and shook his head at his companion's shyness. Margaret watched them closely as they walked directly towards her instead of finding a table facing the door as was their routine.

They stopped in front of her and Margaret unconsciously grabbed the sides of the table. The vibration emanating from these three was at a higher frequency now that they were closer. The woman's vibration was more of a quick pulse rather than a steady vibration like that of her companions. Again, Margaret wondered what her vibration sounded like to those that could hear it – if anyone else *could* hear it.

"May we join you?" The woman's voice was hypnotic in its delivery.

Margaret stared at them for a few moments, studying them. They were smiling at her – that was good. The woman's smile was a little devious and intimidating – that was bad. Still, friends were friends, and she had been following these particular vampires for weeks and they were finally talking to her – that was good. The shy one was quite attractive – and that was very good.

Finding her tongue paralyzed, she nodded in a bobble head fashion that she wished she could stop, but it was beyond her control.

"I'm Elinor. And you are Margaret." The intimidating woman's stare was intense. And then she laughed quietly as Margaret's expression became distrustful. "I do my homework. The only thing I don't get about you is why you are sequestered to that basement room in that old house."

"Elly, behave yourself." The tall one's tone was warning but without being harsh.

It was Margaret's turn to laugh. Her tongue was still not moving but her brain ran rampant with questions and answers. Her eyes scanned the trio, absorbing details she would not have noticed had she been speaking to them.

"Well, this is Ezra and James," Elinor continued, excusing Margaret's silence with a wave of her hand. She motioned to the tall one and the cute one, respectively.

The tall one, Ezra, was dark – of hair, of eyes, and of complexion. His hair was long, wavy, and black. His lips were full and his eyes were deep brown and dreamy. From his few words, Margaret could not determine his accent. Middle Eastern, perhaps, but she didn't know.

James didn't make eye contact when he was introduced, but Margaret devoured every other aspect of him. He was younger than Ezra, who looked to be in his mid-thirties. His hair was shaggy and red and a splatter of freckles darkened his otherwise white face. A chestnut-colored goatee graced his small chin and mouth, reminding Margaret of the Beatniks from when she was a young girl.

"Why don't you leave him – that beautiful Italian boy that visits you?" Elinor continued. She said *boy* as if she were an old woman reminiscing about her first kiss behind the schoolhouse.

Margaret smiled at her tone and, frankly, at her mere presence in the café.

"Why does he leave you here alone?" Elinor looked to her companions. She was becoming frustrated by this one-sided conversation.

"Can she speak, do you think?" Ezra whispered as if Margaret was not sitting just inches from him.

"Yes," Margaret whispered. Her voice was small and sounded gravelly. She cleared her throat and tried again. "Yes, I can speak."

"Marvelous." Elinor clapped her hands together. Her mouth was smiling although her eyes were not. "So why have you been following us? Why are you studying our every move – even now?"

A sense of fear crept over Margaret and she realized she had allowed herself to be cornered by these three strangers. Suddenly she wished for the door to swing open and Martino to sweep in to rescue her. But she knew that was not going to happen. His warnings about the outside world were spot on and she needed to get going now.

There may be things she couldn't do like feel emotions deeply like she read in books or saw in the movies. Or remember parts of her past that she should remember like her family or important dates. But she could sense when she was trapped and should be leaving. "This was a mistake. I'm sorry but I need to go now." Margaret edged her behind off her seat and found her knees too wobbly to support her properly. "I hadn't realized how late it was." Her voice broke but she kept eye contact with Elinor without wavering.

"It's quite early and we're just getting to know each other." Again, Elinor's words didn't match her tone or clearly malicious intent.

"Just let her go, Elly," James finally spoke.

Elinor shot him a piercing look. She was clearly unaccustomed to being contradicted and disrespected, especially in public.

Margaret swallowed hard. The three stared at her in different ways. Elinor looked guarded and accusing. Ezra like he was loving the conflict that was unfolding, and James looked apologetic and embarrassed.

"Just sit down and talk to us. From what I've seen, you don't talk to a lot of people."

Ezra shifted uneasily in his seat as Elinor spoke, and for the first time Margaret noticed he had a dagger strapped under his arm in a holster much like she had seen on police programs on TV. Against the tan leather vest he wore tight against his firm, well-shaped chest was a beautifully carved bone handle sticking out from its leather holder.

A lump rose in Margaret's throat and she pushed herself from her seat once again.

Her memory went from trying to walk from her seat in the café to walking down this deserted road covered in blood. She tried to walk out – no, she *did* walk out – out into the darkness and realized the night had gotten colder.

Memories of pulling her jacket closed as she skillfully kept her head low enough to avoid attention but high enough not to appear out of place. Just as she was about to round the corner of the building safely away from the café and her new frenemies, a hand grasped her arm and she was stopped.

Looking up, she saw James's blue eyes twinkling in the darkness. She liked that twinkle, but what she didn't like was his hand on her arm stopping her from walking. He was strong, probably much older than she – though she couldn't determine how much older. Another thing she didn't like was that Elinor and Ezra were waiting not far behind. Watching and waiting.

Then her memory of the night's events ended. Margaret walked on, seeing her house in the distance. She fought the blackness of her memory. "Come on, step by step," she told herself. It was what Martino always said when she couldn't remember something from her past.

Step by step. James's hand on her arm. His eyes twinkling in the moonlight. Elinor's fake toothy grin. James ushering her back to the café entrance. She got scared again – hadn't she? "Think, Maisie, think." Those were her father's words. Step by step. *Think, Maisie, think.* Scared of what? Was it Elinor? Probably. Ezra, no.

The wind whipped at her body as she made her way farther up the mountain road. She racked her brain for more information. She remembered crying but she was alone when that happened, wasn't she? She closed her eyes and visualized where she was when she was crying. An alleyway? No, it was a public park. She could see the gazebo and the deserted children's playground not far away.

Margaret shook her head clear of images of the park. She had finally reached the house. Home sweet home, she thought. It was still early, no signs of dawn on the horizon just yet. There was plenty of time to slip out of her bloody clothes and into a blessedly hot bath. Sink down in the bubbles and blot out any further memories of this awful night.

But a bath was not in her future. When Margaret approached the house, she saw a light burning in the kitchen. As she opened the back door, she was met with anger and accusation. "Where have you been?" The end of the question that Martino confronted her with died on his lips when he saw the condition of Margaret's body. Not another word came from him until she was cleaned, dressed, and sitting on the basement sofa ready for his interrogation.

Her brown hair was still dripping from the shower he forced her into as she sat and waited for him to begin.

"Do you wish to tell me what has happened?"

Margaret bit her lower lip and tugged on her wet hair. "I don't remember."

The anger in Martino's eyes was like nothing she had ever seen before. Since the day he gave her this horrible thirst and locked her in this room, since the day her memories were deleted and her emotions put on pause, since that day, she had never once seen Martino angry. Frustrated, confused, and strict. That's how she described him in her diaries but never angry. Today was different.

Today he knew she was disobeying him. Today he found out that her brain still contained the rebellion function key and she used it.

"You don't remember why you were covered in blood and trudging home from only God knows where?" His hands covered his face as he tried to control his emotions. It didn't seem to be working.

"I know where I was. I just don't remember how I got covered in blood. My memory just shut off." She cut her hand through the air as if to say that was it. "I went into town."

"Into town? You are not supposed to leave the house without me."

She didn't look at him and the vibration coming from him was a slow steady hum that made her want to hug him. She squeezed her eyes shut, trying to block out those feelings for now. "I know," she whispered. "But I wanted to see what was out there."

"Nothing. There is nothing out there for you. Nothing besides death. I hope this little outing has taught you something?"

Now he sounded like her father. The little bit she remembered of her father was his tone. *You need to be more aware of your surroundings, Maisie. You should take better care of your little sister, Maisie.* Margaret didn't like this tone one bit.

"How did you get out anyway? The lock is not broken."

"I had help."

CHAPTER SEVENTEEN

The night Deanna knew for sure that she was done with this curse and done with this and any other lifetime was the night she got a phone call from her brother.

She was sitting in the living room at Mount Orion with a warm cup of tea in her hands, a blanket around her shoulders, two warm dogs at her feet, and a horrible sense of foreboding in her bones. It had been working on her all day. She kept checking her phone for missed calls or messages. Every time a door opened, she was sure it was someone with bad news.

The room was toasty warm with the fire blazing in the fireplace. Eric continually stoked it, and it roared at his command. Thor rolled onto his back with his belly turned to face the hearth. His tail curled up between his legs, covering his bits and pieces, making Deanna think of a Playgirl centerfold shot. Attila stretched and groaned as Eric stepped over him, returning to the sofa beside Sari.

Two days ago, Sari had come to pick Deanna up just like she planned and never went home. The plan was to run back home this weekend, cancel her apartment lease, and pick up her stuff. Apparently, Eric had convinced her that this *weird world* was the one she wanted to stay in. Secretly, Deanna was glad. She watched as Sari snuggled – hair a blazing orange – into the crook of Eric's shoulder while keeping her eye on some asinine cable series.

Martino had returned just a few hours ago from somewhere. He told Deanna he needed to sort a few things out. Now, he and Richard were in the sitting room arguing about something Deanna could not follow. She could hear some words, but their voices were muffled and it was clear they did not want to be heard. Their conversation dissolved into a few head shakes and curt comments as Tabitha and Abby entered the room.

Abby gave Gail a quick peck on the cheek and disappeared quickly out the front door. Tabitha was not far behind as she tapped on her phone for Chelsea to meet them in town. Richard followed them out and closed the door behind him with a strict warning from Martino to keep it between them, whatever it was.

"Are we alone tonight?" Gail sat wrapped in a blanket on a chaise beside the fireplace. Her head lay drowsily on the back, but her eyes were firmly on Deanna.

"He was upsetting the dogs, so I asked him for some space. I've not heard from him since yesterday." She shrugged, knowing they were talking about Devin. Martino took a seat beside her.

"And that did it?" Gail sounded amazed.

"It was just as strange to me. He doesn't usually do what I ask. Not so easily, anyway. I'm sure he's just pissed or something. I'll deal with the backlash later. For now, I'm enjoying the quiet." She took a deep breath and listened to the silence in her mind. Bliss.

She took a deep sip of her tea and loved the comfort she was feeling in this moment. The warmth of the blanket, the press of Martino's arm against hers, and the relaxing feeling of being around others that understood her unique place in the grand design of the universe. *Or something like that.* Under the serenity there still loomed that overwhelming sense of bad things coming; that harbinger of doom. Whatever you wanted to call it, it still hung over her like a heavy rain cloud. Any moment it could burst and dowse her with its negativity.

She checked her phone again. Her foot began to tap involuntarily, and she pulled her feet up onto the sofa. Deanna pulled Martino's arm around her and rested her head on his chest. She could feel the warmth coming from his skin and she knew he must have snuck out to hunt while she was waiting for him. It was better than the icy, corpse-like cold that sent shivers through her when he didn't feed. Better warm than cold.

She looked to Gail. A small half smile turned up the corners of her mouth. Deanna narrowed her eyes, silently warning her to stop reading her thoughts. She only received a small chuckle in response and Gail closed her eyes.

"Don't bother. Half the time she doesn't know she's even doing it," Eric said from across the room. He sat silently watching everything in the room.

"I still don't like it. It's . . ."

"Intrusive, I know. But there's nothing you can do." He rolled his eyes and laughed as if to say *don't fight it.*

"About what?" Sari looked up from the television program.

"Gail and her annoying habits." Eric kissed her sparkly, orange scalp and she returned to her show. Deanna shook her head, annoyed. She picked up her cell phone, making sure she had not missed a message or call.

"You're acting a bit jumpy. Are you alright?" Martino whispered to her.

She nodded and pressed the power button on her phone, shutting off the screen. She took a deep breath and closed her eyes, wishing that Sari would turn off the television. The silence was blissful, but she couldn't chase those damned doom feelings away when she had to listen to people bitching about drug money and stolen guns.

When her phone rang, Deanna was dozing on Martino's shoulder. The heat radiating from his body was relaxing, and it was pulling her into a meditative state that helped her fight the doom and gloom. The sound of Chewbacca's growling was the ringtone set for her brother, Bobby, and her first thought when she heard it was, "Shit!"

The phone bobbled in her hand as she tried to retain her grip on it. "Hello, hello, Bobby? What's up?" She jumped to her feet and the dogs followed suit. As she listened to her brother's voice on the other end of the phone, she walked into the kitchen for some privacy.

After his first three words, Deanna didn't hear anything else. Her heart froze mid-beat and her brain shut down. All she could think was *this is all my fault.* He was saying that she should come home. The funeral, the family, John was in the hospital.

Now, Deanna was glad Gail could read minds and didn't listen to her only minutes ago. A hand touched her shoulder as Bobby's first three words rang in her ears. Sari took the phone from her and spoke to Bobby as he expected his sister to speak to him. But she couldn't. Words didn't come. Thoughts were frozen in time. After his first three words, she wanted to crawl into a ball and cry until she couldn't anymore.

As Deanna stared at Sari speaking into *her* phone to *her* twin brother, she thought of those three words and knew they couldn't be true. They were lies. Lies to make her come home. She'd been gone a week and her friends missed her. It was a hoax. Not true. It couldn't be.

She turned as Thor whined at her feet for attention and found Jordan standing in the doorway of the basement. He wasn't there before; he heard those words. She knew it. His black eyes were like x-rays. He knew her thoughts. He knew Bobby's first three words. He knew it wasn't a hoax. Tears started pooling in her eyes and Jordan's face became blurry like she was looking at him through a waterfall.

Her bottom lip trembled as those words passed her lips. Three of the nastiest words ever spoken, three of the cruelest words, three of the truest words.

"Max is dead," she said and the room went black.

Sometime in the middle of the night, lying in her bed, Deanna was dreaming. It wasn't a real dream because it felt like a movie. She knew even as she lay unconscious that it was Devin causing these scenes to race through her mind. He'd done it in the past. When he couldn't tell her the truth himself, he would tell her sleeping mind and when she woke, she'd know the truth.

She could see Max in a car, but she knew it wasn't Max at all. It was Devin. He was inside Max just like the time they made love. The car was tumbling, rolling over on its side and then onto the roof and repeat. The trees flew past through the windshield as Devin fought to hold on to Max's life force. It was weak and he was losing his grip. There was dirt and sky and then dirt and sky again as he forced himself away from the driver's door. Deanna could hear screams from far away.

As if in slow motion, he looked to his passenger. With Max's eyes, now hazy and blood filled, Devin saw the passenger side door was open. And then closed. Too smashed to close completely anymore, too disfigured to even resemble a door anymore.

His passenger was John Stone. They were drinking, Max and John, only hours ago. They were always drinking so it was easy for Devin to easily slip behind the wheel of Max's brain and take him for a spin. John never noticed. Devin had done it a few times since that first time with Deanna in bed. Not since that time had she allowed him to use Max to make love to her, but he was able to experience life again in Max's body.

He drank with John and Bobby; he devoured meals big enough for two. Devin made love to many women as Max. Devin missed being human. Missed the rapture of an orgasm; missed the feeling of a full stomach. Missed walking in the rain or feeling the cold snow against his skin. Max's weak constitution allowed him to relive life and now it appeared he would relive death as well.

Deanna hated Devin for showing her this. Hated him for everything.

His grip on Max was waning. The strength of his life was petering out and Devin's hold was slipping. Devin heard the screaming again, this time closer. There were sirens in the distance. Help was on its way. As Max's head hit the ceiling for the final time, Devin could feel his neck fall awkwardly to the side. His head too heavy for Devin to hold up any longer.

Devin's thoughts were with Deanna as the car came to rest at the bottom of the hill. She would lose her mind when she found out what he'd done. She would never understand that racing cars at night was part of the experience and it *was* John's idea.

He tried to clear his thoughts and concentrate his remaining energy on Max. The broken bones, the bruises covering half his body, the blood pouring out of the gash in his left side where the stick shift penetrated his organs.

It was no use. Devin's energy was diminishing. He'd held on too long this time. Hours of drinking, reckless driving, and dying had taken its toll on him. Now there was nothing left that he could do. Max's injuries were too bad. He knew he should let go and see if Max could survive on his own, but Devin knew he couldn't.

The heart was still beating because Devin willed it and as the car found its ground and came to a rocking roll on the roof, he let go of Max's body. Devin watched as Max gurgled through the blood in his throat, not really sure if it was involuntary or not; he felt sympathy for this man. If not for Max, Devin would not have lived. If not for Devin, Max would not have died.

Devin turned away. He wished to give him a proper Viking death in flames but there was no more power in him to will it. He hovered for only a moment more and pulled away. High above the car, he saw John Stone, limping and dragging his battered body down the hill, screaming Max's name.

The scar caused by the crash ran from skidmarks on the highway over the now crushed barrier and fifty feet down the embankment. The car had stopped just feet from the river. A true Viking burial would have been appropriate, but not even the fates allowed Devin to give this poor man that.

The dream came to an abrupt stop and Deanna woke flushed and out of breath. Gail sat beside her, holding her hand. Her face immediately told Deanna that she had seen the dream and experienced the horrifying crash that took Max's life.

"Try to sleep," she said.

Deanna closed her eyes again, seeing only Max's limp body as it hung upside down in the car seat. She could hear Gail humming and she tried to concentrate on her voice and not the sound of screeching tires. Soon she was sleeping again. This time she did not dream.

Two days later, there were at least thirty people stuffed into her small apartment. Max's family were talking quietly in the kitchen, avoiding eye contact with her and making it obvious that in some small way they blamed her for his reckless behavior. Had she not broken up with him, he would not have been drinking and racing cars. They were right. But not in the way they thought they were. Had she not broken up with Max and been distracted by Martino and his world, she could have kept a better eye on Devin.

The food was disappearing quickly as it usually does at a wake. The food and the liquor. Apparently, getting over a death required lots of food and liquor. Deanna started picking up plates and glasses and stacking them in the sink.

"Stop. What are you doing?" Maggie stood behind her. Her face was red and blotchy from crying and the black dress she wore looked like it was borrowed from her oldest living relative with its manly cut and overall lack of femininity. "We will clean up later. Come sit down and talk to us."

Deanna allowed herself to be led to the living room where her friends sat commiserating together. It was a sorry-looking group that appeared to be down by one. She could still envision Max lying on the couch with a beer in his hand. John was covered in bruises and had a cast on his arm and wrist. His left eye was swimming in blood and a large bruise covered the left side of his face. He could not meet Deanna's eye when she walked up.

Bobby got to his feet and pulled his sister to him for a hug. It wasn't until then that Deanna felt like crying. When he let her go, she could see the tears filling his eyes as well.

"I don't blame you," she whispered to John as she sat beside him. "Not one bit." His eyes searched hers and she found that it was difficult to follow them. The left eye was floating on its own, independent of the right one, but tears spilled from them in unison.

Connie blew her nose and stuffed the tissue into her sleeve. "To Max." She held up her beer.

The glass bottles clanged together, and everyone drank one last beer for Max Brewer. Deanna could feel the tears forcing their way up her chest and into her throat. A shudder ran through her and she rubbed the tears away with the heel of her hand. She felt a strong need to escape to Mount Orion. She had destroyed this world, so why not move on to the next? Deanna was starting to believe that she didn't fit in anywhere except with the dead.

"Mom said she'll stop by later after everyone has gone. You know how she hates funerals." Bobby squeezed Deanna's hand and didn't let go.

She nodded. Her mother had hated funerals since her own mother died. Blair Belamy had always said she hated the smell of the flowers and the music, but what she really hated was what everyone hated. The death. The loss. And the sadness. Deanna had no intention of being here when her mother arrived. What Deanna hated more than death was her mother telling her that everything happens for a reason.

Deanna looked up and caught an angry stare from Max's oldest sister. It was hard, cold, and said everything that Deanna was feeling. She brushed away the tears around her nose with the back of her hand. "They blame me," she whispered.

"Did they say that?" Maggie's tone was bordering on outrage.

"No, but they do. I didn't take care of Max the way I was supposed to. And they're right. He may not have been perfect, but I was a terrible girlfriend."

"We were racing. This was an accident. You did nothing wrong." John wrapped his good arm around her shoulders.

"Yeah, but he wouldn't have been out there if I was home." She wiped her eyes again.

There was a silence between them that told Deanna that she was right. The looks exchanged when they thought she wasn't looking spoke volumes about her guilt. She looked around and found she didn't want to be here any longer. Every book, plate, piece of furniture, everything reminded her of Max and how she had failed him.

"I'm moving, guys," Sari spoke up quickly and downed half of the beer in her hand. "In with Eric."

"Just to the city, right?" Maggie's voice was small and pleading. "You promised to be my maid of honor. I don't think I can do this without you." Bobby reached for her hand and gave it a reassuring squeeze.

"He lives upstate. But not that far. I can come home again whenever you need me. I mean, he's not giving up his place in the city, so I'll stay there and we can shop for dresses and stuff. You know, at that place on TV. I'll bring this one too." Sari pointed to Deanna with her thumb like she was hitchhiking.

"Whoa, what do you mean bring this one?" Bobby nearly knocked over his beer bottle as he spoke. Deanna's shy smile did nothing to help his anger. "Mom's gonna shit."

"No, she won't if you don't tell her. I don't know how long I'll be gone anyway. I just know I can't be here." She wiped her face again with her hand. "And if I stay, Mom will demand I go home and I can't do that!"

An uncomfortable laughter erupted from the group, sparking a new round of angry glances from Max's family.

"Please don't say anything, Bob. Please. I'm begging you. Eric's friend offered me a place to stay for a while so I can clear my head and get a fresh perspective. Then I'll be home, I promise." *Lies, all lies,* she thought to herself.

"You can't move, D." Bobby sounded exactly the same as he did when she told him she was going to sleepaway horse camp without him. The tone, the unsteadiness of his voice: he was ten years old again and his twin sister was leaving him forever. "How far away is that?"

"About four hours. Couple hundred miles."

"You'll be back by Christmas, right? We're having an engagement party – Mom doesn't know about that either. I want you back by then."

"I'll keep your secret if you keep mine. One word about me extending my stay upstate and I spill the beans about you not letting your mother help plan your engagement party." She held out her index finger like a hook. Bobby stared at her with a distrustful glare and then shook his head.

"Fine." He linked his forefinger onto hers and they shook like they were twelve years old again. Secrets kept sealed with the secret handshake. "Womb to tomb."

"Birth to earth," she finished.

Again, she looked around the apartment and felt a wave of relief wash over her.

"Ready to go yet, Mouse?"

"More than you know." She was still angry with Devin, but something deep inside needed to have him here with her.

"Another chapter closed, then?"

Deanna squeezed Bobby's hand and kissed his cheek. "I think I'll miss you most of all, Scarecrow." The lost look in his eyes hurt more than she could have imagined. "I love you, baby brother."

No, the chapter wouldn't be closed. Not yet.

CHAPTER EIGHTEEN

As Eric drove to his Manhattan apartment, he knew what he was doing or about to do was the right thing. Martino was insisting on it. Tell Sari, he told him over and over again, even before he got Deanna's text message. Jordan was with them two hours ago, but he wasn't offering an opinion. Yet Eric knew he knew everything.

Everything.

He knew who Eric's sire was. He knew Sari was catching on to Eric's secret. And he knew what Devin had done to drive Eric away from Jacenta in the first place. Jordan's gift of telepathy was stronger than Gail's and he was more apt to use it than she was. But knowing and interfering were different things to Jordan. He'd interfered with too many lives during the wars; he wasn't about to do it now.

Entering the city was a nightmare. Every traffic light, every blaring horn demanded that he tell Sari tonight and he would never need to return to this apartment again. He enjoyed the apartment, if it was anywhere else in the world, but the traffic and congestion in New York was something he would not miss one bit.

Finally, the apartment building was in sight and Eric looked up to the top floor windows. Darkness. He tapped in the six-digit code for the parking garage and pulled in. The elevator was empty at one in the morning. He slid his key into the keyhole for the penthouse and the doors slid shut.

Deanna's text said that Sari was scared. Little things were creeping up on her. Little things like Eric's sleeping schedule and big things like his eating habits. The funeral, she said, had brought up questions and fears that she had been ignoring. Deanna wondered if she should tell Sari the truth. Martino told her no.

Eric now wondered if it would have been easier to just let Deanna spill the beans for him.

The apartment was dark. He could hear heartbeats and breathing. He could feel Sari's anxiety in her sleep. What he didn't hear, or feel, was Devin, and he was thankful for that. He flipped on the kitchen light. The whole room glowed with warm light, extending into the living area and floor-to-ceiling windows with glorious views of Central Park.

He wondered how to tell her. The one piece of advice Jordan did suggest was that he not worry about Sari's feelings. Tell her or show her, he said. Eric and Jordan knew that Sari was somehow catching on to the big secret, no matter how he thought he was deceiving her. There were just too many little eccentricities that could not be explained away by saying he was sensitive to light or had many food allergies. The pull only did so much to cloak the mortal mind to his differences.

"When did you get home?" Sari stood at the bottom of the stairs wearing a thin cotton nightgown that left nothing to his imagination. Her hair was clean of any color, the way he preferred it, and her eyes were rimmed in red from crying herself to sleep.

"Just now. Deanna said you were frightened." He wanted to walk towards her but there was something in her stance that told him not to.

"The funeral is messing with my emotions. Packing up my stuff to move to the cabin is scaring me too." She smiled a thin toothless smile that told him she was more frightened than she was letting on.

He nodded, allowing her to conceal her fear from him. There would be plenty of time to see horror in her face. Plenty of time for her to blame him for ruining her life. "I think we need to talk."

"Do we?" She looked exhausted and he could feel it in every muscle in her body. Her eyes blinked slowly as she stared at him. She trudged to the living room and collapsed onto the sofa.

"What are you afraid of?"

"Nothing." Her voiced sounded dreamy and distant like she was drifting off to sleep.

"So, there is nothing about me that scares you?" He was feeling her out for the truth.

A laugh seemed to hiccup out of her and then she said "no," still sounding sleepy, maybe a little sad too.

"Nothing?"

Sari didn't answer. He could hear her breathing as it slowly raised her chest, exhaling with a little snore. She'd fallen asleep. Eric nudged her shoulder with his finger. "Nothing?" he whispered in her ear.

She stretched, taking in a deep breath and blowing it out. Her eyes were still closed. "Just your teeth." Her eyes rolled under their closed lids.

"I gave her a sedative earlier." Deanna stood in the darkest part of the living room with the city lights making her look like a wraith in the darkness. "She's been in and out for the past few hours."

Eric turned to face her. "Did she just say she's afraid of my teeth?"

"She said that?" Deanna half laughed, and half cringed. "I guess it's a good place to start. I would have said your thirst; that's what scares me about Martino but it's pretty much in the same ballpark. Were you going to tell her?"

"That was the plan. Seems she knows already." He watched as Deanna walked into the kitchen as if it were her own apartment and pulled down a mug. She filled the teapot with water and set it on the stove to boil. He thought of Jacenta as he watched her. He thought of all the times he'd held Jacenta in his arms as she cried over Devin's interference in her life and how Deanna had ruined everything. Even after hundreds of years, the pain Deanna had caused her was still fresh and the wound was still bleeding.

"Give her a day to sleep it off and tell her when she's awake." Deanna smiled as she opened a tin of tea bags. She sniffed one before dropping it into her cup.

"Deanna? There is something I must tell you." He moved into the kitchen as she was pouring the boiling water into her cup. He could clearly see Jacenta's beautiful face as he looked at Deanna. He wasn't sure if this was the right thing to do, but he pushed through his doubt.

"What's up?" Her movements were fluid and relaxed as she sipped her tea. She was clearly very comfortable being Deanna Belamy. Eric wondered if she even remembered being Deanna Cullen or if she remembered the pain she'd caused Jacenta all those years ago.

"I know Ja . . ."

"Eric?" Sari sat up rubbing her eyes. "When did you get home?"

Eric looked to Deanna and smiled. "Those must have been some sedatives." He walked into the living room. "Feeling better? I needed to see you." He leaned over to the switch and flipped it. The recessed lights burst the room into full color.

It took a few moments but finally Sari sat up. Eric could now clearly see the reddened skin around her nose from blowing it. Her eyes were puffy and red. Her hair was still damp from a recent shower and had lost all of the orange coloring from only days ago. He raised his arms, beckoning her to come to him. Momentarily, she resisted and then broke down crying and collapsed in his arms. It took several minutes for Sari to regain control enough to speak. He waited patiently, stroking her hair and holding her close to his chest.

The shuddering of her body was rhythmic as she sobbed. "I'm being stupid," she said finally. Her words were muddled by emotion. "Deanna called you, didn't she?" She eyed Deanna from across the room. Deanna only giggled.

"Something like that." He looked at her, wanting so badly to kiss her. "You said something while you were asleep that concerned me."

"Were you here while I slept?" she asked so innocently that he wanted to take her right there. Her blue eyes sparkled with tears and she ran her hand over her towel dried hair.

Restraining himself, he said, "It was only a few minutes ago. You said you were afraid of my teeth."

"Oh." She dropped her head, not looking at him.

"What did that mean?"

"Can I ask you something?" She searched his eyes. Her hands reached out to touch his. "I'm just going to blurt this out and if it's ridiculous, then tell me. But if not – are you a vampire?" She was still not looking at him. Her eyes were cast down to her lap as if she was waiting for the impact of something to hit her.

Eric laughed. It was a soul-releasing, anxiety-relieving laugh that felt wonderful to release.

"I knew it was ridiculous." She didn't sound convinced.

"No. It's not ridiculous. Not at all."

"So you are? Or you're not? I don't get it." Her eyes drooped again as if she would fall asleep the instant her lids closed. She fought it with all her might.

He kissed her hard, wanting to let her know the truth with his actions and not words that didn't seem easy to formulate. As he pulled away, he watched as her blue eyes clouded and became gray like storm clouds. She was devouring every detail of him with those stormy eyes. She searched his eyes, hands, his skin, and even his hair.

She took a few deep breaths. "I'm still trying to process the fact that you are dead. Or undead or something." She got to her feet and paced in front of him. "And everyone that I know now could potentially kill me at any moment. Is that right? Everyone is like you. I'm living in a nightmare that I'll never wake up from."

Eric remained silent, watching as she paced and thought out loud.

"And Gail! No wonder; oh my God! Did I drink blood? Is that why my hangover miraculously disappeared? Is that why I loved Mount Orion so much?"

Eric laughed to himself. "You loved it because you wanted to. Gail's blood only helped you to accept what you weren't ready to consciously know."

"Oh, it really was blood. How could I have been so stupid? I was alone all day. You were right there all the whole time, weren't you? Downstairs? That's why you kept me drunk during that party." Sari was ranting now. "There was always something off. When I talked to Connie and Mags, they saw it. They knew you weren't right. I'd always agree with them until we were together. Then it always seemed right. Just like being with Gail seemed right." Sari was still pacing and ranting. "Is it mind control? Do I really love you or is it this weird woozy feeling I get around you that I mistake for love?"

Eric stopped her. His movements were too quick that Sari looked as if she had gotten dizzy for a moment. "I don't control your thoughts or your emotions. What you're describing is the pull. It's my soul calling to yours. Drawing you to me. I love you and I know you love me. There is no supernatural absurdity. Is it wrong for me to want to be with you forever?"

She didn't have an answer for him. She looked to Deanna, who was still sitting in the kitchen drinking her tea and listening to every word. "Do you feel this pull with Martino? This loss of control?"

"Absolutely. It's something they can't control. It makes me dizzy unless I just surrender to it."

Sari studied her friend. She looked back to Eric. "Give me a few days, okay? Go back to Mount Orion. We planned on going back on Wednesday. I'll think and then we'll talk."

CHAPTER NINETEEN

Eric was sitting on the sofa in the upstairs living room, waiting for Sari to arrive. It was Wednesday, and she promised to meet him tonight. The fire was burning in the fireplace, warming him comfortably. Gail had gone out earlier and he didn't expect her back anytime soon. She was agitated when she left. It was a mood that she entertained a lot lately, especially when Jordan was away. But most especially because of Deanna and her constant badgering to help end this curse.

Eric still wasn't sure he believed that this curse could be ended. He truly believed that Devin didn't want that to happen and it was clear that what Devin wanted, Devin got. He ran his hands over his face, wondering if this was the best place to be when it got real. When Gail realized what Eric already knew and when the details of Deanna's curse came to light.

He had been entertaining ideas of taking Sari far away until all of this blew over. Now that she knew what he was and seemed to be coming to terms with the reality of it, he fully intended to take her with him wherever he decided to go. Abandoning Gail was not really part of his plan but if he had to deal with Deanna's constant harassment of Gail, he would kill her, ending all problems as far as he could see. Well, until she was reincarnated again and returned.

And Devin. Would he follow her if she died or would he continue to aggravate them?

Devin. That was one name Eric didn't think he'd ever hear again since he had left his sire years ago. The problems that surrounded this household had stemmed from her and Eric refused to accept them as his own. He was a victim as much as Gail was a victim from fallout of this curse. None of this had anything to do with him. It just concerned him as to why Devin hadn't told Deanna of Eric's involvement from the start.

As he sat staring at the fire, the front door opened with an argument that started somewhere in the driveway. "Just because I don't agree doesn't mean I don't care," Sari was saying as she fell into Eric's arms. She kissed him gently and collapsed against him again. He led her to the sofa.

"Gail's out." He motioned for Deanna to take a seat.

Deanna only nodded but didn't sit. Instead Eric watched as she nervously scanned the room with her eyes. He waited patiently for her to relax.

"Is Martino around?" she said finally.

Eric smiled, knowing that's what she had wanted all along. "Downstairs. He should be up soon. I know he's heard your voice."

Deanna smiled nervously and walked to the kitchen to wait. The tapping of her heels could be heard loudly in the living room.

"If I were Tino, I'd escape out the back door." Eric laughed. "What's with her?"

Sari shrugged and snuggled closer to his chest. The scent of her freshly washed hair and skin was intoxicating as he pressed his lips to her head.

"She's been jumpy the entire trip. Something to do with Devin, I'm sure. I didn't ask."

Devin again. Eric thought again of taking Sari and running away. Then something occurred to him in such a strong wave that he jumped, almost throwing Sari to the floor.

"What the hell?" Sari's arms went out. Her hands thrust out in front of her, stopping her descent into the coffee table.

"She told you about Devin?"

"Yes, Jesus. Calm the frickin' hell down!" Sari sat beside him again but not so snuggled now. "She figured that since I was already figuring this whole thing out." She waved her hands in circles, motioning to him and the air around them. "It was probably a good time to dump one more impossibility on top of the insanity sundae I was enjoying."

"What did she tell you?"

"The whole kit and caboodle. Reincarnation, Devin, Gail, and how it was her best friend that did it to her. It all makes me feel stupid." Sari's mouth twisted as she spoke.

"How so?"

"You are not what I thought. Deanna is not either. Makes me wonder who else in my life is not who they say they are." Sari played with his hands, running her fingers over each knuckle and massaging his palm with hers. "Now I know everything and I'm not sure who I can trust. How are you doing with all of this?"

"Wow, did you just channel Gail?" He sounded astonished and pulled away from her slightly. "Which part do you mean? The constant presence of humans in the house? The incessant talk of spirits and curses? Or the fact that Gail is slowly losing her mind to all of this nonsense?"

Sari stared blankly at him when he finished his tirade. All the things he should have said to Gail just came bubbling over on Sari. The blankness of her expression fascinated him. But as he watched, it slowly turned to a quiet sadness, and he regretted saying every word. She didn't deserve his anger or frustration. She also didn't understand it. He would share it all with her once she was with him forever, but there was no need to overwhelm her until she could truly handle it.

Her blue eyes glistened with possible tears if she allowed them to push through. Those beautiful blue eyes that only a short time ago were covered in black eyeliner, clumpy mascara, and poorly applied gray eyeshadow considered him quietly.

His brows met slightly and he frowned.

"I just meant with me knowing about you . . . Gail and the others . . . Chelsea." Her voice was thick with the impending emotion.

Quickly, Eric kissed her hard and desperately on the mouth. He was grateful to feel her collapse against him as he held her. He could feel her hands clinging to him.

"I should be asking you how you are dealing with it. I'm asking a lot from you. We haven't really talked about it, have we?" He took her hand and pressed it to his lips. The sadness in

Sari's face had dissolved into one of devilish amusement that he didn't quite understand. Eric kissed her again. "Do you have any questions that Gail hasn't already answered?"

"I haven't spoken with Gail about it. I wasn't sure if she knew I knew. I get the feeling the others are avoiding me. I haven't seen anyone in days." She twisted her mouth in a vague expression of *that's the way it goes*. Eric could see that she was trying to come up with something to ask. She searched the room and his face for a bit of inspiration. The light in her eyes brightened just as a flood of questions erupted.

"How old are you exactly? Where are you from originally? Who made you like this? Are they dead or alive? What did you do before you were changed? Are movies right about what it's like to be what you are?" And on and on.

Eric laughed out loud, unable to contain his astonishment and joy at her interest in him. There were no questions about Gail; she was interested in Eric alone. And he loved her immensely for it. It did, however, concern him that she was still unable to verbalize what he was, but that would come in time. He hoped.

"I became *what I am*," he teased, "in the mid-1600s in a small English village, my home. My sire was the love of my life and to my knowledge she is still living, though where, I do not know." A little white lie never hurt anyone, he thought. He went on for hours, answering Sari's questions as honestly as he could except when it came to his sire. She wasn't ready for that yet, nor was he.

He enjoyed dispelling all of the myths and superstitions with which modern movies and literature had filled the minds of ignorant humans. The religious myths such as crosses and holy water fascinated Sari the most. There were misconceptions about one head vampire that if killed would in effect kill all other vampires. And Eric's favorite, the shapeshifting fallacies. Oh, he wished he could shapeshift into a bat or wolf, but it was just not true. Thank you, Hollywood, he thought.

They spoke into the night about his fears when he was first changed and his fears now that he had finally found someone that he loved again. And what he would do if Sari decided not to join him for eternity. Although she didn't ask, Eric explained how he'd met Gail and how they had come to build the cabin and live at Mount Orion.

Sari sat enraptured by his tales of the world and the other immortals that he'd met. At some point during the night, Gail had returned and joined them beside the fire. Even though he could not read her thoughts, like she could read his, Eric knew Gail was avoiding Deanna and her issues. Perhaps even Gail had her limits with these unsolvable problems. Perhaps tonight she just wanted to be an immortal and enjoy the history of that part of her life.

The fire was still burning an hour later, and Gail still sat on the chaise, lost in her thoughts. Eric and Sari had gone for a walk around the lake. She loved watching the interaction between Sari and Eric now that his little secret had been revealed. The questions! So many questions. She couldn't remember if any of those she had turned had been that curious.

No, she was wrong. Nadia had been curious. Sometimes too curious. When Gail didn't want her to know about something, Nadia would find a way. Somehow.

She was human, too, when Gail revealed her nature to her. Nadia hadn't been as accepting as Sari. Instead of questioning those myths and superstitions, Nadia had experimented. Thrown holy water in their faces, strung garlic around the house, even locked them in rooms to see if they could slip through a keyhole by turning into mist.

Gail laughed to herself.

The fire popped, sending sparks into the flue. The crackling drew Gail's thoughts back to the impending problems in this chapter of her life.

Martino had taken Deanna out for a while, but he warned that he couldn't keep her out all night. Gail had giggled. She didn't want that. She just wanted some time alone to think about how to sort out this whole mess. Without Jordan.

She missed him. Not because he was the only rational mind in her life, which always helped, but because he was her strength. Tumbling into his arms after a long night was what she longed for and dreamt about when she awoke each day. Keeping him here was wrong. Jordan was never satisfied if he felt trapped. So, Gail always let him go and sow whatever needed sowing in his life and then he would come back to her happy. Until he got restless again.

She heard the back door open and close quickly. No talking, quiet humming. One, not two. Abby, Gail smiled to herself. Not Martino and Deanna. She was not ready for them yet.

"All alone." Abby kissed Gail's cheek.

"For now." Gail patted the space beside her on the chaise. Abby snuggled up close and put her head on Gail's shoulder.

"I saw Eric and Sari down by the lake." Her voice sounded sleepy and almost dreamy. "I guess the other one is around then?"

Gail softly kissed her forehead. "Martino took her out for a while."

"You sound relieved. Getting tired of the problems that come from that world?" Abby didn't care for humans. She disliked having them at the cabin. She was very anxious for Eric to change Sari, hoping it would put an end to Deanna's visits.

Gail shrugged. "It's exhausting at times. I just wish Jordan hadn't gone." She pulled her shawl around herself and Abby.

"He was right to leave. For his sanity. I think they drive him just as buggy as they drive me."

"I know. I promised to help. I just don't know how." Gail's eyes returned to the fire and her thoughts returned to Nadia. How did she deal with the myriad of supernatural creatures in one household without losing her mind? A thought sparkled from deep in Gail's subconscious; a thought she hadn't felt in years. *I wish Nadia was here.*

Abby lay with Gail for the better part of the rest of the night. They spoke minimally and watched as the fire started to peter out. Gail was grateful for Abby's attention, especially with her uncertainty about Deanna. Also, with her newfound appreciation for what Nadia had endured as a human surrounded by immortals, Gail was finding the past was not her friend this evening.

Eric and Sari had returned an hour or so before dawn, as had Martino and Deanna. After only minutes in front of the fire, Sari found she was exhausted from her journey, and she urged Eric to lay with her until she fell asleep. He was only too glad to oblige.

Martino and Abby tried hard to keep Deanna's attention off of Gail. They spoke of world events, movies, and television – anything that would distract Deanna and not upset Gail.

Looking at Abby and Martino, Gail felt proud. Two people that would never have known one another had she not intervened in their lives. They were so different. Martino with his quiet retrospection and Abby with her obstinate determination.

Then her eyes fell on Deanna. At one time, she was also her daughter, Elizabeth. Another person that would never have been here had it not been in some small way due to Gail. At least she liked to think so.

Gail watched as Deanna tried to keep up with the conversation. She had to laugh as she drew from Deanna's thoughts a confusion both on topic and from the speed of dialogue exchange. In the last few months, Abby and Martino had become rather comfortable debating on any subject.

"I'm lost." Gail pulled her shawl around her. "You two have covered too many subjects for me to follow." She closed her eyes and rested her head against the chair.

"We should go up. You've had a long journey and must be tired." Martino stood and grabbed Deanna's hands.

Deanna looked to Gail, who had been listening with her eyes closed. "I wanted to talk to Gail about something. And I'm not tired, Tino."

Gail smiled. With her eyes closed, she could picture Elizabeth at five years old lying on Virgil's shoulder, begging not to be put to bed. And Gail realized that Deanna's voice was almost identical to Elizabeth's. She raised her head and reached out for Deanna's hand. "Tomorrow." When her eyes closed again, it was Elizabeth's face that she saw pouting, eyes puffy and tired.

"But I don't want to go to bed, Tino." *Daddy.*

"Come," he said gently as if he really were speaking to a five-year-old.

Their footsteps on the stairs confirmed Deanna's surrender. Abby returned to the chaise beside Gail with her head on her shoulder. Gail wrapped her arms around Abby and sighed deeply.

"You don't have to help her if you don't want to. You know that, right?" Abby didn't lift her head.

Gail said nothing.

"Why do you feel you owe her anything?"

"I don't," Gail whispered.

"I know you do. This is not an easy thing to fix. It's a curse. I don't know much about them, but what I do know from Joss is that they are not easy to break." Abby sat up, suddenly facing the fire. "Does Deanna even know what the spell was? Was it something she drank or words that were said? Who cast it?"

Gail smiled. "Look at you, interested all of a sudden. Where did that come from?"

"I think better when I talk it through. I'm only trying to help you, not them."

"Careful, you may do both in the process." Gail could hear footsteps on the stairs and the low murmur of male voices. "Asleep?" she asked Eric and Martino.

They nodded. "Shall we adjourn to the basement?" Eric took her hand. "We can talk more easily down there. Without waking our guests."

"Martino, has Deanna spoken to you about the curse? The actual incantation and what it involved?" Gail asked as Eric started a fire in the fireplace.

"Minimally. She either doesn't remember or doesn't want to."

"I'll tell you who would remember. Devin." Abby was rolling wood with newspaper to help ignite the stubborn fire. "But since she's the only one that can hear him, she may not tell us the truth." There was a silence. Eric kept stoking the already burning fire. "Are you all right? Abby took the fireplace tongs from him. He didn't answer. "You can't hear him at all, can you?" she asked Gail.

"No," she whispered, eyeing Eric and finding his behavior curious all of a sudden.

"Can Jordan? Joss might be able to help."

"Because she was such a great help the last time. No way."

"She knows spells and curses."

"No." Gail was firm.

"Jordan's sire is clairvoyant as well, isn't he? Do you think he would be able to hear him?"

Gail shrugged. "Jordan can sense Devin more than I can. If he can hear him, he wouldn't tell me. He blocks out spirits that try to contact him. Trevor, on the other hand, I can't even begin to know where to look for him to ask."

"Good, Bith would not want him around," Martino interrupted sharply.

"So I've heard." Gail raised her eyebrows. "She's not fond of Jordan either."

Abby smirked and caught Gail glaring at her.

"Trevor is a very strong immortal and equally as strong are his gifts. If anyone could hear Devin, it would be him." Gail rested her head on Martino's shoulder. "Perhaps when Jordan returns, we can ask if he knows where to find him."

Martino shifted uncomfortably.

"I'm sorry if his presence here will cause problems for Tabitha, but we may need him if these problems are ever to go away. Your friends will have to understand some things are unavoidable." Gail closed her eyes again.

The basement rooms were so quiet and comforting. She could already smell the lavender incense that Abby was burning.

She didn't know if its soothing effects were real or imagined but either way, she felt the pressures of her problems melting away.

"You sure you're OK?" Gail heard Abby whisper. "You look a bit on edge."

"I'm fine. Just thinking." Eric's voice was soft and distant.

"Anything you want to talk about?" Gail said with her eyes closed. She was much too tired to try to read his thoughts. He had always found it intrusive, so she tried as much as possible to respect his privacy. When he didn't answer, Gail opened her eyes to look at him. "Eric? What's wrong? You were fine until we mentioned Trevor. Do you not care for him as well?"

"I don't even know him. I'm fine, alright!" he snapped. "Just leave it alone."

Gail stared at him for a while, hurt by his short answer and concerned by his sudden change in attitude. She couldn't worry about him now. She couldn't worry about anything else tonight.

Two days later, Jordan returned, and Gail was sure he felt that she needed him.

"Where is Trevor?"

Jordan hadn't been home for more than an hour when Abby came to him. "Why?" He was curious. Abby rarely spoke to him. He knew she had never trusted him. Always blamed him for hurting Gail.

He was sitting in his favorite chair, in his favorite room – the basement study. It was always his belief that Gail had designed and built this room specifically for him. He loved the smell of the old books that lined the walls, and the leather chairs were perfectly broken in. Every month, Gail would treat the leather and the wood floors herself with oils from Europe. The smell was comforting to him.

Abby was standing in the doorway with the light of the outer rooms creating a halo around her. She was beautiful with her soft chestnut hair and delicate features. Somehow the time away from the cabin made Jordan wish she trusted him. There could be a great friendship if only she would forgive him for something he'd never done to her.

"Have you spoken with Gail?" She took one step into the room but no more. He wasn't sure if she was respecting his private space or just afraid to come closer.

Jordan stood and urged her to enter the room. "Not regarding Trevor. What's this about?"

Again, Abby only took one step farther into the room. Jordan resumed his seat and pulled the other leather chair closer for Abby.

"Sit, please." He didn't know if it was the time away from all the problems that came with living here or simply the lighting around her that made him want to speak with her.

"We, Gail and I, were curious to know if he would be able to help us with Deanna and her . . . problem." She took the seat that Jordan offered but only sat at the edge. She appeared nervous.

Jordan didn't speak. He was really curious now. But was he understanding correctly? Gail wanted Trevor here? Of course, Jordan knew where Trevor was. He always knew. He would see Trevor every time he left the cabin. The two had only just separated a week ago in Argentina. Whether he wanted to share this information with Gail, he couldn't decide.

But why would they think Trevor could or even would help Deanna? Trevor detested any talk of the spirit world or witchcraft of any kind.

"We're not convinced that Deanna is being straight with us about Devin. Gail can't hear him and she says you won't hear him . . ."

Won't hear him? Jordan smiled and shook his head. Keep on topic.

"So . . . um, we, I thought perhaps if Trevor is stronger than you . . . psychically, maybe he could hear Devin." Abby stood up quickly, almost upending the chair.

Was she afraid of him? Jordan suppressed a smile. "I could call him," he said quietly, rubbing his chin. "It is possible that he may be strong enough to hear Devin. But it's been my understanding that the curse involved blood magic. Only Deanna and those that share her blood may be able to hear him. And bringing him here may cause other complications as well."

Abby's steps reversed slowly toward the door. "I know, Martino said Bith hates him."

Jordan chuckled. "Yes, Tabitha does present a myriad of issues. But Trevor enjoys creating trouble, more now than in the past. It's my belief that he's growing bored with his life and enjoys inventing his own adventures." He shook his head, slightly irritated.

Abby nodded and took another step toward the door.

"Does Gail know you are here?" He noticed a slight tremble in her hands as she reached the door.

She swallowed hard before answering. "I couldn't be sure that Gail would ask you to call Trevor. There's always been a bit of jealousy when it came to him," she whispered. "I just want this all to be over. I want the old Gail back." Her voice was quivering with tears that she fought to suppress.

"Perhaps when Devin is finally done draining her of energy."

"You've noticed too?"

He nodded. Jordan got to his feet and reached out for her. She recoiled, not trusting his intentions. "But unfortunately, this is Gail. She thrives on this madness." He studied the anger growing in her expression. There it was, the need to protect Gail from Jordan's harsh words. Yet this time if she listened to him, she'd know he was right. "I know you think she's the fun-loving companion that you see in between the drama she creates. But she's not. I've fallen for that as well." Jordan took her hand.

"When Deanna is gone," he continued, "there will be another that will take Gail's sanity away again. I can't explain it. We are not enough for her." A tear burned his eye. "I fear we never will be."

Abby wiped a tear from her cheek and nodded. She knew

Jordan was right. How else could Gail have fallen this deep so quickly?

CHAPTER TWENTY

The sky had darkened as she sat in church. It was the church she was raised in, made her first communion and confirmation. The church where her mother hoped she'd get married. They were locking up and she still hadn't figured anything out. Walking from the church, a fine mist of rain covered Sari. Thunder approached in the distance and the sky lit up at least a mile away. A bit of fear ran though her as her pace quickened. Sari was sorry now that she had walked across town. Again, a clap of thunder sounded, this time closer than before. The rain came down heavier and the drops were larger. She put her jacket over her head and walked a bit faster.

Nothing was solved as she sat in that church. Weren't miracles supposed to happen every once in a while? She needed some divine intervention right about now. Of course, why would He help her in her decision to commit suicide? God had bigger problems than some random girl that was determined to damn her own soul. Sari felt just as guilty as she had earlier that day. It was the guilt that had led her to the church. *Useless church.*

"Why do you feel guilty?"

Sari jumped as the voice spoke from behind her. Turning around, she saw Gail, soaked from the rain, yet smiling as if it was a beautiful evening. She motioned for Sari to follow her into the Dunkin Donuts on the corner up ahead.

They ordered a cocoa and a donut for Sari and a cup of coffee for Gail.

Sari blew on her cocoa as she slowly sipped it. "You don't drink coffee, do you?"

"I enjoy the warmth on my hands and the smell . . ." Gail inhaled the pleasant aromas. "The donut is a bit sweet for my senses."

"Sorry." Sari pulled it away.

"No. It's fine. I order the coffee so as not to appear out of place. You'll see. There are little tricks we use to blend in." Her eyes sparkled as she stared at Sari across the table. "Now tell me why should you feel guilty about this decision? True, most of us don't have the luxury of contemplating whether we wanted it or not, but there shouldn't be any guilt." Gail took her hand. "This is what you want, right?"

"I don't know. How can I be sure if becoming . . ."?

"Immortal," Gail finished her sentence.

"How can I be sure that will be the right decision?" The rain poured out of the sky and Sari was happy to be out of it for a while.

"Sari." Gail held her cup between her hands. "You know it is right. I know it's right. You love Mount Orion and the family life that exists there. The family life you never really had, right?"

Sari swallowed hard.

The lightning flashed, and thunder drowned out the drops of rain hitting the pavement. Sari looked long and hard at Gail. She absorbed the graceful movements that pushed back her dripping hair. The chalky white complexion that had an iridescence that Sari wanted to touch. Her stance was relaxed as she shoved her hands deep into the heavy raincoat that she wore.

She could feel the same magnetizing pull that she felt when she was close to Eric, even from across the table. She wanted to agree with Gail, knowing it was wrong to do so, but that pull was not allowing her free will to flow.

"Your free will is still there if you don't fight it. Fighting it only confuses your mind into submission. It's something you will learn to appreciate once you're . . ." Again, she insinuated that Sari's decision had already been made. "Will you come to Mount Orion tonight? Eric is expecting you."

Sari took a deep breath. "I need some time to think."

Gail nodded and stared out the window.

"Why is this important to you?"

Gail squinted momentarily, watching the strong headlights of a car pulling into the lot. "Eric wants it. I care what he wants."

"He told me you wanted me to do this," Sari whispered.

Gail laughed. "I want you to think about something. Eric has been an immortal since, I'd say, the late seventeenth century. I, on the other hand, was brought into this life in 1884. That's almost a three-hundred-year difference." She paused, examining the confused look on Sari's face and scanning her thoughts for some understanding. "Do you really think I could influence an immortal of his age?"

Sari shook her head, no.

"My only concern is and will always be whether your transformation will affect the inhabitants of Mount Orion as long as you are there. That's all."

"I'd live with you at the cabin?" Tears welled in Sari's eyes.

Gail laid her hand on Sari's face. "Of course, if that's what you want." She smiled. "You're right. Why don't you take tonight to think it over? Actually, take as long as you wish. We're not going anywhere."

Sari watched as Gail got up to leave. The clacking of her heels echoed on the pavement outside as she disappeared into the darkness. She looked around the donut shop. The lights were bright and harsh, and for some reason it made her feel safe. The patrons were her age, college students. They laughed and talked about politics, movies, and other assorted ridiculousness that would have seemed important to Sari five months ago.

But now she was making the hardest decision of her life. How do you choose the damnation of your own soul? Sari knew she wanted to live at Mount Orion, and she couldn't do that as a mortal. She also wanted to share her life with Eric and that was definitely impossible as a human.

Not knowing her motivation, Sari picked up her cell phone and pressed the button marked HOME. A deep sickening feeling struck her in the pit of her stomach. The phone rang at least six times before a harsh voice said hello.

"Hi, Mom," Sari whispered.

"Did your friend tell you I called?" Her tone was mean and unyielding.

"No, she didn't. How is everyone?" Sari swallowed hard. The soreness in her throat burned as she fought the tears.

"What do you want, Sari Ann?" There was nothing motherly in this woman's tone. Nothing loving. Sari's thoughts immediately went to Gail and how tender she was.

She paused for a moment, lost in thought and not knowing what to say. "I, we haven't seen each other or spoken in months. I just thought . . ."

"Oh, I understand. You need money. Have you squandered the last check we sent? I know you got it because it was cashed. No use lying about it. You'll have to wait until next month."

Sari held back the tears burning in her eyes and the lump steadily rising in her throat. She knew this was the perfect time to hang up. The perfect time to sever all ties.

Then she heard: "It's your daughter. She needs money."

The phone changed hands and the gruff voice of her father drifted through the receiver. "How much do you need?" he said simply. It was the perfect Dad question, Sari thought. Protests from her mother could be clearly heard in the distance.

"No, I don't need money, Dad. I just called to say hello." *Or goodbye.* "Mom just assumed."

"Well, I'll let you sort things out with your mother. I'm going to watch the game. Bye, Sari."

"Bye, Daddy." Several tears trickled down her cheeks. She hung up before her mother had another chance to degrade her.

An hour later, the skies cleared, and the moon was hanging bright above the cabin. Walking up to the door felt strange. This was it, the decision. She had decided as soon as she pressed and deleted the cell phone button marked HOME. That was no longer her home. It hadn't been home for almost a year, but she had finally accepted that her real family waited beyond the doors of this cabin.

There was nothing for her outside the cabin. Not even her friends were more important than how she felt every time she walked through this door. She took a deep breath and turned the knob. The reception she got wasn't quite what she expected. Gail was curled up on the sofa, her legs pulled beneath her and her arm cradled her head. Deanna sat across from her and only glanced up as Sari walked in.

"Is Eric around?" Sari asked softly.

Deanna said that he was downstairs with Abby and Richard. *Downstairs? Could she go downstairs now? Those mysterious rooms that were just feet away. Those rooms where she knew they slept during the day.*

She looked to Gail for approval. "The door's open. Just go on down."

That's it. Just go on down. The forbidden doors had opened.

Gail laughed. "Something like that."

She saw the inquisitive look on Deanna's face and thought she caught a hint of understanding and disapproval in her eyes. Choosing to ignore it, Sari walked to the door but hesitated. There it was: the staircase that led to the downstairs rooms. The staircase that opened up a whole new world. She exhaled audibly. The high-pitched laughter of Abby carried all the way up the stairs. *Everyone is the same as they were yesterday. Nothing is any different, except that by walking down the stairs, I have accepted the chalice of immortality. No, the cloak of immortality, the shield . . .*

"Oh my God, just go down," Gail shouted from the living room. She shouted from the *upstairs* living room.

Sari took her first step towards the downstairs living room and felt herself getting lightheaded. *She wasn't ready for this. Another time; this is not the right time.* She turned quickly on the stairs to find Gail standing behind her.

"You're ready. Go to him." Gail gently turned Sari's shoulders to go back down the stairs.

Eric, Abby, and Richard were sitting in a sunken living room that could have been taken out of a page of *Better Homes and Gardens*. Sari couldn't believe her eyes; it was nothing like she'd pictured. No creepy sounds, no furnace room, no dead bodies. The walls had beautiful paintings that Sari could have sworn were in her art history books from her half semester in college. The fireplace was lit, and she could feel the warmth from the stairs. *Why would anyone go upstairs?* she thought.

"Hi," she said as Eric looked up to her.

There was a hesitation at first when they saw her. *I'm not supposed to be here and they know it. That's it. I'm not supposed to be here.*

"Yes, you are." Jordan was standing in a doorway down the hall. He held a newspaper in his hand, and he was beckoning her to come to him. She had seen him so many times upstairs, reading the newspaper. Now looking at him, she couldn't move her legs to walk toward him.

He smiled and started to walk toward her. "Sari, welcome. Sit with us." He grasped her hands and pulled her gently towards the sofa. As she sat, she still was devouring the room. The lighting was dim, electric recessed lights. There was soft music playing. Sari would have expected classical but instead it was Maroon 5.

"Is that disappointing? Should we be more clichéd?" Jordan laughed.

"No." Sari could hardly find enough strength to speak louder than a whisper. "It's great down here." She felt ridiculous. Her hands would not stop shaking.

Jordan placed a hand on hers and gently squeezed. "Richard, Abby . . . may we have a moment?"

Richard smiled and ran his hand over Sari's hair. Abby, not really understanding, felt slighted and off-put by being told to leave. It took only a moment for them to ascend the stairs and the door at the top was closed behind them.

Eric moved closer to Sari. "So, you've made a decision?"

She looked to Jordan first and then to Eric. "I think so." *No, I don't.*

Jordan squeezed her hand again. "I'll leave you alone." He caught Eric's eye as he left and knew he was elated. Jordan closed the door as he went upstairs.

Somewhere outside she heard the dogs barking and for a moment she was back in her nightmare. A slight shiver ran through her as her eyes met Eric's and she felt a wave of nausea course through her. Then the sound of Richard shouting at the dogs to *be quiet* and she knew this was real and not her dream.

Eric ran his fingers through her hair. His kiss was hard and desperate. Sari felt the urgency in his movements. She didn't want to pull away, but he was hurting her. *Is this going to happen? Here?* She pulled away and looked him in the eyes. His eyes were brown at some point in his life; now they were hazel with some iridescent green flecks. She kissed him again.

That magnetic yank clamped on her insides and dragged her to him. She couldn't fight it if she wanted to. Did she really want to do this or was this maddening pull overpowering her? *Yes, I do want this.* Sari pulled Eric to her and allowed him to take her. She tried to surrender to the pull like Gail suggested. Don't fight it and it won't fight you.

Lying back on the sofa, he was on top of her before she could accept her own decision. He was rough and frantic at the start but slowed his pace so as not to scare her. She could see bruises already forming on her upper arms. His hands were everywhere at once, her breasts, her thighs, and her neck. His kisses were brisk and stinging. *Stinging?* Her neck was suddenly on fire with his mouth pressing against it. Her shoulders ached under the pressure. She felt lightheaded again. Sari thought of her moment on the stairs when she thought this was not what she wanted.

She could feel her limbs weak from Eric drinking from her. Her fingers and toes tingled. She grabbed his shoulders, pulling him closer. The need to feel his body pressed against hers was confoundingly urgent. Sari dragged her nails across his back and pulled them through his hair.

An audible moan escaped her, and she thought of those in the rooms above. They were so far away now. It was only her and Eric sharing this moment that would be only theirs. As he pulled away from her, she uncontrollably clutched him. "Don't," was all she could muster.

He sat up looking at her as she lay exhausted, motionless before him. *That can't be it?* Sari didn't feel any different. Except she was craving something . . . something she could not . . . sitting up, a pain in her abdomen struck her and she cried out. "Be still," she heard Eric say but it was as if he was miles away. His voice was muffled and distant. Again, she tried to sit up, fighting the pain in her stomach. Sari craved something that was right in front of her.

He was on top of her again, suddenly. The burning in her shoulder, the pain as he drew even more of the blood from her body. The weight of his body seemed to be less pressing than it had been moments before. He was pulling away slowly this time. She watched as he used his fingernail to slice his own chest. The blood seeped out and Eric took her head and led her mouth to the blood.

Sari kissed his chest and tasted the sweetness of his blood. She suckled from the wound on his chest until he gently pushed her away. Kissing her neck and lips, he lifted himself off of her. The weakness in her limbs was intensifying the nausea, but the smell of his skin was calming at the same time.

She wanted to touch the velvety hair on his arms. She wanted to nestle her face into the cleft in his chin. To touch the soft skin behind his ears and on the nape of his neck. Her senses were alert. The sense of smell was ever-increasing. Touch, the need was inescapable. And taste . . .

Eric.

With no knowledge of how to accomplish what she needed, Sari climbed to her knees. The pain was crushing her insides and she felt the pressure rising as if she needed to vomit again. Taking a few panting breaths, she tried to overcome the nausea. "Don't fight." His voice was so far away. *Why can't I hear him? I need to do this.*

Sari didn't know why she had such a great need, but there it was sitting before her. The steak dinner that had been denied her for her entire life. The caviar garnish around the suckling pig. She didn't even know if those went together. But it sure sounded good.

Eric.

The need outweighed the pain and nausea. She'd vomit later. *Maybe.* She was pulling herself to him again and he wasn't stopping her. Kissing his skin didn't seem like enough any longer. Taste was conquering touch. There was warmth just below, sweet, liquid warmth that she needed to taste. A sharp pain cut through her stomach and she collapsed against him.

How is this done? Do I just bite? And she did. Biting was easy as soon as she realized that daggers protruding from her jaw were part of her prize package. *Of course. Fangs!* They sliced through his skin and the beautiful liquid warmth flowed into her mouth. It was the best orgasm she had ever experienced. Her breathing sped and the liquid warmth kept flowing.

Along with the liquid warmth were thoughts and memories. Thoughts and memories that were not hers. *The cabin, Gail, bloodied bodies. A red-haired woman, a glass vase smashed against the wall, fear. Sari, the red-haired woman, and Devin.* She realized that these were Eric's thoughts that she was seeing. With the liquid warmth came shared thoughts.

What had he seen from my liquid warmth?

Slowly, Eric pulled away, still holding Sari in his arms. The pain in her stomach was less but the nausea was pushing up again. She stared at him, desperate to run to the bathroom. He stroked her face with the back of his hand. "There's a door at the end of the hall. It leads outside."

Sari ran for it.

CHAPTER TWENTY-ONE

Gail sat back in her chair and stared out the window. The yard was alive with talking and approaching headlights. The driveway was already filling with cars, and a few were forced to park on the grass. She smiled to herself, happy that it was almost winter and her flowers were already gone.

Behind her, the men were discussing the current situation, trying desperately to come up with a solution. Gail was nervous. She didn't want to have this party, but Trevor thought it was a good way to get everyone together to get a feel for the overall climate of the situation.

Trevor.

He had arrived a week ago and had successfully enchanted everyone he came in contact with. Sari was absolutely enthralled by him. Visually he was perfect. His brown eyes were large, a little too large for his face, making him appear like he stepped out of a big-eyed Margaret Keane painting. His high forehead and angular face were imperfect but pleasing to gaze upon. A flurry of reddish-brown hair was cut short but left longer in the front so it would fall effortlessly on his forehead.

Almost as if he was torn from the pages of GQ magazine, he was dressed simply but dazzling at the same time. Jeans and a button-down shirt were complemented with a black velvet jacket that he had borrowed from Eric. His jewelry was also modest yet somehow made a statement regarding his personality. A large watch, one ring on each hand, and Gail had seen a sparkle in his ears from diamond studs.

The clothes, the jewelry, even the haircut exuded confidence and a bit of arrogance that she wasn't fond of and didn't really trust.

When he arrived, it was all business with a subtle humor and a glimmer in his eye that added to the lack of trust his outward appearance had already instilled. Gail tried to present him with the facts and gauge his interest accordingly. He was skeptical of the curse and was openly hostile at the idea of being used as a conduit to this spirit. He showed interest in one thing and one thing only: Deanna.

From the moment he was introduced to her, he fawned over her. He kissed her hand and when he spoke to her, it was in a very intimate manner that outraged both Devin and Martino. The tantrums that Devin threw were titanic in proportion – smashing, slamming, throwing; no one knew he was capable of such destruction until Trevor arrived. Gail was forced to remove Deanna from the cabin just not to lose any of her more precious heirlooms.

With Deanna out of the house, Trevor's interest turned to the curse and the one that cast it.

"What did you say her name was?"

"Jacenta." Gail was exhausted by the last few days of chaos in the cabin. Her tone was short and to the point.

"And she's not one of us. She's dead?" His question was oddly directed toward Eric, but Gail answered.

"Correct." She pulled her hair around her shoulder and rubbed her eyes as if they hurt. They were bloodshot and dark rings stood out under them. Devin's constant presence was taking its toll on her, but at Deanna's demand, he was no longer draining her energy – though as of yet she had not felt a significant difference.

"Why?" Jordan swirled the dark red liquid in the goblet in his hand. "What are you not saying?" He was tired as well and was in no mood for Trevor's games.

Trevor simply shrugged. "Not a common name – Jacenta. But it's familiar." Again, he looked to Eric. Eric's expression was placid, but his eyes were like burning coals directed at Trevor.

"I'd drop it if I were you," Jordan warned.

At the time, the exchange was lost on Gail, who was too drained to do much of anything but fight to keep her eyes open. Now as she sat thinking back on it, her head filled with questions.

Trevor was an enigma and he was prone to playing games. Gail looked at him now as he stood comfortably in her upstairs bedroom; he was clearly at home wherever he stood.

Beside him, now and for the last week, was Jordan. Tonight, he was dressed in a cornflower blue sweater and black pants. His hair hung down around his shoulders, exactly how she loved it, but his face showed none of his usual confidence. His black eyes were smoky, almost steely gray, and there was a permanent dimple between his brows from his constant expressions of disapproval since Trevor had arrived. Specifically, he was against this party and wanted nothing to do with it.

On this point, Gail heartily agreed. It was a matter that should not be spread too far around. It was a matter better handled by the few already involved. But Gail was quickly learning that you didn't oppose Trevor. He didn't like it.

In the reflection of the window, she saw a face peeping in the doorway.

"Get out!" she heard Jordan say. He was angry and projecting it on everyone except Trevor, who actually deserved it.

Looking up, she caught a glimpse of Adrian's face as Eric pushed him out the door. She smiled. Seeing Adrian again was like revisiting the past. A past she wasn't sure she wanted to revisit. Thoughts of the night Adrian was reborn washed over her quickly and she tried to push them away. He was rebellious and a real pain in the ass; still she loved him as she loved all her immortal children.

Martino, Abby, Adrian, and Nadia.

All four had changed her in some way. They had allowed her to grow and become the immortal she was today. A chuff of a laugh escaped her chest. They were poignant, these memories. She sighed slightly and returned her gaze to the window.

"Who else did you tell about this?" Eric asked Jordan.

"Besides the ones that already know, I contacted Jocelyn at Gail's request." Jordan swept away lint from his trousers offhandedly.

Trevor rolled his eyes and exhaled, clearly annoyed.

"I hope that's not going to be a problem." Jordan raised an eyebrow as he glared at Trevor.

"If you think having that witch here is going to solve your problems, then who am I to stand in your way?" His jaw was tense as he spoke.

"Jocelyn has been a great help to us in the past. I just thought . . ." Gail started looking to Jordan for support. "I don't want her presence here to start any problems." Jordan squeezed her shoulder lovingly.

"She and I don't see eye to eye." Trevor smiled slyly. "If there is to be a problem, I'll be sure to take it outside."

"There won't be any problems." Again, Jordan glared at his sire. "Jocelyn is welcome here. You, on the other hand . . ." He sneered lightheartedly, and Trevor pretended not to notice.

Gail was getting tired of these little jibes and taunts toward each other. All week, Trevor was playing games with them. First it started with the cottage and Trevor's intention to stay there instead of being squished like a sardine in the basement rooms. The cottage was huge and completely empty — that was his argument. After that battle had consumed the cabin for two days, Gail, a hundred-and-thirty-year-old immortal, made it quite clear to Trevor, a two-thousand-year-old immortal, that if he set foot in that cottage, she would incinerate him. Taking her at her word, Trevor called a truce and a mutual respect was formed — Trevor moved into the guest rooms on the second floor of the cabin.

Jordan had warned her that Trevor would not be easy to live with — she was starting to believe him.

"We'll see," Trevor commented, walking to the window beside Gail to look out at those approaching the house.

"We're not going to have a problem, are we?" Jordan interjected, clearly agitated. His jaw muscles were clenched and pulsating.

Trevor shrugged and walked to the door. "She's your witch." This calm disconnection of Trevor's infuriated Jordan. It was something Gail knew Jordan detested in others, although he'd done it to her countless times. She suppressed a smile as she watched Jordan fume. Her eyes watched the men as they paced the room before her.

There was silence between the four of them. Jordan reached out his hand to Gail. *"Time to get this over with,"* he said silently to her with a private smile.

Trevor smiled sarcastically, squinting his eyes as the men faced each other. He'd heard Jordan's comment and didn't appreciate it. "You called me, remember? I could go."

"It's always an option." Jordan pulled Gail to her feet and slipped his hand around her small waist. "You may want to sneak out the back way. Tabitha is downstairs."

"You should fear her more than I." Trevor's large eyes narrowed.

"I wouldn't be so sure. She detests you." Jordan laughed in a low derisive manner.

Before Trevor could respond with a quip of his own, Gail interjected. "Boys, please. This is supposed to be a party, not a pissing contest." She took a deep breath and linked her arm through the arm Eric offered. "Stop acting like children and let's get this over with."

Quite aware that she had just restated the very comment that had started the argument, Gail gave Eric a sideways glance. There was a look of surprise and humor stretched across his face. His dark eyebrows rested high on his forehead in disbelief as he cast his eyes down so as not to laugh in front of Trevor and Jordan.

Gail laughed out loud despite the anger she felt following her to the stairs.

CHAPTER TWENTY-TWO

As the party droned on, Sari retreated to the porch. After her Chelsea's friend, Noelle showed up and stole her attention, Sari wanted to be alone. Eric was distracted and had been for days. Nothing she did could break him out of his funk. The party, Trevor's arrival, and the constant talk of this witch, Jacenta, was somehow taking its toll on him.

The porch fireplace was roaring, and Deanna sat alone curled up on the cushioned Adirondack chair with a glass of wine twirling in her hand. Her hazel eyes were glassy and staring blankly at the fire. Stopping as her heel hit the stones on the porch floor, Sari didn't want to intrude. Seeing Deanna sitting lost in her own thoughts was sad to her. But the need to escape the party was pushing Sari on to the porch.

The last few weeks were a whirlwind. Since that fateful night two weeks ago when she allowed Eric to drink her blood and she shared his – along with many of his memories and thoughts – her life was topsy-turvy. She didn't realize how difficult it was to learn to be a vampire. Cheesy horror movies hadn't prepared her for the changes both mental and physical that she was enduring.

The word alone – vampire -- made her cringe. It brought to mind images of Bela Lugosi, William Marshall, and Gary Oldman in scores of Dracula movies. She thought of his minions and the many brides of Dracula. The mental institutions and dark cobwebby castles. The crosses, holy water, and stakes through the heart. It was a word that was impregnated with mythology and superstition.

Vampire. She hated the V word.

Eric had done his best to dispel most of the superstition. Yet he could never undo what hundreds of years of folklore and decades of horror movies had done to saturate a young girl's imagination.

None of those around her fit into the horror genre that had been so perfectly mapped out in her brain. Bith and Chelsea were in no way the brides of Dracula. She could never see them being mind-controlled by a man, doing his bidding and whims. Those two did the controlling.

Eric could be Dracula. He was sexy enough, but not sure enough. There was always something that lurked below the surface with Eric. Something he was hiding. Dracula was confident and alluring. He didn't need to hide what he was.

Even in her thoughts she could not say the *V* word.

The hunt was an adventure. Sari could never have guessed how deeply the need for the blood would go. From the pit of her stomach to her taste buds, every vein, every cell screamed for it. The desire – no, not desire – the compulsion for the blood caused her intense and immediate pain nightly. Eric assured her the pain would subside as she learned to control and quench it adequately.

Tonight, the pain was almost nonexistent. Chelsea had introduced her to her first human kill –first, second, and third human kill and it was that blood her body needed. What her body craved. Her body was adequately quenched. No pain.

For the first weeks, Eric started her hunting animals. Teaching her to listen for danger and other predators in the vicinity. Rabbits and deer were easily spooked, and it was almost impossible for Sari to be patient. The scent of the blood and the fear her presence stirred up in the animals was pulling her. Drawing her into the woods, listening for them, wanting their warm flesh in her hands. *In her mouth*. Eric held her back several times, only releasing her when the time was right or when he felt she could learn from her failure.

The last few nights with Chelsea had taught her that humans were easier. They possessed absolutely no instincts for recognizing danger. There was nothing that said *you're being stalked* or *you're about to die.* Millions of years convincing themselves that they were at the top of the food chain had removed any fear of falling prey to something wanting to eat them.

Being on the other end of the pull was sweet. Her first human started to fight, and then the pull anesthetized them. They all but gave themselves over to her. It was amazing.

Chelsea challenged Sari. Eric had not. He had killed her first meal to satisfy the intense blood lust that had started the moment she was reborn. Chelsea, on the other hand, stood back and watched. Assistance came only when Sari faltered or lost her nerve – and sometimes not even then.

Eric taught her to be a predator. Fulfill the need. Chelsea was teaching her to be a hunter. It was all about the sport.

Standing on the porch, she could smell the aromas surrounding her. The air smelled like snow, crisp and clean. It had been snowing off and on, but nothing had really stuck just yet. It was going to be a green Christmas. The evergreen and fir trees surrounding the property were so fragrant. The wood in the fire smelled like maple. Gail's scent was all over the porch; Sari inhaled deeply. *Jasmine.*

Deanna's wine smelled like honey and was a bit nutty too. The scent Sari was trying to avoid was Deanna herself. The smell of her skin, the mixture of coconut hand lotion, and the light fragrance of lavender body spray. The strongest scent was her distress. The stress hormones were raging, increasing her heart rate and blood flow. Deanna's heart pounded in Sari's ears. She swallowed hard.

Her palms were sweaty, and Sari could feel her muscles tensing like they had when she was stalking her prey. The angle of her spine dipped slightly, putting her in perfect position to pounce if Deanna made a single move. It didn't make any sense. She'd been with Deanna in the past few weeks and she hadn't needed to control herself until today.

Shaking herself free of the predatory instincts that were now part of her nature, Sari realized it was the human blood that had done all of this. The taste, the smell. It awakened all five senses. She held her breath and closed her eyes. Deanna's heart pounded in her ears and her muscles fluttered uncontrollably. Again, she found her limbs were preparing to attack.

Weakness in her legs caused her to stumble as she took another step towards Deanna. The wine glass twirled innocently and obliviously between her fingers. Deanna's mind was miles away from where she sat.

Another step. Sari was not in control of her movements now. As her foot slid one more time, a hand grasped her arm, halting her forward motion. Her senses switched from predator to prey and she pulled away, feeling trapped. Her body flexed as she took in all the scents surrounding her. The mix of musky cologne and anger filled her nostrils as Eric dug his fingers deep into her upper arm.

With his face pressed against hers, Sari could almost taste his anger. He pulled her into the kitchen and closed the porch door, leaving Deanna safely on the other side.

"Now I know why you've been avoiding me all night." His eyes were fierce and he had yet to let go of her arm.

She pulled away but his fingers dug in deeper. "You're hurting me."

"I doubt that very much."

A small crowd gathered around them and Eric felt a need to escape. Chelsea stood in the kitchen doorway, taking in the spectacle with an arrogant smile. Noelle stood behind her. Her eyes showed concern and a kind of embarrassment for what was enfolding. Sari looked to the two women, and only those two, for direction. When Chelsea started to speak, Noelle silenced her with a gesture as simple as a hand on her shoulder.

Coming between a master and his pupil was frowned upon and Chelsea had stepped too far over the line already. Sari stared at them as Eric pulled her toward the back door. The backyard was deserted except for Attila and Thor, who were more than happy to have some company – especially Sari.

Once outside, she struggled in his grasp until Eric threw her farther into the yard and slammed the door behind him. The windows rattled on the verge of explosion and the door frame splintered. The dogs expressed their displeasure of his aggression toward Sari with a low growl. Eric glared at them and they turned, tail between their legs and ears back submissively. They sat near the kitchen door and waited. An alpha had been established for now.

"What do you think you're doing?" She rubbed her upper arm vigorously. The red marks from his fingers looked like war paint on her arm, and she tried to rub them away.

Eric charged her, wrapping his hands around her face. Sari had time to take only one step back before he was on her. His movements were too quick even for her and her breath sputtered. A burning tear stung her eye and her hands flew up to stop his advance – too late.

"Do you have any idea why I was keeping you from humans? Do you?" His voice was gruff and almost a growl. He reminded Sari of the dogs. His eyes pulsed as he stared at her. For the first time since she met Eric, she was frightened of him.

She lowered her eyes and nodded. A slight tremble shook her shoulders and her head lowered.

"You are not capable of separating friends from prey at this early stage." His voice and his tone softened, but only to keep the others from coming out to separate them. "You could have killed her."

"I'm sorry." Her voice was barely audible.

"What?" he said ferociously.

"I'm sorry! But it made the pain go away." She sounded like a child who was being chastised by her father, and she hated Eric for making her feel this way. "I needed it. Chelsea was trying to help." Her hands were shaking, and the dogs whined in unison. They walked, tails stiff and angled down, to the right and left of Sari. They watched Eric as he was watching them.

Eric approached Sari, cautiously watching Attila and Thor as they flanked her protectively. He reached out and took her face in his hands again. This time in a loving, not at all aggressive manner. A low warning growl escaped Thor, and his tail tensed. "Don't go near Deanna unless you're with one of us. If you feel yourself losing control – remove yourself immediately." He kissed her and pulled away quickly, a look of realization in his eyes.

"You've drunk Chelsea's blood, haven't you?" He was still holding the sides of her head. His voice sounded accusing, but hidden far beyond the anger and frustration, Sari detected his hurt.

Her eyes searched his for some form of understanding, but there was none. Even the hurt that she had felt a minute ago was gone, being quickly replaced by fury. The light amber flecks in his eyes were gone and only a thin brown trim outlined his large, dilated pupils.

"Why are you so angry?" She stepped behind the dogs for protection. "What's the difference to you? You're here and then you're not. At least she wants to help me learn!" Immediate regret stabbed at her as the words flew from her lips.

"Learn? Is that what's happening here? She deliberately took you away to teach you something she knew would only cause trouble. Chelsea and her games." He shook his head; his face twisted in an expression that Sari hoped she would never see again. His eyes vibrated and bloodshot, his mouth in a snarl that Attila would envy, and his hair standing up in a bristly mess. Dr. Jekyll had become Hyde.

Sari knew that she should accept her guilt and leave it alone. But something was egging her on, something pushed her to continue. "You don't want me to learn anything. Why did you want me to be like this if your plan was to abandon me afterwards?"

"We're going away. I'm taking you far from here where you can't be manipulated by . . . others." *Others* came out forced as if he wanted to say so much more but thought better of it. He approached her as if to grab her and again stopped himself.

"You're scaring me. Stop it. I'm not going anywhere." She was demanding through her tears, still keeping her voice controlled. "I want to talk to Gail." Tears escaped the corners of her eyes and she wiped them away.

The dogs started barking and circling Sari's legs. Eric wasn't the only one whose hackles were up. She reached out, calming them with a scratch behind their large upright ears. It did no good. They continued to bark frantically, staying protectively between Eric and Sari.

    Eric closed his eyes to regain his composure. It was not an easy feat. "Go away!" he growled through his teeth. The volume of his voice was so low that Sari barely heard him.

    "Are you serious?" She looked at him in amazement.

    "Go!" His voice was louder and full of venom.

    The dogs erupted into a fierce fit of howling.

    "You are unbelievable," Sari spit out. She pushed past him to return indoors before she started to bawl uncontrollably. A tightening in her throat caught any other words that she wanted to scream at him.

    Quickly, Eric's arm flew out to stop her. Again, his movements were too quick for her to stop him. "Not you." He wasn't looking at her, but she knew he was talking to her. "Close your eyes." The hazel flecks in his eyes had returned, and the pupils shined with iridescent light. The hardness of his face, the tension in his jawline, softened when he looked at her now. "Trust me." He took her hands, feeling her apprehension. "If you concentrate, you can feel Devin feeding off our energy. I usually feel it here." He circled his stomach with his hand.

    Her hands were still trembling as Eric held them. Sari wasn't sure what she was feeling for. With her eyes closed, every movement became amplified. The tickle of the dogs' hair against her bare leg, the breeze pushing her hair around, the gentle pressure of Eric's thumbs as they massaged the knuckles on her hands delicately. Nothing. She felt nothing.

    A loud whistle startled her. "Quiet," Eric silenced the dogs.

    She tried to block out the sounds of the party inside the cabin. Gail was in the kitchen talking with Richard. Both making sure that Sari and Eric were all right. Chelsea hovered somewhere in the background, not far from Gail. Sari could hear Noelle reprimanding her for her part in Eric's anger. A car was starting around front and tires dug into the gravel and dirt. Still she felt nothing from Devin.

"He must have gone." The words squeaked from her dry tender throat. The need to cry wasn't prevalent, but the urge was lying in wait for her brain to give the go ahead. Sari didn't open her eyes when a flutter between her shoulder blades caused her to twitch. A deeper tingle and the flutter continued. It moved across from shoulder to shoulder and then faded. "Devin," she whispered with a smile and a bite of her lip. "I felt him."

Eric nodded, his brows tense as he felt Devin withdraw. "It starts as a tickle or an itch but as he feeds, it gets more intense." He ran his hands over his face as if trying to rub the scowl from his features. "He exhausts our energy, and he gets stronger. I wouldn't want to know what he'd do if he was fully charged."

Back inside, Sari assured Gail that she was fine. The flutter ran across her shoulders again; this time she was expecting it and welcoming it. She smiled, knowing Devin was with her. She wanted to run and tell Deanna that she had felt Devin, but just as she reached the porch door, Sari stopped.

Standing with her hand on the door, the flutter crossed her shoulders once again, but a deeper pain hurt her heart. She remembered Eric's words of warning regarding Deanna and took her hand off the doorknob.

CHAPTER TWENTY-THREE

The party started breaking up somewhere around 4 a.m. So many vampires came and went throughout the night, but the core group hung around until the end. Gail circled – always the perfect host – as she tried to get a feel for who was willing to help or not.

The questions or topics weren't specific, nor was the problem being presented. She nonchalantly worked it into conversation – if you could ever nonchalantly work a curse into conversation. Martino watched as it was becoming abundantly clear that no one had any idea or interest in that particular subject.

"We'll be fine," he reassured Gail when she started losing hope.

"Where's Deanna?"

"Porch. She's been there all night." He knew Deanna expected nothing and everything from the party's outcome. Gail had built up the evening in Deanna's mind so much that any outcome would fall short of her expectations. Although he had been noticing that she was becoming more difficult to deal with, as they were no closer to helping her solve her problem.

Withdrawing to the porch early in the evening with a bottle of wine was becoming her favorite form of passive aggressive reaction. The whole night was not without its exciting moments. Eric and Sari had a rousing round of *this is not what I expected from this life*. A popular fight between a sire and offspring, Martino was finding out. He remembered having that exact fight with Gail years ago. And with Margaret every time he visited her.

There were less cars when Martino walked outside just before dawn. "Are we staying tonight?" he called to Deanna, who was still on the porch.

"I suppose. No use going home now." She stood and leaned on the railing overlooking the front yard. The dark circles stood out under her eyes as she tried to stifle a yawn. Even exhausted, Martino loved how she looked. Yes, her eyes were glassy from too much wine mixed with exhaustion. Yes, her hair was a mess – she must have dozed on the porch chair over the course of the night. And yes, she never looked more beautiful to him.

When she was tired, Deanna was real. Her movements unrehearsed and languid. Her expressions soft and natural. He wanted to lie beside her for the rest of his life. "We should go back in then. You're exhausted." He leaned against Phillipe's blue Astin Martin convertible; Phillipe had left with Bith earlier in the night, following her big fight with Trevor and the bombshell he dropped on her regarding Aaron.

Deanna shrugged and smiled, clearly exhausted but fighting it as long as she could. She was forever the little girl that refused to be put to bed. Even when he woke her when she fell asleep in his arms, she would insist that she was not tired and hadn't even fallen asleep.

"Come on, little girl. Time for bed." He took a step toward her as the front door opened.

Gail stepped out on the stoop, followed closely by Jake and Rhea. Martino didn't like them. In truth, he didn't really know them at all. They were part of Gail's recent past. A past that he was not part of and, from talking to Jordan, a past he was happily not part of. Jake was one of Gail's greatest blunders – to use a Jordan expression – and Rhea was family. That was all Gail would tell Martino about her. *Family.* It was such a strong word for Gail. It meant everything. She had her human family and her immortal family, but as long as family was part of the phrasing, it was important to Gail.

Now, Martino watched as Gail hugged them both and said her goodnights. Promises of getting together soon were shared with the underlying knowledge that it would never happen. Gail smiled and returned to the house. Abby rushed by just as Gail stepped a foot into the house. She raised a hand and waved to Martino with a nod and a smile as she closed the front door.

"Promised Phillipe that I would put the top up. Looks like rain this morning." Abby jingled Phillipe's keys at Martino. As she slunk down into the leather seats, a sigh of delight escaped her lips. "Oh, wow, this is nice. Wanna go for a spin?" She raised a single eyebrow playfully at Martino. "I bet this thing can move." The engine sprang to life and Abby pushed the button to raise the roof.

Martino laughed and approached the car. "If he's not back by tonight, you are on." He smelled the leather upholstery and part of him wished the sunrise was not less than a half an hour away.

Rhea and Jake passed in front of the car, whispering to each other. "She's definitely up to something." The only words Martino could make out or even cared to.

"Not up to anything," he called to them as they reached Jake's Porsche. "We just have a situation that is taking up a lot of her time and energy. Gail thought we might find someone willing or even able to give some insight."

Rhea was staring at him as he spoke with an incredulous look on her face. She walked around the silver sports car and opened the passenger side door. "Oh, come on, it's got to be more than that. Why would Joss be here? She never gets involved with anything. She's practically a recluse these days." She leaned on the roof above the open car door without getting in.

Martino shrugged. "Believe what you will. But . . ."

"What about all those weird questions and the fights that kept breaking out?" Rhea interrupted. "I can feel when something's amiss. My *Spidey* senses were going nuts in there."

There was a long silence that hung in the air like a pause, but no one really wanted to continue but Rhea. "Just do me a favor and leave us off the guest list for your next party. I can't be pulled into this insanity that seems to circle Gail." She looked to her father, Jake, who was urging her to get into the car.

Martino's hands were clenched into fists that he forced into his jacket pockets.

The Porsche's engine roared as Jake depressed the gas pedal several times.

"Looks like it's time for you to go now." His words were overlaying a *get the hell out of here* subtext.

"Just be careful. Something doesn't feel quite right." Her green eyes were intense and locked on Martino's brown eyes. "There's more than a curse here. Something felt off when I talked to your girlfriend, there." She raised her chin to Deanna, who was standing on the porch riveted with curiosity. "I don't know. Goodbye, Martino. See ya, Abby." Rhea blew Abby a kiss, dropped into the low seat beside her father, and shut the door.

Martino stood completely still for a moment, trying to absorb what Rhea had just told him. A tickle in his lower back told him Devin was near and loving Martino's distress. Quickly, before they could pull out of the driveway, he flagged Rhea to stop for a minute. She pulled down her window to speak with him.

"What did you feel?" He bent close to the car speaking so low it was impossible to hear him unless you possessed preternatural gifts.

Rhea looked to him carefully and smiled. It was a sad smile that seemed to say *I'm sorry* and *what have you gotten yourself into* at the same time. "When I spoke to her earlier." She motioned with her head again to Deanna, who was still watching the silent interaction with mounting interest. "I can't really explain it. I felt she wasn't whole. If that makes any sense."

It didn't, but he was interested. "Whole? How?" Martino's face crumpled in confusion. He wanted to shake the answers from Rhea. This was not the time to be cryptic.

The expression on Rhea's face told him she knew his thoughts, and she did. As part of Gail's family, Rhea was the last in the family bloodline to be born with the gift of telepathy. "Look, I only know what I felt. I just can't explain it. It reminded me of my sister, Renee. She always made me feel the same way."

"Maybe I should talk to her then."

"You're welcome to try. She's up on the hill. Second gravestone from the left." Rhea's eyes looked to the cottage briefly and then they dropped to her lap. "If this is a curse, it's one that has not only enslaved a soul but splintered it as well."

"How is that possible?"

Rhea shrugged, unable to formulate her thoughts into words. "Somehow this girl is connected to something or someone. Her soul . . . it's fragmented. I don't know if that's even what going on here. Just promise me something, Martino."

He stared at her, helpless and feeling lost at the same time.

"If you do figure this thing out, end it. Don't try to save anyone. Trying to save them only hurts everyone. You can't fix a splintered soul. Just end it." Rhea reached out and touched Martino's hand lightly. Then she sat back in her seat, and the window slid silently up into the door frame.

"You all right?" Abby was beside him, jingling Phillipe's keys in her right hand absentmindedly.

He jumped slightly. He'd forgotten she was even still outside.

"Ending it would solve everyone's problems. I'd trust what she says. Rhea's *Spidey senses* are usually dead on." She twisted her mouth as if to say Rhea was right. The Porsche sped down the driveway, stopping briefly near the lake and then continued on to the main road. Martino watched until the car's rear lights were no longer visible. *Just end it.* He knew what she meant but didn't want to face it. Ending it meant killing Deanna with Devin. Ending it meant he couldn't save her. Like he tried with Margaret.

He didn't even notice how choppy the usually calm lake waters had become.

A long sigh escaped his chest as he turned towards Deanna again. The look on her face said she heard Abby's comment and was putting two and two together regarding the silent conversation with Rhea. Her eyes, watery and red, were pulsing with rage that was building in her. Her lips were a thin white line, and her jaw was tight and square.

He'd seen it coming before it hit him, but Martino let the wine and glass that Deanna hurled hit him in the chest. Stopping it would have been impossible and trying to avoid it would only have made her angrier. He figured, let her hit me and get it off her chest.

There were no words – yet. He fully expected to be a verbal punching bag for the next several minutes. Until the sun rose, before he went back into the house, and then she would be talking to herself. He laughed at the prospect – quietly to himself, of course.

The humor of the situation was lost on Deanna and Devin alike. Martino could feel the tingle in his lower back again, but it was now burning and stinging as well. Devin was evidently as angry as Deanna, maybe more. The burning was painful and stronger than usual. All the arguing in the house tonight must have fueled Devin to a full tank of gas. But Martino took the abuse from Devin too. Might as well get it out of their system. Might as well take it out on Martino rather than someone who didn't deserve it like Gail.

Or Abby.

"Seems like it would solve your problems as well." Abby laughed, looking at the wine stain on his shirt as she opened the front door. "Come inside and get cleaned up."

Martino heard the dogs first. The horrible howling from inside the cabin. The sad mournful wailing like a banshee. The static in the air was uncomfortable, and he knew Devin was furious. He looked to Deanna as if to say *call Devin back,* but it was too late for words or even a single thought. Abby cried out in unison with the dogs. A painful heart-wrenching scream that echoed off the trees surrounding the property as her feet rose off the ground.

Her head twisted swiftly as her body was thrown across the hood of Phillipe's car. Abby's spine cracked like a tree branch, and the sound was horrifying. Martino rushed to her only to be thrown back. He hadn't felt hands on his body, just a wall of energy that surrounded Abby's battered body. Lifting himself to his feet, Martino watched helplessly as blood poured from her mouth and tears from her pleading eyes.

"Help her!" he screamed at Deanna. His voice trembled with anger. Deanna only turned and sat back down on the porch chair.

Another scream echoed above the chaos; it was Gail. Standing at the front door, watching helplessly as Devin impeded her exit from the cabin. Tears poured from her eyes as she held her hands up to an invisible barrier, pushing with all her might to escape. Beside her, Jordan held her, and Eric watched almost unemotionally as it all unfolded.

Again, Martino ran toward Abby. It appeared that dual barriers were too much for Devin's strength, even if he was at full capacity from the night's events. Martino threw his body against what he expected to be a solid obstruction, only to fall against Abby and the car with great force.

When he looked at her body, there was so much blood he couldn't stop it. It poured from every orifice. Her blood-stained tears covered her face; as she tried to speak, blood spit with every attempted word. Martino quieted her as he tried with great effort to move her. An earsplitting, blood-tainted scream exploded from her mouth as he pulled her body from the dented car.

"Abby," he whispered through his own tears. "I have to move you. We have to get inside. It's dawn." Her eyes moved over his face as more crimson tears streamed from the corners. The iridescence in her eyes was dim and clouded. Halted, gasping breaths escaped her as he laid her on the ground beside the car. "I have to. Please."

Her hand shook violently as she placed it on Martino's chest. She swallowed the blood in her mouth with difficulty like she had a sore throat. Again, her tear-filled eyes searched his face for some understanding; words quivered in her throat, sounding sodden and choked.

Martino knew what her eyes were saying to him, and he couldn't face it alone. He looked back to Gail, still trapped behind the barrier; he had never seen her look so lost. The sky was brightening, and the horizon showed the beginnings of sunrise. A small stitch of panic stabbed his chest. "Let them say goodbye. Please, Devin."

It took only seconds for Gail to reach them after the barrier disappeared. Her body collapsed beside Abby on the gravel, and Martino moved away to give her time to say goodbye. Gail gently wiped the tears from Abby's face and the blood from her mouth. Her fingers trembled as she brushed her hair from her forehead as she expressed her love over and over again in whispers.

"Gail, it's time to go." Jordan bent beside her and took her shoulders in his hands. Quickly, he took Abby's hand in his and touched it to his lips. Eric's goodbye was tearful but swift. He bent to kiss her lips and followed Jordan and Gail, urging Martino to follow.

In the house, Jordan held Gail as a croaking, guttural cry came from her body as the sun had fully risen, and Abby's final cry could be heard as the burning rays charred her flesh. Gail collapsed in his arms as he carried her to her room. As her body buckled in Jordan's waiting arms, Martino felt for Devin. The air was still, the static electricity that he had felt just before Abby's attack was gone, and even the usual tickle of his presence in Martino's back was non-existent.

The forlorn looks on everyone's faces was a puzzle to Martino. His sadness was over; he felt only rage. Rage toward Devin. Rage toward Deanna. *Just end it.* Those words were tattooed on the backs of his eyelids as he retreated to the basement rooms and fell into a restless daytime slumber.

CHAPTER TWENTY-FOUR

Left lying on her back on the cold gavel of the driveway, the pain in Abby's back is excruciating. Worse than anything she thought she was capable of feeling. Second only to the numbness weighing down her extremities. A sensation she hasn't felt since she was human, her legs feel like they are asleep, and she can only let them lie heavy on the ground, waiting for the painful tingles to accompany the blood flowing back into them.

But the tingles will never come. Her legs will never move again, neither will her arms. In moments she will be dead. Abby knows this and is slowly making her peace with it. The sky above her is starting to lighten. Through the potential rain clouds, the rays of the sun were burning away the darkness and replacing it with grays and yellows. So pretty, she thought.

Alone beside Phillipe's car, she tried to move her neck again. It didn't move and along with the pain (and lack of pain), Abby is visited by an old familiar friend. One she hasn't spoken to in decades. Fear. Fear of death. Fear of being alone. Dying alone.

When she first tried to move her neck, it was only to see Jordan dragging Gail from her side. She wanted to reach out to her, to call her name or at least turn her head to watch her go. But she couldn't. She could do nothing but hear Gail crying as she was all but carried into the house.

Martino held her hand. She saw him holding it but couldn't feel it. He looked angry and Abby couldn't get enough blood to her brain to reason why. Then it was Eric's turn to say goodbye and she felt his cool, dry lips on her skin. A single tear fell on her cheek from his eye and he brushed it away. Again, just like with Gail, she wished she could touch him.

Martino's goodbye was quick. He stood over her for a second looking down on her, looking angrier than she'd ever seen him. His eyes fell to the horizon and he was gone. No time for explanations, no time for a lifesaving transfusion.

The sun was almost up and soon it would creep over her body like little fingers of fire.

Fear, like an old friend, took her in its embrace. Alone.

Abby hoped against hope that the storm clouds or perhaps the shade of Phillipe's car – the car she wished she had taken for a spin after all – would protect her. Give her a few more precious moments to reflect on her life.

The sky was bright and as the storm clouds separated, she could see blue. Abby stared at it, trying to remember the last time she'd seen the sky any color other than black. Over a half a century.

It occurred to her as she stood on the precipice of oblivion that she would be almost eighty had she remained human. A good long life, she thought.

Ashes to ashes. The sun was peeking through the clouds now and she could feel the warmth of its rays as it crept up the driveway. Hope against hope, she thought, no rain today. Perhaps the shade of the car will protect her, and then she saw her arm, lying helpless beyond the car's shadow. Unprotected. It would start there. She knew it.

The long fingers of fire reached out for her, piercing holes in her white, almost pearlescent flesh. Helplessly, Abby watched as it crawled up her arms. She held her tongue as long as she could, tears pouring down her cheeks. Within seconds her arm was blackened and charred and when her chest became a furnace, she lost her silent battle and screamed until there was no face left to scream with.

Abby was dead.

CHAPTER TWENTY-FIVE

"Gail? Eric?" Sari walked in the back door of the cabin just after sunset. "You left the dogs out all day. Richard's gonna be pissed." She sang her words of warning to soften them, but Richard really would be pissed.

Attila and Thor raced into the cabin, following Sari to the food bowl. She searched through several cupboards before finding a large bag of dry kibble. A fleeting thought of Old Mother Hubbard grazed her mind as she fought the dogs for a space near the food bowl.

"Come on, guys, give me a break." She pushed them with her legs, edging her way between them as their nails scratched the wood floors. "Eat up." The time lapse between the food hitting the bowl and the dogs devouring it was about two minutes. With full bellies, they sniffed around the house for signs of life.

The basement door was open, and she could hear a movement, very subtle movement, but it was there. Sari bounded down the stairs, looking around the empty room, anxiously hoping to find Eric. The smile on her face quickly faded as she was greeted with an empty room. No candles lit, no fire. It felt empty like a tomb.

"Anyone down here?" Her voice was small like a frightened child. The movement she had heard from the kitchen returned and it was coming from Jordan's study, yet he had not answered her. The sound of her own footsteps was too loud for a reason she couldn't explain. Sari kicked off her shoes and walked toward the hallway in the back of the house.

Jordan was sitting in his usual chair, a book open on his lap, and a large brandy snifter full of blood stood untouched beside him. He was not reading, though. His eyes had a far-off gaze and he appeared to be deep in thought. The fingers of his left hand gently rubbed the center of his forehead as if to rub out a terrible headache or perhaps flatten the crease that was puckered between his brows.

"Jordan? Where is everybody? Is something going on?" Sari bit her lower lip and leaned on one leg nervously as she stood in the doorway of the study.

"Is something going on?" He repeated the words slowly and deliberately. "Gail is upstairs in one of the worst states I've ever seen. I've asked Eric to stay with her for a while so I may have a moment to think. And Martino is probably outside with Trevor." His answer was thorough but still enigmatic.

Sari stood in the door, leaning on the frame, waiting, hoping he would continue. But he did not. He simply lifted the book from his lap, placed it beside his untouched glass, and shifted his position on the leather chair. His eyes met hers and she hoped that he would continue, but the lost look said enough. It told her that Jordan was not the one to ask; usually he was the one with all the answers. But those glassy black eyes and the deep creases surrounding them spoke volumes all by themselves.

Back in the kitchen, she refilled two large water bowls for the dogs and gave them each a treat. The pounding of their tails echoed through the house, making it feel abandoned and creepy.

"Sari." Eric's voice was a welcome sound. Even after their fight at the party last night, she was so ready to fall into his arms, but he was clearly not in the mood for cuddling. "Can you please stay with Gail? I need to help Martino and Trevor. She's in her room."

His eyes were just as glassy and tired as Jordan's. They were bloodshot and red-rimmed with dark circles surrounding them, almost entirely. The feeling that hit Sari the hardest was that he looked lost – just like Jordan. Her first instinct was to protect him. She held out her arms and wrapped them around his neck. A tense, hesitant hug melted into a vanquished, desperate embrace. For several minutes, Sari held Eric, letting go only when he prompted it. The flutter of his breathing told her there was so much going on that she couldn't possibly imagine.

He gently kissed her lips and when he pulled away, she watched a tear trickle down his cheek. "Just sit with her, please." The front door opened and closed, and Eric disappeared so quickly that it was as if she had imagined the entire exchange.

At the top of the stairs, she stared down the darkened hallway. It was quiet, too quiet, and she was hesitant, afraid of what Gail might tell her when she entered her room. Gail's room was absolute darkness. No candles, nightlight, not even a digital clock illuminated the darkness. The electric blinds were closed and sealed off all possible light from the outside. Sari could hear talking from the front of the house, and a strong pang of curiosity was pulling her to the window.

As her eyes adjusted to the darkness, which they did incredibly well as a vampire, she could see a shape lying in bed. The comforter that usually covered the neatly made bed and had been in perfect place since Sari's first visit to Mount Orion was wrapped around Gail's body like a cocoon. Only the top of her head peeked out like a black beanie capping off a butterfly chrysalis.

A chair sat beside the bed right where Gail's head would be if it weren't encased in coverings. Sari walked as quietly as possible and sat beside the bed. Looking around the room, she marveled at how detailed her night vision had become. The picture frames with their ghosts of the Gail's past. The open jewelry box with gems rarer than Sari had ever beheld. The jars and bottles lining her dresser all sat motionless in the darkness.

The shape beneath the covers sighed. It was soft, not really a sigh as much as an audible exhale, like she had been holding her breath for a long time. Sari watched Gail as directed but listened to those one floor down, just outside her window.

"We can't make any decisions until we speak with Gail." It was Trevor. His authoritative tone was unmistakable. "And since she is temporarily unavailable, we can put her in the cottage."

Sari swallowed hard as she heard mention of the cottage. Put who in the cottage? Her eyes darted to the lump under the blankets. There was still no noise, but the lump began to tremble, and Sari knew Gail was listening to the conversation in the front yard too.

"Absolutely not," Martino adamantly protested.

"I agree. We don't want to upset Gail any more than she already is. There must be another option." Sari felt a chill run up and down on her skin. Eric was standing up to Trevor. It was a little arousing – she was ashamed to admit it and hoped Gail didn't hone in on that particular thought in her head.

"The only other option would be far more upsetting for Gail."

"What about the barn?"

"Very well." Trevor's voice was steady and calculating. "When Gail is up to talking about it – arrangements can be made then."

The word arrangements brought to mind funerals and picking out caskets. It also brought to mind her grandmother's funeral when she was a child. Her mother was a wreck, much like Gail except she was crying and screaming, not catatonic. Sari had gone with her father to choose the casket. Grandma requested that Sari help choose her finally resting home. Grandma: the word also brought images to mind. Images of a smiling face when there was none at her own house. The scent of pasta and meat sauce. The feeling of warm hugs and sounds of laughter. Grandma was a good word.

The word arrangements scared her into remembering Grandma in the casket looking plastic and fake, wearing the dress she hated and lipstick that she thought was too red. Arrangements meant someone was dead and needed to be "dealt with." *Let me go and deal with this,* she heard her father saying about the funeral home. *Can you just deal with my mother's body? My wife and I are in no state to deal with her ourselves.* At the time, Sari couldn't understand what it all meant. But now she knew it meant pushing Grandma into the ground, so they didn't have to *deal with her* any longer.

She straightened her back in the chair and shook the human problems from her mind. They were no longer her problems. They belonged in the past. Leave them there.

The voices were silent outside. They didn't come into the cabin and she didn't hear them leave. She figured they must have gone up to the cottage to do whatever it was they were doing. The lump hadn't moved at all since the talking stopped. Sari ran her hand over what she assumed was Gail's shoulder. As she sat back down on the chair, she could see an eye peeking out from between the folds in the blankets.

One small, bloodshot, teary eye peered out and Sari felt her heart stop for one brief moment. It was that eye coming to the surface like a submarine's periscope that confirmed Sari's suspicions. Someone was dead.

And from beneath the sheets and blankets, Gail struggled to free herself. Shifting this way and that, kicking out until the blankets were no longer a cocoon around her but simply draped over her small frame. The blankets rose as Gail lifted one arm and Sari thought she meant to rise. Words of protest rose in Sari's throat, stopped only by the realization that Gail was beckoning her under the covers.

There were no words as Gail nestled Sari in her arms, yet Sari felt she might cry. The strength of Gail's embrace seemed desperate and clingy. The sound of her silent crying was causing a deep stabbing pain in Sari's chest. Footsteps signaled the return of Trevor, Eric, and Martino from the barn.

"Phillipe is going to be pissed." Eric sounded like he was only making idle conversation.

"Can we hose this area off a bit?" Trevor asked. "No evidence. Yes?"

There was a muffled answer of agreement. The front door opened and closed.

"I'll go check on her." Martino's voice sounded stiff and false. Footsteps on the stairs stopped as Sari heard him thank Eric and Trevor each for their help.

"Send Sari down, will you? She should be told." Eric sounded exhausted.

She already knew someone had died. The only news would be who.

"Abby." Even in her grief, Gail easily read her thoughts. Her voice was gravelly and strained. "Abby is dead." She said it again as if confirming it to herself.

Now the how was a huge question weighing on Sari's mind. Not one to be answered by Gail.

She didn't know how to respond. She would miss Abby, that was certain, but whether it brought emotions of loss or desperation – she didn't know yet. She wouldn't know until that first time there was no one to call Martino out on his pain in the ass attitude or when there was no one to roll her eyes with as Jordan said something conceited and aggravating.

Would Sari cry when she sat on the porch and there was no one there to invite her out for *drinks*? Or would she cry thinking of how angry Deanna's human presence made Abby? What would set her off and how would she find a way to stop when the emotion began?

"Sari?" Martino's lilting accent rolled over the "r" in her name. "Eric is asking for you."

She waited, saying nothing, not moving and not even breathing. Leaving felt wrong. She closed her eyes, scrunching them tight, and buried her face into Gail's unnervingly warm neck.

"Go." A breath of a word. And a small kiss on her forehead. Gail's embrace relaxed, her hands ran up and down Sari's arms.

By the door, she reached for Martino's hand and squeezed it. Looking into his eyes was not what she expected. The lost, pitiful look that she had seen in Eric and Jordan's eyes was not present. Martino's brown eyes were glassy and moist yet hard and furious. Chills ran up Sari's spine and fear crept in beside the myriad of emotions that she was feeling right now.

"Thank you, dear." Gail sat up, still completely surrounded in blankets. Her hair was a wreck and she was wiping at the lake of tears that surrounded her eyes. "Go to Eric and hold him close tonight. Remind each other what it means to be in love."

Gail's words stayed with her as she descended the stairs into the living room. It was as empty as it had been an hour ago. In the kitchen, seated on the hardwood floor in a style that immediately reminded Sari of kindergarten – crisscross apple sauce – Trevor played roughly with Attila and Thor. He was growling as he teased them and dragged his long slender fingers through their dense coats. He looked up to Sari as his mouth pulled into an emotionless grin.

She didn't return the gesture and turned to go downstairs without a word.

A fire was blazing in the fireplace and Eric sat before it, staring at it like he was watching TV. *Hold him close tonight.* She heard Gail's words as she wrapped her arms around him and buried her face in his chest. It was then he explained to her in horrible detail what happened to Abby. The screaming, the blood, saying goodbye.

"Did Martino tell you who died?" Eric's voice was thick with emotion after his tale was finished.

"No, Gail."

"She spoke?" Jordan was suddenly in the room.

Sari nodded and smiled sadly. "Not much, but when Tino came in, she did."

Without another word, he flew towards the stairs and up to the third-floor rooms.

"What happened to Deanna?" She was almost afraid to ask.

Eric shrugged. "There was a blanket covering Abby's body, which I assume she provided. But she left this morning as far as we can tell. Cleaned out her room as well. Just don't mention her name to Martino. He's livid – actually, that may be too mild a word. The party, as they say, is over."

CHAPTER TWENTY-SIX

About the time Sari was discovering the horrors that Abby had to endure, Deanna was struggling to free her suitcase from the back of the closet. It was stuck. Trapped behind old shoes, Max's skiing equipment, and an old typewriter that belonged to her great grandmother. She never went anywhere so there was no reason for it to be accessible.

Except now she had to pack up her apartment, their apartment. Hers and Max's. It sat unused, unloved. Deanna had successfully avoided returning to the apartment for over a month now. And had it not been for Devin's cataclysmic mistake, when she found she had nowhere else to go, she would never have returned at all.

Driving from Mount Orion, in her second hour on the New York Thruway going south, she stewed over her options. There weren't many. The top options were: her parent's house where there were too many questions to answer, the apartment where there were so many memories, or staying with her friends where there would be the constant reminder that she had been lying to them for months. She had even contemplated going to Eric's apartment in the city. Sari's keys were in her purse. She put a pin in that option for further review after she had packed up everything from her life with Max.

Memories had won out. Better to be alone with her memories than to be badgered with questions from friends.

The apartment was dark when she first entered. It felt wrong to be there. The darkness said so. There was always a light left on, always a welcoming sign that she had come home. But no light and the room smelled stale like cigarette smoke. On the coffee table sat a full ashtray and four empty bottles of beer. The gang's final goodbye to Max, she guessed.

Max's school books were neatly stacked exactly where she left them after the funeral. It wasn't right; they should be spread all over the living room. Exams were in a few weeks. Max should be studying for them and Deanna should be pulling her hair out over the mess he was making.

He shouldn't be buried across town in the same cemetery they had been in less than four months ago.

A dull throb ached behind her eyes and Deanna checked the medicine cabinet for some aspirin. As she closed the mirrored cabinet, Deanna didn't recognize the face staring back at her. With the stress of the last twenty-four hours weighing down on her, she didn't remember who she expected to see. Was it Elizabeth with her high cheekbones and slender nose? Or perhaps Sophie with her plump face and full bow-like lips. Could she expect to see Gemma with her deep-set eyes and heavy, almost masculine, brow? Maybe Agatha? Dear Aggie, who was almost blind would never have been looking into the mirror at all.

The thought of Aggie was almost comical to Deanna. She remembered seeing only large blurry shapes. Sunlight – she loved sunlight. Its intensity made those blurry shapes more distinguishable. But mirrors were her enemy. In fact, her parents had removed them from her room when she was a child after she smashed them out of frustration.

Deanna remembered that frustration clearly. Sight was something she never took for granted ever again. Even with an eternal soul, human frailties plagued her. Devin was her salvation in those days. He was her eyes.

A stitch of pain caused her to flinch as if she had just received a shot from the doctor. *"Devin, where are you?"* she thought. He had not returned since last night and she was afraid that he had gone too far this time. Another stab of pain in her chest sent chills through her body and she breathed deeply.

Looking into the mirror now, she saw an exhausted twenty-three-year-old that had aged twenty years in the span of a day. Deep circles bruised her already pale skin, and lines cut into her forehead and around her mouth like she was carved from stone. The brown in her hair was dull and matted with pieces of ash littered throughout, pieces of Abby.

A burning tear slid down her face as she stared into the mirror. The tear cut a trail through the ash that had deadened her complexion. So much had gone wrong. So much. So quickly.

First there was Devin and his terrifying energy. He was so strong. Deanna knew that the negative energy that was building at the party had fueled him. She knew he was feeding off of it all night and yet she did nothing to stop it. It was her fault from the start.

Then Martino and Rhea had their private conference that infuriated her. It was clear from Rhea's gestures that they were discussing her. And Martino was believing her, all the lies she was telling him. He fell for them hook, line, and sinker.

Finally, Abby telling him to end it. It would be better if he'd just end it. Deanna could feel the anger in her rising now just remembering it. *Just end it.* Standing on the porch last night, she assumed it was Devin causing her anger, but it wasn't. He was with Abby. Listening.

He was silent for once. Silent and calm. The anger that was causing her heartbeat to race and the blood to pound in her ears, it was all hers. And the more she centered on those words, *just end it,* the louder the pressure in her ears sounded, and her vision was becoming blurry.

She could see the lake water was steadily rising. The dock by the lake had all but disappeared. The waves were submerging it and receding. Over and over again until it seemed the small body of water had a current of its own. Waves crested on the shore, pushing the upside-down rowboat farther up the hill.

The Porsche carrying Adrian and Rhea away from the cabin stopped near the lake. Deanna knew she needed to calm herself or they would return, maybe this time carrying their tales of doom to Gail. Thankfully the brake lights disappeared, and they continued on their journey away from the cabin.

It was then that Deanna felt Devin. He wasn't near her, but he had felt her anger. His energy was stronger than she had ever felt it, yet he kept drawing from her negative energy. The static in the air was tickling her nose, causing her eyes to tear and her hair to rise.

The rest was a blur. Abby's screaming, Martino's pleas for help, Gail's crying.

Now surrounded in boxes and empty suitcases, Deanna breathed deeply, trying to summon a positive thought through all the painful ones. *Breathe and breathe again.* She repeated it several times, hoping it would calm her muscles and unclench the knot forming in her stomach. It didn't work.

Be here now. Be here now. Repetition was key. *Be here now.* With her eyes closed, she reached for her clothes and threw them into the suitcase haphazardly. *Be here now. Come on, Deanna, be here now!* Not working. *Forget the past and be here now.*

Last night's sleep was a restless one. Bad dreams, fantasies of moving shadows, and strangely, she heard crying. At first, she thought it was a dream, but it continued well into her struggle with the suitcases and getting the supplies to start packing up the apartment. It wasn't in the apartment at all. She heard it at the supply store where she purchased cardboard boxes, markers, packing tape, and post-it notes. It was in her. The crying was coming from inside her.

Determined to finish the task, Deanna concentrated on her own belongings first. Clothes, books, CDs, DVDs, photo albums, jewelry. Some of it would come with her to wherever she found herself next, and the rest would find a home in a storage unit. Max's things were harder to separate. After avoiding his things for most of the morning, she wrote labels on three large boxes: **Garbage, Donate,** and **For John & Bobby**.

The **Garbage** box was filling quickly with school papers, hot rod and motorcycle magazines that Max refused to throw away himself, and random other trash that was not worth saving. **Donate** had mostly clothes that would never fit either John or Bobby. The last box was for John and Bobby to go through and keep whatever they wanted to save or use for themselves. Sports equipment, car models, a multitude of heavy metal biographies, and Max's massive collection of vinyl albums.

The only thing that Max owned that was worth any kind of money was his car, and that was destroyed in the wreck. Any insurance money went to his parents to help cover medical and funeral expenses.

As the apartment slowly emptied into cardboard boxes and Rubbermaid containers and Deanna made arrangements for the furniture to be picked up by Goodwill, sadness started to creep in, and her mantra was no longer working. *Be here now.* She tried, but thoughts of her short life with Max were becoming overwhelming. Somehow, packing up the apartment was harder than attending the funeral. Somehow more final.

She sat on the sofa and pulled a photo album from one of the bins she intended to keep. VACATION PHOTOS was printed across the front with a sunny beach with swaying palm trees and clear ocean water. Inside the book, however, the pages were filled with smiling faces of Max and Deanna everywhere except a tropical beach.

Their Florida trip was first. St. Augustine, Daytona, and Walt Disney World. Then trips with the gang to Atlantic City, surfing in California, and skiing in Vermont. Max had even driven a stock car in Dover, Maryland – the Monster Mile. Deanna ran her hand down one of the pages and felt peaceful for a moment. So many pictures of her and Sari laughing together.

A photo of the four girls, Maggie, Connie, Sari, and Deanna, on the beach in California made her smile. Bobby was photobombing them by popping up behind Maggie's head. Deanna Belamy's life was a good life, she thought. But now it was fucked up. Best to start all over again. Start from scratch; time to check out.

Her cell phone rang as she tossed the photo album back into the box and taped it shut. The final **Donation** box was also ready to be taped and moved to the front of the apartment. Filled with plates, glasses, mugs, and so much silverware, it was an extremely heavy box. Getting on her knees, Deanna pushed the box with all her might.

Again, her phone rang and she ignored it. Instead, she pushed the box with her hands and head and still was only able to shimmy it a few feet. Breathing heavily, she leaned on the box and pulled her phone from her pocket. Deanna nearly dropped her phone as she stared at the name in disbelief.

It was Sari. The photo showed an eighteen-year-old girl with bright pink spikey hair, dark eyeliner and shadow, with the brightest of smiles.

A shudder quaked through her entire body and she was unsure whether she could even press the green button to answer the call. It took all her nerve to find her voice to say hello.

"Sari?" Her voice caught and she couldn't say much more.

"Hi, D." It didn't sound like Sari. Her voice was barely more than a whisper and without much inflection at all. "Want to tell me your side of the story? Where are you?" Tough and to the point.

Deanna could tell Sari was not in the cabin. The wind was blowing, and she could hear the wind chime that hung on the dock at the lake. "I'm home back in Torry. Packing up. I thought I could stay here but it's way too hard." Her voice broke again. "I won't be here long. How's Gail?"

There was a long pause on Sari's end and Deanna knew that she was trying to figure out if she should be honest or polite. And then softly, "Not good. Jesus, D, what the fuck happened last night? Everyone is a mess. *Everyone.* Even Jordan and seeing him upset has got to be the freakiest thing for me. He's always so together, you know."

Deanna listened, not knowing what to say, or did she even care to comment at this point? Was it really worth it? She wanted to scream, *I don't care how this is affecting Jordan!* But she didn't and allowed Sari to continue.

"I have never seen Gail this upset. She's finally speaking, barely, but it's better than before. When Eric told me what went on, I thought he was joking. That this was some cruel form of hazing. *You* really need to tell me what happened. What set Devin off this time? I mean this is bad, really bad. Like no one is even mentioning your name. You're like Voldemort or something. I feel like if I say your name, I'll be attacked by Death Eaters." It was a joke but not a very funny one and Sari knew it.

"Listen, there's so much you don't know. So much I don't even know."

"Enlighten me." Sari sounded frighteningly like Gail all of a sudden.

Deanna stared around the empty apartment and decided not to fight with Sari. This was going to be the last time they spoke – ever. Better to be honest and kind. "I can't blame Devin entirely for this one. I got angry too and stuff started to happen that I couldn't control, and frankly, I didn't want to control. I let a lot happen that I shouldn't have. Listen, tell Gail I'm sorry. I didn't mean for any of this to happen." It was her intention to press the end button after that but found she couldn't do it.

"What are you saying? *You* killed Abby?"

"Yes. I'm to blame. I may not have killed her with my actions, but I'm no less guilty."

Sari was silent, trying to process the information she was just given.

"How's Martino?" Deanna's voice was surprisingly calm, but the fear of hearing the answer to this question was evident.

"What can I say; he's pissed. Furious! Like I'm afraid to be alone with him furious. I feel like he's going to blame me by association and if Eric wasn't with me, I'd be dead. I'm not even kidding about that. I can't wait for Bith and others to return just so he'll project his anger anywhere else but at me."

"I'm sorry. I'm sorry that you were touched by any of this. If I could turn back time, I would have not dated Max, and then you and I would never have met each other and he would still be alive too." She swallowed hard, suddenly wishing she hadn't packed up the glasses so she would have something to smash against the wall to alleviate the sadness and anger that she was feeling.

Again, there was an extended silence coming from Sari's end, and only the sound of the wind chimes tinkling could be heard through the phone.

"No," Deanna continued without waiting to hear what Sari was thinking, "I'm sorry I fucked up your life, but I wouldn't have traded your friendship for anything. I love you, you freak." Her chest was heaving and if Sari could see her, she would have told Deanna that she was an ugly crier and laughed. At least, she would have joked like that two days ago; now Deanna had no idea.

"No, you don't get to say that. Shit is going down here and you ran away without talking to me. You don't get to tell me you love me like it's goodbye, and what, just disappear?" Sari's voice was thick with emotion. "You're not just walking away from this mess. I want, no, I *expect* you to get your ass back here and clean this up!"

Deanna smiled to herself. That was as close to an *I love you too* as Sari was going to get. "That's not going to happen and you know it. I'm Voldemort, remember? I just killed Dumbledore. There's no way I'll ever be welcomed back into Hogwarts." She laughed through her tears.

"Did you even read those books?" Sari laughed and sniffled. "I'll work that out on my end. Where will you go now until things can be smoothed over at the cabin?"

"Well, to tell you the truth, I was going to stow away at Eric's old place for a while. Do you think he'll mind?" She tried to lighten the conversation, but it was hard.

"You've still got my keys, right? Yeah, I don't think he'll mind – I'll talk to him privately so no one else will know. He never goes there anymore." Sari paused and seemed distracted by something on her end. "I've got to go. Maybe I'll stop by soon and check on you." She was gone.

It took Deanna another full day to finish cleaning the apartment from top to bottom. She left the keys with the landlord and told him to expect Goodwill to pick up the donations in a day or two. Driving into the city was somehow calming. Although she had not actually said goodbye to Sari, the implication was there, and she knew Sari knew it too. The next time Sari saw Deanna would be when she found her lifeless body on the floor of Eric's apartment.

CHAPTER TWENTY-SEVEN

The common room was fairly empty. Sabina sat in front of the fire pit reading a book, and Gwen lounged across from her, staring at the flames. It was past the newbies' curfew so with Callie tucked safely away in her room, Gwen was free to relax. There were no words between the women, just calm tranquility. Tranquility that was about to be disrupted by anger and fighting. A regular occurrence in the last few days.

Down the hall, not far from the common room, voices could be heard. An argument that had begun somewhere farther away, probably in the tech wing, but it was getting louder and more heated as it reached the common room and its occupants that were trying to enjoy the last moments of silence and solitude before the sunrise.

"Who's leading all immortals?" Jacenta was ranting when she entered the room. She was in the middle of a heated discussion with Gabriel regarding whether she was capable of continuing to lead the ongoing and growing community of immortals. Her hands were flailing over her head as she walked through the door.

"You certainly are not!" Gabriel was hot on her heels, keeping up step for step and word for word.

Without looking to the others in the room or caring if their loud voices were disturbing anyone, she wheeled around to face him. "I'm not trying to. If you haven't noticed, I'm finding it hard enough keeping this place from collapsing in on itself."

"I beg your pardon?"

"I've read your emails and texts. I know what you and Thecia are planning. And don't pretend that taking steps to push me out is not part of your grand scheme."

"Uh oh, something's about to hit the fan." Sabina put her book to the side, exchanging a worried look with Gwen. Both were preparing themselves to spring into action.

Gabriel ran his hands through his hair. It looked as if he had acquired a few more grays since Jacenta came to visit. "Let me get this straight. You hacked into my private, very personal correspondence, misunderstood everything that you read, and are now holding me accountable for your stupidity? Typical."

It wasn't clear which one got to her feet first, but Sabina and Gwen jumped up before Jacenta could react with a proper response that was due after being called stupid. Their movements were so swift that they almost collided trying to get across the room to separate Jacenta and Gabriel.

"OK, enough." Sabina held Jacenta by the shoulders. She could feel the vibration as Jacenta trembled with anger. "Can we please call a truce? The two of you have been fighting for days. If it's not one thing, it's another."

She could feel that if she let go of Jacenta's shoulders, she would fly at him.

"Am I hearing things, or did he just call me stupid?" Jacenta said as if Sabina hadn't spoken a word.

"What do you call admitting your crimes and then your inability to comprehend that crime? Stupid!"

"Stop calling her that! And what unforgivable crime has she committed, exactly?" Gwen was standing beside Gabriel, hoping her presence would stop his rants. It didn't.

"I didn't steal those emails or hack into anything. Roderick gave them to me. He thought we could work together. Now if you want to talk about stupid . . ."

"Wow, you both sound like you're four years old. Can we stop using that word? Now sit! Both of you." Sabina let go of Jacenta's shoulders, still unsure if she would attack; she felt that the sudden burst of anger may have sedated the others for the moment. "Now speak. One at a time. Like adults. And if you can't handle that, we're going to lock you in a room together and see which one makes it out alive."

Gwen snickered behind her hand.

She motioned to Gabriel to begin.

"Thecia and I are not trying to push you out." His words sounded like he had carefully selected them.

Sabina nodded, good start.

"Did you know we have a history? Thecia and I?"

"She told me." His eyes were cold and unfeeling as he spoke.

Jacenta nodded. She wasn't making eye contact and was still visibly angry. "If there are any further correspondence with any Haven, it needs to come from me. Fair enough?"

This time Gabriel nodded. "May I go now?" He looked to Sabina, who smiled warmly at him.

His exit was swift and without ceremony. Gwen followed him out, leaving Sabina with a quick humorous, exasperated expression. Sabina shook her head and laughed.

A few minutes passed before the silence between the two women was broken. Sabina had hoped that Jacenta would tell her on her own that it was Devin causing all of this trouble, but she didn't. Devin had been back for more than a month and had not left Jacenta's side for a moment. It was clear that she was being emotionally drained by his presence but was refusing to speak about it. Now was the time for things to change.

"So," she started slowly, "what is he doing here?"

"Apparently, he's conspiring against me." Jacenta's jaw was clenched and her cheeks puffed out like a child pouting when she didn't get her way.

"Not Gabriel. Devin."

Jacenta didn't answer. Her eyes searched the room, actively trying to avoid Sabina's accusing gaze. "He's using me to avoid his problems with Deanna."

"What's new? Look, *he's* your problem here, not Gabriel. You didn't argue this much with Gabriel until Devin came back. In fact, I thought you were starting a relationship of sorts."

"But Devin's causing the issues. He's causing your anger. True, it doesn't help that Gabriel has a temper and will react to just about anything you throw at him. It also doesn't help that you are attracted to him and, frankly, jealous of everything he does without you." She searched Jacenta's face for agreement. It was tattooed on her face. "It also doesn't help that Devin refuses to allow you to love anyone but him."

Sabina waited for both their reactions. Jacenta's and Devin's. Nothing came from either. "Your issues with Thecia are your own. I can't or won't advise you on that. But letting the war go and the problems that came with it is a good start." She took a deep breath and extended her hand. "I want you to stay with me tonight. In my rooms. Devin knows better than to enter my dwelling. You can get a better rest than you've had all month."

Jacenta took her hand and kissed it gently. "Thank you."

"Tomorrow, we'll discuss everything else."

The next night, Jacenta was sitting alone in the tech wing, trying to follow the dozens of email communications between Gabriel and the many Havens he had already reached out to. She could feel Devin beside her. He hadn't spoken yet, but his silence was worse than his ranting.

Slipping out of Sabina's room proved easier than she thought it would. When Jacenta awoke, she was alone and free to roam on her own. She had been sure that Sabina would be watching over her the whole night. Now, she continued to read the sometimes-incoherent messages between two vampires that were clearly uncomfortable with the format of communication. In a folder on the table before her, Roderick had printed out some text communication from Gabriel's phone. The emails were from all over – Portland, Dallas, London, but the contraband texts were mostly between Gabriel and Thecia.

Sabina, God love her, was right. Jacenta was jealous. She hated Thecia and had for centuries, but that wasn't the problem. The real problem was Gabriel. She still didn't completely trust him and at the same time found herself unwilling to admit why.

Whatever the problem, they still needed to find a way to work together. Jacenta knew that if she finished reading the emails, she'd have a better, clearer understanding of Gabriel's true vision. Not the vision that Devin had been using to cloud her mind.

Thecia's exact location had not been established in the texts. Quickly, she drew a large question mark at the top of the page and wrote "Where?" beside it. It was dangerous to know where Thecia called home these days. Paying her a visit to settle an old score was not out of the question, especially now that Devin was constantly getting under her skin with old memories.

"Stop it!" she said aloud. Looking around, several other immortals stared back at her from their cubicles. "*I need to concentrate, and you are not helping with that.*"

"*What am I doing, my love?*"

"*You know damn well that you are affecting my judgement. Now go away.*"

The negative energy around her diminished and she continued to read the papers in her hand.

There were pages of flirtatious banter cloaked as Haven business. And for reasons she didn't care to admit, Jacenta's jealousy was escalating. He said he'd visit Thecia within the month. That was well over two months ago. Had he visited her while Jacenta was in Connecticut?

"*Stop hovering and speak, if you must.*" She tore her eyes away from the sheets of text messages.

"*Is that the turncoat Thecia? That was how many years ago? Three hundred?*" It felt like Devin was looking over her shoulder.

"None other," she mumbled and turned the pages over on the table. Now he was playing dumb, like he hadn't heard her argument with Gabriel last night. "*So, what's with you?*"

"*This world is getting smaller by the minute.*"

"*Why? Who else have you run into?*" So many names ran through her head, too many that she was sure she'd not want to speak to again. Much like Thecia. How did she come to run a Haven, especially without Jacenta's knowledge? Finding out which Haven had fallen into the clutches of this vile being was first on her agenda, then finding out what exactly existed between Thecia and Gabriel.

Devin chuckled at her jealousy. *"So many lovers for you. So many."*

"Stop being so damned mysterious and spit it out. Talk. Tell me the awful truth about Deanna and what she did to you this time. Maybe it will cheer me up." She laughed and closed her laptop. No more work – it was more fun to gossip with Devin.

"I wish there was gossip to share." He read her thoughts easily as always. *"I fear this time I've let my emotions carry me too far."*

What else is new? she thought. Trying to protect her thoughts and trying not to laugh at the same time was extremely difficult. "So, what'd you do?" Finally, Devin might actually be ready to spill what horrible incident had led him to her this time and for so long. She was practically dancing in her seat with anticipation. He'd never stayed away from Deanna for so long without good reason, and he showed absolutely no signs of leaving anytime soon.

"There you are." Sabina came up from behind her. She pressed her lips to Jacenta's head. "All alone tonight?"

Jacenta turned and scanned the room. She was unaware that sometime during the evening the room slowly emptied out. "Trying to finish up this paperwork. And then Devin started to open up a bit. So, if you don't mind." She tipped her head to the left, hoping Sabina would get the hint and leave. She didn't.

"I can't hear him. Spill away. I want to read some of this top-secret correspondence." She pulled the laptop toward her and turned it back on. "Let me guess? Your password is something to do with Eric."

Jacenta nodded and stared at her.

"Are you going to give it to me?"

"If I do, can you please take the laptop into another cubicle? ERIC1666." Eric's rebirth year.

Sabina smiled as she typed the characters into the computer. "It would be nice to see him again. Don't you think? Still no clue where he is?"

"How would I know? I told you he's gone like smoke."

"He's in New York," Devin said. Like he was telling her the time of day. *He's in New York. It's 11:15 p.m.*

"What?"

"What?" Sabina was suddenly interested.

"Devin said he's in New York. How do you know that?" She spoke to both at the same time.

"He's with Deanna." Again, without much feeling. *It's sunny and 70 degrees.*

"WHAT?"

"Hey, your eyes are bulging. What did he say?"

"He's with Deanna. Eric — my Eric — is with Deanna. How the hell did that happen?"

"You didn't lose another man to her, did you?" Sabina teased.

"She's trying to break the curse with help from your kind." His tone was full of disdain, not so matter-of-fact now.

"That won't work," Jacenta said under her breath. She repeated what Devin said to Sabina and cringed a little, hoping he wouldn't notice.

"Oh, he needs to spill it all. Go on, translate. Start from the beginning, Devin." Sabina closed the laptop again and sat up straight in her chair, waiting for the hottest gossip she could possibly imagine.

Like turning a spigot, he spoke uninterrupted for almost an hour. The only other sound in the otherwise empty room was Jacenta translating what he was saying to Sabina and adding her own commentary. He started with breaking out of Lizzy's Restaurant and Hotel, seeing Eric with other vampires, searching the restaurant. He told them how he tried to scare them away. Then when he found Deanna again. He told them about her human friends and Martino. Eric's relationship with Sari came next and then Deanna meeting her mother from the past and how she was going to help break this unbreakable curse.

Max's death and Devin's ability to possess humans and animals was particularly interesting to Sabina. She had never considered that he would be able to take over another's body. But there would be plenty of time for questions after the tale was told. Finally, he explained what happened to Abby and why he could never return to Deanna.

"Holy God. That's more than I anticipated learning when I woke up this evening." Jacenta laughed. "Where in New York exactly? City or state? Why haven't the scouts detected them?"

"They're so inexperienced. If they are hidden away somewhere, the scouts wouldn't know where to look," Sabina said.

"It's a large piece of property. Gail calls it Mount Orion. Deanna adores it and always has," Devin explained further. *"Eric lives there with Sari. She's his first, I believe."*

Jacenta was silent for a while after reiterating what Devin had said. Eric's first child. She wanted to meet her. To know why he loved her. To know why he chose her.

The story was enthralling Sabina. She couldn't imagine a coven of vampires hidden in plain sight without a hint of detection from the scouts. Over the last few weeks, while Jacenta spent her time arguing with Gabriel, Sabina was spending her time with Roderick. He was filling her in on his side of this operation called Haven. Gabriel was the dreamer, but Roderick was the doer. Recruiting and getting the word out that there was a safe haven for any immortal that needed it.

The scouts travelled in quadrants close to their facility not more than a hundred miles in any direction. They were trained to meet others and share experiences. There were rumors of a band of older vampires travelling the east coast – mostly the northeast – but their age frightened off most of the scouts. No one had gotten close enough to make an identification of any of them. The only thing she was sure of that tied all the rumors together was that they travelled in the company of two large dogs.

Roderick was aware of the drawbacks of his scouts, and it was primarily that they were young and inexperienced. Training would do them a world of good, but there were few that had the time or the patience to take on such a task.

Sabina thought of the trackers the Council had utilized to catch rebels during the wars. They were young but well-trained and afraid of nothing. She had trained them well. Taking them out of their comfort zone, out of their environment. They were trained like wolves. Taught to trust their instincts and not their thoughts. It had taken less than a month to turn out three of the best trackers the Council had ever seen, and the Rebels would live to fear. Perhaps she should offer her services to Roderick while she was here, she thought.

"Do you think I should go?" Jacenta whispered, returning Sabina's thoughts to the present time.

"I can see that you want to, but you do have commitments here. After this girl's death, this Abby, where did Deanna go?" she spoke into the air to Devin.

"He doesn't know. He left immediately and hasn't returned." Jacenta paraphrased his lengthy response. "I really think it's time to face her. But I can't leave this to Gabriel. I can't . . . I've got to sort this mess out first. As soon as I know Haven is secure, then I'll go."

"Go where?" Gabriel entered the room like a celebrity on the red carpet. He was sporting what Devin would call vampire casual attire. A simple tailored pair of black pants with silk shirt and maroon vest. He looked quite stunning.

Jacenta thought fast. "Home. As soon as all of this is worked out, I'll go home. Callie is thriving here. At least I think so; I haven't seen her lately." She laughed uncomfortably.

His eyes looked distrustful, but whatever thoughts he had he kept to himself.

"It's midnight and I'm sure you've been staring at that small computer screen for hours. Come, sit with me and we'll talk through these problems we've been having. I am tired of fighting as I hope you are too. Sabina, you are welcome to join us, of course." He offered his hand to Jacenta.

"No, I wouldn't dream of interfering in your peace talks. I have some things to discuss with Roderick, so I'll leave you. And bid you goodnight." As she leaned in to kiss Jacenta's cheek, she whispered that she should do something to ensure Devin's departure.

Jacenta did.

They were in his study surrounded by blueprints and scale models of buildings that could be the future of Haven if Jacenta would only stop being so pigheaded. Those were Gabriel's words and that was when the peace talks ended, and the argument began, as usual. This time, however, it was stopped by a sudden jolt to her system that knocked Jacenta off her feet. It was a pain that she hadn't experienced – ever. Unlike the familiar tug that she associated with Deanna's birth and the stabbing that came with her departure, it was almost a blending of the two. A pump in her heart with a blinding intense jab that took her breath.

"What is it? Are you all right?" Gabriel was at her side, completely forgetting that they were in the middle of their usual heated discussion regarding Haven.

"Fine. Just something unusual." She exhaled and felt again for the pain. It was gone, almost as quickly as it had come.

He wrapped his arms around her waist and carried her to the nearest seat. Beside her chair was a small model constructed out of balsa wood that looked strangely similar to the Haven she had started in Amsterdam centuries ago but had burned to the ground by the Council during the Wars. She studied it as Gabriel pulled a beautiful crystal decanter from his bottom desk drawer.

"Drink," he said, pouring the red liquid into an equally beautiful crystal glass.

"I'm fine. Really. I have these episodes every once in a while." She laughed and rubbed her head to clear her mind of the uncomfortable thoughts that were running through it now. Thoughts of Deanna and if she was alive. Thoughts of whether she should tell Devin of her fears, and strangely there were thoughts swimming around about the Council's outrage and burning of the Haven in Amsterdam and how she and many others had almost burned to death. Too many thoughts.

"Don't fuss, drink. It's not the good stuff but it will suffice." He pushed the glass into her hand and watched her take her first sip. "Now tell me what happened. You said this has happened before?"

Jacenta nodded, keenly aware that his hands were rubbing her thighs. She didn't really want to discuss it, but knowing Gabriel wasn't one to be waved away, she continued. "Not often but yes. It's usually a tug or stabbing pain in the center of my chest. But this was somehow different and completely unexpected."

"Are there tell-tale signs that an episode is coming on?" His concern was almost so heart-warming that Jacenta could not believe she ever allowed herself to be angry with this man. His hand went to her face, tugging at the skin below her eye. He checked both eyes the same way and didn't remove his hand from her face after he was finished.

"Usually."

Usually, Deanna was old and would suffer heart attacks or strokes before the end. Those would come in the form of light tremors that were easily ignored, but Jacenta always knew that the end was near and she should prepare herself for the pain – both physical and emotional – of losing Deanna again.

"Do you know what causes it? It's quite unusual for our kind to feel pain except in battle or death and even then, it's minimal. Or so I hear." He laughed.

Jacenta smiled and looked at him. She enjoyed him like this. Caring, playful, relaxed.

"Better?" He saw that her glass was empty. Taking it from her, Gabriel fluffed a few pillows and urged her to lie down. Jacenta did as she was told and watched as he pulled a throw from a nearby chest to cover her. "Rest and if you don't mind, I'm going to take a blood sample just in case."

"It won't tell you anything. It's not physiological. It's metaphysical." Her mouth twisted into a half smile and half *here's-where-you-think-I'm-crazy* expression.

"So, you do know what causes it."

CHAPTER TWENTY-EIGHT

As Jacenta and Gabriel were resuming their peace talks following her episode, Gail knocked on Eric's New York City apartment door. The apartment felt empty when Gail opened the door. She had knocked three times but there was no answer. After knocking, she felt around in her pocket for the set of keys Eric had given her. Three keys on a simple silver metal ring. Front door, back door, and the storage unit.

Eric had simply handed her the keys with absolutely no offer to come with. This was a one-man operation, he said, with a great chance of crying and yelling. No thank you.

Gail laughed.

It was the first time in almost two months that she even wanted to laugh. And it felt wonderful. The pain of Abby's death was slowly subsiding, being replaced by memories. In the first few days, there was only blinding pain. Every fiber of her body ached when she tried to move, and speaking was such a struggle that she had said as little as possible. Jordan tried everything to break her out of her spiral. Nothing worked.

As the days went on, the pain was replaced by a dull nagging ache deep in her heart. Sari had suggested that she keep a journal of anything she could remember about Abby. Years of therapy had taught Sari that most grief counselors believed that the pain was caused by fear of losing your grip on the one you lost.

Abby memories led to Martino memories and almost an entire book of Jordan memories. Then there were memories of her human parents, husband, and children. Those fading thoughts led her full circle back to the reason she was keeping the journal in the first place – Deanna and the mess she caused.

But it wasn't Deanna that had led her to Eric's New York apartment. It was Martino. While Gail got better, Martino was getting worse. The anger that was building in him was horrible. He rarely talked to anyone and when he did, it was sarcastic and heated. Sari was becoming the target of most of his rage. She was the easiest target. Deanna's best friend, the youngest vampire that couldn't fight back and worst of all, she knew where Deanna was and wasn't telling anyone.

It was Jordan that had convinced Gail to reconnect with Deanna. Perhaps some closure would solve everyone's issues with her. Now standing in the doorway of Eric's apartment, Gail was feeling a little bit more than apprehensive.

She had never visited Eric's apartment. Never needed to. This was how he stayed close to Sari until she came to live at Mount Orion. How he appeared normal before she knew what he truly was. It was funny to Gail that Deanna would end up here. Going from one lair to another.

The key slid in easily and she opened the door. With the door still open, Gail stood in the foyer. The smell in the apartment was unusual. There was a faint trace of Eric's cologne mixed with an even fainter human scent. Not a good human scent; this smelled spoiled. The scent struck her as bitter or even a bit sour like garbage that is going bad but had not turned completely yet. It made Gail stop and listen, rather than smell.

She heard something but couldn't put her finger on what it was. Shuffling? Dragging? A shuffling drag? Maybe. Then she knew she heard a distinct thump like a bag of mulch being dropped on the roof. Or perhaps a human body falling to the floor? The overall feeling of the apartment told her that she was alone, but somewhere deep within she could hear a heartbeat. It was weak but still there.

The phone in her pocket vibrated as she stood listening to the slow heartbeat. Sari's picture was on the screen as she pressed the green answer button. Without saying hello, Gail whispered, "I need you."

Waiting in the lobby of Eric's building, Sari didn't bother to answer. She didn't need to. The sound of Gail's voice and the circumstances she was walking into told Sari that things had gone from bad to worse and asking a lot of stupid questions would only slow down the process. Taking the stairs and not the elevator was better than having to count the floors as they dinged by in the elevator. As she took her first step into the apartment, she stopped short, nearly knocking Gail to the floor.

"Oh shit! You scared me! Why are you looming in the door . . .?" Sari stopped when she caught wind of the scent permeating the entryway. "You don't think?"

Gail watched as the elevator of Sari's usual peppy personality plummeted from the top floor to the basement within seconds. She put her hand gently on Sari's arm. "No, not yet. She's alive. Just barely, but alive."

"Is he here?"

Gail shrugged, not wanting to speak of Devin. The name would only bring back the pain of Abby's death. The death he caused.

"Have you walked around at least?" Sari was sounding antsy.

Again, Gail silently answered, this time with a gentle head shake.

With an audible huff, Sari pushed passed Gail and literally followed her nose. Gail followed close behind cautiously, expecting a bloodbath. Down the small entry hallway, Sari turned left, feeling completely comfortable with her surroundings, and the entire apartment opened up before them. The walls were brick with several large floor to ceiling windows looking out on to the night sky and cityscape. The living room, kitchen, and dining area were spread out before them, all facing a large gas fireplace. Gail walked around the centered open staircase and looked into the loft above them.

The scent was stronger as they approached the staircase. At the foot of the stairs was a pool of vomit that was speckled with blood and looked as if someone had been dragged through it and up the stairs.

"D? Deanna?" Sari called out. Her voice was anxious and tense. "Deanna, answer me."

Gail nodded that she was sure Deanna was in the loft. Whether she was willing to be the first to climb the stairs was another story. Both women paused and exchanged a look like they were terrified of what they were inevitably going to find.

Sari took the first step and then another and finally she found her panic was good fuel for her forward motion. She took the stairs two at a time, almost flying to the top. The stairs led to Eric's office and farther up to the roof deck. But she never made it to the roof. She found Deanna's lifeless body lying behind Eric's desk still clutching a medicine bottle.

"No, no, nononono!" she cried as she pushed the large leather chair out of the way. Sari slid on her knees to Deanna's unconscious body. The cami she wore was soaked through with either sweat or vomit, probably both, and her sweatpants had streaks of vomit stains from her knees to her ankles. With two years of CPR training that she had never needed to use until today, she checked Deanna's pulse and breathing, hoping she would not need to start chest compressions. Both were shallow and faint but still there; a good sign but not great.

When Gail reached the top step only seconds after Sari, a few things were determined. "She took my leftover Percocet. From my wisdom teeth. She's still breathing." Quickly, Sari took Deanna by the shoulders and called her name several times. She shook her roughly. Deanna's eyes rolled under her closed eyelids and her breathing sputtered, but she did not regain consciousness.

"How many were in here?" Gail held the empty medicine bottle. "How many?"

"I don't know. Almost the whole bottle, I guess. They made me dizzy. I only took one or two." Sari searched her pockets for her phone.

"What are you doing?" Gail slapped the phone to the floor.

"Calling 911. What do you think?" Sari reached for the phone again. "She needs an ambulance."

"No, she doesn't. We are all she needs." Gail stared at Sari for a moment and then pulled the sleeve up on her sweater. Quickly and without much preparation, she slashed the center of her forearm with her thumbnail.

"NO! You'll kill her. Worse, you'll make her like that other one . . . Margaret. She's like a zombie or something, isn't she? No, you're not doing this. Just let her die or let me call 911, for God's sake!" Sari screamed. Pulling Deanna's lifeless body close to her own, she was protecting her from Gail and getting Deanna's vomit all over herself. "Don't. Just let me call 911, please."

"I'm not going to turn her. You drank my blood. Remember how it made you feel? It will help her heal. Speed up the process a bit. But if we don't do it now, we will definitely lose her. I have no idea what those painkillers will do to her brain. So, release her and let me do this."

Gail gently brushed Deanna's hair back from her face and kissed her forehead. "It will be fine, baby. Just drink." The gash on her arm was barely visible, covered in blood. She pressed her wounded arm against Deanna's mouth and waited for her to accept the offering. Deanna didn't move. Again, her eyes rolled as her head pivoted on her neck. "Open her mouth a little."

Sari pulled Deanna's lower lip down until her mouth gaped in a codfish kind of way.

Gail pinched the wound on her arm and winced. Blood dribbled out into Deanna's open mouth. "Drink, baby, drink," she pleaded. It was slow and felt like a newborn finally finding the nipple on its mother's breast, but Deanna started to drink as Gail cradled her in her arms.

Her dark brown hair was dull and lifeless as Gail smoothed it back and Deanna drank the blood. The drinking became more of a sucking and Gail knew she had had enough. Pulling away from Deanna's grip proved to be more of a trial than anticipated. Her jaw was locked and her lips were suctioned onto Gail's arm.

"Pull her back."

"D, let go. Let go."

A loud suction breaking noise followed as Deanna was torn free from the healing fluids that ran through Gail's veins. The effects were slow. First, her eyes opened and she looked around, dazed and disoriented. It was clear that she was having a hard time focusing on any one object. Her hazel eyes rolled in her head again and she fought for focus, blinking over and over.

"Welcome back, baby." Gail smiled. "Do you know who I am?"

"Mother." Her voice was soft but raspy.

Gail laughed and cried at the same time. She wasn't ready to lose another person she loved. Not yet. "How do you feel?"

"Strange. Like I'm floating. Am I floating?" she asked.

"That'll last a few days." Sari rolled her eyes and snickered.

"What happened?"

"Looks like you tried to check out early." Sari held the empty bottle of Percocet in Deanna's face.

Deanna looked into her lap but didn't respond.

"Why?" Gail asked.

"Why here?" Sari pulled herself up on to her feet with the edge of Eric's desk.

Still not looking directly at Sari or Gail, Deanna said, "I was trying to get to the deck. Figured if nobody found me, at least I wouldn't make the whole building wretch." Her words were followed by a small shrug and an ironic snicker.

"Didn't quite get there, did you?"

Deanna looked to Sari. The look they exchanged was clear that they were both glad she hadn't checked out so soon.

"Why?" Gail asked again, this time taking the pill bottle from Sari and throwing it into Deanna's lap. "Answer me. Why end it now?" Her tone sounded very maternal.

Deanna got to her wobbly feet without looking at Gail and walked down to the living room, clutching the banister and half dragging her unsupportive legs as she did. She covered her mouth and nose as she passed the puddle of vomit at the bottom of the stairs.

"Deanna, don't walk away from me. I expect an answer. Were you trying to completely throw me over the edge? Abby wasn't enough. Let's have Gail find my dead body too. Is that what you were thinking?" She was ranting but couldn't help herself. Two months of emotions that had been bottled up were spilling over like a shaken bottle of Coke.

"I'll just go into the bedroom and give you guys some privacy." Sari slipped out of the room without another word.

"What were you thinking?"

"What do you care? I haven't heard from you in almost two months. I just figured better to start over somewhere new. Get rid of this body and start again." She breathed deeply. "Wow, I need to walk around. My heart is racing."

"Just don't fight it. And I do care. I have always cared." She held Deanna's face in her hands. "I lost Abby. Probably one of the most painful experiences of my life, ever. I didn't know how to go on."

"I know. I'm sorry. I really am. I just couldn't lose everything. You, Martino, Devin. All gone." Deanna pulled away from Gail's touch.

"Devin?"

"I haven't heard from him since the night it happened. He's gone." She collapsed on the sofa and looked up to Gail with tears in her eyes. "Be careful what you wish for, right?"

Taking Deanna in her arms, Gail held her tight. Tighter than she would have normally held her, but since taking the blood, Deanna had at least one full day of unbelievable strength protecting her. Tears poured down as they held each other, and Gail couldn't help but be reminded of the night she held Elizabeth after her father died. Holding her daughter in her arms, crying and feeling the loss of Virgil so deeply that she could barely remember how to breathe.

"Promise me you won't try this again."

"It's over. This dream of breaking this damn curse. Without Devin, I'm stuck here. And without Martino, I'm stuck here alone." Deanna started to cry softly at first and then soul-emptying tears poured out of her as if she had never cried in her life. The hazel in her eyes turned steadily into a deep mossy green that was darkening as she cried.

Gail could see rain clouds accumulate faster than she ever thought was possible. The sound of thunder clapped somewhere in the distance and the rain pelted the wall of windows.

"It's not over until it's over. Right?" Gail held her and laughed. "There must be a way with or without Devin. Martino, however, is a very different story. I'll need reinforcements to work with him. But we'll do it. Trust me."

Deanna laughed through her tears. The rain slowed as she settled down and she watched as the rivers of water running down the windows evaporated.

"Everything cool?" Sari was wiping her arms with a towel as she entered the room.

Deanna nodded. "What's with the towel?"

"Well, you screwed up the plumbing or something. The tub was full, so I was trying to drain it and then it started to bubble and some crazy whirlpool thing happened. The water finally went down but only after it stopped freaking out. The bathroom's soaked. Maybe I should call a plumber before Eric finds out."

"I'll take care of it." Deanna wiped the tears from her face. Her eyes were hazel again. "I'm the one who caused it after all." She smiled and looked to Gail. Gail only looked at her with quiet observation, somewhere deep inside knowing that Deanna *did* actually cause the tub to overflow.

CHAPTER TWENTY-NINE

"Jordan, you don't need to be here." Martino's voice was calm but sounded strained as if he were biting his tongue as he spoke. He was – not literally – and Jordan knew it. He was holding back the many thoughts that Jordan could easily read. So many hateful, disparaging thoughts regarding Deanna and Devin and even Gail.

"Believe me, this is the last place I wish to be this evening." Jordan didn't hold back his annoyance at all. "However, for the sake of Gail's sanity and in the interest of getting all this business over and done with, I have begrudgingly agreed to mediate."

Martino was pacing now as Jordan watched him comfortably from his window seat where he could easily see Deanna's approach. His legs were comfortably crossed, and he reached for his goblet of blood. It was animal blood from what Gail jokingly called the finest vineyards on Mount Orion. The stores would have to appease him for now; later he knew only the hunt would release the tension this encounter would inevitably cause.

Outside the forecasted snow had begun its slow descent from the leaden clouds. Not much in the way of accumulation was expected, maybe four or five inches, but enough to slow Deanna's arrival – which would also slow his escape out of this torment of mediation. Jordan was not a good mediator; he never had been. His strong suits were accusation and punishment. Hearing testimony bored him, and he could feel his otherwise comfortably crossed legs start to twitch with the need to leave.

"Where is she?" Martino turned toward him quickly.

Jordan didn't answer. He wondered the same thing but refused to allow Martino the pleasure of his growing agitation. On the table in front of him sat a two-day-old newspaper that he pulled toward him and began to scan with his eyes. He wasn't reading, just distracting himself from the impending torment of mediation.

From the corner of his eye, Jordan spied a silver Prius making its way gingerly down the snow-dusted gravel road. He could already feel Deanna's apprehension and taste the tears that were saturating her face. Gail explained Deanna's condition as a "delicate emotional state" and that Jordan should be "patient and understanding." He wasn't sure if he could do it.

The heavy clouds were lower than they were only moments before – Jordan was sure -- and a squall had kicked up as Deanna's car approached the cabin. The flurry of snow had grown significantly in the last few minutes and it looked like they could be looking into the face of a blizzard.

When Deanna's car skidded to a stop in the driveway beside Eric's Lexus, he could see she was well prepared for the coming snowstorm, small as it was. A heavy, white, quilted coat covered her body almost completely, giving her the look of an enormous walking marshmallow. Her boots were massive hiking snow boots and made it difficult for her to negotiate the simple path to the front door without stumbling several times.

Her dark hair pushed out the sides of her hood as Jordan watched her hazel eyes scan the front of the cabin before entering. He thought she looked helpless and childlike in that one instant. He found he wanted, against his better judgement, to protect her and enfold her in his arms. For that he blamed Gail for getting into his head.

It was then just before her hand touched the doorknob that Martino finally caught her scent and heard her approaching footsteps on the stoop. Jordan looked away from Deanna's helpless image at the window and couldn't believe Martino still was so unaware of his surroundings. How did he survive all these years with no basic survival instincts, he thought?

One would have thought that years with Tabitha, some of her natural survival skills would have rubbed off on him. "Calm yourself," he said as he watched Martino fill with anger and rage as the front door slowly opened.

Deanna, covered in her marshmallow coat and oversized boots, stood dripping in the doorway. Not more than two months ago, they were sure she would never set foot in the house again. But here she stood looking frightened and secretly wishing Gail hadn't saved her life a few days ago. Here she stood, not a hundred feet from where Abby died, thinking this was a big mistake.

"No, it's not." Jordan startled her with his swift approach. "Take off your coat and boots and sit beside the fire. You are still weak. May we get you anything?" He took her face in his hands, studying the dark circles beneath her eyes and the small, busted capillaries in her green eyes from excessive crying.

Before answering, Deanna closed her eyes and leaned into his cool, gentle hands. "No, I'm fine. Thanks." Her words were weak and barely above a whisper. Jordan could also sense a hint of distrust in her tone. And rightfully so; they had cultivated a good crop of suspicion and blame over the last six months and it was blooming beautifully until now.

He took her marshmallow coat and oversized boots and left them to dry near the front door.

"They've upgraded the storm. We're supposed to get a foot now. Glad I made it before it really started to come down. I should have rented an SUV instead of that piece of crap. It sucks in the snow and there's no accumulation yet." She laughed nervously, looking to Martino, hating herself for having to make small talk to a man that was supposed to love her.

"Is he here?" Martino came at her quickly and without compassion.

Deanna looked as if she had been slapped. Jordan felt that uncharacteristic urge to defend or protect her again, until he saw her eyes clear. They went from surprised and watery to angry and hard within seconds. He decided to allow this conversation to unfold before he interfered. After all, Deanna was the oldest soul in the room. She could handle herself no matter what Gail thought.

She didn't answer right away and grabbed Jordan's hands for comfort or control, he couldn't tell.

"Where is Devin, Deanna?"

"I don't know. I don't know. I don't know!" The third time she said it she was yelling. "He left that night and hasn't been back since. Don't ask me questions I know you know the answers to. Gail must have told you all of this."

Jordan's quick hand squeeze confirmed this.

"Devin killed Abby and disappeared. Okay? He's gone. Gone! To you, to me – gone. Happy now? You don't have to be troubled by his presence anymore." She paused but was far from done. "I tried to check out too. Just to make your life that much easier. But unfortunately for you, Gail was able to prevent that from happening. So, I'm sorry for disrupting your precious life, but at least you are done with one of us."

Martino simply stared at her as she delivered her tirade and said nothing. His fists were clenched, and he turned and began pacing again.

Jordan could hear the jumble of thoughts racing through his head but could make no sense of any of them. Thoughts of Margaret, of seeing Deanna at a bar, various intimate moments between them, arguing about Devin, and Margaret again. Lots of anger accompanied thoughts of Margaret. Anger that Jordan couldn't distinguish between hurt, fear, or hatred. It was dizzying.

Deanna looked to Jordan and released his hands with an embarrassed expression that told him she hadn't realized she was still holding them.

"What do we do now?" she asked.

"Martino, stop that infernal pacing for a moment and sit," Jordan demanded.

He did – reluctantly and cantankerously – mumbling the entire way. Not beside Deanna but across from her. The hurt on her face was evident.

"Do you mind if I speak with Martino alone?" Deanna asked Jordan. "You'll know when we need you. I'm sure you'll be able to hear us." She laughed nervously again.

There were a few moments after Jordan left the room that Deanna felt there was no hope for her relationship with Martino. He refused to meet her eyes and the hardness of his expression was frightening.

"Why are you so angry? Gail forgave me or is trying. Why can't you?"

He didn't answer.

"Wow, I really didn't think we'd end like this." She got to her feet and headed for the front door.

"Like what?"

"With you hating me as much as you do. I'm sorry about what happened to Abby. I really am, and I take full responsibility for my part in that horrible event, but I don't deserve this. I've lived way too long and have learned over those hundreds of years that no one is allowed to make me ashamed of who I am. Not even you, Martino." She stopped and sat on the stairs to put her boots back on. "I love you. I really love you and I don't think I realized how much until you gave up on me. And it hurts, a lot, but I'll get over it. Next lifetime, I won't even know you. And without Devin, maybe I won't even remember all of this. Life will begin again for me. Next time maybe I'll finally get it right."

She clomped over to the hook her coat was drying on and saw Martino was now standing but still saying nothing. Behind him, she could see the snow was coming down harder than before; at least a half an inch covered the ground.

"So, it looks like there's nothing more to say – or in your case nothing to say at all – so I'll be going." Her jaw was clenched so tight to stop from crying that it was beginning to hurt.

"You can't go out in this." Jordan was at the kitchen door. "Take those ridiculous boots off your feet and sit back down." He took her hand and whispered. "Looks like you needed me sooner than you thought."

"I just need a place to stay tonight and I'll be gone in the morning."

"It's what you do best, run away." Martino was glaring at her.

Jordan and Deanna stared at him as if he'd never spoken a single word in his life and his first words were full of disdain.

"Yup, it works. Why stay where I'm not wanted?"

"Or refuse to face any consequences?"

"Wow, this is a new side of you." Deanna was shaking her head. "I think I hate it. Devin was right about you all along."

"Yes, I'm not to be trusted. You've told me this fairy tale before. How about the one where Deanna finally faces up to her guilt in the murder of an innocent person? Or is that too much to ask?"

"I have! I do! I'm trying," she screamed, tears streaming down her cheeks. She turned to Jordan. "Tell Gail I'm sorry. This was a horrible mistake. I'll take my chances with the storm."

Just as she turned to leave, Jordan reached out his hand and grabbed her arm. The color in her eyes had gone from hazel to an earthy green but Jordan didn't notice. His concentration was on the goblet that he had left on the end table beside the window. It was bubbling as if it was being heated by an invisible flame.

The expression on Deanna's face confirmed that she was causing the phenomenon. Her mouth twitched with emotion. Her eyes, now completely green, were watering and refused to meet his eyes, searching the room for a resting point. They found purchase at the window, which was now completely white from the spontaneous blizzard.

"That's you?" Jordan nodded to the goblet.

She swallowed hard and nodded.

"And that's you?" He flicked his chin at the snow-covered window.

"It was supposed to snow . . . just not this hard." She took his hand in hers. Her eyes were already slowly turning back to hazel. "It's the only real power that I have. But I can only summon it when I'm upset. When Abby died, the lake overflowed. It rained all day at Max's funeral. When Devin died, there were gale force winds with hurricane conditions. The rivers swelled. That was the worst one, I think."

Jordan nodded his understanding, but this was something he hadn't banked on. Deanna had power without Devin. She was a real, honest-to-God, bonafide witch. "Does Gail know?"

"Yes." Gail stood in the center of the room beside Martino. Her entrance went unnoticed by all of them. Her long black hair was free around her shoulders, making her appear ethereal, and when she spoke everyone stared at her as if they could see through her. "I wasn't sure at first but after Max's funeral, I started remembering things when you were a child." She looked to Martino and grabbed his hand. "Little things like your bath water overflowing on its own. It was never much, just oddities that stuck in my mind, and I didn't recall until you were crying so hard for Max and the strength of the rain changed with your outbursts."

She shrugged as if it was no big deal.

"Now, we need to settle this between you two. Because we are going to continue with this little quest of ours. Whether you two reconcile or not, it would just make it easier if you would. Deanna, sit beside me. Martino, you right there." She pointed to the seat behind him. "Abby's death was a horrible, horrible thing. But I will not lose you as well. So, tell Martino how you feel."

Jordan stood by the window and watched as the falling snow slowed to a flurry once again. The look of amazement in his eyes made Deanna smile. She cleared her throat and spoke.

"I've already told him. He doesn't want to hear. I've said I love him. I've said I'm sorry. I don't know what else to say. Devin's gone. I can't promise it will be forever. He may come back tomorrow. I don't know. You really hurt me when you didn't come after me."

"Come after you? Why weren't you here? Where was I supposed to look?" His voice was strained and emotional, making his accent sound muddy and indistinguishable. "I was angry. You turned away when I asked you to stop him. Why?"

Deanna didn't have an answer. "I don't know. I was angry too. No, I was furious. She told you to end my life. She told you to kill me and you were listening to her. I couldn't believe . . ." The tears burst through once more.

Jordan burst out with an astonished laugh as he stared out at the snow. "It's coming down again!"

"Come away from the window." Gail sounded embarrassed.

Deanna composed herself as Jordan took a seat facing the bay window, so he could monitor the ebb and flow of the storm to her emotions.

"That was Rhea that told me to end it. Not Abby . . ."

"I know," she shot back at him before he could finish his thought. "But he was really strong that night and I was really hurt. It got away from me and from his disappearance, I think it got away from him as well."

"Abby is not the issue here." Gail's voice tripped over Abby's name, but everyone pretended not to notice.

"No, she's not. I have no control here and I think that night was the culmination of that fact for me. I couldn't help Abby. I couldn't stop Devin. I couldn't control you. I've felt helpless and very much alone since this whole thing started. I ran away as well."

"I didn't realize that we were leaving you out. I'm so sorry." Deanna walked to him and knelt at his feet. "Is that why you've been so angry?"

"Most of my anger tonight has little to do with you, any of you. It's because of Margaret."

Deanna tensed at the mention of the name. She knew Margaret was alive somewhere, but she hated the mention of her name. Gail looked to Jordan, who had finally looked away from the window and was staring at Martino, waiting for him to continue.

"That's where I went when I ran away. Colorado. That's where she is. Although she's not as locked away as I was led to believe. She's found her way out and has been exploring in between my visits. She never showed any interest before but for the last few months she's been different."

It was as if he was talking to himself, confirming information that he already knew as he spoke it aloud.

"Different how?" Jordan asked.

"More talkative. More secretive. More active." He held Deanna's hand firmly as he spoke.

"Just in the last say seven or eight months?"

Martino kissed Deanna's hand warily and nodded. He was feeling a great deal of his anger melting away as the heat of her body against his leg warmed him.

"What are you thinking?" Gail was studying his thoughts and behavior.

"Devin has found Margaret," Jordan said plainly and without reservation. "He showed her the way out of the house and he has sparked a lust for life that captivity had stifled in her. Shame on you for keeping her captive in the first place. She could have lost her mind and without a soul, who knows what she would have been capable of."

"I know what she's capable of." Martino's eyes locked with Jordan's for a minute and he was sure he got the full gist of what Margaret had done recently.

"She can't be left alone any longer," Jordan whispered, still only looking at Martino.

He nodded.

"Do you think he's there?" Deanna asked.

"He wasn't there when I was this week. He's not with Margaret."

"Maybe we should go there, and he'll come to us," Gail suggested.

Jordan laughed. "What do you mean we? Frankly, I'm happy Devin is gone. And now that these two are happily ever after again, I'm done here. That's all I promised I do. But if you go, you must bring her back with you. Do not leave her alone a moment longer."

Gail rolled her eyes as he headed for his study in the basement.

Jordan stopped at the basement door. "I would, however, like to discuss this power over water you have, Deanna. When you get back from, what was it you called it, your quest? That is one thing that is fascinating to me."

Deanna smiled and nodded. It was unsettling to have Jordan interested in her. "So, when are we going to Colorado?"

CHAPTER THIRTY

Then, two days later, Deanna found herself on a plane to Colorado. It was too quick for second thoughts and she was sure that was why Gail booked the flight. She was flying solo and the others, whichever others wanted to join the crazy train, flew out last night and had arrived in Colorado in the early hours this morning. Martino had texted Deanna when they arrived. She didn't want to be separated from Martino, especially after finally reconciling, but Gail insisted that Deanna go ahead and do her exploring – her words exactly – so that when they awoke, they could get right down to business.

Landing in Colorado was surreal. She hadn't grown old as Margaret. She was ripped from her body without warning, giving her no opportunity to say goodbyes or prepare for the next life. It felt like she was stepping into a chapter of a book that she hadn't finished. The book had closed suddenly, leaving her lost and unfulfilled.

Driving to Boulder brought back memories of childhood. The parks she played in, the streets she walked, the schools she attended. They were all still there waiting for her to finish the story. But she wasn't here to finish the story, was she? She was here to – well, she wasn't sure what she was here for. Gail thought Devin might return if they brought Margaret back to Mount Orion, and Jordan thought that Margaret shouldn't be left alone for some reason that was kept between Martino and himself.

The only thing Deanna could guess was that she was violent or could become violent. The potential for violence was enough to lock her up in the first place; at least that's what Martino had alluded to. But was he being honest? For the first time since she'd met him, Deanna was sure Martino was lying to her.

The taxi let her out in front of a midcentury cape cod that was well maintained and had the look that a lovely little family of four lived there. The husband, an accountant, and the wife an overly involved stay-at-home mom and homemaker. The children, two girls – the oldest the apple of her father's eye, of course – both were just cute as buttons. Don't forget Fido. Deanna could picture a golden retriever or some mix that said family dog.

Standing in front of the house, she searched her purse for the keys that Martino had entrusted to her. There were a few rules.

"One: Do not unlock the basement door – no matter what you hear. Two: Feel free to snoop into anything, just don't move things around. She hates that. Three: If she's not there or there but out of the basement, leave and text me immediately."

The last rule frightened Deanna. She wasn't ready to see Margaret on her own and if there was even the slightest chance that she could be wandering the house . . .

She didn't want to think about it. In fact, she pushed the thought to the furthest part of mind that was reserved for her true feelings for Jacenta and what she was going to do if they did break the curse. The keys stuck in the lock but after a few jiggles she heard the deadbolt slide back into the door frame. And she turned the knob.

The house was small and dated. The furniture was straight out of *Better Homes and Gardens* magazine circa 1960. The armless sofa was red and sat in the center of the room with a few chairs flanking it to make a conversation nook, as her mother would have called it. The dining room shared the same space with a small dinette set and very avant-garde style chairs.

Nothing looked familiar. The furniture was new – dated but new.

Deanna dropped her bags and listened to the stillness of the house. She looked at her watch. 3:30 p.m. Two or three hours before sunset, two or three hours alone.

It wasn't until just after sunset that Deanna started to hear noises coming from the basement. She had spent her time searching the house. There were three small bedrooms upstairs with very little closet space and very little of anything else in any of the rooms. The beds were small and unused – Deanna could see if she was going to spend the night here, she would need to change the dust-covered sheets.

The one room she remembered vaguely as being hers as a child had a single twin bed and a dresser. Otherwise, it was completely empty. Her parents' room and her sister's room were much the same. Nothing held what she would have expected – nostalgia. It was just a house that looked familiar but not in any particular way.

She washed up in the one bathroom on the second floor and it was then that she started to realize what a horrible place this was to be trapped in for fifty years. Looking around, she saw the pea green toilet, a sink and tub. It was a really small tub that made Deanna feel claustrophobic just looking at it.

She'd looked in every drawer and all of two closets. One bedroom didn't even have a closet, just a large armoire with a mirror. It was her sister Patty's room. Inside the armoire she found pencil etchings of Patty's name and her schoolgirl crush's name. Deanna's hopes were to find something to connect Margaret to this house. A piece of mail, a notepad with her writing on it, even a book that looked familiar.

There was nothing. If there was some connection, Martino had gotten rid of it years ago.

The noises coming from the basement started just after 6 p.m. were just normal moving-around noises that anyone would make; however, Deanna had horrible images in her mind that she couldn't shake. Images of zombies, thanks to Sari for that one – she spoke incessantly of *The Walking Dead* since last night. Other images included white-faced, mindless vampires with blood pouring from their mouths. It wasn't a pretty image.

Gail and Martino were expected within the hour; they had gotten a hotel room for the day and would arrive soon. At least that's what Martino texted her just before sunrise. As she sat in the tiny boring living room watching the minute hand glacially move around the clock on the wall, she could feel something.

"*I saw her.*" The disembodied voice was low in her ear. Almost a hum. "*You were very pretty.*"

She jumped slightly and felt the relief wash over her like standing under a waterfall. Deanna closed her eyes and suppressed a smile. "I've missed you." Her voice was breathy as if he had just caught her from falling.

"*I'm glad to hear it, Mouse. I was afraid that you didn't want me back.*"

"Never," she said intimately inside her head. "I made mistakes and I'm sorry. You had me scared for a minute, Brodie. I thought you were never coming back."

He was silent for a moment. "*And you were going to move on without me?*"

"How did you know about that?" Even the voice in her head sounded astonished that he had learned about her suicide attempt.

"*Remember, we're in this together. Don't leave without me.*"

"Never again, I promise."

"*Good, now that we've settled that . . . I could open that door if you'd like to see her for yourself.*" The hum was a warm vibration behind her ear that was relaxing to the point of making her drowsy and she didn't realize how much she missed it until just then. "*She's just sitting. Her eyes are closed, out of pure boredom, I presume. Although your love has surrounded her with all your favorite books. There's even a Victrola.*"

"No, I promised Martino I wouldn't open the door." Her eyes shifted to the basement door just beyond the kitchen entryway. It was locked. The knob wouldn't turn when she tried it. Tried it, pulled it, and pounded on it.

"*It would be very easy for me to turn the lock on either side.*" He stopped, teasing her, knowing she wanted to hear all of what he saw. Dying to see it herself.

Deanna couldn't help herself. "Have you been here before? Jordan guessed that you had," she said aloud.

"Yes," he said without reservation.

"How? I mean, how did you find her?"

"Loverboy. I simply followed him. He led me right to her. He comes here a lot. A lot more than he tells you."

The minute hand clicked another minute and she walked into the kitchen. It was small, too. All the appliances were harvest gold, giving the room an almost sepia tone. Deanna felt as if she were stepping into the past. Everything was new. The electric stove appeared to never have been used. The toaster and percolating coffee pot were covered in dust but brand new.

The yellow linoleum was not worn in the usual wear spots. By the sink or by the back door, after fifty years there should have been tread wear. Nothing. It was like new. Nothing looked familiar in here either. Martino had changed everything.

The basement door was beside the back door, leading to the yard. As Deanna walked into the room, she tried the knob again. It was a desperate hope that Devin had unlocked it or that Margaret had silently climbed the stairs and turned the deadbolt on her side.

Still locked. She walked to the refrigerator, in another desperate attempt that something had changed since she had arrived. Again, she was disappointed. If the others didn't arrive soon, she would have to take the long walk to the grocery store in town.

The sun had set and Deanna expected to see Gail and Martino any minute. She sat at the kitchen-slash-dining room table and put her head in her hands. They needed to get here soon or she was going to tear down the basement door herself. It was with that thought that she heard it again. The noises from the basement. Rustling.

A shuffling of feet.

The feeling, without seeing anyone else, that she was not alone.

The tingle on the back of your neck when someone is standing behind you.

"Is the prospect of meeting your former self intimidating, Mouse?" The hum of Devin's presence tickled the nape of her neck.

Deanna listened at the basement door. At first, she didn't hear anything. Dead silence. Then she heard the rustling again, as if Margaret wasn't picking up her feet as she walked. Deanna imagined her as a monster in the old horror movies. Movies that Margaret loved and would see every Saturday afternoon with her sister, Patty. Patty loved going to the movies with her big sister and her friends. The smell of popcorn; the boys in the back heckling the scary parts making them not so scary; still being scared when someone jumped out. Saturday afternoons were Margaret's favorite part of the week. When it rained, it was the best. No adults telling you to enjoy the sunshine. She could sit in the dark with her sister and pretend to be the brave one.

Sadly, Margaret was now living the horror movies that she had loved as a child.

"What is she doing now?" Deanna whispered. "Devin?"

The rustling became low thumps on the stairs. One step and then another, Deanna stepped back from the door, petrified.

Thump!

Her pace was slow but didn't sound labored. Still Deanna had the image of a rotting corpse trudging up the stairs, pulling its weight on the banister, one foot hanging lifeless, dragging behind, slowing the progress.

Thump! Another foot hit the step closer to the top.

"Devin, are you doing this? Are you playing games? It's not funny." *Please answer me.* She pleaded silently.

Thump! A final step taken.

Margaret was on the other side of the door. Deanna could almost feel her standing there. Slowly she placed her hand on the door, feeling the cool metal of the door, envisioning Margaret doing the same.

She laid her head on the cool door and listened. She tried to envision how she was as Margaret but couldn't picture anything past ten years old. She remembered swinging in the back yard. Her dark hair tied up in a ponytail so tight that it made the skin on her forehead taut and shiny. She was swinging by herself. Patty was napping.

The swings faced her mother's flower garden and it was full of butterflies. Margaret was making up songs about the butterflies. Singing and swinging. Butterflies and flowers.

Deanna smiled, remembering herself that happy and content. Then a knock came from the other side of the door. A soft faint knock that seemed timid and questioning. Then Deanna realized that while she was reminiscing, she had been drumming lightly on the door with her fingertips. Drumming the sweet song about butterflies and flowers.

The knock came again, this time a bit harder. Deanna stepped back. She didn't know if she should knock back. So many questions flooded her mind. Should she respond? Should she say something? Where the hell were Martino and the others?

She started to hum the song from long ago, the song that she had written and Margaret had performed. The sound started low in her throat but as she continued, the tune and lyrics were coming back.

Butterfly, oh Butterfly . . . Fly away with me . . . Butterfly, oh Butterfly . . . I so long to be free.

Deanna pressed herself against the door again and continued to sing the words she could remember and hum when she could not.

"Deanna, what are you doing?"

With a start, Deanna pulled herself away from the door, letting a little scream replace her singing. Behind her, Gail, dressed in a long black cape coat and elbow-length gloves, was smiling inquisitively. Just coming into the kitchen were Martino, Sari, and Eric.

As Gail stood waiting for a response, she pulled off her gloves and casually tossed them on the countertop. Her movements were swift but graceful.

"Come away from the door." Martino took Deanna's hand and led her to the sofa in the adjoining room.

"She's right there. On the other side of that door. Margaret. I heard her. Listen, I know you will too. She's been knocking." Deanna found she was more excited now than frightened.

Gail and Martino exchanged a look.

"Well, let's open it." Sari pulled her coat off and tossed it on the loveseat to her left. She had none of the grace of Gail. Deanna could clearly see that Sari was exhausted and had probably not even fed yet. Still she was anxious to get a look at Margaret. "You got the key, Tino? Come on."

Eric looked at her, annoyed. He, too, was clearly exhausted and he held none of the enthusiasm for this encounter as his protégé did. The sound of Margaret's knocking stopped his sarcastic retort and made Deanna jump with excitement.

"See. She started moving at sunset. Do you think she can sense the sunset even if she can't see it?"

Gail and Martino exchanged another look.

"What?" Deanna asked. "That's the second time you've looked at each other. Am I not supposed to wonder about her? Or are you just saying, *poor sweet, demented Deanna*?"

"No, I'm happy that you are excited and not frightened by her." Gail sat beside Deanna. "But I don't want you to get too overwhelmed by all of this. Martino has a lot to go over with us before we open that door. One of the many points is that he believes that you two may hold some kind of connection. She may not be reacting to the sunset as much as she's reacting to your presence in the house."

Deanna's face crumpled in confusion.

"She senses you, remembers you . . . that's why she's knocking."

"Remembers me? You think she's retained all my memories? How is that possible?"

"When you left you took your soul, not your brain." Gail smiled patiently.

"Should we let her out?" Sari asked still staring at the door. A bit of her enthusiasm was snuffed with Margaret's sad and lonely knock.

Martino shook his head. "I'd rather not confront her like this. It would be much better if she was calm and preferably still sleeping."

Deanna looked to Sari and then to Gail and Martino. "We can't just leave her there."

"She's been there for over fifty years; I don't think a few more hours will do her any harm," Eric spoke up.

CHAPTER THIRTY-ONE

Margaret wasn't sure if she should continue knocking. The singing had stopped – that song, the one about the butterflies. She remembered making up that song. She remembered singing it when she was happily playing or when she was scared during thunderstorms or when her parents were arguing, which they did a lot.

It was her. The one Martino told her about or at least tried to tell her about. Margaret refused to listen and even went so far as to cover her ears when he brought up the subject of the girl. He showed her a picture and called her Deanna. He said they were the same person and that it all came back to that damn curse.

The knocking wasn't doing anything now. Martino had arrived and he was still angry with her. There was no way he was going to open the basement door; it was like he was punishing her. Still she hadn't left the basement, just like she promised. She stayed in her closet and wrote constantly for the last few months.

It was odd to have Martino back this soon. He never visited this often – not in years. There were other voices she heard as well. The girl, Martino, and at least three others.

They were like her, what Martino called immortals. Their vibration was numbing her brain. The different pitches and pulses. Two different women were beyond the basement door. Two different tones. She tried to listen, but one was too erratic to follow. The other was quick as well but had a more pulsated rhythm to it, much like Elinor from that fateful night at the cafe.

Then there was Martino. His vibration was slow and steady and the pitch was distinctive. The fourth one was a man as well. His vibration was slow but deeper in pitch than any of the others. His reminded Margaret of Elinor's friend, Ezra – he must be older than the others.

She sat on the top step for a while, listening to the voices in the living room. The glow was back. She had missed it. This singing girl, Deanna, her other self, spoke to the glow. Spoke to it as if having a conversation with it. It answered her. She called it Devin.

The glow – Devin – was there when she woke this evening. He hovered close, drawing her to the stairs. But he didn't wake her. There was a hum in her head like the sound the needle on a turntable makes at the end of a record.

At first, she thought he had meant to open the door again. The promise she made to Martino hung over her as she walked slowly, following the floating orb up the stairs one step at a time. But he didn't unlock the door. The glow disappeared at the top of the stairs and she noticed something that she hadn't before. The hum was louder and was accompanied by a force field feeling.

It made her hands and feet vibrate. It was hard to breathe being close to this girl. A single slab of steel stood between the two women, and the discomfort was unbearable. She could hear Martino drawing her away from the door, and Margaret waved her away with her hand. Move away, she thought. The farther Deanna's steps moved from the kitchen door, the less pressure Margaret felt and the easier it was to breathe.

She took a deep breath and closed her eyes. Margaret still felt the numbness in her fingers and the pressure in her chest even as she descended the stairs. She wasn't sure she wanted Martino to open the door now. What would happen if she came face to face with this girl? What would happen if the pressure became so great that she found it impossible to breathe?

Sitting in her closet, she no longer felt any pressure or tingling. She only heard whispers of voices from upstairs and tried with all her might to block out what they may be saying about her. Grabbing a black ball point pen, she opened her journal and let her emotion flow out onto the pages. By the time the sun rose, she could no longer hear any movement from upstairs, and the glow was her only companion.

Margaret walked out of her closet and sat on the sofa, watching as the glow hovered beside her. No sunlight could harm her where she was, and fatigue was not something her body was accustomed to feeling unless she hadn't eaten in a while. She kicked off her shoes and reclined comfortably.

"At sunset when they awake, will you open the door for me, Devin?" The brilliance of Devin's essence was blinding for a moment, and Margaret took that to mean yes. When he returned to his usual dim glow, she lowered her hand from her eyes. "I wish I could hear you like she can." Again, he brightened but not as much as before.

Margaret smiled and closed her eyes. Sleep would make the time pass quickly, she thought. "What will you do when we are all asleep?" she asked, knowing she would not get a response.

The next time she opened her eyes, the sun had set and the sound of footsteps on the stairs startled her. Margaret grabbed her shoes and locked herself in her closet.

CHAPTER THIRTY-TWO

"Ready?" Martino asked after unlocking the basement door but before he pulled the door open.

Deanna didn't think anything could ready her for what lay beyond that door. She swallowed hard and reached for Gail's unseen hand. There were no words on her lips, just a tremble that ushered in the tears standing in her eyes. She looked to Gail and shook her head, no.

"You don't have to go. Devin's back. That's what we wanted." Gail placed her hand on Deanna's hair and gently stroked it. "You don't need to be brave," she whispered.

Now as she squeezed the banister with one hand and Martino's arm with the other, she wished she had taken Gail's option to remain in the kitchen with her and the others. Deanna could feel Devin was near, but he wasn't talking. He had seen Margaret yesterday and she knew he had visited her before they started down the stairs. Whether she was awake and expecting them or still resting, Deanna did not know.

As her foot fell on the final step, she felt a shudder in her chest. Last night and just before they began their little adventure down the rabbit hole, Martino had told her of his beliefs that she and Margaret might still hold a connection to one another. Two bodies, one soul. There had to be something that bound them together. Some spark. That's what frightened Deanna most of all. What if Martino was wrong? What if there wasn't a connection? What if Margaret was merely a walking, talking shell of what she used to be?

Not much light in the rabbit hole, Deanna thought as she looked around. Again, a horrible image of Margaret filled her mind. Not the decaying corpse but a Nosferatu-like vampire with glowing eyes. A creature that didn't need light to survive. A cannibalistic cave-dwelling monster that hissed when approached and cowered from the light. Suddenly, Deanna felt that she should be carrying a torch to wave at the creature when it approached.

Martino hit the switch at the bottom of the stairs. The light faded all thoughts of monsters and corpses. Deanna was taken aback by what lay before her; to the left of the staircase was a sitting room. A room that looked like it had been taken out of the pages of *Better Homes and Gardens* circa 1967. The room was decorated in what her mother, Blair Belamy, would call midcentury modern, but really it was just old and dated. This was no brainchild of an eccentric decorator; it was a room lost in time. Forgotten by the world. This was not new. This was home. It brought back images of her life with the Coopers.

While the furniture was dated, the electronics were not. Sitting on what Junelyn Cooper would have called the credenza was a flat screen television with a wireless cable box. On the beautiful roll top desk, beside the typewriter, was an opened laptop. The walls were lined with adjustable shelving that held books, DVDs, CDs, records, and photo albums. In the corner behind the sectional sofa was a full stereo system; it had a turntable, iPod dock, tape deck, 8-track player, a CD player, and a radio. Martino had thought of everything and had continued to update the technology over the years.

"You did all of this?" Deanna asked. She walked into the room without waiting for an answer. Touching everything she passed, Deanna found herself drawn to the photos placed decoratively on the shelves and end tables. There were photos of Margaret and her sister Patty; Margaret and Martino – she remembered taking that one. A beautiful night together under the stars. Deanna glanced to Martino and saw he was smiling.

Continuing her trip down memory lane, there was a picture of her golden retriever Perry and several of her parents. A tear slipped down Deanna's cheek as she studied the photos.

"They're in Denver. At least your mother and sister are. George and Perry died not long after you. There was a fire upstairs. Your dad fell asleep with a cigarette in his hand. Set fire to the whole ground floor."

"Mom is still alive? What is she? Ninety?"

"About that. Patty got married, has couple of kids, I think. She may be a widow, I'm not sure. I stopped caring after Margaret stopped asking about them. But I bought this place when they moved and repaired the damage. I thought she would feel at home." He looked up to the dropped ceiling as if surveying the work he'd done. "I don't really think she cares either way."

Deanna watched as Martino explained what happened after she died. It was so matter of fact.

Still looking around, the room was nothing like she anticipated. She expected to see a dirt floor covered with half-eaten carcasses strewn about. There were chairs and pillows; a coffee table; even a hostess tray set that Deanna could guarantee was stolen from Margaret's grandmother's house.

"Where is she?" Deanna whispered. There was a closet in the right-hand corner of the room beneath the staircase. As Deanna reached for the knob, Martino turned to the right of the stairs.

"She's probably this way," he said.

The other room was dimly lit, and Deanna's thoughts returned to the torch. "Is there a light in here?" she asked.

"Behind you."

The recessed lights brightened the darkened room. A dated washer and dryer sat unused in the corner, but the focal point of the room was the enormous coffin sitting beside the stairs. It was closed with a thick layer of dust covering it and when Deanna approached it, Martino said, "She's not in there. She detests it. I should have removed it years ago."

Deanna pulled her hand away as if she almost touched fire. "Where are you?" Her whisper was barely audible to the human ear.

Martino continued down a short hallway and stopped in front of a large double door. He looked to Deanna and turned the knob slowly. The door creaked on its hinges and when it finally opened, a foul odor filled the hallway.

"Oh!" Deanna held her nose and covered her mouth. "What is that stench?" she said through her hand.

Martino motioned to the bones on the floor. There were pieces of at least five humans and many animals. From the look of it, Margaret had survived on rodents and cats with a human on special occasions. The urge to run was building quickly in Deanna and she found that she didn't want to fight it. The air upstairs was less putrid, and the thought of innocent creatures dying right where she stood was making her lightheaded.

"I haven't pushed her to clean up in months." He shrugged and shut the door. "Stay here," he said without looking back.

"Please don't leave me alone," she pleaded.

He didn't look at her or respond. She remained in front of what was obviously the rooms where Margaret did all her sleeping and eating. The difference between the two sides of the basement was immeasurable. The sitting room gave an appearance of normality, but this side was the animalistic side of Margaret materialized. She could feel her hands trembling but was powerless to stop them. There was no noise from the rest of the basement. Deanna could hear whispering coming from the kitchen but that was all.

Without a second thought, Deanna began walking. Slowly, she passed the unused washer and dryer and then the unused dust-covered coffin. The whispering upstairs was louder, and she could see Sari standing at the top of the stairs, waiting to be allowed down. "Tino?" Deanna whispered as if she was disturbing someone.

"We're in here." His voice sounded as if it came from beneath the stairs, and Deanna remembered the closet door that she wanted to open. Had she opened the door, she would never have to see the room of skeletons and smell that atrocious smell.

We're in here. Deanna's feet felt heavy like she was dreaming. Margaret was on the other side of the stairs with Tino.

"Do you need help, Mouse?" Devin was suddenly surrounding her. *"They're waiting for you."*

"*I know. Where have you been? Did you see what I just did? I needed you.*" She took a few deep breaths. "*I'm frightened, Devin,*" she said only to him and quickly wiped away a tear.

His energy encompassed her, and she felt warm. The warmth permeated her skin and flowed into her chest. For a moment she felt safe, like nothing in the world could harm her. "*I will always protect you, Mouse.*"

As he spoke, Deanna could feel the strength in her legs disintegrate and her pulse speed up. Though Devin was calming her, his love was coming at a price. Her energy. Her strength. It was his now; he was taking it and feeding off it as he did when she was angry.

"Stop," she said aloud, and she tried in her weakened state to shake him off. "Get off me," she demanded. When Devin pulled away, Deanna found she could not stand on her own. He was somehow supporting her as he physically depleted her. She fell to her knees.

"D? Are you all right?" Sari came bounding down the stairs with Gail close behind.

Deanna slumped on the floor, trying to build up enough strength to push herself up. With her eyes closed and deep breaths, she concentrated on her limp limbs and racing heartbeat. As she sat folded on the floor at the foot of the stairs, she felt hands on her head. Warm, gentle, kind hands reached for her arms, offering to help her to her feet. She thought it was Gail that was holding her, but she was wrong.

"D." She could see Sari's feet at the bottom of the stairs, but she sounded far away.

"Deanna." Gail sounded distant like she was in a tunnel.

Both sounded scared and worried.

Using what strength she could muster, Deanna raised her head. Squatting on the floor right in front of her, holding her arms for support was Margaret. Deanna's body trembled violently, and she fell back, hitting the coffin with her head. "M . . . M . . . Margaret." Her own voice was in a tunnel and echoing in her head.

"Shhh." Margaret looked Deanna in the eyes and brushed away the tears pouring down her cheeks.

For a moment, Deanna absorbed the woman helping her to her feet. Her soft, glossy iridescent hazel emotionless eyes; her pale, flawless face; her straight, brown hair and despite not having seen the sun in half a century, it was highlighted beautifully with auburn streaks. Then Margaret pulled Deanna to her feet and ushered her passed Martino into the sitting room. At the same time, she held her own chest like she was having a heart attack.

Deanna's legs felt numb as Margaret dropped her on the sofa. She couldn't take her eyes off the woman before her. A pressure pressed on her chest and she took a deep breath to alleviate the stress. Margaret stood there staring at her, her expression unreadable. "Thank you," Deanna said, keenly aware that she was staring at herself.

"Margaret." Martino came up from behind her. "Sit down."

She smiled without showing any emotion in her soft hazel eyes. It was unnerving to see a perfectly formed smile without emotion.

Sari and Gail joined them as Margaret took a seat beside Martino opposite Deanna. Gail sat beside Deanna, and Sari took the chair to their left. Eric appeared at the bottom of the stairs. He said nothing and took a seat beside Sari.

Suddenly, Deanna felt outnumbered. Five against one. She eyed those around her. Gail sat beside her, holding her hand and whispering for her to be calm. Deanna awkwardly looked around the room again. Comparing the photos of Margaret with the real Margaret, she could clearly see the difference. It was the eyes. The photos showed her smiling and laughing, her eyes dancing with emotion. The cold indifference in Margaret's eyes now was unsettling. She tried not to stare but she could not help it.

"I'll always protect you, Mouse." Devin was back.

"Go away." Deanna was still weak from their last encounter and was not in the mood to replicate the incident. *"When I need you, you'll know."*

Margaret's emotionless eyes seemed to follow Devin's movements.

"Can you sense him? Or hear him?" Deanna asked her former self.

Margaret's eyes stopped their dance and met Deanna's gaze intently.

"Does she speak?" Gail asked Martino.

He nodded. "Rarely."

CHAPTER THIRTY-THREE

The time dragged by as Margaret watched everyone arguing around her – about her. She couldn't grasp the problem. It wasn't a problem that she could figure out. If they wanted problems, she could give them problems. Let them meet Elinor or Ezra or even James. Well, not James. James was dead – of that much she was certain. But Elinor would give them plenty of problems, especially now that Margaret had gone berserk and attacked them.

She bit her lip as she thought of those three vampires she had met what seemed like forever ago. Looking up, she saw that girl pacing again. The girl that gave her pain in her chest. Margaret found that when she looked at her, the pressure in her chest intensified and made her short of breath. Her hand pressed against her chest to dull the sensation somewhat. That mixed with the vibration she was picking up from these vampires was killing her. Taking a deep breath, she pressed her fist into her sternum.

"Are you alright?" the younger one, Sari, asked. That one could count her age in months if not weeks, Margaret could tell from the pitch of her vibration. It seemed that the older the vampire, the lower the pitch. She learned that thanks to Elinor and now the good-looking silent one, Eric. His pitch was quite low and his rhythm was not as quick or erratic as Sari's.

Margaret followed everyone's gaze until they were all locked on her. She had not realized that she was crumbled in her seat protecting herself from the rhythms filling the room.

"Margaret, honey, are you in pain?" Gail asked. Margaret winced at the utterance of her own name and the maternal tone that this beautiful vampire was addressing her. Gail crouched beside her and pushed back her hair. "Can we help you?"

The sound of her voice was like music. So soft and sweet, yet sure and strong. Gail's name was familiar. She had heard

Martino speak of Gail with love, with joy, and in anger. She knew she was his sire. So many questions filled her head. She wanted to know what Martino was like outside of this house, the details of his rebirth, who were his friends.

Gail continued to smile, looking directly into her eyes. "In due time," she whispered.

Margaret's heart stopped. Did she just read my mind, she thought? And again, Gail smiled but this time only winked. Margaret broke eye contact and looked to Martino, mesmerized. He only rolled his eyes, looking very annoyed.

"We need to get her to speak." Sari slapped Eric's thigh.

"She does speak. Just not that often," Martino sniped.

Who exactly do I have to speak to? Margaret thought to herself.

Gail laughed a little and covered her mouth as if it were inappropriate to laugh. Everyone looked puzzled but Gail gently dismissed them with a simple wave of her hand. Margaret was feeling more comfortable.

"There's a glow," she whispered finally. She raised her index finger to point it out around Deanna's head. "I see it there. It comes to me sometimes."

When Margaret finished speaking, she could see Deanna's eyes fill with water. A nervous laugh escaped her lips and she touched Sari's hand beside her. "You see him?" She was laughing and crying at the same time. Strange. Margaret wondered why someone would mix those two emotions.

She looked to Martino for an explanation.

"What you are seeing is a spirit. The spirit of a man that died over six hundred years ago. Can you hear him as well?"

Margaret shook her head, no. "You can." It was more of a statement rather than a question. She already knew Deanna could hear him and speak with him.

Deanna smiled and nodded, wiping tears from her cheeks with a tissue.

"I heard you singing last night. He led me to you." She turned toward Deanna again. "I know that song. I remember it."

Deanna sat forward on the sofa. The glow encircled her again and Margaret saw the girl shake it off again. "His name is Devin." The glow brightened at the utterance of its name and she watched it become a brilliant orb above Deanna's head.

Devin came towards her and then stopped. It appeared that Deanna was distracted, perhaps by the orb. Margaret watched closely as Deanna's expression changed dramatically from crying and laughing to annoyed and jealous. The orb expanded into a glow and surrounded Deanna. The light dimmed substantially.

"What did you say to him?" Margaret asked.

"Did you hear him?" Gail asked.

"No," she said plainly. "His light dimmed like he had been reprimanded. I envisioned him as a child that had been scolded for doing something naughty." Margaret looked to Devin's glow. "His essence expanded too."

There was a silence in the room. Margaret thought of Deanna's singing last night. The soft melody about butterflies that she remembered from her childhood.

"May I ask you something? Do you feel any different when I'm near you?" Margaret was intense. This was perhaps the most important question that she needed answered.

"How do you mean?" Deanna's brows met.

"I feel a pressure in my chest when I'm near you. Do you feel that too?"

Deanna looked around, taking a few short breaths as if she was trying to feel something. "I have been feeling a slight pressure, I guess. I just thought it was exhaustion. Is yours all over or just in your chest?"

"Mostly in my chest, but it's being disrupted by the vibration from these guys."

"What vibration are you talking about? From us?" This was the first time Eric spoke this entire time and it made Margaret smile. She studied Eric's face as she had studied Sari's. His skin was much smoother and whiter than her own or even Martino's. He was beautiful to look at; she only wished she could have appreciated that beauty when he was human. His mannerisms spoke volumes to her. He was well educated and cultured. He didn't wish to be here but was obligated by something – perhaps the girl beside him.

Margaret couldn't read his accent. She could only assume that years of living and travelling had muddled it into an amalgam of sounds. His true accent probably came forth when he was angry, she smiled to herself.

"You don't hear that either." Margaret was dejected. "Why is it that only I can feel or hear these things?"

"Perhaps the chamber that houses the soul is compensating for the lost soul. It is empty now and fills itself with energies of those around it." Eric looked around, pleased with his assessment.

"That was pretty good, baby." Sari humored him.

Gail laughed and shook her head, amused.

Margaret wasn't sure if he was right, but it would explain a lot of what she felt when she was around anyone. Humans had a vibration to her as well, just not as intense. Theirs was more of a hum, like the one coming from Deanna, except hers was masked by the pressure and numbness.

"I'm finding it hard to breathe when I'm this close to you. Like an elephant is sitting on my chest." Margaret stood and walked across the room. "This is a better distance."

"Wow, yeah, I didn't notice it until you pointed it out, but I feel less congested. That's what it feels like to me. Like I have a chest cold and my lungs aren't getting enough air." Deanna pounded on her chest with her hand.

CHAPTER THIRTY-FOUR

As they were boarding a night flight back to Albany International Airport, Deanna slipped her hand into her pocket. Pushing aside a folded piece of paper, she wrapped her fingers around something the TSA had missed at their security checkpoint — a crystal that held Devin's blood. A slight tingle travelled up her arm and into her chest. The tremor she felt was not as intense as the first time she held it or even as intense as it was when she placed the crystal in her pocket this morning. Deanna was unsure if it was due to her anticipation of the tremor or not; she was just glad that she wasn't having a heart attack anymore when she touched it.

Devin's blood. How she knew it was Devin's blood was all in the touch. She didn't think she would have any reaction to her own blood and if it was Jacenta's, well, she always imagined hers to be black. In truth, it was just a feeling. A deep, tingly feeling that pulsed through her when she first touched it and reminded her of the feeling she got whenever Devin was around her. A flutter in her heart that could be love, but she knew it was just his energy threatening to kill her at any moment.

She had been snooping around the basement when she found it tucked away in Margaret's private belongings. Deanna left the others in the living room. All of their attention had been on Margaret for the past hour and she felt it was the perfect time to experience the basement for herself. To see what it was like to be trapped down there for years.

Once down there, she looked in every drawer, every cubby, every nook. Margaret had unfortunately retained many of Deanna's own hoarding tendencies even without her soul to guide her. There were drawers filled with notes. Each book on the over-crammed bookshelf had a proper bookmark and at least one receipt or scrap of paper placed between the pages. To anyone else these were receipts indicating when the item was purchased, but to Deanna these were additional place markers saving the pages that Margaret like to reread, sometimes multiple times. She knew this from her own bookshelves. Textbooks she never resold back to the school so she could continue her learning, literature that held quotes that she lived by, and her favorite authors that created the characters that she carried with her and helped her to adapt to her day-to-day, year-to-year life.

The closet where Margaret had hidden on her first day was behind her. Something told her to tread with care. If she knew Margaret as well as she thought she did – as well as she knew herself – this closet held secrets. That's why she was in there on that first night. She wasn't hiding; she was protecting.

Deanna took a deep breath and hesitated before going to the closet. She scanned the desk briefly. The laptop still stood open. She didn't bother looking at it. She knew Margaret had never touched it. Martino bought it, turned it on, and there it sat. He, knowing just as little about computers as Margaret, was in no place to teach her anything about them.

She turned towards the closet again. And again, she hesitated. Her hands started fidgeting with the desk drawers. As she pulled them open, they all appeared to be as untouched as the laptop but contained items far older. Fountain pens, letterhead stationery, a journal embossed with Margaret's initials and gilded pages, extra watermarked typewriter paper, a typewriter eraser. These were not items you find in a desk in the twenty-first century.

Deanna briefly ran her fingers over the embossed letters on the journal.

MAC. Margaret Anne Cooper.

It was finally time to face her demons or at least Margaret's demons. Her demons.

She listened for voices or footfalls upstairs. She could hear Sari and Eric speaking to each other. Sari interrupting Eric as usual. Martino was whispering. Deanna could barely hear him even as she strained at the bottom of the stairs. Margaret saw the glow and marveled at it. Devin was hovering and listening. Gail was on her cell phone. Deanna didn't try to hear who she was talking to, as long as she was distracted for now.

The closet was only a few feet away, but she took her time getting to the door. No rush. No one seemed to miss her upstairs, thankfully. Still, time was a consideration; Margaret could only hold Devin's attention for so long.

The door of the closet was cut to fit the space under the stairs. It opened easily, no lock or door jamb. A small latch kept the door closed for convenience rather than utility, Deanna guessed.

Inside was a treasure trove of stuff. A hoarder's wet dream. Shelves of knick-knacks, books, snow globes, dishes holding more trinkets. Where the shelves ended a few feet above the floor, there were boxes of magazines and newspapers, and paperback books.

Just as she was about to turn her attention to the small desk nestled under the stairs, something stopped her in her tracks. Mixed in with all the other unimportant trinkets and baubles was a small glass bottle filled with red liquid. Blood. Devin's blood to be precise.

Deanna lifted the bottle and held it up to the light. A soft purr came from the vial of blood like the vial was happy to be home again. The glass was foggy and scratched. And the cord that she carried it around her neck on was long since broken. Just a simple vial of red liquid. But it was so much more – this could break the spell.

When her hand wrapped around the glass, the familiar sensation of putting a butter knife into a toaster shot up her arm. The numbing, painful energy pulsed up her arm into her shoulder. Her neck spasmed and threw her head to the right painfully fast. Deanna dropped it into her jacket pocket. The feeling frightened her, and she had completely forgotten what it felt like to touch the vial for the first time.

Each lifetime the vial found its way back to her. Each lifetime she suspected Devin of placing it where she would find it.

He was the keeper of the vial. Still, Deanna could not remember how Margaret had come to have it since Devin never met her. She pulled the vial from her pocket, holding it between her index finger and thumb so the pain would not be so intense.

She stared at it. *How did you get here?* And she dropped it back into her pocket with the intention of asking Devin about it later. For now, it was her secret to keep. Somehow this blood, perhaps merged with her own, would bring an end to the curse. A secret inner smile warmed her, and she turned to the desk behind her.

It was the desk from her room as a child. A survivor of the fire that killed her father and dog. A survivor along with Patty's old armoire. She ran her hands over the scarred wood that had been sanded and repainted too many times to count. The desk was littered with postcards, journals, plastic Bic pens, nubby pencils, worn down erasers, and notecards with quotes, drawings or both.

Deanna ducked her head so as not to slam it on the underside of the staircase to get a closer look at the desktop. This was Margaret's space. Her thoughts were overflowing on the pages of the journals. Not leather-bound journals with gilded pages; there were no engraved initials on these. These were a mix of Moleskine, wirebound office supply store notebooks, and marbled composition notebooks. Every page was covered front to back. In the margins, top and side, there were afterthoughts and ideas. The writing looked harried and without punctuation. *Oh, Sister Agnes would be so angry with young Margaret Anne.* Deanna laughed to herself. Thoughts of nuns slapping her knuckles until they bled because she had disregarded their lessons on punctuation during a test were unhappy ones and Deanna laughed again. This time a sad, sardonic laugh.

Her writing may have been harried but her penmanship was exquisite. The beautiful lines and careful lettering that the nuns had beat into her at an early age had stuck. Maybe too well. Deanna's handwriting now was identical to Margaret's.

Looking closer at the pages, it was clear that Margaret was writing quickly and without stopping until she filled a notebook completely. The wastebasket was filled with empty pens and crumped pieces of paper that had been ripped from the journals.

Deanna reached into the trash to retrieve a crumpled ball of paper. She flattened it out on the desk top and started reading the passage.

Martino visited today He was acting strangely He kept asking me questions about the curse That damnable curse that has left me lost and confused most of the time I know somewhere my soul has been reincarnated into another body but whether that body has any remembrance of me or even cares that I sit alone and suffer day after day I don't know But he keeps asking and it's frightening me why does he care now he didn't believe me when I told him about it at first He has also asked about Devin I know this name but I don't know the name I remember but then again I don't

I don't want Martino to return I am happier when he does not visit, I can leave this basement and wander the town I saw the others again The others like me They keep their distance but they know what I am just like I know what they are

It ended abruptly and Deanna wondered how this passage differed from any of the others that Margaret had written. Why did she throw this one away? Deanna touched the pages lightly with her fingers. A slight pain stabbed her chest and she could feel a tightening in her throat.

"D." It was Sari. It was funny how strange her voice sounded now – almost as if she were speaking into a microphone. "Gail wants you upstairs. Meeting."

Deanna nodded. Taking a deep breath, she folded the paper and placed it in her pocket beside the vial.

Deanna entered the living room clutching the vial of blood in her pocket. Her thoughts were racing over the one journal page that she read and the rediscovered heirloom that she had unearthed in Margaret's personal space. She wanted to sit and talk with Margaret but now was not the time.

Gail looked serious as she sat in one of the armless chairs. The cell phone sitting in her lap told Deanna that she was waiting for another call or text from whomever she had been speaking to.

"What's up?" Deanna sat beside Martino. He, too, looked serious but his expression was closer to concern or distress rather than anger. It was a nice change from the last few days.

Margaret sat beautifully composed beside Eric. Not at all the same person that scribbled books of ramblings alone in the basement rooms. It made Deanna smile to see her sitting just a few feet away. She had been so many women over the last six centuries and thanks to Martino's mistake or selfishness or whatever you call it, she was able to meet the woman that she was and speak to her.

"I spoke to Jordan. He wants us to bring Margaret back to the cabin. In fact, he was quite adamant about it."

Deanna sat listening to the words, unable to formulate a single sentence around the multitude of thoughts streaming through her brain. She took Martino's freezing hand in her own, only briefly thinking that he would not be very agreeable until he hunted – and she was right.

"What do you think?" she asked Martino.

"Well, Jordan knows best. Doesn't he?" He shot out of his seat and began pacing.

"Is there a problem? I thought you were on board with this plan?" Gail didn't look at him as she spoke.

"Isn't it better that she's not left alone?" Deanna's voice was beseeching.

Nods came from all around except Martino and Margaret, who hadn't taken her eyes off of Martino as he paced.

"What do you think . . . Margaret?" Gail's words stopped Martino's pacing.

Margaret continued to gaze almost lovingly at Martino and then she blinked twice as if woken from a dream. She looked to

Gail and then to what Deanna could only assume was Devin hovering above the assembly.

"Margaret, would you like to come home with us? With Martino and Devin?" Gail tried to keep her attention with names that gave her comfort.

Her eyes slowly panned down to Gail again. She sized her up affectionately.

"Yes. I think I would." She looked to Martino, who stared as if she'd never before spoken. "It might solve a few problems in the process."

He rolled his eyes and shook his head, making it clear he didn't wish to discuss it.

Gail looked to Martino as she got flashes of three powerful vampires and Margaret washing blood off her body from Margaret's mind. Maybe this was a mistake, she thought and immediately texted Jordan what she'd seen.

"What did you do?" It was the first time Sari spoke during the meeting. She promised Eric she'd keep her opinions to herself, but this just sounded too good to miss.

Margaret smiled. "I went into town . . ." Her words were so low that it was as if she had only mouthed the words to Sari.

Sari's eyes popped with excitement. "OMG, tell me everything!"

"Stop!" Martino shouted. Deanna knew that if there was anyone out on the road, they were sure to have heard him. "This is not the point."

"What exactly is the point, Tino?" Deanna chimed in. "We want her to go. She wants to go. You're the only obstacle. Why?"

"Tino. I like that," Margaret whispered to herself.

Deanna bit her lip and felt a flutter in her chest. She remembered hearing the nickname for the first time and saying that exact thing. Martino looked to Margaret and then back to Deanna. His eyes glazed over with tears. He wiped it away quickly.

"She needs to come home with us and we'll sort out any indiscretions once were there. I've told Jordan that she may need some protection and he's graciously agreed to help us with that, if needs be." Gail put her cell on the table and stood. "So, we'll need to do a few things. Pack? Is there anything you wish to bring? We can send for everything else if you wish to stay with us but I think a simple suitcase will be fine for now."

Margaret smiled a bright emotion-filled smile that Martino had thought her incapable of.

"I'll help you." Sari was immediately at her side and laughed. "And you can fill me in on your *indiscretions*."

The room was silent after Sari and Margaret went into the basement. Gail returned to her seat and placed her head in her hands. Martino sat beside Eric and waited for Gail to berate him; holding him responsible for deeds Margaret had done. But it wasn't Gail that spoke up first, it was Deanna.

"What did she do that she needs protection?"

Martino shrugged and looked to Gail, who still had her face in her palms. "That's just it. I don't know what she's done. Two months ago, I found that she had been sneaking out of the house and she returned covered in blood. Covered."

"What did she say happened?"

"She hasn't. I don't think she knows. My fear is that she blacks out and loses control. It's why I locked her up in the first place. She disappeared just after she was reborn, and days went by without any word. Then she came home, not knowing where she was or what she had done. I couldn't trust her."

Deanna looked to Eric and then to Gail, who was now looking up again. They were all thinking the same thing. "Why didn't you just keep her with you rather than lock her up?" Her tone was accusatory, and she had no shame in expressing it.

He looked around at the critical stares and his shoulders dropped several inches. "I was scared of her. I didn't know what I was doing, and she frightened the hell out of me. It took years before I could turn my back and not expect her to attack me."

"We'll see how she does at Mount Orion. I don't want to lock her up again, but if Jordan's wrong about this, so help me I'll lock him up with her." Gail's laugh was nervous and drained.

Now sitting on the plane, Deanna sat beside the closed window in first class and thought of their options. Now with the vial in her pocket, they actually had options. She searched out the others seated around her. Margaret chose a seat several rows away from Deanna – the pressure in her chest was not getting any better. Neither was Deanna's so she was thankful when Margaret chose the farthest seat.

On either side of her were Gail and Martino, watching over her protectively. Eric and Sari sat behind Deanna, both actively trying not to draw attention to themselves on the overcrowded flight. Deanna closed her eyes and for the first time since last night, she realized that Devin was not with her.

CHAPTER THIRTY-FIVE

Devin was back. And he was acting up. Slamming doors, throwing chairs, upsetting the horses on the nearby farm. Jacenta thought that since he'd gone back to Deanna, she wouldn't hear from him for a while. No such luck.

Jacenta couldn't talk to him, nor did she wish to when he was like this.

Her desire was to leave. Where to? She was still unsure. Return home to Brazil or go to wherever Deanna and Eric were. Following her recent episode in Gabriel's room, she felt stronger now than ever that she needed to see Deanna again. If only to make sure she was still alive. The feelings frightened her as much as excited her.

Seeing Deanna again would awaken the anger and, more importantly, the regret she had been repressing for centuries. Each lifetime, she saw who Deanna was. She experienced what Deanna – her former best friend, the only woman to ever break her heart – had become. Each lifetime, Jacenta gave Deanna that one chance to repent. That vial of blood. Devin's blood. She'd stolen it when Gemma died and given it to Cristine and then from Cristine to Sophie. On and on. It was her out. If Deanna could figure out which spell was used, then Jacenta would have offered the rest and ended it.

But she never did. Never tried.

Jacenta threw another item of clothing into her suitcase. She was annoyed at Deanna's laziness. She could have figured this all out years ago. But somewhere between wanting to be rid of Devin and clinging to the only way of life she ever knew, something was stopping her.

Where was that vial now? Without Devin, Jacenta found it harder to keep track of Deanna. The last she knew – the last time she cared to know even though she lied about it to Sabina –

Deanna was in Colorado. The vial was hidden in her jewelry box by Jacenta as the six-year-old, Margaret Cooper, slept peacefully. Since then she didn't know where it had gone.

Now Jacenta sat on the bed pushing the packing to the side. She looked around the room. She was going to miss Connecticut. Miss the conveniences and technology; she was going to miss Gabriel. But it was time to go. Time to let go. Six weeks passed quickly – passed and kept going. Jacenta had extended her stay into five months and was now ready to go home. Gabriel and Roderick had the changes well in hand. There was talk of having a meeting with all the directors of all the Havens across the globe. She promised to be there. Until then, she'd leave Gabriel and Roderick to their dreaming.

Her reason for coming had pulled a disappearing act. Callie was so settled in that she rarely visited with Jacenta in the last few weeks. Jacenta wasn't even sure where she was sleeping recently. If her closet wasn't upset regularly, she would be convinced that Callie had left Haven all together. But her closet was raided regularly – nothing was returned. It was clear Callie was enjoying the vintage clothing that Jacenta refused to dispose of.

Walking around the room, she made sure that everything she wanted to take with her was in the suitcase. As she started folding a few new articles of clothing she had acquired on a shopping trip with Sabina and Gwen, the door blew open and slammed shut.

"Must you do that?" she shouted into the air.

No answer.

Jacenta continued folding the cashmere sweater with antique pearl buttons that she had seen in a vintage shop and just had to have. Carefully she placed it on top of the dresses and suits that Gwen was determined to buy for her. *Someone so pretty shouldn't be wearing camouflage*, she told her as she filled her arms with hanger after hanger of dresses.

Gwendolyn was quickly becoming a good friend. She was a permanent resident at Haven but travelled regularly. Just a few days ago, she had said goodbye to Jacenta; she was heading to meet someone in Spain. She wouldn't divulge whom she intended to meet, but she did promise to visit Jacenta in Brazil within the next few months. Gwendolyn was excited to meet Piper and Hunter and see how Haven was meant to function originally.

A chair flew past Jacenta as she collected her jewelry and placed it into her travel bag, crashing against the wall splintering one of the legs. "Stop it, Devin," she said calmly. The closet doors vibrated violently. "If you're ready to talk, then talk. Otherwise, go away; I'm trying to pack." Jacenta waved Devin away as if he were an obnoxious fly.

Still nothing.

The door to the hall opened and Jacenta braced herself for the slam, but it didn't come. "Leaving already?" Gabriel poked his head into the room. "Why rush off?"

"Rush? It's been almost five months. That's double the time I usually give my newbies." She laughed, completely aware that she didn't stay that duration just for Callie. She had stayed for Gabriel and he knew it.

He entered slowly, trying to come up with a reason to make her stay. "You are not leaving because of what happened between us, are you?"

Jacenta dropped the silk blouse in her hand and looked to Gabriel. "That's a reason to stay, not leave. You are always welcome to come with me." Her smile felt false and she hoped it didn't appear that way. Deep down she wasn't sure if she actually wanted him to come with her to Brazil. There was that underlying fear that he may want to change things. Things with Haven, things with her.

The closet door opened and closed. Jacenta smiled uncomfortably. Again, the door opened and closed, a little harder this time.

"What's that? I thought you were alone." Gabriel stepped closer to the closet and took the glass knob in his hand.

"I am and I'm not." She took a deep breath and resumed packing.

"That makes perfect sense," he said mockingly, opening the door and peering inside. "Would you care to explain or should I just come up with my own bizarre explanation?" His eyes sparkled with the lights reflecting off the closet's glass fixtures.

She giggled. "I'm going to miss your wit." Their eyes met and she wanted to be in his arms. "Among other things," she finished playfully.

"My rapier wit, dashing good looks, impeccable style . . ." He wrapped his arms around her waist from behind and rested his chin just below her ear. Kissing her neck and ear several times, he held Jacenta's hands, keeping her from her task. "My breaking heart," he whispered in her ear.

The closet door opened wide and slammed shut, making the two jump.

"Okay, what is that?" Gabriel pulled away. The anger in his voice was evident and something Jacenta had not heard for some time.

Jacenta grabbed his hands and pulled him close to her. His embrace was tense and distracted as she pressed her body against his. "Just ignore it. Someone's having a tantrum," she said more to Devin than to him.

He pushed her away. "I'm sorry, someone's having a tantrum? Who are you talking about?"

"Devin." The bedside lamp toppled to the floor at the utterance of his name. "And I wish he would STOP!" The expression on Gabriel's face was almost comical and would have been pleasing for Jacenta twenty weeks ago, but now it hurt her to see him confused and somewhat frightened. "He's a spirit that keeps me in a constant state of apprehension and frustration."

Jacenta watched as Gabriel righted the lamp and sat in the wing chair beside the fireplace, giving him a very aristocratic air. She humorously thought that a pipe and a hunting dog would complete the picture.

"Spirit? You did say spirit, didn't you?" He shook his head in disbelief.

"Long story." She started folding again.

"He's always with you? Has been here the whole time? When we were together?"

"No-no-nonononono." She laughed. "He comes and goes. He's been with me for years but in a child of divorce sort of way. I guess. I get him every other weekend and for two months during the summer." Jacenta laughed again, but she was the only one. "Look, it's a painfully long story that doesn't end well and doesn't paint a very flattering picture of me, but he was not with me at any point that you and I have been together." *Except maybe the first day,* she thought. "He's having his tantrum about something that doesn't matter in the slightest to me – I'm sure. But yay, I get to experience the fallout from someone else's screw-up." She was getting herself upset talking about it. "Let's talk about something else."

"Who gets him the rest of the time?"

"Sorry?" Jacenta started tossing items into her travelling cases haphazardly, trying to distract herself and expedite the process. She threw items that she didn't intend to pack in an attempt to sidetrack the conversation. "Can you help me zip this?"

"If you have him every other weekend, who has him the rest of the week?" Gabriel's eyes pulsed as he waited for an answer.

"There's so much to explain and no time for it. Another day, perhaps."

"Jace, talk to me. You are clearly bothered by this presence. Can I help?" He sat forward, steepling his hands as he spoke.

She watched him, knowing that he would never understand and even if he did, the mere knowledge of what she had done would forever ruin their relationship. How do you explain to someone that you callously murdered your husband and enslaved his soul? And regret your actions every damn day of your life.

"So, what will you do with yourself once I'm gone? Who will you find to argue with?" She smiled, pulling the overstuffed suitcase off the bed, placing it next to the door.

"Don't do that?"

"What?"

"Change the subject. Tell me who this Devin is and why he's slamming doors."

Jacenta stared at him, caught between wanting to tell him everything and trying to find a way to pick a fight so he would forget about this undesirable topic of conversation. "He's . . ." She found it hard to even verbalize what Devin was to her. "He *was* my husband. He's dead."

"You killed me." Devin was eager to join the conversation. *"Don't forget to tell him that. Loverboy will love to know that you are a cold-blooded killer."*

His words made Jacenta laugh. Not a cynical, derisive laugh but a funny ha-ha, I may wet my pants kind of laugh. She doubled over with her hands on her stomach and her hair falling in her face as her laugh became somewhat of a cackle. In that moment, hearing those words *cold blooded killer*, she realized how ridiculous it was that she feared what Gabriel thought of her actions over six hundred years ago.

Looking at him as he sat in the chair across the room, the confused look on his face made her laugh harder. The fact that his expression would have been a triumph when she first arrived was not lost on Jacenta. It actually added to her hysterical display.

"Jace, what's going on?"

"Yes, Jace, what's going on?" Devin mocked him.

"I'm sorry," she said to both of them. "He's Devin. My husband. He's dead because I killed him in a jealous rage over six hundred years ago. I also made the biggest mistake of my life by enslaving his soul with blood magic. He's also bound to what was once my best friend. She presents a whole different set of problems. Ta-da, my life story in a nutshell." She took a deep breath and waited for his response.

"*Biggest mistake of your life?*" Devin actually sounded hurt.

The closet door slammed shut and the light bulbs in the ceiling chandelier exploded above their heads. Jacenta knew Devin was gone.

"Well, that did it. Maybe I should tell the truth more often." She shrugged with a laugh.

Gabriel sat back in his chair watching the chandelier swing like a pendulum. "And that episode you had last week? That's tied into this as well? Is she immortal?"

Jacenta nodded slowly as he pieced the puzzle together.

"But not one of us?"

She shook her head from side to side, keeping her eyes steadily on him.

"I think I'm going to someplace called Mount Orion when I leave here. This whole thing . . ." She twirled her finger around in a circle between them. ". . . kind of made up my mind. Care to come with?"

"To meet a six-hundred-year-old woman that causes you to have fainting spells and is tied to your ghost husband?" He reached into his jacket and pulled out a thin cigar. He ran the stick under his nose and sniffed it.

"I could use the support and the company." She smiled, playfully twirling her hair between her fingers.

Gabriel pulled Jacenta into his lap. "Ghost husband?"

"Forget him. He's gone for now. All he wants is attention. He thrives on it. I find if I ignore him long enough, he'll go away." She ran her hands through his hair playfully. "Now do you want to talk about Devin or try to convince me to stay here some more?"

CHAPTER THIRTY-SIX

A few nights later, Gail was disoriented when she opened her eyes. The bed was unfamiliar to her, comfortable but not encompassing like her own. She waited for her eyes and head to clear and she looked around. Books stacked around the room. That wonderful musky, masculine aroma that made her feel safe. Jordan's room.

The bed was empty beside her but still warm to the touch. She listened carefully to the movements of the house. No steps, no one walking above her. She did hear shuffling, possibly of blankets. Arguing. She definitely heard arguing.

Gail pulled the covers to her throat and buried herself deep within them. Block out the fighting, she told herself. No need to hear unpleasant things yet. She listened again. Pages being turned. A glass touching wood. Jordan was in the study, no doubt. She smiled slightly. She could feel that he was happy and content.

Last night had put her in a similar state of happiness and contentment. Taking a deep breath, Gail could see herself walking with Jordan in town. Talking of the past, the future, and anything that wasn't related to their present state of unhappiness in the cabin. They had even walked past what was once Lizzy's Restaurant and Hotel – now a hole in the ground barricaded with caution tape and fencing. Not a word passed between them as they went by the hole; Gail was glad it was gone. Hopes of other problems disappearing as easily as that building calmed her.

She and Jordan hunted together, something they didn't do often.

By sunrise, Gail found herself unable and completely unwilling to separate herself from him. His hands, his lips, covering her body, helping her to remember why she had fallen in love with him. She trembled when he touched her, and Gail realized how much she missed his touch. All the fighting, all the problems – recent and long past—melted away as they held each other.

The night was young, she could feel it. Not much past five o'clock. Daylight savings and winter. Short days and long nights; she adored it. Gail slipped out of bed silently, pulling on Jordan's shirt that he had worn last night. The room was littered with books and articles that Jordan had either printed out or clipped from the newspapers he collected.

The dresser was covered in cologne bottles, various jewelry pieces – which she had never seen him wear except the watches, his money clip, and a stack of photos. Thumbing through the photos, Gail didn't know most of the people smiling up at her. She carefully replaced the stack on the dresser.

His gray tweed jacket was carelessly tossed over the suit rack; like the shirt she wore, removed hastily anxious to be in her arms. Gail let a smile grace her lips as she picked up the jacket. As she lifted it, his wallet fell from the breast pocket. Gail looked to the money clip on the dresser and then to the leather wallet as it tumbled to the floor, hitting his black oxford leather shoes.

The wallet contained credit cards, many more than she expected him to have and more photos. Unlike the stack on the dresser, Gail knew these faces. A photo clearly cropped to center on her and Nadia laughing together, one of Nadia's children, Rhea and Renee, just before the end of Renee's life and another of Gail, alone, sitting on her favorite chair in the cottage. There were others, a few but not many. She flipped back to the one of her and Nadia.

"Stop snooping." Jordan's hand closed the wallet and placed it on the dresser.

"Why?"

"It's rude." He pushed her hair away from her neck and kissed it gingerly.

"No, why do you have those?" She pointed to the wallet, her voice thickening with emotion.

He pulled her shoulders, forcing her to face him. "I like to remember even if you don't." Jordan kissed her firmly on the lips.

Gail's lips parted, wanting to be kissed, wanting to be held. Not wanting to think about those pictures and the pain it caused just seeing them. She could feel Jordan was trying to be accommodating to her. He didn't wish to argue and she didn't either. His kiss was urgent and unyielding, and she was happily losing her battle with the past. It would not win out today, she thought.

"You are so beautiful." Jordan was staring at her. "Why don't I see it more often?" She smiled and sucked on her lower lip. His stare made her feel young and vulnerable; she shuddered as she ran his finger over her lips. "Let's get away," he offered.

"What are you saying? Now?"

"Nothing is changing. Nothing is going to change. They can do without you for a month or so." He said *they* with disdain, meaning Deanna and Devin. "I want you all to myself. We'll go anywhere you'd like, my love."

That fluttering in her heart was distracting and her hands were shaking. "I can't leave." *Can I?*

"*Yes, you can.*" Jordan easily read her thoughts. "*I love you. I need you.*" He spoke to her heart and mind. "Did last night mean nothing? That passion I felt from you . . . I thought I'd lost that years ago."

"So did I," she whispered. "Yes. Yes, I'll go," she said quickly and absolutely.

"Where? Anywhere you choose, we shall go."

Gail thought on the question for a moment and remembered something Tabitha had told her. "Spain."

Jordan nodded, clearly elated. "Any reason?"

"Bith spoke of a shelter or something."

A shadow came over Jordan's face but was quickly replaced by a smile and almost playful roll of his eyes. "Haven."

"Yes, that's what she called it!" Gail exclaimed. "She called it a hidden gem in the center of everything. It's been there for centuries. For our kind."

Again, he nodded and pursed his lips, suppressing a knowing smile. "We can't go there."

"You said anywhere? What's wrong with this Haven place? Bith said I'd love it and . . ."

"Of course, she did. Another shot at me, no doubt. Gail, do you know what Haven actually is? Did you even bother to ask?"

Her expression was innocently vacant.

"It *was* a hideout for criminals, centuries ago. Hiding from the judgement of the Council. Hiding from me." He laughed this time, a cynical laugh that told Gail that he thought Tabitha played a good game. "I can't go there. It would be duplicitous."

"Not anymore it's been centuries. Who's going to care? Bith described it more like a hostel. Sounded cozy and different, for me anyway. Please, it sounded perfect." Gail wrapped her arms around his waist and reached up to kiss his lips. "Please?"

He breathed deeply, looking down at her pleading eyes. "Fine. Whatever you want. You shall have."

Jordan kissed her again, pulling her down onto the bed. He unbuttoned the shirt – his shirt that he found so enticing on her – and kissed her throat and breasts. Holding him to her, Gail felt his teeth sink into her shoulder. She did nothing to suppress the moan that came from her soul. He drank from her deeply and desperately, kissing the wound that was healing quickly as he pulled away.

Sliding on top of him, Gail pulled his shirt apart, popping the ivory buttons as she did so. As his blood slid down her throat, she could feel his hands grasping her back in orgasmic pleasure. His thoughts usually well hidden from her were becoming transparent. He held images of Nadia, Chelsea, and Tabitha locked away in his internal vault. She saw raids and fires. Screaming immortals as they met their fiery end. She felt his need and desire to be with her and the fear he felt that she was losing her mind to this precarious situation.

She felt him pull her away and she collapsed beside him on the bed. Blood always calmed her; Jordan's blood brought her to a transcendent place. Was it that he was her sire or that she loved him so deeply? She didn't know? But lying beside him, her thoughts were clear and painful. Abby was in the forefront of her mind. The sunrise, her screams, Gail's inability to help. "Let's go tonight." She was eager to run away again and Jordan was just as eager to help. "We'll tell everyone we're just going for a few days."

Jordan smiled as he sat up. "You're certain?"

Walking up the stairs felt odd to Gail. Somehow the cabin held an alien feel to her this evening. She wished to linger in the basement beside Jordan – in his bed – together. The sound of Deanna whispering, although very soft to the human ear, was excruciating to Gail. The sound was pathetic and lost. She stopped with her hand on the doorknob listening for any other movement in the cabin.

Jordan had returned to his study and she could hear his pen softly scratching against the paper in his journal. He would wait for her to tell Deanna and then they would leave.

Deanna's whispering stopped momentarily, and Gail recognized her halting thoughts as how she silently spoke to Devin. Somewhere in the distance, she heard a car. Gail didn't know if it was close enough to be on her private road or just background noise of the Northway. If she concentrated, she could hear Eric and Sari by the lake, laughing and frolicking, free of Margaret for once.

Gail turned the knob and stepped out into the kitchen to face whatever adventures the night would bring her way. Deanna's whispering and halting thoughts had broken out to heated one-sided conversation. She was trying to be quiet, but her anger was causing her to lose control of the volume of her voice.

"How long have you known?" she was saying as Gail hovered in the kitchen doorway. "What else are you not telling me, Devin? Stop calling me that! I will not calm down!"

The monologue went on like this and was increasing in volume when Gail decided to join the conversation. "Deanna?" she said softly. "Anything you'd like to share with me?"

"She's here." Deanna's tone was stoic and somewhat unemotional.

"Who?" Gail said, already knowing the answer. *Jacenta.*

Two lights caught her eye through the bay window; a car was coming up the driveway.

"How?" Another ridiculous question that she had already answered on her own. *How long have you known,* Deanna had said to Devin? Gail was beginning to piece it together that Jacenta was an immortal, like she was. At least the playing field was even – sort of.

Deanna didn't answer, nor was she moving. Her hands, still clutching wet, makeup-smeared tissues, were folded neatly in her lap. Her eyes, half closed, stared straight ahead and held no expression whatsoever. Her mind was closed, probably to Devin but it also closed Gail out as well.

The approaching headlights were blinding as a long black limousine pulled up into the circle drive and stopped. The lights illuminated the front of the cabin. The driver turned off the engine but didn't get out of the car. As the rear door opened, Gail walked to the window to get a better look at her guest.

From the back of the car, a tall good-looking man emerged. He was clearly immortal from his pallor and the iridescent sheen in his eyes as he caught a reflection of the lights from the window. He was well dressed, and he seemed to absorb his surroundings before offering his hand to another still waiting in the car.

Gail was impressed by the care he was taking as his blue eyes scanned the house and the movement within and without. He was much older than she and possibly older than Jordan but by how much she was uncertain. A wave of alarm washed over her. Dealing with Jacenta, who had to be easily six hundred years old, was one thing, but this immortal was much older than that. A small part of her mind wished that Tabitha was at the cabin. Or

Trevor. But their visits were becoming more and more sporadic and Gail couldn't determine when they would return.

As a small hand reached out of the car, Gail felt a shudder creep up her chest into her throat. The anticipation of meeting this woman was making her shake slightly. Then a small woman with a mane of red hair stood beside the car looking fairly frightened.

Like her companion, her eyes circled the area. She studied the cabin's façade for some time. Possibly listening as the other did, possibly contemplating her next move. The night was so dark that the lake was almost invisible from this distance. Then her eyes fell to the cottage on the hill. The moonlight illuminated it like a halo, giving it an ethereal appearance. Gail could see the questions forming in Jacenta's mind and in her eyes.

Her handsome companion took her hand with the kindness of a lover and guided her toward the cabin's front door. A slight hesitation made Jacenta stop and turn back towards the car. Again her companion took her hand, kissing it this time, and steered her back on course.

The nervousness in Gail's chest subsided some as she saw how anxious Jacenta was, also.

"Deanna, get the door." Jordan was suddenly in the room. "You have guests." His tone was harsh and demanding.

Gail turned just as they tapped lightly on the front door. "I'll . . ."

"No, she'll do it."

Deanna didn't move.

They tapped again.

"You started this. Now you'll finish it." Jordan was impatient with her. He took her arm and lifted her from the sofa. The tissues in her hand tumbled to the floor as her feet left it.

Still not saying a word, Deanna allowed Jordan to usher her to the foyer. The only thought Gail heard was, "Devin, don't." An attempt to stop Devin from hurting Jordan, she could only assume.

The door opened before Deanna could touch the knob. Jacenta stood before her in mid-knock, still holding her friend's hand tightly. For a moment, the four stood staring at each other. Deanna, Jacenta, Jordan, and the handsome stranger.

Jordan waited for Deanna to speak, run, strike out, but she did none of those things. She stood staring, not at the new arrivals, just staring past them as if she had opened the door and no one was there.

The handsome stranger, as Gail was coming to think of him, cleared his throat and nudged Jacenta with his shoulder gently. "Hi . . ." She stopped and took a deep breath, seeing that Deanna had no reaction. *"Is this her?"* Gail heard Jacenta say to Devin silently. Her topaz-colored eyes seemed to devour Deanna's face. "It is you," she said aloud. "The eyes. They never change. I always know you from your eyes. Quite amazing. The eyes, I guess, truly are the windows to the soul."

Deanna still had no reaction.

"Hello, I'm Jacenta." She looked to Jordan, hoping for a warmer welcome. There was a look of shared recognition and horror in their eyes. Jacenta recoiled a bit as Jordan touched her hand to his lips and smiled.

"Please come in." Gail approached the door. "I'm Gail; welcome to my home." She stepped back, allowing them to step into the foyer.

Jacenta passed Deanna without another word. Her eyes devoured the room as she stepped into it. Jordan took their coats, hung them in the closet, and remained slightly removed from the assembly. Jacenta walked to the fireplace and studied the photos on the mantel. "Lovely," she said softly.

"Thank you." Gail smiled. "I hate to admit how eager I am to speak with you. Please sit unless you'd like to freshen up after your journey. We have rooms if you'd like to rest before we speak." She was agonizingly aware that she was stumbling over herself to accommodate these strangers.

There was a momentary silence. Deanna stood in the doorway with the heavy front door still open, although she didn't seem to notice. The handsome stranger was beside her standing guarded but open to their hospitality. He came around Deanna and closed the door. "Shall we sit?" He took Deanna's arm, not expecting her to respond.

Deanna remained silent through the introductions and pleasantries. It was all very polite and unnerving to Gail. She was used to her human way of life. Dinner parties, dates, coffee shops, movies. What she wasn't used to was welcoming elder immortals into her home and having them respond to the normality of her life in a positive way.

From the corner of her eye, Gail watched Deanna. She sat just where the handsome stranger, Gabriel, had set her down. Her hands were folded as before, no tissues this time. No tears either. Her eyes were dry, and her mind was closed to everyone.

Jordan was taken with Gabriel. The two spoke of their recent travels and Gabriel even remembered Jordan from his Council days. Jacenta stared at Jordan as if she were staring at a monster but then caught herself and looked away. Jordan, never too keen on the subject of the wars, smiled and detoured the conversation to other subjects.

Gail studied Jacenta as she sat beside Gabriel. She was still enjoying her surroundings, as if she'd never been in a house before. The photographs throughout the room drew most of her attention. "I know her." She said softly to Gail, not wanting to disturb the men in their conversation. "Little Red. I mean, Rhea. I call her Little Red, well, for obvious reasons." She laughed softly, motioning to her own red hair.

Smiling, and very curious, Gail wanted to know how she knew one of her closest friends.

Without asking for an explanation, Jacenta offered it. "She is a frequent visitor in Salvador."

"Brazil? You know Adrian, no doubt. Rhea's father."

Jacenta's brows met slightly. "She's always alone. She seems to prefer it that way."

Gail was very curious now, almost forgetting Deanna and why they were all gathered together. "What's in Brazil?"

"Haven. You've never heard of it?" Jacenta said more in astonishment rather than a question. "It's a shelter for wanderers. A community for all that need it." She glanced to Jordan like she was afraid to continue, afraid of what he might say, but Gail urged her. "Connecticut is the closest. Gabriel is a resident and . . ." She trailed off as the front door burst open.

Sari was running and laughing – followed closely by Eric, who was in hot pursuit. She shrieked happily as he caught her; the two laughed, very embarrassed, as Gail stood and cleared her throat.

"What's with the limo?" Sari giggled.

"Eric?" Jacenta turned from her place on the sofa. "Eric."

There was a mix of emotions on his face. He walked into the room, ignoring everyone except Jacenta. Opening his arms, she approached almost cautiously. Staring at his face, she looked like she wanted to touch him but couldn't – memories, both painful and tender, kept her at arm's length until he pulled her to him. Jacenta nestled her face beneath his chin and seemed to melt there, fused to him for a moment.

The two locked together broke from their embrace as Jordan and Gabriel rose and walked toward them. "This is him." Jacenta beamed, holding tight to Eric's arm. Taking Gabriel's hand, she introduced the two and it became evident to Gail that these were the two most important men in her life – and then there was Devin.

Eric looked uncomfortable yet elated at the same time. The way only Eric could. He introduced Sari to Jacenta. Awkward as it was, Gail could feel Sari's excitement bubbling beneath the flimsy surface of her emotions.

"Shall we sit?" Gail offered. Grabbing Eric's arm, she gave him an inquisitive look.

"She's my sire," he said simply.

"WHAT?" Deanna burst out. Gail lowered her head into her hands, hoping that this could have been avoided. "I can take the false polite conversation. I can even take the fake comradery building between those two." She motioned to Jordan and

Gabriel. "But seriously, you know him!" Deanna jumped to her feet and was wagging her finger in everyone's face. "How long since you've put it all together? Since the beginning? Yesterday? When?" She railed at Eric.

"D, this is not Eric's fault," Sari jumped in.

"Isn't it? Do you realize how much plotting and planning we've been doing, and he sat there watching us . . . probably laughing the whole time, knowing the truth. How long, Eric?"

Eric stood still for a while, not saying anything, not wanting to pour fuel on Deanna's fire.

"How long have you been laughing every time I mentioned her name? At what point were you going to tell us?" Deanna's face was reddening as she screamed.

"I didn't intend to tell you," he burst out finally. "My plan was to watch you fail and hope to God that you would go away. And while we're pointing fingers, where was Devin in this witch hunt? He knew for as long as she's been alive. Do you know where he goes when he's not with you? For all those months or weeks that he disappears? I do." Eric pointed to Jacenta as she stood staring, open-mouthed, as he delivered his tirade.

"For years, he was with us. Years. Off and on, but there just the same. It wasn't her name I was hiding from; it was his. And when you think of being self-righteous, little girl, you just think of Abby and your friend, Max. Just remember who your friends are and what we're protecting you from."

Deanna took a step closer to Eric, ready to respond when Jacenta stepped forward.

"Enough. That's enough. No more fighting, no more threats. This is what I was afraid would happen and the reason I didn't really want to come here today."

It appeared as if Deanna was ready to explode. Her eyes were red and watery and around the edges the hazel was darkening into an earthy green.

"Oh, calm yourself, Deanna. Let's keep our finger in the dike, shall we? No need to cause a typhoon." Jacenta stood facing her ex-best friend. "This is not Eric's fault or anybody's really. If you wanted to break this curse, you had the answer all along."

Deanna's jaw clenched and when she spoke, she hissed through her teeth. "You don't get to speak to me."

"Deanna, please," Gail finally spoke up as well.

"No, it's fine." Jacenta sounded patient. "This is the Deanna I remember. So glad the years haven't changed you at all." She looked to the air, possibly listening for Devin, who hadn't spoken since Jacenta drove up.

A faint sound of the basement door opening and closing followed by footsteps concerned Gail. It sounded like several bodies had entered the cabin. If she concentrated, Gail could pinpoint who it was from their thoughts, but there was no hope of concentrating on anything other than the issue before her.

She only hoped that they remained in the basement. Looking to Jordan, she saw his concern as well, but his familiar need to escape to his study was filling his thoughts. Sending Gabriel with him – and possibly Eric and Sari – might help defuse a potentially explosive situation. With that thought, she heard voices coming closer and footfalls ascending the stairs.

Now she could hear them: Martino with Margaret in tow, Tabitha and Chelsea arguing playfully, and others that could only be Phillipe and Richard. The dogs were the first to enter the room, running to Sari as was their custom before finding their place on the carpet in front of the hearth. Following them, the others felt as if they had walked into an awkward situation.

Then suddenly, Chelsea burst out gleefully and hugged Jacenta. Turning to face the assembly, Jacenta said, "Sorry, we're old friends. She was one of my first newbies."

"Small world." Gabriel smirked, eyeing Jacenta playfully.

"We shouldn't be here. We'll catch up later." Chelsea kissed Jacenta's cheek quickly and motioned to Bith and the others to follow her to the lake.

"No, please stay. This won't take long." Deanna was still fuming. "Are you going to help us or not?" Deanna demanded.

"Oh, I'm sorry. Am I allowed to speak to you now?" Jacenta looked to those around her, Gail, Eric, and Gabriel, and smirked. "Who is us, Deanna? Don't you mean *you?* Won't I help you?" She rubbed her chin as if she was thinking. "Tough question."

Deanna was seething.

Eric squeezed Jacenta's hand, warning her not to be cruel. Gabriel stood back with Jordan, Chelsea, and Bith taking it all in.

"Why should I? I came here with every intention of helping you. I did. I don't know how you feel, but I hate that Devin is with me constantly. He slams doors, throws things. His tantrums are what convinced me to come." She stopped and watched Deanna's reaction. When there was none, she smiled. "Did you know that adultery is a crime punishable by death?" She stopped. "But that's only in some countries. The church says it's a crime punishable by eternal damnation. Eternal damnation, Deanna. Eternal."

"It's been six hundred years; you're still carrying that around? Most women would have moved on with their lives by now." Deanna put her head in her hands.

"Most woman would have killed you both six hundred years ago and not given you this second chance."

Gail nodded, knowing she would have killed her husband had he cheated on her. Chelsea looked down, remembering always being the other woman, and Tabitha simply raised her eyebrows in agreement.

Deanna didn't care if anyone else agreed with Jacenta. "What kind of second chance did you give me? A second chance to do what? Die? I've done that too many times to count. To realize that Devin and I were wrong for one another? That he really always belonged with you? Well, cheers, my friend. You hit that one right on the head. You can have him. Just give me my freedom on your way out."

The heavy front door opened and slammed shut. Everyone except Jacenta and Deanna jumped. Margaret laughed and watched Devin's light move through the room. The dogs howled and Gail watched helplessly as Devin threw several lamps to the floor and shattered a mirror near the stairs.

Jacenta ignored Devin's tantrum. She stared at Deanna studying her. "You don't get it, do you?" She shook her head, defeated.

"Yes, Deanna, this isn't helping." Gail interrupted. "Why don't we discuss this rationally?"

Everyone shifted uncomfortably in their seats. Chelsea whispered something to Bith, and Martino nudged Richard cautiously. Even Gabriel looked anxious. Jacenta followed everyone's movements without moving her head. She was suspicious of what their next move would be. She took a deep breath.

"First of all, you may all go," Gail said to the others. "I don't see how this is helping. You're making our guest nervous and frankly, you're making me a little uneasy as well." She smiled at Jacenta. "The only one that needs to be here is Deanna." She walked them to the door. "You too, Sari and Eric, please. It may make the going easier." Gail put her hand on Eric's shoulder.

Eric quickly kissed Jacenta's cheek and got to his feet. He nodded to Gail and Deanna. Sari was a little peeved at having to walk out in the middle of what she thought of as the negotiations. "I'm sure we'll hear all about it later," he whispered in her ear.

"I'll be downstairs," Gabriel whispered to Jacenta and followed Jordan to the basement.

"Nicely done." Jacenta crossed her legs. "And thank you. I was feeling a bit cornered."

Gail sat down across from Jacenta. "Do you agree that this had gone on long enough?"

Jacenta didn't answer at first. *Long enough for whom? What was the statute of limitations on betrayal? Betrayal from a husband and betrayal from your best friend, your sister? Exactly when does it stop hurting to look into the eyes of the one that deceived you?*

"Fair enough." Gail read Jacenta's thoughts.

Jacenta was taken aback by the intrusion on her thoughts. "Don't do that," she said coldly.

Gail swallowed hard.

"Listen, let's take this one step at a time. You have Devin's blood, right? The vial you collected years ago?" Jacenta looked to Deanna. Deanna nodded. "So, all you need is the words and . . ."

She devoured the confused expressions that crossed Gail's and Deanna's faces. "Did you think that all you had to do was combine Devin's blood and yours and poof! The spell would be broken? Well, this isn't some cheap Lifetime movie." She giggled. "This is real witchcraft. You should know better than anyone, Deanna. It was your spell, after all."

"What is needed?" Gail asked with due caution.

"Me." Jacenta smiled, loving this temporary control she had. "My blood." She tapped her temple. "The three of us have been tied together for centuries by the blood. We can hear Devin, sense each other, and know when the other dies. I've known every lifetime you've had. Not because of Devin but because of a sharp stabbing pain I feel . . ." She tapped her heart. "Every time you die."

Deanna stared at her intently.

"I'm sure without knowing what it was, you felt when I almost died over three centuries ago at the hands of the Council. Maybe you thought it was a heart attack or just indigestion, but I know you felt it. Just like you felt when Devin broke out of that restaurant. I felt it. I didn't know what it was, but I felt something." Her cell phone vibrated. Jacenta glanced down at the screen to see who was calling her – Piper – and she ignored it.

There was no reaction from Deanna. She just continued to stare.

Jacenta looked to Gail and shook her head with impatience. "You'll get my blood and my help when I'm good and ready." With that, she left.

Gail sat down after Jacenta slammed the front door shut. "I need to talk to Eric. He'll need to talk to her and convince her to help." She watched as Deanna sat staring at the floor. "She's still really pissed at you."

Deanna had no reaction.

"She's angry with *you,* not Devin as much. You really hurt her. I could feel that from her." Gail raised Deanna's face in her hand. "You need to make some kind of amends with her."

Deanna scoffed and got off the sofa.

"If you want any of this to happen, you need to come to terms with what you did to that woman. You've been so good at playing the victim, but now you must take ownership of your part in this mess." Her eyes followed Deanna as she paced the room.

"Ownership? I didn't do this. I didn't kill Devin! I am the victim. Whose side are you on, anyway?" Deanna paced more frantically.

"Your side. I'm always on your side, but you did sleep with her husband. You betrayed her trust." Gail said calmly. "You slept with your best friend's husband. Even now, with morals being at their lowest point, where there are cougars and teen pregnancies and weird open relationships, what you did sucks."

Deanna stopped pacing. "She's still mad at me? Not Devin? But me?"

Gail nodded. "She loved you. Still very much so."

"She loved Devin too. Why is this all about me?"

"Wow, you really don't get it, do you? You've told me you were like sisters. He was just a man. You kind of get it when a man hurts you. But not your sister." Gail held Deanna's face for a moment. "That's what you need to own. You hurt her. She hurt you. Make amends, my love." Gail walked to the kitchen and looked back. "What did she mean that it was your spell?"

Deanna didn't answer.

CHAPTER THIRTY-SEVEN

As Jacenta stepped outside the cabin door, she was keenly aware that she had left Gabriel in the basement with Jordan. *Wow, that was Jordan Glynn*, she thought. The last time she'd seen his face was at the other end of a broad sword. A group of rebels had been caught and she was with them. *And was that the Warrior Tabitha? The same Tabitha that had saved her life and the lives of countless novice Warriors?*

Coming to this cabin, she expected to dredge up parts of her past that she would have preferred stayed buried, but this was a completely different set of parts that she didn't expect to unearth. Warriors, Council members, Chelsea – one of the first lost souls she took in before Haven was really Haven. She had become a great tracker for the Council, hadn't she? But Jordan was the one that stopped her in her tracks. Not as awe-inspiring as she remembered him to be, of course now he wasn't threatening her life while she wept on her knees before him.

Jordan knew things that no one else knew. He could read their thoughts and knew their secrets. There were so many threats made by the Council. As a warning, she watched as one of her companions was decapitated before her – not by Jordan but an equally awe-inspiring figure, a woman named Olivia. It was then that Jacenta had decided to remove herself from the Warriors and return to Sabina.

She couldn't believe Jordan was here, now downstairs talking to Gabriel, living with Eric. Her head was reeling. So much had taken place in the space of the last hour that she could hardly take it all in.

The moon was hidden behind the clouds now, cloaking the property in darkness. She could see the moon hiding but wasn't sure if it was ready to come out to play. The limousine driver leaned against the car smoking a cigarette, paying no attention to Jacenta.

The screen on her iPhone showed Piper's face and vibrated in her hand before she hit the green answer button.

"Piper? What's wrong now?" Her harsh tone was caused by and meant for Deanna but had its target on Piper.

"Just checking in." The sweet, bubbly voice drew Jacenta away from the cabin and back to Salvador. "Are you all right? You sound stressed." A note of concern crept into the conversation, but Piper's usual cheerful personality lifted Jacenta's mood.

"Way too much to explain."

"How's Connecticut?"

Jacenta could almost hear Piper twirling her ponytails between her middle and forefinger. For the first time in over two months, she wanted to go home. She wanted to walk through the door to Haven and smell the fire burning, see the smiling faces of Piper, Hunter, and probably Sydney. She wanted to sit in her chair and feel the *good stuff* as it permeated every cell of her body.

"Not there anymore. On a road trip, of sorts. Any news that I should be concerned about?"

Piper laughed a quick chirpy laugh that Jacenta always found both slightly irritating and completely loveable at the same time. "We're all fine here. Nothing new to report in the way of newbies. Callie do okay with her new digs?"

"Hmmm." Jacenta was gnawing on her cuticles, nervously looking back to the cabin.

"J, you still with me?" There was some whispering in the background. "Hunter says hi." She hushed him and returned to the call. "What about Callie? She, uh, fitting in?"

Jacenta remembered all her clothes that kept disappearing as the weeks went on at Connecticut Haven and seeing Callie less and less. "She's doing fine. Nothing to worry about there. She's got a new cell phone. I'll text you the number if you want to call her."

"You sound really distracted. Sure you're okay? I could fly out there and we could road trip it together?"

A warmth consumed her chest. A smile and a tear graced her face. Piper. The best and biggest pain in the ass that Jacenta ever had the privilege of knowing. The Pipers of the world made it worth risking her life and her sanity to keep Haven up and running. "No, I'll be . . . well, this trip kind of sucks so far, but I met someone that makes it all worth it. And I hope to finish this business soon and be home by the end of the week. Fingers crossed."

"Hey, quick question. Are we upgrading our systems or something? 'Cause I got a call from some guy in Portland . . . Haven in Portland, asking about our computer systems. I forget his name, something like Nathan or Newman; anyway, what's he talking about?"

Jacenta exhaled a large burst of air like she was preparing to blow up a balloon and closed her eyes. "If they call again, tell them to get in contact with Connecticut. The US Havens are moving in a different direction. Not one I'm all that thrilled with, but Roderick is spearheading it. Let him field the calls."

"Wait, what? Are we changing too? Shut up, I'm trying to hear!" There was a ruckus in the background on Piper's side. Hunter was listening to the conversation and expressing his displeasure into Piper's ear.

"Look, you don't need to worry about this. There's nothing to worry about." She took a deep breath and exhaled audibly. Bouncing back and forth on the balls of her feet helped Jacenta to calm down. "Hey, stop fighting! I'm dealing with something right now. Personal stuff. When it's done, I'll be home and we'll talk. If you keep getting phone calls, tell them to call Connecticut."

After saying goodbye and reassuring Piper that she didn't need to come to the States, Jacenta stuffed her phone back into her jacket pocket. Finally, the moon had come out from behind the clouds again and the property was under a giant spotlight. She looked to the cabin and saw Deanna still sitting in the same spot where she left her.

Jacenta sent the limo driver away, telling him that they would call if they needed him again this evening, which was highly unlikely. As she watched the long sleek car pull away down the driveway, the headlights shone on a lake and the group of curious immortals gathered there. It made Jacenta smile, although she wasn't quite sure why – maybe because they were watching her and now she was watching them.

The air was crisp and a breeze blew her hair as she walked swiftly toward the lake. The water rippled to the shore and Jacenta watched as the moonlight caught the crests and illuminated the water. Eric was the first to approach her, and he was loving and unexpectedly passionate. He grabbed her waist and kissed her neck roughly – like he used to do years ago.

"So, have you reconciled with Sabina?" Hearing his voice again was incredible.

She smiled, staring towards the lake. "Hmm-hmm. In Connecticut."

"Where you met this Gabriel?"

Again, she smiled hearing the old jealousy in his voice. She broke free from his embrace and kissed his hands as they held hers. "Yes. She's training their scouts as we speak. She asked about you. In fact, it was her persistence that got Devin to divulge your whereabouts," she said playfully.

His face lost all of its humor and he raised his eyebrows in response.

"They'll be well trained." Chelsea appeared from the shadows. "She trained the trackers back in the day. Great lady."

Jacenta smiled warmly and whispered, "Yes, she is."

"Are you still running Haven?"

A warm spot formed in her chest that made Jacenta instantly fall in love with Chelsea again. She remembered the fear in her eyes over three centuries ago when she found her huddled in an abandoned farmhouse just outside of London. She, like so many others, assumed the name of where she was born. Jacenta was glad to see it stuck. "Yes. Brazil is my home, but Haven has survived despite . . ." She rolled her eyes, letting the thought linger in the air.

Chelsea chuckled, knowing exactly what Jacenta was getting at.

From the shadows, the others filled the edge of the lake. Sari and Margaret were farthest away, watching and listening. Richard and Phillipe introduced themselves and stepped back. Tabitha's approach was next, and it made a nervous laugh bubble up in Jacenta's throat.

"You think this is funny? This mess that seems to start and end with you?" Tabitha's dark hair flowed carelessly around her shoulders. Jacenta envied how relaxed and at home she appeared in this setting even as her tone dripped with acid.

Jacenta studied Tabitha carefully. "I remember you," she said without thinking.

Tabitha looked at her accusingly and she could see Chelsea take a step towards her in a protective manner even though Jacenta was older than her by centuries. She assumed it was more to stop Tabitha than protect Jacenta.

"I remember how everyone envied you." Jacenta smiled. "You were the 'it' girl in those days. Aaron's right hand."

"Feared more than envied, I'd say." Tabitha took a deep breath, full of regret, and dropped her defensive stance.

Jacenta nodded. "You scared me. With that sword . . . you were something." The sword was a large steel blade that Tabitha always carried slung to her back. The handle was adorned with jewels that sparkled behind her head like a halo. "You probably don't remember it, but I was there at the Battle of Toulon when you and Aaron were captured. The Haven there was destroyed in that battle."

A light went out in Tabitha's eyes as she remembered the details of the battle and the small hidden compound that served as a hideout for her fellow militia. "The end of the war," she whispered. Tabitha saw the confused looks surrounding her. "So, you were a rebel or a supporter?"

Again, Jacenta nodded. "Both. Sabina was in the mix for a while and I joined before she stepped away. She's what they call today a conscientious objector. My time as a Warrior didn't last long. Olivia . . . and Jordan saw to that."

"Sabina was a war profiteer if I remember correctly. She worked both sides for her own gains." Eric laughed. Jacenta opened her mouth to correct him but thought better of it, especially in present company.

Tabitha nodded approvingly as if there was a certain respect that came with being a fellow Warrior. "I remember Sabina," she said as if she both agreed with Eric and still respected her at the same time. "I remember you as well. The safe houses before and after the wars; the taverns and inns that welcomed our kind. You helped a lot of Warriors in your time. Why?"

Jacenta had been keeping her fellow immortals safe for years. "Reparation. Atonement. Redemption. Whatever you want to call it. Making up for evils of the past, I guess." Jacenta smiled nervously.

There was a sense of some distorted friendship beginning with these creatures that Jacenta hadn't thought was possible when she first left the cabin. The delicate sound of wind chimes tinkling on the small dock across the way helped calm her. She looked to Eric, who was now pulling Sari closer to the front of the group.

"So, this is Sari." Jacenta grabbed Sari's hands playfully. "You need to tell me all about yourself, my dear. Of course, Devin has filled me in on the superficial details. But I want to know how this all came to be and what are your intentions with my Eric?"

Sari's expression was guarded and suspicious yet awestruck underneath it all. "I'm young. I'm inexperienced and yet . . . very territorial."

Jacenta's sly cunning smile dissolved into astonishment and then laughter as she looked to Eric and then back to Sari. "Well played. I like this one."

Just two hours before sunrise, the others left the cabin and its problems behind. Eric found himself alone with Jacenta. It had been years since they sat alone in the same room together and he could see the uneasiness in her face. The last time they had spoken, their words were harsh toward one another. Now he was sure it was Devin's doing that had caused their break, but at the time Eric couldn't spend another minute in Jacenta's company.

There were pleasant memories, if he searched for them, but the outstanding ones were painful and cruel. Devin had been with them for longer than usual. Like now, he would visit and irritate them for longer than either he or Jacenta desired, and then he returned to whichever incarnation of Deanna was alive. Deanna was Emily when he and Jacenta parted ways. And Emily was having none of Devin.

Jacenta had confided that Emily refused to acknowledge him since puberty. Devin was hurt and angry and was their problem for the duration of Emily's life. There were times Eric and Jacenta would plot Emily's death just to rid themselves of Devin. In the end, they did nothing but argue and accuse.

Sabina was with them when they split. She and Jacenta fought as well. They fought over Eric, among other things. Jacenta would rail over why Sabina was attracted to him and that she should leave them in peace.

The sound of the ocean from the windows of the small shack that he and Jacenta called home was the first pleasant memory that returned as he stared at her sitting uncomfortably in front of the fire. He remembered sitting on the beach watching Jacenta and Sabina play in the surf. They'd build a fire and lie in each other's arms under the stars. Those were the good memories. The ocean and the wind. The howling wind threatening to decimate their humble home. How the walls would scream under the pressure of the forceful wind; it made Eric laugh now.

"What's so funny?" Her voice sounded far away and strangely unsure of herself.

"Just thinking of that abysmal shack we had. Right on the beach. We were totally unprotected and really didn't care." He chuckled and got up to stoke the fire.

He could feel Jacenta watching him. As he turned from the fire to face her, he could see the sparkle of the fire in her blue eyes. Her posture was more relaxed now. Her legs were pulled in a knot in front of her as she considered him lovingly.

"I guess I should apologize for . . ."

"Nothing," she interrupted him. "You have nothing to apologize for. If time has taught me anything, it's that you need to forgive and move on with your life. And let's be honest, my love, Devin was a big part of why we went our separate ways. Devin and Haven."

Eric was reluctant to remember that side of the arguments. Those parts had nothing to do with Devin. He was jealous of Jacenta's growing reputation and pressed her many times to give up her failing cause. The fear that it was his jealousy after all and not Devin that had driven them apart was eating at him.

She continued, "If we're being honest, I've been looking for you for years."

"Have you?" Eric sat beside Jacenta on the sofa.

She nodded. "With or without Devin, your hatred of Haven aside, there is not a day that goes by that something inconsequential doesn't make me think of you. And I laugh and then I cry. Sabina couldn't believe we haven't seen each other since . . . then. She still fancies you."

That made Eric laugh out loud.

"What did she call you? Tall, dark, and dreamy, I believe." Her mouth twisted into a pout-ish smile that made Eric want to kiss her. His intentions must have been apparent because Jacenta dropped her eyes and bit her lip like an innocent schoolgirl. He did kiss her and happily felt her body melt into his as she bit his lower lip now. The cool touch of her hand against his skin made him pull her closer, and she giggled as their mouths glided together again.

"Time out, we can't do this. There are others we need to think of now." She pulled away, catching her breath, all the time still smiling.

"Devin?"

"He's thankfully absent from my mind and this room but Gabriel is downstairs, and Sari . . . tell me about Sari." She straightened up and knotted her legs again.

"You met her."

"Tell me why you chose her. After all these years, you haven't chosen someone to spend your life with until now. You must love her very much." Her eyes sparkled again in the firelight and her smile was honest and tender.

"I do. She's so part of this world. Do you understand? She grounds me. And for some indescribable reason she puts up with all of this and still loves me." He chuffed.

"There's a lot to love. I'm happy for you, baby. I really am. A little jealous when I see how she looks at you and you at her, but otherwise, very happy." Her cool hand stroked his face and Eric closed his eyes, knowing this might be the last time they spent a moment alone. He quickly took her hand and kissed her palm.

"Quid pro quo. Gabriel, really?" Eric laughed again, enjoying the growing easiness between them.

"I know, Sabina said the same thing. I don't know. We fight constantly. About everything. He's stubborn and maddening and frustrating. But he gets me if that's the right wordage. He calls me out when I'm obsessing, and he knows Haven. More than I want him to, but he understands that part of my insanity." She shrugged and looked into the fire. "He's loving and gentle. He's the first man I've loved since you."

Eric listened to her words and watched how animated she became as she spoke about Gabriel. He was happy for her as well. He just wasn't sure if he trusted Gabriel yet.

They sat in silence for almost an hour, watching the fire as it slowly petered out. Jacenta rested her head on his chest as his arms encompassed her. She fit so perfectly in his arms. Yet he noticed that she took the opposite side to Sari. She was the mirror of her. His missing puzzle piece in an alternate universe.

"Almost dawn." Gail appeared in the doorway behind them. "I was being honest with you before: we do have a spare room for you to stay here if you wish." She came around the sofa and looked to Jacenta without a hint of judgement as she lay in Eric's arms.

"Thank you. I think I'd like that." The women stared at each other for a moment, one sizing up the other.

"Good, I was hoping you'd like it here."

"I adore Mt. Orion. The land, or what I've seen of it, is beautiful." Jacenta sat up and patted the seat beside her. "It reminds me of my home in Ireland."

"Your home with Devin?" Gail sat in the chair facing them. The sun was just coming over horizon, and she kept her eyes locked on the trees lining the shore of the lake.

Jacenta nodded. "It was gorgeous. It had not a lake like yours but a creek that ran near the house." She sat back a little. "When the sun was high, the creek would sparkle as if it were lined with diamonds." She took a deep breath and allowed herself to remember just a little of her past. "The house, not as large as yours, was quite large for houses then. My boys loved to play in the fields that lay behind the house."

"Do you miss it? That life, I mean, with a husband and children?" Gail still didn't look at Jacenta but kept her eyes glued to the horizon and her impending doom.

"Don't you?" Jacenta stood, sensing Gail's uneasiness regarding the hour.

Gail jumped, startled by the sudden movement. She turned toward Jacenta. "I don't miss it, no." She paused. "I never really lost it. Jordan replaced my husband."

"He's your siempre," Jacenta said softly.

"I'm sorry?"

"Siempre means always. Something a friend told me once. The one that will always be in your heart."

Gail smiled. "I like that. Well, Martino and the others are my children. Being immortal has never really changed my life."

Jacenta stared at Gail and reached out her hand. "Have you ever been sorry that you missed the whole *experience*?"

Gail thought on her answer for a while. She had travelled as far as any immortal and had experienced the kill with unimaginable passion. She couldn't imagine what the *experience* actually was. Glancing down at Jacenta's extended hand, there was a ring on the third finger of her left hand. "Do you miss it?" Gail asked again, this time motioning to the ring.

Raising her hand, Jacenta stared at the ring before her. The ring Devin put on her finger on their wedding day. She hadn't taken it off since. It was gold and engraved with images from Devin's family crest. Jacenta laughed. "Tough question," she said simply. "I miss Devin as a husband as much as you miss Virgil."

Gail nodded, understanding completely. She took Jacenta's hand and followed her towards the basement rooms. Then she thought on Jacenta's last words. "How did you know about Virgil?"

Jacenta smiled slyly. "I've always known where Deanna was. Never very far away, you might say."

Gail wasn't sure if she should ask the countless questions that were filling her head. Instead she stayed quiet and let Jacenta continue.

"That's why I hesitate. I don't know how to live without Devin. Deanna and I have a lot of unresolved issues before I do anything, but . . . wow, living without Devin. I don't know if I know how to do that?" Both women were silent as they followed Eric down the final steps into the basement living room.

"You are still down here? Swapping war stories?" Gail laughed as she fell on the sofa beside Jordan. "Too late to go upstairs. I trust Sari is safe."

Eric nodded. "With Chelsea, I assume." He ignored the uncomfortable looks his irritated tone had generated.

"I'm sorry I can't offer you better accommodations your first day here."

Jacenta smiled. Her eyes closed to the sound of Jordan and Gabriel, continuing a story that had been started hours ago.

CHAPTER THIRTY-EIGHT

The next evening, Jacenta woke to arguing. She had slept in, thanks to a bit of the good stuff before bed this morning. It always gave her what could loosely be referred to as a hangover but not in the human sense. Gabriel called them *blood relics*. The after-effects of the extra immortal blood in her system. Her hangovers or blood relics made her sleep in hours (once it was days) past sunset, and she found her hunger was doubled. This time was no different and when she went upstairs, she had hoped just to slip out for a bite to eat. The fates had another plan in mind.

When she entered the living room, everyone turned toward her.

"You need to lay off the sauce, m'Lady," Gabriel whispered in her ear as she kissed him. "You should have slipped out the back door to appease your blood relic. There will be no time now."

"What's going on?" she said quietly but loud enough for the others to hear.

Gail sat on the sofa staring at Jacenta. Jordan and Martino were seated close by but rose when she looked to them. Deanna approached from behind with a glass of water in her faintly trembling hands. Within a matter of minutes, the room cleared — a little too quickly for Jacenta's taste. She was hoping this confrontation with Deanna was going to be avoided or at least postponed for a while.

They were completely alone in the house now. There was no one. Jordan and Gabriel told them all to leave, even Gail who was the most resistant one. Martino gave a little opposition but in the end the elders had won out. Gabriel knew it was time that Jacenta and Deanna work out their business. It was a word he used whenever describing this problem.

Business of the past.
Betrayal business.

At times it sounded almost insufferable; at times she knew exactly what he meant. Jordan, on the other hand, was just eager to have their business over and done. He was tired of the intrusion in his life.

So, they had all gone. Jacenta listened carefully to the surrounding area outside. She was sure some would go to the lake to wait out the storm, but she didn't hear so much as a breath coming from that direction.

She looked to Deanna as she waited by the kitchen entry. *A good place for a quick escape.* Jacenta knew Deanna didn't trust her and it made her smile inside. Funny how the tables had turned. Now Devin was keeping secrets from her; now Jacenta had the upper hand in the deception.

"Come sit with me." Jacenta gestured toward the large comfy chair across from her, near the fire. "Please, Deanna."

Deanna's cold, angry, distrusting eyes looked from Jacenta to the chair and back again. "I'll stand." Her tone was as cold as her eyes.

"Suit yourself, but the fire is quite enjoyable." Jacenta sat back on the sofa. Fluffing pillows beside her, she pulled her legs up comfortably. Her hunger was weakening her, and she wished she could have hunted just to clear her head. But that wasn't to be.

"Devin? I know you're here. Have you anything to say before we start?" She could feel him as he circled her and watched as Deanna fought to ignore him as he neared her.

"Sit, Mouse. Take the first step towards repairing this bond."

Jacenta smiled. "Which one of us are you playing with that line?"

Deanna's eyes quickly met Jacenta's and they softened for a moment with a bit of her old humor.

"Go on, Devin. Let us girls work this out," Jacenta continued, not breaking the gaze she held with Deanna.

"Mouse, do you wish me to go?"

"Mouse? A term of endearment?" Jacenta questioned them both. "I quite like that you're Deanna again. Seems fitting and I've always been very fond of the name." Her eyes sparkled in the firelight and a small private smile graced her lips.

Deanna took her first steps toward the big comfy chair and stopped. "Should we set some ground rules?" She tilted her head inquisitively.

"If you'd like." Jacenta played along.

Deanna sat on the edge of the chair. "First. Don't try to get Devin to take sides. And you can't take sides either, Devin. We're both big girls and can hold our own."

Jacenta held back a laugh. "Well said. Second?"

"Um, second. I don't know. Don't kill me, I guess." Deanna's worried expression was bordering on the comical.

Jacenta laughed, this time, without reservation. "No promises," she joked.

There was a silence between them. A feeling that they both desperately missed from the other. Friendship. Without looking up, Deanna was the first to break the silence. "Gail said I need to take ownership in my part of this mess. That I should stop being the victim."

"Smart lady," she whispered.

"So here goes: my part, I guess, was that I slept with Devin. I was lonely and he comforted me. Too much. So, I'm sorry I slept with your husband." The last words were fast to leave her lips as if they were too rehearsed and had lost their meaning.

Jacenta waited until she was sure that Deanna had finished her thought. She looked at Deanna, studied her as she is now, and remembered how she was then. Her hair, much darker than it was then, was pinned up in a perfect bun, making her eyes look cold and severe. She was still beautiful, maybe more now than before, but those cold, unemotional eyes were just the same.

"Well," she started, "you certainly took some broad strokes over that canvas, didn't you?"

"I'm apologizing. I thought that's what you wanted. Now it's your turn."

"*Wow, this went bad quickly, didn't it?*" Devin chuckled to the women.

Jacenta tried to ignore him, but he was right. She had hoped that momentary comradery only minutes ago would be the beginning of mending what was broken. But if Deanna thought she deserved an apology, they were further from the mending than she thought.

"You want me to apologize to you? For what, pray tell?"

"You killed Devin for starters!"

"That's between me and Devin. That has nothing to do with you." She shook her head, annoyed.

"You cursed us! You lied! You stroll in here acting like you own the place . . ."

"What did I lie about?" she interrupted.

"You're alive!" Deanna's voice was getting loud and the rim of her eyes were deepening in color.

"How did I lie? Devin lied. He knew what I was from day one. I didn't lie." Jacenta was fuming.

Deanna rolled her eyes. "Semantics. That still doesn't explain why you're here getting all buddy-buddy with my friends."

Jacenta stared at her silently, unable to verbalize all the thoughts filling her head. She closed her eyes briefly and tried to compose herself. Deanna was jealous of her new relationship with Gail and Tabitha. She took a deep breath and tried to continue calmly. "I'm here because I thought I'd help you. Devin told me you were looking to break the curse. I thought if after six centuries you were finally ready for it all to be over – maybe I was too. So, I came to help you."

"Why . . . why now?" Deanna's voice was shaking when she got to her feet.

"Because you wanted it. I've followed you for so long and you never tried, not once, to really break the spell. Yet I know you could."

"I tried." Deanna sounded small.

"I even gave you Devin's blood again and again. And still nothing. It was incredibly frustrating."

Deanna looked into Jacenta's eyes. The green in her own eyes faded back to hazel. She grasped the vial that was now hanging around her neck all the time. "I tried," she repeated.

"No, you didn't. Not really. Well, I'm wrong . . . Agatha got close. Real close and I thought that was going to be it. Devin was going to be gone and you were going to figure it out. But then you – I don't know – you got cold feet or something. That drive went away, and who was next . . ." She counted lives on her fingers.

"Emily," Deanna said quietly.

"Yes, Emily. Emily didn't even care." Her voice sound astounded. "She was the one I was most thrown by. Just one lifetime before you were determined to end this thing and then Emily comes along . . . I can't believe that was even you. To tell you the truth. She didn't even acknowledge Devin. At all!" Jacenta covered her face with her hands to stop them from flailing. "Thanks to you, I got to spend almost seventy fun-filled years with him without interruption. I was ready to kill her – you." She took a deep breath in between rants. "That's when I lost Eric." Her voice broke and she barely got the last sentence out.

Deanna licked her lips and diverted her eyes from Jacenta.

Back on track, Jacenta continued. "Then Elizabeth locked him up completely. Looks like your magic still works now and then. You were smart enough by then to figure out the spell on your own. Why didn't you?" Jacenta watched Deanna fall back into the chair. Her face was ashen, and sadness was replacing the anger in her eyes. "Listen, do you remember when we used to play around with spells? Writing them, saying them, hoping something would happen? Do you remember that?"

Deanna nodded a small forlorn nod that hurt Jacenta's heart.

"Nothing ever worked. We would write and brew and play with my crystals. Nothing. Until that one night."

Deanna's eyes searched as if the memory would materialize before her. "When one worked."

"Yes, one worked. It happened. We made a connection with the fates. We felt it. Something happened that night. Our souls were joined, fused, attached in some way. Remember?" Jacenta reached out her hand and reluctantly, Deanna took it. "Then it all worked. All the spells, all the charms, every incantation, everything clicked."

The light in Deanna's eyes was working, flickering like it was trying to find a connection. A lightbulb searching for a spark. "It was a full moon, wasn't it? You wanted it so bad – the magic – but could never achieve it on your own. But together. My mother would have said the Goddess smiled on us that night."

Jacenta watched her eyes dance. "My intention with that *curse* was to punish Devin, not you. The spell we wrote, I didn't know what I was doing. I wanted to keep him at arm's length from you, always. Fitting punishment, I thought. So, I combined all our blood, said the spell we had written, and that was it." Jacenta stared at the fire. "I was hurt . . . and angry. So angry. He had said such hurtful things to me. Things about you; things I don't think I will ever really forgive him for. I hated him." Jacenta shrugged. "I had no idea you'd kill yourself. The waters swelled for days after, flooding a good portion of the land around the river. So many people accused you of witchcraft and that you'd cursed them." Jacenta laughed at the irony.

The frames on the mantel quaked, reminding the women that Devin was still with them.

Deanna's mind was full of questions, and she pulled her hand from Jacenta's grasp. "That spell we wrote didn't have anything to do with my soul. It was just spirit enslavement. Remember the cat? The power of three. Your blood, my blood, and the cat's." Her hand went to her lips as she remembered how they sacrificed a cat to test the spell. Its soul had left its body and was released with a simple blood and spell mixing. "I can break that spell. Easy. I did it then. That's the one you used?"

Jacenta nodded, pleased with herself.

"What did you do to me?"

"Nothing." She paused, enraptured by Deanna's confusion and mounting interest. "Your reincarnation didn't start until I died. When we were playing and our souls connected, they *really* connected. I live forever and so do you."

"But I was dead . . . for years?" Deanna was bewildered.

"The universe works in mysterious ways. Since we were linked, I assume your soul was lying in wait. If I had died naturally, you would have moved on, I assume. But I didn't, so you didn't." Jacenta held her breath, waiting for Deanna's explosion. "I often wondered what might have been different if you were alive when I was turned. Would you be immortal rather than like this? I don't know."

Jacenta remembered feeling something when she was turned into a vampire. It felt like she regained the second half of her heart. At the time, she thought it was a normal part of the process, but over the years whenever Deanna died or was reborn, she felt it. The loss, the gain, over and over. The tug on her heart.

"I can free Devin with the blood. I know that. That part is easy, but how do we separate you and me?" Deanna was surprisingly calm.

"We created the first spell. We have to figure out how to reverse it. Together."

CHAPTER THIRTY-NINE

Two days later, Deanna was alone in the cabin. It was almost 10 a.m. and the cabin was silent. The kitchen door stood open as she sat on the porch. Somewhere deep inside she wished it was 10 p.m. and Jacenta was standing in that doorway. She wanted so much to finish their conversation from last night and the night before. It was an ongoing discussion about the past – Jacenta's past, Deanna's past, and their past together.

Last night they were talking about the tug Jacenta felt when Deanna was born or died. Deanna never had the privilege of feeling Jacenta's death – she had never died. Even her rebirth was a mystery to her; Deanna was being reborn at the exact moment and had sadly missed out on the connection their hearts had created.

Deanna felt she should sleep like the rest of the inhabitants of the cabin. Gabriel kept warning her that her mind and body would give out if she didn't get the sleep she so greatly needed. The deep bruises under her eyes and her sluggish thinking were clear indications to everyone that she was still not sleeping.

She never slept anymore. Any day now, she and Jacenta would come up with the parting spell and she would be free to die. *Free to die*. Those words brought feelings of happiness and terror with them. Free to live only one more lifetime. Free to become one with the elements. Her body returning to nature and her soul – well, Deanna had no idea where her soul would end up.

The only dead person she knew was Devin and he was still here.

Her feet were perched on the railing of the porch and she felt the hot sun burning its mark on her delicate skin. Skin that hadn't seen the sun in many weeks. But now she wanted to drink in the sun, the moon, the rain, the flowers. She wanted to absorb all of Mother Earth's beauty before she said goodbye to it all. *Free to die.* Again, the doubts as to where she would go after this world pained her.

She had never been religious – not in any lifetime. She faked it – faked it very well but the concepts of heaven and hell, in God or the Devil, or even the goddesses that she was taught to follow, they were all alien to her. God the all-powerful being that had foreseen this curse and allowed it to happen. That was the concept she refused to embrace.

A squirrel scurried onto the porch and noshed on some sunflower seeds Sari had left for them. It stood on its hind quarters with a seed in its paws, trying to crack the shell, its eyes carefully surveying the area. The whiteness of its chest fascinated Deanna, such stark contrast to the dark gray back and tail.

Sari swore she saw a blonde squirrel months ago in the autumn months before her rebirth. The squirrels were massive in the fall. They were fattening up for a long winter. Seeds and berries were on the porch to entice the blonde squirrel back. Sari wanted to see him again before she left.

The plan was in a few days, possibly sooner; Sari and Chelsea were leaving. They had been planning and plotting destinations where Sari had always dreamed to travel. San Francisco was their first planned stop, and after that, maybe Monte Carlo. Jacenta suggested Salvador. She offered the use of her rental overlooking the beach and the city or they would be welcome to stay at Haven. Piper would love Sari. She would be good for her as well.

Jacenta gushed about the music, the smell of the salty ocean breeze, the calm that came with sitting on her balcony with her eyes closed drinking it all in. It made Deanna want to go herself. Chelsea was excited by the prospect of hunting in the Amazon. The animals, the dense jungle, it all brought to mind the animalistic side of their nature. The Amazon fascinated Deanna; she wondered how Martino would fare in such a primitive setting. She thought of Gail as well or strangely even Jordan. They all seemed so sophisticated and part of this world — not at all in touch with the internal animal that made them crave blood.

All of Chelsea and Sari's plans hinged on Eric. He, after some prodding and lengthy discussions, offered to transport Margaret to Haven in Connecticut. Once she was settled, he would meet Sari wherever she was. But Deanna was getting the distinct impression that Sari was more interested in seeing the Connecticut Haven as opposed to the less desirable Amazonian Haven (as she came to call it). The Amazon frightened Sari and she was still fighting the jealousy that Margaret stirred in her.

It was Gabriel's suggestion to send Margaret to Connecticut. The state-of-the-art facility offered every possible form of protection for her as well as stimulating her need to be around other immortals. A call to Roderick told him that the staff of doctors and psychologists were informed of her condition and excited for a new case study.

Case study. Those two harmless words ignited a feud that raged for the past few days. Martino was the most surprising one to be offended by the words. He didn't want to send Margaret somewhere she would be used as a lab rat. Jacenta laughed at his tirade, which angered him beyond words.

"You mustn't get caught up on their jargon. It angered me as well. They speak of recruiting and testing." She was getting worked up just talking about it, and strangely her emotions were calming Martino. "It all seems so . . ."

"Clinical?" Martino offered. His tone was respectful but still frustrated.

"No, like a cult. I hated it. Still do, believe me." She looked to Gabriel, who watched her with brazen humor, and she sneered at him playfully. "But they are well meaning and amazing at what they do. She'll be fine."

Devin was not as easy to calm. His usual tantrums were followed by tirades, daily for Deanna and nightly to Jacenta. *How could they send her to that horrid place? She needs to be with family and not strangers. She'll become like everyone else. She'll lose her sparkle.*

The sparkle he spoke of was himself. Margaret could see him when no one else could and he loved it. He loved entertaining her. He loved watching her eyes as they followed him around the room. He became very protective of Margaret since he met her and now refused to let her go.

Deanna agreed with his arguments but felt that without her or Devin to watch over Margaret, Connecticut was the best place for her. And she trusted Jacenta when she promised to visit Connecticut often to check in on her.

"I still don't want her to go."

Having been lost in her thoughts, Devin's unexpected appearance startled Deanna. Her sudden movements sent the squirrel running, upending the dish of sunflower seeds as he went.

"What do you want them to do with her? I can't expect Martino to babysit her forever," she spoke aloud to him. "I won't be here much longer and neither will you. Everyone else is making plans as well. The cabin will be empty when it comes our time to depart."

"Depart? Don't use his words."

Depart was a word Gabriel had been using recently to mask the unpleasant knowledge that Deanna would be dying in a matter of days. He did it for Jacenta and Gail more than Deanna. The idea of death was not in the forefront of her mind. She was worried about Margaret and Devin's departure before her own.

"Sorry," she said silently, feeling something like regret but not knowing exactly why. "I just want to know that she is safe before I go. Don't you? No loose ends, right?"

"What if I said I am not ready to go? Would you stay with me?" His voice was a soft whisper in her ear, and she felt the familiar tickle and loved it.

"No." Her answer was short, but her voice trailed off as if she wasn't sure of herself. "I can't do this again. I can't keep going like this."

"You needn't continue as you are. Let Jacenta do the parting spell and finish your life as Deanna Belamy. Just give me

one more lifetime. You and me, please, Mouse." His voice broke as he pleaded with her.

She smiled, letting the idea sink in. One last lifetime. The prospect was tempting. She would avoid the goodbyes, avoid the enduring the pain in her mother's eyes when she lied to her about moving away. But then what about Martino?

"I know you're scared. I am too. I've never crossed over to whatever's out there. Maybe there's nothing, but at least we'll be there together." The voice in her head sounded wrong, like she was lying to herself and not just to Devin.

CHAPTER FORTY

"I don't know how to tell her." Jacenta's heart was racing as she started to tell Gail of her recent revelation. Her heart felt as if it was going to explode out of her chest. She needed the good stuff more than ever right now, but it was all gone. Still, she looked around Jordan's study hoping for a little reprieve in the form of a flask or decanter.

"You're sure?" Gail's head was in her hands as Jacenta explained the details of her discovery and how it was the only way to end the connection that she and Deanna shared.

Devin hovered beside the women, knowing all the details already but wanting to hear Gail's reaction. Secretly he loved the idea but knew he was alone in that appraisal of the plan.

"There's no other way unless she wants to continue this endless cycle of living and dying. But she'd be doing it with Devin. Forever. I think he's made his decision pretty clear."

Devin chuckled in Jacenta's ear. She really had no idea what his decision truly was. The new plan threw a wrench into the works. He could have Deanna with him forever if he could convince her to stay with him. No flesh, just energy. He let them continue their conversation without further interruption.

Gail threw her head back and took a deep exhaling breath. "It's not Deanna I'm worried about; it's Martino. Frankly, I don't think she'll have a problem with any of this. But he had hopes of having her forever after you . . . you know." Her voice trailed off as she realized how ridiculous her words sounded.

"You know that's impossible. Even if it were possible, she doesn't want it – you know that."

Gail nodded in a very defeated manner that broke Jacenta's heart.

"Here you two are. I've been looking everywhere." Sari poked her head in the study, staying safely outside until she was invited. "What's up? You two don't look so good."

"We figured it out." Jacenta held out her hand for Sari to come to her.

"Oh." Sari entered the room, much like Abby several months before, guarded and tentative. "And you're not going to be able to save her, are you?"

Jacenta shook her head and dropped her eyes.

"Apparently, the only way is to enslave her soul like Devin's and . . ."

"And use the same reversal on them both. Brilliant, but . . . oh." Sari's eyes searched Gail's for some hope, but there was none. "Does she know?"

Again, Jacenta shook her head. "The plan was to tell her tonight, but now we're not sure how to break it to her . . . with or without Martino."

Sari was thinking for a while and stopped suddenly. "Does it matter? I know he'll hate this idea but he's not going to die. She is. She should know that you've figured it out. You need to think only of Deanna and Devin right now. Harsh as that sounds, this curse is all about them." Devin tickled the back of Sari's neck gently and she giggled. "Glad you approve."

Jacenta touched Sari's hand slightly. "It affects all of us. I don't want to lose her any more than Martino or Gail or even you. Devin only likes the idea because if she agrees to it and it works like it's supposed to, she'll be with him as a spirit. But you're right; ultimately it's about Deanna and how she wants to proceed."

An hour later whether she was ready or not, Jacenta sat on the upstairs sofa facing Deanna and holding Gabriel's hand as if it were her job to keep him in place. Everyone was anxious. Deanna seemed to be the only one smiling. Martino was skeptical, mostly because Gail refused to answer any of his questions and wanted to leave when everyone arrived.

Jordan was interested in what was unfolding and had stopped Gail from leaving. He felt that she was a vital part in all of this, and she should be there to support Deanna – no matter what her decision. Eric, Margaret, and Sari were hovering in the doorway of the kitchen listening and Jacenta motioned for them to take a seat. It was making her nervous having them standing behind her.

"So, since we're all here, I'm guessing you came up with something. I've been racking my brain, but I've got nothing. I don't even know how we accomplished it to begin with, so . . . how do you fix something like that, you know?" Deanna laughed, realizing she was the only one. Her eyes scanned those before her, and her smile faded.

"Yes, I think I've come up with some kind of solution. Before I say anything, nothing is written in stone. You have every opportunity to think on it and decide whether it's worth trying." Jacenta swallowed hard and unconsciously dug her nails into the back Gabriel's hand.

"I understand." She smiled weakly. "Just spit it out. I can take it."

Jacenta stared at Deanna, wanting to continue but finding that she couldn't formulate the words in her throat. Her eyes searched the assembly for Gail, but she was actively avoiding eye contact with anyone.

"Wow, that bad, huh?" Deanna looked to Martino.

"The only way is to enslave your soul like Devin's and then release you." Sari's voice broke as she said *release you*.

"I see." Her voice was small, barely a whisper.

"She has no choices with this plan?" Martino sounded amazed more than angry, but anger was cruising right below the surface of amazement.

His question was answered with silence.

"You'll be with me. Finally, and completely, you and me together."

Jacenta smiled hearing Devin's words and she looked to Deanna, who was already looking at her. "If you choose not to be released, then you will be together. Hopefully not around me, though."

Gabriel laughed this time.

"How do we begin?"

"Wait, you're not seriously considering this preposterous plan? You will die." The surface of Martino's amazement was finally breached by the anger. And it was bubbling.

"Tino, that was the plan all along. Just because you refused to acknowledge it doesn't make it any less true. I love you but this needs to end and if I have to die first, then so be it. How is it any different than me dying after the spell is broken?" Deanna was calm and her words were well thought out. "We haven't even heard the plan yet. How about we not get ahead of ourselves?"

Jacenta watched the interaction between Deanna and Martino with quiet admiration and a little bit of awe. Again, her eyes found Gail and she had the same look of wonderment on her face.

"So how do we begin?" Deanna said once again.

"First, you must . . . you know, depart, and then we will do exactly what I did six centuries ago. Mix the blood, say the words, and hopefully that will do it. I do need you to write down the counter-spell, so I'll be able to release you both together." Jacenta let go of Gabriel's hand and was a little more in control of her emotions for now.

"Wait, wait, when Dee dies, won't her soul be reincarnated like immediately?" Sari interjected.

"Shit, I hadn't thought of that. We'll have to be fast, I guess?"

A silence descended on the room again as the plan fell apart before them. Martino's angry expression had changed to a look of vindication.

"She didn't reincarnate when you were sleeping," Devin offered.

"Yes!" Jacenta burst out.

"What does that mean?" Deanna asked, looking around to the equally confused faces circling her.

"Almost fifty years ago, I was freaking out. Long story, but I went underground like some of us do for around two decades. When I emerged, I immediately felt that tug that I get when Deanna is reborn. I didn't think anything of it at the time, just thought it was coincidence. But Devin told me, God, months back, that Deanna had not reincarnated while I was asleep." She looked around, grabbing Gabriel's hand again this time in joy. "So, if I go underground, temporarily, maybe, just maybe it will buy us some time to snatch her soul and keep it in one place."

"Brilliant," Sari exploded.

"Wait, was Chynna so sick because you were underground? Did I die then because you were asleep?" Deanna was piecing a puzzle together.

"I don't know. Maybe. She's the only one that died young and then you were stuck until I awoke. Maybe."

"Will I get sick if you go underground this time?" Deanna was looking for some broad pieces in the puzzle now.

"Not if you do it quickly," Sari offered.

CHAPTER FORTY-ONE

Not if you do it quick?

Deanna tried not to think about it. While everyone else finalized plans and their role in the breaking of this curse, she needed to figure out how to die. She had died so many times. Drowning, heart attack, cancer, pneumonia. It was all done without fear knowing that she would be coming back. But now this was it. The final goodbye.

Must give herself a proper send-off. She looked down at her things to do list and scratched off the first item on the list. Take a blood sample.

That was done, thankfully. It was Gabriel that took the blood. They were in Jordan's study alone. Deanna had never been in this room before, never been in the basement. But Gabriel insisted that they be completely alone and without distraction.

The room, by itself, was a distraction. It was reminiscent of her father's study at home. The leather chairs, the huge, hulking desk, and the delightfully intoxicating smell of books. She looked around, seeing Jordan in every detail. The delicate etched bottle displayed on the minibar, surrounded by glasses that she had seen him drink from many times. The journals stacked on the shelves were aged and worn. Deanna wanted to pick one up and flip through it.

Returning her eyes to the task before her, she saw Gabriel standing ready and waiting, equipped with a needle and vial. He was curiously gentle in his technique. After tying a belt to the top of her arm, his large surprisingly warm fingers felt for a useable vein. Not looking up from his task, Deanna heard his frustrated exhale when a vein did not present itself easily. Then he found one. Eureka.

She watched as her blood travelled down from her arm through a thin tube into a blood collection vial just like at the doctor's office. When it was full, he carefully pulled the needle from her arm and covered it with cotton. His hands were warm and kind as he held her arm in place.

"Hold that right there," he said softly. Next, he placed a bandage over the cotton and smiled. "You're all done. Sorry I don't have a lollipop for you."

Deanna laughed and immediately saw why Jacenta loved this immortal. He was dressed in a simple white button-down shirt – that probably cost more than her whole outfit – and jeans tonight. Deanna wasn't sure if he chose his outfit to make her feel comfortable or not, but it did. There was just something unnerving about someone in a velvet frock coat taking your blood that beckoned images of Dr. Frankenstein.

"Do you take blood a lot? I mean, with a needle?" She stammered over her words.

As he looked up at her, his blue eyes showed amusement, but the rest of his face was emotionless. "One of my passions is blood. Knowing its properties and how it affects immortals."

"Just immortals? I would think you could use your knowledge to help humans as well." She swallowed hard, knowing what his answer would be.

"Humans are fallible. Helping them is ultimately useless. Eventually they will die, no matter what medical miracles are performed. Don't you agree?" Deanna didn't answer and found it hard to meet his eye. "You above all should understand the human dilemma. There is only one outcome. But for immortals, death is not an eventuality that we fear. So, finding better means to become stronger and more capable of facing the years is what I strive for."

The blue in his eyes seemed to deepen as his argument became more impassioned and Deanna found herself getting lost in his words. "But you do die. Abby died. Immortality is an illusion."

"From speaking with Jordan, Abby's death was completely preventable had emotion not clouded the situation. She could have been healed with the use of immortal blood. It's been done before." Knowing what he said was true, Deanna said nothing in response. She watched Gabriel as he labeled the vial with her name and dated it. Just like at the hospital.

"Are you a real doctor?" His head was down, and she studied the waves and interweaving of grays through the brown. She thought it made him appear rugged and sexy.

"No, but I play one on television." He laughed at his own joke.

That was last night, and now with the sunlight flooding through the kitchen windows, she looked at the second item on her things to do list: Visit Mom and Dad. Deanna drew a large question mark beside the number two and moved to number three. Write counter-spell.

First, she had to remember the original spell and how it was cast. Then she would remember the reversal spell. She had done it once to a cat. They had killed the cat and controlled its spirit and then released the soul to the universe. It seemed easy enough.

Deanna remembered vaguely actually performing the spell.

"Collect his blood in the saucer," young Deanna Cullen had told an even younger Jacenta Brodie over six hundred years ago. They were in Jacenta's kitchen. Devin and the children were conveniently absent for a few hours.

A dead cat was lying on the table before them. Surrounding the table, candles were lit to keep the spirit close to them. Next to the cat were three saucers and a bowl; two saucers contained blood, the bowl held water, and the third saucer sat empty for now. It was that third saucer that Jacenta obediently grabbed and roughly shook the cat's body over to collect enough blood for the spell.

Deanna's eyes were closed as she instructed Jacenta further. "We'll pour the three saucers into the bowl and we'll both recite the spell." She took one saucer in hand while Jacenta had two and they poured as they recited from memory the spell that they had written. After the blood was poured into the bowl, they each held hands and placed a hand on the cat's body to complete the circle.

"Sky above me, Earth below, Spirit hear my cry. I summon you from the other side. Come to me and cross the great divide. Stay with me until this spell does break. By the power of three this bond I make."

With their eyes closed, they waited for something to happen. Anything to happen.

Deanna opened one eye and looked to Jacenta, who was looking back at her clearly disappointed.

"We killed my daughter's cat for nothing. Devin will be quite angry with me." She started to collect the saucers and the other implements they had used to cut their own arms for the spell to work. Jacenta winced slightly as she pressed a slice of bread against the wound on her forearm. "We won't be able to do this anymore. He'll be furious that we were attempting to summon the devil."

"Not the devil. Surely, you know that. My mother was able to control the spirits and speak with them. Is it wrong for us to want the same?"

"Devin won't understand. He's frightened of the spirits. The Brodies have always been deeply religious and easily frightened by the tales of the little people and the sprites."

"Sean as well, God rest him. But we haven't done anything. I've hurt my arm plenty of times whilst working the farm, you as well. We've done nothing wrong. We'll tell Brina that her cat got in a tangle with the dog from down the road."

Jacenta nodded and continued to stack the dishes for washing.

"I'll bury the cat. Can I borrow a bit of cloth to wrap him in?"

It wasn't until days later that Jacenta started hearing the cat's cries in her home. The crying in the morning was the loudest, echoing off the walls, and she also heard the cat scamper through the rooms. Sitting in front of the fire, while Devin read and she sewed, Jacenta heard purring beside her.

"Do you hear it too?" she asked Deanna when they found a moment alone. It had been days that she had been comforting her daughter over the loss of her cat while still secretly hearing the cat every waking minute of the day.

"He's still here; that is why you hear him, and I do not. His spirit is not accustomed to travel." Deanna laughed. "My mother told me of these spirits. They get trapped and don't move around."

A hissing sound made Deanna jump. She turned and found nothing behind her.

"Oooh, he does not like you." Jacenta laughed.

"We should put him to rest." Deanna was shaken to her core. They had done it. They had trapped the soul of another being and kept it from passing on to heaven.

They reopened the same wound on their arms and spilled their blood into the same saucers. The cat's blood was coagulated and drying but with hopes that it was still useful, they put it into the saucer beside their own. Just as they did the first time, they poured the blood into the water filled bowl, held hands (and paw), and recited the reversal spell.

"Sky above me, Earth below, Spirit hear my cry. A spell was cast, now make it past. You are free. The spell is done, so mote it be."

Standing in the kitchen of Mount Orion six hundred years later, Deanna was smiling as she jotted down what she remembered word for word. Quickly, she crossed out the third item on her list and looked to the fourth. The smile faded from her face as she stared at the paper with her pen in hand.

Decide how to die.

Trevor was the first one up on the day Deanna figured out how to end her life. She was sitting comfortably on the side porch when he appeared at the door.

"Would you like me to build a fire?" His smile was bright and with his large eyes sparkling, he looked angelic. Looking at him, it struck her again how young he was when he became immortal. His feet were bare, and he wore jeans and a loose-fitting gray tee shirt that he must have rummaged out of one of Martino's boxes in the basement. His hair was mussed like he'd been running his fingers through it in frustration.

Deanna shook her head, no, and patted the seat beside her. "Sit."

There was definitely a nip in the air and she should have said yes to his offer but sharing the blanket with him seemed much more inviting than a fire. Thor and Attila lounged at her feet and the thump of their tails against the wood floor as Trevor approached reminded her that they were there.

"They sense your sadness." He scratched their necks as he sat. "So do I. Am I right in guessing that a decision has been made?"

Deanna didn't answer, but the shift of her eyes spoke volumes, especially to a vampire that could read her mind.

"You must not think of this as an ending to life. It's an ending to your misery. Rebirth couldn't have been pleasant. Childhood, adolescence, old age, senility. Dying in the prime of your life sounds cruel but solves so many problems for someone like you."

She couldn't help but stare at him as he spoke. The large angelic eyes coupled with the iridescent sheen of his skin made him appear downright ethereal. And when she realized that she had been staring at him far longer than he had been speaking, Deanna's face reddened with embarrassment.

"I don't even remember old age. I haven't lived past sixty in over a century." Her laugh was a mix of sad and embarrassed, and her eyes were planted firmly on the empty fireplace.

Trevor smiled, knowing her feelings. "How have you decided to end it, if I may ask?" He slipped down to the floor between the dogs.

She was silent, watching him playfully tease Thor. "I want to talk to Gail before I make a decision." She lied and he knew it. The look in his eyes was disappointed, but he shrugged and continued to dig his fingers into Thor's massive coat, sending a flurry of hair into the air.

"She's with Jordan now." He didn't look at her. "She'll be up presently. If you haven't quite made up your mind, why so melancholy?" His tone was suspicious.

"Martino, I suppose. He's been ducking me all week. I want him to support me in this decision. Hoping that he would understand is a waste. But can't he just be with me now, so close to the end?" With her jaw clenched, she fought the tears.

"Do you want me to speak with him?"

"No. That would be worse. I don't want his support out of obligation or, worse, fear. If it doesn't manifest itself from love, then he can leave me to die alone."

Trevor was smiling when she finally mustered enough nerve to meet his gaze. It was a look of approval mixed with a bit of surprise. "Come, let's go downstairs and hash out the details once and for all." He jumped to his feet and the dogs followed.

Taking her hand, he led her to the basement living room. Attila and Thor forced them to the left side of the stairs as they bounded down, excitedly making their way to Sari. A happy squeal accompanied their arrival on her lap.

"Hey, D. What are you doing down here? Is something wrong?"

Deanna could hear a smidge of displeasure in her tone. She was clearly annoyed that Trevor had brought a human into the basement. An immediate comparison to Abby formed in her mind and she shook it off.

"Gabriel beat me to it by two days." Without needing to read her thoughts, Trevor answered her tone instead.

"He took my blood in Jordan's study the other day," Deanna explained. "I can go upstairs if it makes you uncomfortable."

"Nonsense." Gabriel appeared at the bottom of the stairs. "Another myth propagated by Hollywood. The myth of a lair is fabricated by caped, eastern European Hollywood fops, and I detest it. The sanctuary of an immortal is only forbidden to anyone outside of the circle of trust. Deanna is not outside that circle. Don't you agree?"

Gail stood silently watching from Jordan's bedroom door. "Completely. Deanna, you are welcome to stay." Her smile was lukewarm, and Deanna could clearly see she was just as uncomfortable with the prospect as Sari.

"Where's Jacenta?" Deanna watched as Gabriel took a seat beside the hearth.

"After an early intrusion by Devin, she said she needed some air. I don't care to know what he said, but it upset her significantly. There needs to be a way to keep him from her if she is to prepare for a peaceful rest. I don't believe he understands the control he holds over her."

"Oh, he knows," Deanna said. "But I'm sorry for the early disturbance; it's probably my fault. I've been in his ear all day. I'll talk to him about leaving her alone."

Gabriel nodded but said nothing.

"I know we shouldn't discuss this without Jacenta, but I need to know. And if we are to keep on schedule . . . what have you decided?" Gail leaned on the sofa behind Sari.

Deanna stared at her for what seemed like eternity and then glanced to Sari, Trevor, and finally Gabriel. "I'm not completely decided yet. I mean, there's so much to go over but I think I want Margaret to do it."

"What?" Sari burst out.

"Why Margaret?" Jacenta glided down the stairs as if she were floating.

"Well, for one, I don't think anyone else could go through with it, and I'd be in the same boat I am right now. And two, it's natural. We're the same person. I was her, she's me. I don't know. It made sense when I was ranting about it this morning and half the afternoon."

"To Devin, I know. I got an earful when I woke." Jacenta came around and sat with Sari and what little room Attila left on the sofa.

"I thought of other ways. Devin and I came up with millions of scenarios. Drowning, pills, Gabriel could give me something from that portable medicine cabinet he carries around – but with everything else there was a chance of failure. I have a pretty strong will and I'm afraid the strongest of poisons wouldn't kill me."

"Have you spoken to Margaret yet?" Trevor asked.

Deanna shook her head. "Not yet. She's with Martino nonstop and finding him these days is like trying to catch a breeze in your hand."

The glances shared between those before her made Deanna angry. "I already know he's not on board with this. But I need Margaret. He can stay hidden for all I care, but we need to find her." The thought of Martino made Deanna furious, and she felt Trevor's hand on her shoulder for comfort.

CHAPTER FORTY-TWO

"Connecticut has underground accommodations for me? Is that what you just said?" Jacenta stopped Gabriel mid-sentence to make sure she was hearing him correctly. They were sitting on the side porch discussing her part in what Sari humorously coined as Operation: Deep Sleep.

"With all your fighting, you never gave me the chance to show you that level." He was quite jovial, especially in the last few days, and it made Jacenta uneasy.

The night air was pleasant as they sat talking of their plans. Richard played with the dogs in the front yard, pretending not to listen but still hearing every word. Jacenta was well aware that Martino was getting his information from Richard about the plan. On the porch, Gail, Deanna, Margaret, and Sari listened intently to Gabriel's ideas. Tabitha, who was rarely around recently, stood in the kitchen doorway trying to catch up on the live soap opera called Mount Orion playing out right in front of her.

"Are there others?" Jacenta asked.

He nodded. "There are rooms. You will have your own room and monitors will be set up, so we know when you reach your deepest sleep and won't be easily woken. And since it's the intention to bring Margaret there as well, perhaps you can take her with you and save Eric the trip."

"But she's D's exit plan?" Sari interjected.

"It's a better place for Deanna to depart and they can properly dispose of her body afterwards."

Deanna and Margaret said nothing. To them, the place was inconsequential. But it was Gail who rose with arguments against the idea.

"I want her buried here. I don't want her departure to be too antiseptic. It needs to be done surrounded by those she loves and who love her."

"Despite opinions to the contrary, Haven is not antiseptic. It's very welcoming and is very much like a resort on the surface. Suites, pools, library – beneath those layers, you will find a technologically advanced state-of-the-art facility designed to house, care, and cater to immortals."

Jacenta smirked as she saw how annoyed he was that her opinions about the Connecticut Haven had infected everyone.

"Even if you are right, I still want her here . . ."

"You may go with her. Roderick would love visitors and you can help Deanna feel comfortable before she departs." He looked to Deanna as he spoke.

"All of us?" Sari jumped in.

"As many as you'd like or deem necessary. There is plenty of room. All that is required is a phone call and rooms will be made ready."

The porch emptied soon after it was decided that Gail, Sari, and Eric were definitely going. Gail still harbored doubts and she reserved the right to cancel the plan if she thought Haven was not the proper place to proceed.

Jacenta remained with Gabriel enjoying the night air and the sound of the frogs near the lake. She snuggled into his chest and watched as Sari and Eric walked toward the lake. A small smile pulled on her mouth watching Eric's patience toward Sari's incessant talking as they got closer to the water.

"I've never gone underground without reason. It's always been to hide or withdraw. What will keep me asleep this time?"

"Your will. Simple as that. You will keep yourself from waking subconsciously. That's how we do it. If you wish, I can give you an injection to help calm your mind for the first stages of the hibernation cycle."

"Injection of what?"

"Blood. Immortal."

"Can't I just take it the old-fashioned way?" She reached up and nipped his earlobe with her teeth. A quick flurry of his concerns rushed through her as his blood touched her tongue and then disappeared as she swallowed. She kissed his cheek quickly. "Thank you."

"For?"

"For being worried about me."

Their eyes met and he took her hand and kissed it gently. "I don't want you in a hibernation room. You'll sleep in my rooms with me. It will be a gentler progression into sleep, and I'll be better able to monitor you."

"You're doing this with me?"

"For better or worse."

Few words passed between them for the remainder of the night, and her mind travelled back to Brazil where she found Rani in his meager hut and his stories of the past. He spoke of what he called his *siempre* wife. The one woman that would always be his no matter where their paths led them. Jacenta had never believed such a thing could be possible for her. *Siempre* spouses were rare. She supposed Jordan and Gail had found their siempre and maybe she had also found hers.

It was another week before she found herself standing in the common room of the Connecticut Haven watching Sari talking to Sabina. Watching them as Sari spoke in her usual animated way, using movie references that Sabina did not understand but was nevertheless entertained by and seeing Eric, whose arm had been taken hostage by Sabina since he arrived, was beautiful in an indescribable way. Sabina laughed like Jacenta hadn't heard in years, completely captivated by her new friends.

Callie loved Sari. They giggled and gossiped and spoke of random unidentifiable topics that only eighteen-year-old girls would appreciate. They spoke using acronyms rather than words; they were excited about things called *Star Wars, The Walking Dead*, Pokemon, and Twenty-One Pilots. Jacenta couldn't believe Sabina was still hanging on to the conversation.

Gail circled the walls of the common room, studying the paintings and the artistic details. Roderick trailed her, answering any questions she had and filling her in on Margaret's future following her evaluation.

Gabriel had gone to make his room ready for her cycle, as he kept referring to it. Jacenta couldn't help thinking of a menstrual cycle and giggled whenever he used the term. Operation: Deep Sleep was to commence in less than one hour. (Or T minus thirty minutes, according to Sari.)

Deanna sat in front of the firepit speaking silently with Devin. Hearing both of their internal voices in her own head, Jacenta sat beside Deanna and put her arms around her for a hug. They sat holding each other for a while before realizing that the room had gone quiet and they were being watched.

"I will be going soon." Jacenta ignored the spectators. "Come back to my room. I want to show you something."

Her room was just as she had left it, minus the horrendous mess that Callie had made of the closet. The clothes were picked up and Jacenta noticed that many were missing. Out of date and out of her closet. Either Sabina had thrown them away or Callie had integrated them into her own wardrobe.

"Gabriel's waiting for me to join him. I don't really have anything to show you except my love. I will miss you. Both of you. When I wake, I should be able to hear you both just as we hear Devin. That's the reason I'm incorporating my blood into your enslavement spell." She watched as Deanna walked around the room inspecting every detail of Jacenta's life.

"So, saying goodbye now is unnecessary." Deanna sounded cold as she pulled out drawers and peered into containers.

"I guess," Jacenta whispered. "Listen, I haven't mentioned anything to her but if you'd like, we can incorporate Gail's blood as well and she'll be linked to you too. What's wrong?"

Deanna stared at herself in the full-length mirror inside the large closet. "Is it wrong what I'm about to do? Is it wrong not wanting to stay with Gail and Sari?"

"And Martino?" she finished her thought.

"He doesn't even know where I am. I thought he'd show before we left but he didn't." She stared at herself, examining her tiny waist and long black hair. "Would you be terribly angry if I changed my mind now? Is it too late?"

Jacenta smiled tenderly. "You're still alive, so no, it's not too late. After Margaret kills you, then it will be too late for regrets. Have you called him?"

She shook her head and turned away from the mirror. "I can't live another lifetime, but I can't leave this one without him. Sounds crazy, right? I can't believe I'm saying it."

"No, not crazy. Look, I have a man waiting for me to fall asleep in his arms and I wouldn't trade that for the world. I'm going to join the man I love and when I wake, whatever you decide will be fine with me. But a little advice, from one sister to another, call him, find him, talk to him. He loves you too. He's hurting and doesn't want to say goodbye. Make him. For both of your sakes."

Jacenta took Deanna's hands in her own and felt her breath catch in her throat. "I'm sorry for all of this. For the lost years, for the unexpected immortality, for the bitterness and secrets we let Devin create between us. But in truth, I loved following you around when I could. I loved seeing you learn from each mistake and when you fell in love with Bryon, so did I. You've made my life whole and I thank you, sister."

The laugh Deanna produced was moist and shaky. "I only wish I knew you were there. I could have used a friend to talk to. I held on to so much pain and resentment, so much anger. I'm so sorry." Tears covered her face as she kept talking. "The day I saw you at Mount Orion standing at the door with Gabriel, I realized how much I hated you and at the same moment, how much I loved you too. And I was scared of what those two emotions, if I allowed them to be released, what they would do."

Jacenta laughed in spite of the burning pain in her chest.

Deanna wiped at her eyes. "I saw your boys in my boys too. I saw Brina in Alice every day of her life. Elizabeth was the hardest lifetime of them all. And strangely the culmination of all my truths. I couldn't take Devin any longer, so she locked him up. I needed to feel real love and her children were everything I could have asked for and more. And she had the best, most loving mother and now I got to know her better. So much pain in that lifetime and yet so much happiness. I only wished deep in my heart that you were there to enjoy it with me – not that I would have admitted it at the time."

Jacenta's arms wrapped around Deanna, afraid to let her go this time. More tears, more words of love. Pulling away, she kissed Deanna on the lips and walked to the door. "Find him. And thank you for being my sister." And before another tear could slip down her cheek, Jacenta pulled the door closed and walked away from her friend forever.

Gabriel was waiting for her in his bedroom. The doors were locked and barricaded except for the one she entered from. A soft hum and harsh beeping came from the monitor beside the bed. Gabriel was clad only in a simple cloth robe, and he stood beside the bed, waiting for her.

"Did you say goodbye?" he asked.

Jacenta wiped the final tears she was to shed for the next month and nodded. "How do we do this?"

Without words, he drew her to him and kissed her lips gently. His fingers started to undo the ivory buttons of the silk shirt he had picked out for her just this morning. The blouse dropped to the floor in a gold silken heap, as did her black pants soon after.

He kissed her mouth, her neck, and her shoulders as he undid her bra and slipped off her panties. The final article of clothing to fall to floor was his robe. As they stood facing each other, naked, Gabriel unceremoniously used his fingernail to slice his chest. Blood flowed freely from the wound and Jacenta stared into his eyes before understanding took hold.

Her mouth and tongue lapped at the dripping blood on his chest. As she drew more blood from the wound, Gabriel moaned and Jacenta pulled harder. She felt a soft pressure on her chest and back as he adhered the monitor probes to her body. He pushed her away, drunk on the ecstasy of her thirst, and she fell, naked and satiated, into his large, overstuffed bed.

"You did this for me?" Her voice was dreamy and detached.

His smile was his only answer. Jacenta casually thought of the enormous bed in Brazil and giggled at what Gabriel would think when he fell into it. The weight of her eyelids pulled her from the delicious sight of his naked body as it climbed into the bed beside her.

Thoughts of Deanna kept her mind in the present, and Jacenta knew she would not be able to complete the hibernation cycle to ensure that her body was truly asleep. Margaret would kill Deanna and her soul would slip away again, starting another lifecycle.

It was those thoughts that fought the effects of Gabriel's blood, and she could hear the erratic beeping of the monitors he had attached to her. Gabriel's cool hands massaged her stomach and breasts as she leaned into the massiveness of his chest as his muscular arms encompassed her. As his warm fingers slipped between her legs, she felt the stinging of his teeth pierce the delicate flesh on the back of her neck.

A shudder coursed through her as the ecstasy covering her body made it impossible to do anything but surrender to it. Her mind was calm and soon there were no thoughts of Deanna or Devin. Gabriel's blood took her away from the present and his touch allowed it to do so.

Jacenta turned toward him and her body collapsed against his. His arms enveloped her as her limbs stiffened and her breathing slowed to where the monitors barely beeped at all.

CHAPTER FORTY-THREE

Jacenta's room became Deanna's room. She figured she deserved it and loved borrowing her clothes. Callie, Sari's new best friend, wore Jacenta's clothes almost exclusively. Deanna wasn't sure if Jacenta minded, didn't care, or even noticed that her closet was being raided on a regular basis. Well, now it was her turn, and for the last month she had been through at least half of what Callie had left hanging in the closet.

"Wake up, sleepyhead, the last day of your life has arrived." Devin was in her ear.

She pulled the pillow over her head and groaned. The feel of the pillowcase covering her head was nothing to groan about; its soft buttery feel made her want to stay in bed until this horrible day was over. "I hate being awake during the day. It's so creepy here with no one else around except the maintenance guys."

"As opposed to being surrounded by bloodthirsty vampires?" He laughed in her head. *"Come now, the library is all yours for hours. Anything on ground level is deserted."*

"What's the point? By the end of the day I won't matter. I'll be dead." She buried her face deeper into the sweet smelling, butter-soft pillow.

"You always matter."

"Ha, you sound like Gail," she teased him.

"Get out of that bed or I'll drag you out." His demands always sounded a scant bit like whining. It made Deanna laugh.

"Dare you." Her teasing was getting serious but without a thought she felt an enormous pull on her midsection, and she was thrown on the floor. "Oh, you are so dead! I swear you will pay for that as soon as I'm dead." She pushed herself up on the palms of her hands.

"I never back down from a dare. You know this. So, are we going to the library on your last day or shall we make a brave escape before anyone else is awake?"

Still on the floor, she yawned and stretched. "Roderick is up. He never sleeps. Just does his research. Did you know he taught at Yale?"

"What did he teach? Ancient history?" Devin snickered as his own joke.

"Seriously. He said he's taught different subjects at a ton of different schools too. Yale being only one of them. He's done it for years. I guess it's a lot easier these days with online classes and emails to your professor rather than appointments and stuff. I don't know, I was impressed."

"Doesn't take much."

"Think about it. How incredible would it be to be taught ancient civilizations from someone who actually lived it? No textbook required. He would teach from memory. Crazy, right?" She flipped the switch in the bathroom and peeled off the tank top and panties she slept in. "You would definitely get your money's worth that semester, I can tell you." She kept talking as she pulled out a heated towel from the rack and selected a scented soap that she thought appropriate in which to die. Sea salt soap with jasmine extracts – Martino's favorite.

Martino promised to be beside her until she died or until Margaret drank enough blood that her body could no longer survive. He'd been back for almost two weeks now and they had spent every moment together.

By the second week of searching for Martino, Deanna believed that she was going to exit this world for the final time alone. All her attempts to contact him had failed. She called him numerous times, texted him even though she knew he was not very tech savvy, and she emailed him. Her final attempt was the good old-fashioned standby of snail mail.

It was a lost art that she didn't realize how much she missed until she sat behind Jacenta's antique writing desk with a quill in hand. The delicate artistic letterhead reminded her of pinstriping on the classic cars that Max had always loved. The paper was just as delicate and very feminine.

All of her emotions overflowed onto the paper. There was something about the scratch of a quill tip against parchment that helped unlock feelings she had been hiding all these months. If Martino didn't get the letter or still refused to come to her, the letter would serve as a goodbye. She hoped it wouldn't come to that but still signed the final page attesting her undying love and eternal thanks for helping her find peace.

Devin had baulked at every form of communication but none so much as the letter. Perhaps it was her honesty and sincerity or perhaps he knew it was the one form of communication Martino would understand and respond to. He was right. Not more than a week passed before Martino was standing uncomfortably in the common room arguing with Gail about going along with this madness.

"You're here." Deanna's surprised voice ended any further arguments. "Apparently the US Postal Service is still good for something."

"I'm still against this . . ."

"I know."

"But I don't want you going through this alone."

Her arms couldn't hug him hard enough or tight enough. Martino laughed as Deanna attached herself to him. For the last two weeks, she avoided talking about the end or the spell whenever Martino was in the room. She found it easier to divert any conversation away from the subjects with kissing or making love.

Now somewhere in this goliath of a building, Martino was sleeping safely. Only nine more hours and he would be either holding her hand as she died or arguing her into eternity. She laughed as she pulled back the shower curtain. Jacenta had given instructions that Deanna's room was to be fully stocked with every human luxury, and the bathroom was by far no exception.

Full, plush heated towels, bath soaps, lotions, and gels. The candles were lit, standing on every surface. The building was maintained by a human staff during the day, and it was clear that they knew she was not staying in her own room. They had fully stocked Jacenta's bathroom instead. "Did you light these?" she asked Devin aloud.

"I thought you might enjoy the ambiance."

She did. The candle glow was beautiful as it shimmered off the polished surfaces.

"What are you doing?" She could feel Devin as he moved the water and soap over her body as she stood in the shower covered in lather. Deanna wondered if she would be able to do the same things Devin could do, or did his abilities develop over time? Would she still be able to touch Martino? Then the unpleasant thoughts of being dead and feeling trapped in a dimension that she could not escape overwhelmed her.

"Stop thinking of things you cannot control, Mouse. Your decision has been made, has it not?"

"Does it hurt?"

"To die? Yes, very much," he teased. *"Especially the way I did it."*

"No, to be trapped in infinity."

"Have I ever given you the impression that I was in pain?"

"No. Do you feel trapped? Do you feel like you're in a box you can't escape?"

"The world is a huge place. I am free to wander. I'm not tethered to you or Jacenta. I chose to stay with you because I love you. I love you both. And the world is a lonely place when you have no one to talk to. My only fear is that you won't be able to hear me. We won't have a blood connection through your spell."

"We're connected now. Why should my death change your curse?"

Devin was silent and then softly whispered. *"It was never a curse for me. I loved being with you every minute."*

Deanna closed her eyes and buried her face in the shower's spray to mask the tears streaming down her cheeks. The gentle massage of Devin's invisible fingers moved lather through her hair. The massaging pressure on her scalp relaxed her and brought to mind all the years Devin had supported and loved her only to be repaid in agitation and resentment.

"I'm sorry," she said as she wrapped a warm towel around her naked body. "I really am truly grateful that you were with me all these years. You helped me to cope with the changes and to accept that I had no alternative than to keep going. You've been my best friend."

Deanna sat on the edge of Jacenta's bed, holding Martino's hand tight enough that her knuckles were completely white. He either didn't mind her tense grip or didn't notice and used his free hand to stroke her back. She was trembling, but only slightly, and Deanna took some deep breaths to calm herself.

"I'm terrified," she said aloud to both Martino and Devin, who was pressing against her. She felt him in the pit of her stomach and even on the nape of her neck. His essence, as Margaret called it, blanketed her and for the first time in six centuries, she loved it.

"You don't need to go through with this . . ." Martino said.

"Madness, I know." She laughed. "I can do it."

As the words exited her mouth, the door to Jacenta's room opened and in walked Margaret. Deanna hadn't seen Margaret for more than a few minutes here or there in between her training. There was something different about her, something Deanna couldn't put her finger on.

Physically she was very much the same as she was the day they found her in that old house in Colorado. The difference was subtle, but when her eyes saw Devin's glow, that sense of wonder was no longer there. They followed him with humor and cunning.

"How would you like to proceed?" Her voice was completely changed. No more uncertainty or fear. It was self-assured and confident. Deanna's mouth hung open as she stared at Margaret.

Still, Deanna had no idea how to proceed. Gail was outside, somewhere, waiting to harness her soul. So, time was crucial. How do you direct a killing machine to aid in your murder/suicide?

She heard Devin chuckle at her thoughts and tried to ignore him. Martino sat calmly beside her, watching Margaret in what could only be described as awe. He, too, could not believe the transformation. Haven was a miracle factory.

"Shouldn't she just bite you?" Devin teased.

"Hush," Deanna said silently.

"This is going to be a very long process if she expects to drain your blood by osmosis." He laughed at his own joke.

"He's very bright. Devin, are you pleased with all of this?" Margaret looked slightly to the left of Deanna's head.

"He's cracking jokes," Deanna answered for him. "I don't know how to begin. I'm afraid it's going to hurt."

"Of course it will hurt. She's digging her saber tooth fangs into your flesh and then draining your blood through the torn flesh. It will probably be the worst pain you've ever experienced."

"Thanks," Deanna said aloud with unfettered sarcasm.

As she turned to Martino, he peeled her hand from his, and she noticed it was numb as her hand fell like lead into her lap. He took her face in his hands and kissed her.

"You're sure?" he asked.

She nodded and closed her eyes, waiting for another kiss. When it came, it was soft and warm. His lips glided against hers as their tongues teased each other playfully. Martino's hands wrapped her up in a safe cocoon that she never wanted to leave.

As his lips left hers and found her earlobe, she could feel the acceleration of his breathing. "I will love you forever," he whispered as she felt the pressure of his teeth pierce through the supple flesh of her neck. The pressure became pain as he withdrew his teeth and imbibed the sweet deliciousness of her warm blood.

Deanna cried out; her mouth tried to form words but couldn't. Instead she searched blindly for a light to draw her away from the pain. Martino's arms drew her close as he gave into the hunger. Deanna had seen him fight the hunger when he tasted her blood but now, he would surrender. He pulled away momentarily to look at her. In her drowsy, weakened state she saw not Martino but the animal he truly was, the vampire.

His eyes were glazed and savage. Blood stained his teeth and lips and his breathing was heavy and fierce. His hand reached up to close her eyes as she felt his teeth rip into her chest. Another cry built up in her body but only a watery gurgle escaped her lips as the blood flowed from her.

"Follow my voice, Mouse. Follow me away from the carnage. Away from the pain." Devin's voice was distant and low.

"Devin," she screamed. *"Devin, I can't hear you. Help me."*

A sensation of being lifted and a weightless flying. Deanna wanted to see what was happening. Hoping to see Martino one last time with her own eyes, but they would not open. All she saw around her was darkness. Blackness.

She wanted to scream but could neither find the voice nor the emotion to do so. The darkness was pressing down on her and she couldn't hear or see anything. Again, she called out for Devin, but he, too, had abandoned her. There was nothing. Blackness devoid of sound. Her only hope was that if this plan failed, she would not remember this nightmarish oblivion in her next life.

CHAPTER FORTY-FOUR

Gail sat in Gabriel's lab, counting the minutes. She was alone and she tried with all her psychic power to hear the moment that Deanna died. Any thoughts, any sounds, something. What good was this power that she possessed, and had possessed since she was a small child, if she couldn't wield it to her whim? A deep blustery frustrated exhale was the only sound in the empty room.

Before her stood four bowls. Carefully laid out and prepared, three contained blood and one contained water. Just as Deanna and Jacenta instructed. The blood – Jacenta's, Deanna's, and Gail's – sat still and dark as she stared at them.

The lab was stark white, exactly how she envisioned a laboratory to be, exactly how the movies always made them out to be. The whiteness of the room was only disturbed by the stainless-steel utensils and the blood. There were countless glass beakers and test tubes along with a multitude of other gadgets Gail couldn't name if she tried.

She sat on a cool stainless-steel stool before an enormous island countertop. Gabriel had cleaned off all of his experiments and research so she would have plenty of room. Gail knew the truth was he didn't want her accidentally messing up any of his developments.

"This could take hours. Why must you torture yourself like this?" Sabina burst into the room as if on a mission. "Come and sit with me. We'll talk of something other than this unpleasantness. Martino will come to you when it's time."

Gail liked Sabina. She was straightforward and honest, a no-nonsense kind of woman that she had always admired and wished she could emulate. But Sabina didn't know that Gail needed to be here. Needed to know the moment Deanna passed.

"Thank you but I should stay. Martino knows I am here."

"Yes, and when he finds that you are not, he will go searching for you. Your stress is not helping anyone. Most of all, you." She held out her hand and patiently waited for Gail to take it.

"I should be with her when she passes."

"You will be, but now is not the time." Sabina pulled the large heavy doors open easily. Gail noticed the *keep out* sign on the entry side of the door as she passed through it. Gabriel protecting his work again, she thought and smiled.

The hallway to the common room was aflutter with some kind of commotion. At least three young immortals, young being relative considering they weren't much more than a decade younger than Gail, approached Sabina in eager anticipation of some unknown event.

"Tomorrow starts the final examinations in their training," Sabina shared in a whisper. "I will take them somewhere unknown to them and they will be tested on their tracking and scouting methods and disciplines. They are over the moon with excitement, as you can see. I am too." She laughed easily and without reservation.

"But you've done this before? Chelsea, one of the others that currently lives with me, mentioned something."

"Chelsea." She whispered the name as if the name itself conjured up some wonderful memory. "So proud of that one. She was amazing. But you know her, so I need not tell you what she's like." She waved her hands as if wiping away her thoughts off a dry erase board.

Gail nodded, feeling like she didn't know Chelsea at all.

"I trained trackers for the Council during the Wars. She was one of my finest protégées." The sense of pride in Sabina's voice was evident.

"The Council. The Wars. Is there no one that is not somehow connected to those dreadful years?"

"If you lived through them without being affected, then you were fortunate. However, not many were that fortunate. I avoided most of the battles by training in remote regions. I didn't have the stomach to fight the Council nor the resilience to join the resistance. I played both sides if you will."

Gail laughed. "The resistance was more militia rather than real troops, wasn't it? I mean, they weren't organized."

"Now that's an interesting way of looking at it. Not as much as you'd think. They were seasoned warriors, most of them. Coming from human wars and bringing their know-how and ingenuity into our battles. Some were turned just for their experience in battle." Sabina stared at Gail for a few moments before opening the door to the common room. "You are too young to be pro-Council. Many of the members, that are still alive, have abandoned any belief in their cause. Where do you get your information?"

Gail bit her lip and frowned. "You don't want to know."

"Please, I'm curious."

"Jordan." It was a statement in the form of a question. Gail prepared herself for the worst but hadn't anticipated what Sabina burst out.

"*The* Jordan? The same Jordan that ran the Council with an iron fist? The same Jordan that, with that ruthless bitch Olivia at his side, murdered and imprisoned hundreds of innocent immortals? *That* Jordan?"

Gail found it hard to meet her eye when she finished her mini tirade. She had never spoken to Jordan regarding his part in the Wars but now was finding it increasingly difficult to protect him without knowing how he fit into the puzzle. Her instincts told her to apologize but for what? She hadn't done anything to be sorry for; she was too young to have any connection with the wars. The only guilt Gail had was befriending two of the top players on both sides: Jordan and Tabitha.

Sabina watched as Gail became increasingly anxious. "I'm sorry. You are not to blame for Jordan's crimes. You are merely an innocent bystander. Even though the battles are over and done, there is a small part of me that would love to see the brave warrior Tabitha face off with Jordan. Just once."

It was impossible to conceal the laughter that bubbled up in Gail's throat. Her lips trembled and her chest vibrated as she threw her hand over her mouth. "We need to talk. Not today. After all this has passed and we have a few hours together. We need to talk."

Sabina looked at her with a mixture of confusion, irritation, and humor.

The common room was empty when the two women finally entered together. The firepit was lit with no one around to enjoy it. Gail collapsed into a bean bag chair while Sabina sat on a nearby chair that was reminiscent of a large potato chip.

"She's in here." Sari's voice filled the room and she wasn't even in it yet. Shortly after her voice, her smiling face appeared in the doorway. Behind her was Eric, looking concerned and agitated but relieved to find Gail with Sabina.

"Any news yet?" He sat cross-legged in front of the fire.

Gail shook her head, dejected.

"Martino's going to do it, isn't he?" Sari picked up the pitcher of water on the counter and began absentmindedly watering the foliage around the room.

"What makes you say that?" Eric and Sabina said in unison.

She shrugged and pulled at the fern surrounding the waterfall wall. "Just the look on his face when he was peeling me off Deanna just before they went in. He was all, like, I'll take care of her and stuff. I don't know. Could have been my imagination but I'd put money on it that Margaret doesn't get to do any of the wet work."

"Lovely imagery you bring to the table." Sabina laughed. Her face dropped quickly, and she bit her lip, thinking. "I hope he does. Seems more fitting. I know she wanted Margaret, but it should be Martino. Right?"

Sari spoke up with a resounding, "Yup." Eric merely nodded almost begrudgingly and Gail, eyes flooding with tears, was beyond words. With the heel of her hand, she rubbed her eyes, wiping away the tears and most of the tiny bit of makeup she applied when she woke.

"He's exactly the kind of man I would have chosen for my daughter." Her words were thick with emotion. The tears poured from her eyes as she said, "I'm going to miss her so much."

Sari rushed to Gail, dropped into the beanbag chair, and wrapped her arms around her as Gail collapsed. A feeling of anxious anticipation leapt from one to the other as Gail tried to compose herself. They weren't quite sure what was happening, but the feeling was palpable.

"What's going on with the waterfall?" Sari lifted herself from the beanbag chair. The water sprayed instead of flowed and it periodically stopped altogether. Sari held her hand out, shielding herself from the pulsating spray. Behind her, the water pitcher bubbled as if it were a boiling kettle and the rapid movement of the water caused the pitcher to explode. Sari screamed and stepped aside just as it sprayed glass and water in her direction as if she predicted the explosion seconds before it occurred.

Gail was staring openmouthed at the events happening around her.

"It's done." Sabina looked to Gail.

She nodded, still enthralled by the startling exploding pitcher.

It took only moments before Margaret found them in the common room. She appeared calm but Gail could sense her trepidation. "Martino would like to see you in Jacenta's room. Just Gail," she said as Sari started to follow them out the door.

Gail rushed down the corridor toward the wing that solely belonged to Jacenta. Without knocking or pausing, she burst through the door to find Martino lying on the bed with Deanna in his arms. She lay on his lap with her arms extended in a somewhat seductive pose. Her eyes were closed and her mouth gaping as Martino's arms held her waist snugly. The forlorn expression on his face told Gail much more than she could read in his mind. The blood on his shirt continued the tale and the marks on Deanna's body brought it to a rousing conclusion.

"We must bring her to Gabriel's lab." She found herself curiously calm. Perhaps it was the need to save Deanna or Martino, she wasn't sure, but the maternal instincts were keeping her calm for now. She would cry later when she could fall into Jordan's arms and lose her mind for what she had done. "Bring her, Tino." He didn't move. Like a small child, he clutched Deanna's body like a rag doll.

With her patience wavering, Gail pulled on his sleeve and demanded that he move. He didn't.

"Martino, please." Margaret was standing behind Gail near the door. "We must finish this. For Deanna. Please."

His eyes, watery from crying, rolled toward Margaret. As he blinked, more tears slipped down his cheeks; he didn't bother to wipe them away. The corners of his mouth twitched as if he were about to cry or speak, but neither happened. He continued to sit and hold Deanna's lifeless body.

"Devin is searching for her. I can see it. His movements are crazy. I don't think he can find her." Margaret spoke to Gail. "She may be lost. We need to help her. Now. What if she's suffering?"

"Martino, carry her or I will. If Margaret is right, I will not wait any longer." The tough loving maternal side peeked its way into her voice and Margaret stepped back a bit. Gail walked to Martino, intent on taking Deanna's body from him.

"No," he said finally, "if she's suffering . . . I can't let that happen."

The lab was cold and sterile, just as she left it. Sabina, Eric, and Sari stood in the center of the room, waiting. Gail barely looked at them as she patted the countertop for Martino to deposit Deanna's body. The bowls of blood and water were just where she left them only one hour ago. She stared at them and nodded to herself. Mustering the courage to complete the spell, she took a few deep breaths and motioned for Sari to light the candles.

Three white candles stood on the countertop near the body. Sari's hand shook slightly as she quickly touched the match to each wick. When it was done, Gail motioned for Margaret's assistance without words.

Gail took two bowls and Margaret took one and they poured the blood into the water together. From her pocket, Gail pulled the slip of paper Deanna had written the spell that they were to recite. She looked to Margaret and when their eyes met, they spoke the words together.

"Sky above me, Earth below, Spirit hear my cry. I summon you from the other side. Come to me and cross the great divide. Stay with me until this spell does break. By the power of three this bond I make."

Nothing happened and a nervous chuckle erupted in Sari's chest that was quickly stifled with one glance from Gail.

"Is Devin here?" Gail asked Margaret. Her voice was barely above a whisper.

Margaret nodded. She lifted her hand to point, then thought better of it and lowered her hand again.

"Do you see anything else?"

Margaret moved her head slowly from side to side.

"It didn't work. I'm not a witch. I knew Jacenta needed to do this, not me." She dropped her head into her hands. "She's probably stuck somewhere until we wake Jacenta and then the cycle will start all over again."

"Not so fast." Sabina had been quietly watching the events unfold. "Deanna said that it didn't work at first, remember. Jacenta heard that cat the next day or later that day. It didn't happen instantaneously."

Gail nodded, not completely convinced that she hadn't just condemned Deanna to another unwanted lifetime of misery.

CHAPTER FORTY-FIVE

The pull was far greater than she imagined it would be. In fact, she hadn't really imagined it at all. The darkness was all around her and if true emotions were possible, Deanna would say she felt fear and depression most of all. For how long, she couldn't say. These things she used to call emotions were stuff of legend in the darkness.

She remembered having emotion but feeling and caring about anything was impossible the longer she stayed confined to this cell of ambiguity. Hope, if that was what it actually was, kept her sane. Hope that Gail would be able to finish the spell and she would be able to see as Devin did and speak to others as Devin did.

When it finally did happen, Deanna was quite unprepared for it. Floating, sitting, lying. She wasn't sure what she was doing but without a body, did it even matter? She had been existing in the darkness and then something strong and uncontrollable pulled her toward it.

There was no light. No vast eternity that she was heading for, just a pull and then she was there. In a stark bright room filled with steel tables and white cabinets. Then Martino came into view. Beautiful, dark-haired, sensitive, arduous Martino. He was standing beside her body.

My God, is that me? she thought.

Her body was lying on the hard countertop like the next patient for an autopsy. Or worse, the next victim of a sadistic serial killer waiting to dismember her body and bury her in the back yard. The thoughts made Deanna laugh. It was hardy and felt good to do it out loud.

She could see Gail and Sari. They were wondering if anything happened. If it worked. The spell had worked, and Deanna ached to let them know that it had worked beautifully.

She was here.

Devin could move things, she thought. Wait, Devin. Where was Devin?

"Right with you, Mouse." His voice was breathy and not at all what she heard in her head as Deanna Belamy or anyone else for that matter. "Welcome back into this world."

"How do I let them know that I'm here?" She was anxious and impatient. "Shouldn't Gail hear me?"

"In time, a relatively short time, she will. Keep working on it and she will hear you." Again, the timber of his voice startled her. There was an echo to it like they were in a long empty room and were speaking to each other from opposite ends.

"Look at me. I'm dead. Martino did it, didn't he? He looks miserable, poor dear. I need to tell him I'm here."

"Be patient and you will be able to move something and touch him slightly. If we had the time, I could teach you to possess someone." The echo voice laughed, and Deanna realized she didn't like it. Not one bit.

"Why would I want to be human again? I just stopped doing that. I've been doing that for too many years. I'm ready for a new adventure." The emotions she was experiencing, now desire, were strong, stronger than she had ever felt. The need to do anything and everything that was before her was voracious.

Deanna moved around the room. So white and sterile in this room, not at all appealing. She moved toward the steel utensils on the back counter. The energy she had become was unable to move them. She swiped at the scalpels, hoping they would fly with the slightest touch. Nothing.

"Bring her body to the morgue, Martino. We will bury her when Jacenta wakes." Gail sounded defeated. Her voice was soft and monotone. "If anyone hears or sees anything unusual, I want to know about it the moment it happens."

Nods from those around her. Sari kept looking into the air as if Deanna would materialize any second, but the disappointment in her eyes said she didn't expect it to really happen. Like looking for Bigfoot, you want to see him but until he materializes, you have no real expectations about it.

Sabina wrapped her strong arm around Gail's back and rubbed it gently for comfort. She whispered a few words of encouragement that Deanna didn't hear but appreciated just the same. Margaret and Martino gently wrapped Deanna's dead body in a sheet that had been left for this exact purpose. (Gabriel thought of everything, Deanna laughed).

Swaddled in a white sheet, the body looked like a mummy, causing Deanna to start laughing again. Margaret looked to the exact spot Deanna was hovering as if something caught her eye and disappeared. Her brows met as she searched the room.

"Did you see something?" Martino's words jumped at her.

She shook her head. "Just Devin. He's been here the whole time. I think he'll let us know when she arrives."

"Only time will tell." He gently lifted the wrapped body and carried it from the room.

As Margaret held the door open for him, she looked back to whatever it was that she had seen. Her eyes fell on what Deanna could only guess was Devin's glow and stared at it for a minute. "Don't be shy, Devin. If she's there, please, tell us." And she left the room.

"*I think she saw you, Mouse.*"

"*Why haven't you told them about me?*"

"*They can't hear me, remember?*"

"*There are other ways and you know it.*"

"*I just want you to myself for a while. They can have you when they can hear you for themselves. Until then, you are all mine.*"

CHAPTER FORTY-SIX

The enslavement spell was successful. As Jacenta opened her eyes after a month of sleeping wrapped in Gabriel's arms, she heard laughter. It was muffled and distant but completely within her own mind. She listened, this time intently, but no matter how hard she tried, the sounds were not getting any louder.

Looking around the room, the first thing she noticed was that Gabriel was gone. If he had slept at all, he had awoken and risen days before her. He laid out a fresh set of clothes for her along with brushes and towels if she'd like to bathe before starting back into the world. From where she lay, Jacenta could see the bathtub had been filled and waiting for her.

She yawned and stretched fully as she pushed back the covers of Gabriel's bed. The monitors were gone, as were the electrode sensors that had been taped to her chest and head. Jacenta rubbed her chest where the sticky tape had left a minute bit of residue on her skin. She remembered movement around her, but she thought it was part of a dream. The wonderful hibernation dream that took her back to Ireland where she was a young girl. Again, she heard the laughter followed this time by conversation. It was like listening through a door or a window. She could make out some words but not all.

The bath was heavenly as she sank deep into the bubbles and hot water. She closed her eyes, enjoying the water flowing around her skin. A few air bubbles tickled her back and travelled up her legs and chest; she giggled, making no sound. The bubbles continued, speeding up like the tub had jets. It didn't and she knew it. Fascinated and amused by the bubbles, she was thrilled that Deanna's first communication was fun and playful.

"Good morning, sunshine." Gabriel entered carrying a medicine bag. His voice was muffled as well but not as much as the ones in her head. Jacenta smiled and waved as she pulled on a robe, indicating with fingers to her throat that she still could not speak. She shrugged and pulled him close for a kiss.

Again, with her hands, she motioned for him to tell her all that he knew and what was going on while she slept. With both hands, she opened and closed them like an infant who was waving goodbye. He touched her hands and kissed her again.

"It's been a month and Deanna is dead." He motioned for Jacenta to sit beside him as he pulled a pen light from his bag and checked her eyes as he spoke. "Gail did splendidly with the spell. They've all indicated that Deanna has contacted them."

She tapped on her chest and mouthed the words "me too," almost too excited to stay seated. Gabriel held her down so he could check other vitals that may have been affected during the hibernation cycle. Her brows met and she drew a question mark in the air, asking how others had been contacted.

"Knocking things over, tingling their skin – mostly knocking things over." He laughed as a picture frame toppled to the floor. "See?"

Jacenta's eyes darted to the fallen frame and the confused expression returned to her face. With her index finger, she tapped her ear three times.

"Last stage of the hibernation cycle. Speech and auditory functions are the last to return. You'll hear her soon enough. Gail has heard her. She cries every time." He rolled his eyes. "Every time."

Jacenta laughed without sound.

"Here, this should help speed up the process." He pulled the bullet-shaped thermos from his bag. "It's human. So, don't get your hopes up. Still, it should help get your strength up."

It took almost a full day for Jacenta's speech and hearing to return. Her first words were ironically, "Shut up, Devin." The sound of Deanna's voice in her head was both enchanting and unnerving. Jacenta had expected that her internal voice would have an Irish accent, but sadly it didn't.

Gabriel was correct. Gail did cry anytime Deanna spoke. It was becoming comical. Even though she heard only half the conversation, sans Devin, it drove her to tears regularly.

Alone – but not really – sitting in her room, Jacenta spoke to the empty space. "Can you see each other?"

"What is there to see?" Deanna's voice chuckled in Jacenta's head. *"I'm just happy that wretched darkness is history."*

"Wretched darkness?"

"After I died the holding cell I was trapped in because you were sleeping was a black hole of nothingness."

"Oh, I'm sorry. Nothing at all?"

"No sound, no light, nothing. I was trapped. Devin wasn't even in there with me. It was the definition of scary. Had I remembered it from the last time, I don't think I would have done it again. Now that's a curse. This, not so much."

"How long were you in there?"

"No clocks in there either." She laughed.

Jacenta fell back on her pillows. As she sank into the mountain of mush, her renewed sense of smell picked up hints of Deanna's perfume. "Have you been sleeping in my bed?"

"A lot more than sleeping."

"Aah! Now I have to burn the sheets," Jacenta teased but took one more whiff before rolling off the side of the bed.

It took only days to formulate a plan as to how they were going to proceed with the final spell. The items needed were cataloged by Gabriel. The blood was most important. What was left of Deanna, Jacenta, and Gail's blood from the entrapment spell had been saved and kept in the cooler with the various stores Gabriel experimented with.

The vial of blood Deanna had obtained from Margaret's house was dried. With Gabriel's help, they scraped as much of the blood out of the vial and sealed it in a container until they were ready to use it.

Saying goodbye was always hard. Saying goodbye after six hundred years, Jacenta found, was nearly impossible. Standing in her room alone, she felt for Devin and Deanna. She didn't want to speak to them, not yet. She wanted to feel them. The tickle on her skin, the breath through her hair, the spike in her emotions.

There was every annoying action that Devin had done to her, every nerve that he got on, every straw that was her last: it all came back in a flood of emotion. She hated him. She loved him. She was jealous of his feelings for Deanna even after his death; especially after his death. Deanna became his entire world. In her effort to keep him at arm's length, she made him more dependent than ever on her for love, friendship, and attention.

Now as she stood on the precipice of the end, she wasn't sure she could live without him. The voice in her head was part of who she was; it was part of every memory she had forged. Starting Haven had come from Devin. Not that he ever knew it, nor was she willing to give him any credit for all her hard work, but he was the first one to suggest helping those hurting from the Wars.

He made her laugh when she wanted to cry. He gave her courage to keep going when she wanted to die. That deep, loving, often irritating, and always uninvited voice that was making her smile now even when she didn't hear it.

And Deanna. She didn't allow her to say goodbye when they were flesh, but now that she was spirit, she had to hear it. And Jacenta had to say it. Goodbye.

"Are all these depressing thoughts really helping you?" Deanna's voice was harsh and sarcastic with an underlying warmth that made Jacenta smile.

"You really are making this easier and easier." She laughed. "Can't we have one moment where you are not demeaning me?"

Deanna laughed.

"Ladies, if these are to be our last moments alone, shouldn't they be filled with our adoration for one another and not our regrets or misgivings?" Devin always trying to be the peacekeeper. If he didn't start the trouble, he usually didn't want any part of it.

"I'm going to miss you, Devin," Jacenta said. It was quick as if she had to spit it out before she could rethink it or before he said something to ruin the thought altogether. "Listen, I'm going to just say what's on my mind and then we'll be done. Are we okay with that?"

Both answered yes and remained quiet for the duration of Jacenta's dialogue.

"I love you both, always have, always will. Yes, I cursed you. And I should take this time to say I'm sorry . . . but I'm not. I loved that you were always here, Devin. I wish you would have been a little more respectful of my relationships and my wishes, but by and large, I wouldn't have changed a thing. You gave me four beautiful children. You made me a wife and you made me who I am. So, thank you." She took a deep breath and continued slowly.

"Deanna, you are my sister and I love you. Thank you for being my friend all those years ago and for a brief time now. Thank you for teaching me that no one is perfect no matter how much you love them. When you go, you will take half my soul and all of my heart."

When she stopped speaking, there was no noise in the room. Not one sound and Jacenta thought for a brief time that she was alone, speaking to the walls.

Deanna was the first to break the silence. *"I'm sorry for hating you for so many years. I blamed you for everything. Anything Devin did, anything that went wrong in whatever life I was living, I blamed you. You didn't deserve that. I know that now. I knew that then but couldn't admit it. Thank you for giving me a second chance to be your sister. I know I didn't deserve it."*

The tears saturated Jacenta's face as she listened to the words in her head. She closed her eyes and could see Deanna from the past speaking to her in her small living room in Ireland. That's the Deanna she wished to remember. The unblemished, beautiful friend from long ago.

She walked toward the door of her room, trying to control her emotions before Gabriel caught sight of her and tried to give her a shot to calm her down. The others were gathered in the lab waiting for her to say her goodbyes to Deanna and Devin.

Gail had been in tears for the last few hours after she had her last moments with Deanna. Sari was a bit more composed, but tears were also shed when she also shared a private moment alone with Deanna (with Gail as a translator). Jacenta was sure her goodbyes would not go in that direction, but she was wrong.

Everyone was there when she opened the door to the lab. Martino, Sari, Gabriel, and Gail.

Sabina had gone off with her scouts and would return in a few weeks.

Margaret was done. She did not wish to be part of the rest of the spell, and Jacenta was okay with that.

She saw the bowls of blood and the water just as she had instructed. Just as they had been six centuries ago. Although the room was not as blindingly white, she could picture two naïve young girls playing around with forces they had no idea about and no control over.

The faces around her were stoic and unreadable. Brave faces, her mother would have called them. *Put on a brave face, Jacenta,* her mother always told her.

She wondered if her face was brave as she stared back at them. Seeing Gabriel standing toward the back of the room, she wanted to fall into his arms and cry her heart out but knew that would happen later. And from the look on his face, she knew he could feel her pain and probably read it all over her face.

Gail stepped up to the table and rested her pale hands on the cold, steel table. Sari took her place on one end of the table to the left of Gail. Martino took a step back behind the harsh lights and watched the proceedings beside Gabriel.

"We will each take a bowl and pour it into the water. All three of us will say the words. Three times. After the spell is completed, you must place the empty bowls around the water. Guardians of the East, West, North, and South. I'll say their names and complete the circle in blood. Closing the circle should break the spell and release them. I hope. With no bodies or personal items, I hope this works. Any questions before we begin?"

Gail shook her head, no. It was quick and she did it without making eye contact.

"Goodbye, D. I love you," Sari whispered. The water bubbled in the bowl, making it overflow a bit, and Sari trembled slightly.

"Okay, take the bowls and begin." As Jacenta took the bowl of Devin's blood in her hand, she felt him tickle the skin behind her ear, and she closed her eyes.

"Perhaps this won't be goodbye, my love. Perhaps we shall exist beyond this realm."

"Perhaps. If there is such an existence beyond us, don't spend your time pining for what you had. Spend it experiencing new adventures, and if you see our children, give them my love." She opened her eyes and nodded for Gail and Sari to pour.

"Sky above me, Earth below, Spirit hear my cry. A spell was cast, now make it past. You are free. The spell is done, by the power of three, so mote it be."

After the words were spoken three times and the blood combined, Jacenta dipped her finger in the bowl of water mixed with all four of their blood. She made a cross in the center of the table like a large plus sign and Gail placed the water bowl in the center. Around the cross she drew a large circle and at each end of the cross a bowl was placed as Jacenta called on each of the guardians of the East, West, North, and South.

"Deanna and Devin, you are free. May your souls wander no more."

CHAPTER FORTY-SEVEN

The cabin was quiet. The sound of the crickets chirping and the frogs by the lake singing their songs were all Martino could hear. The loneliness he felt was heavy, but for now that was how he preferred to be. Living alone, remembering Deanna in his own way, and learning to exist without the care or supervision of others.

If allowed to, Gail would have stayed with him and taken care of him like a child. That was no good for him or for her and thankfully Jordan saw it too. He took Gail on their travels that they had planned. First Spain, and since Haven was on the agenda, Jacenta and Gabriel tagged along as well.

After discovering that Thecia was in Spain, Jacenta found it imperative that she visit and assess the changes that Haven was undergoing there. Gabriel was going as a referee; someone needed to stop them before they killed each other, he joked before they left.

He shuffled around the cabin, enjoying the solitude. Winter had fallen all around him and the beauty that lay just outside his window was exquisite. A heavy snowfall had been laid during the time he slept, and waking up to the moonlight twinkling off the snow hurt his heart somehow. He remembered Deanna with such vivid detail that he could have sworn she was coming up the drive in her little rented Prius covered from head to toe in a marshmallow white coat and not buried up on the hill beside the other gravestones.

By Gail's insistence, they brought Deanna's body back to Mount Orion. A few words, more tears, and she was laid to rest on her own land. She would have liked it that way. Elizabeth would have liked it that way. Martino peered out the window every now and again, just to see the shadow of the stone looking down on him. In his fantasies, he saw her standing beside the stone looking down at him. She was dressed in a long flowing gown that caught the wind. Her hair blew behind her as she raised her hands, beckoning him to come to her. His rational mind told him it was not real, but his broken heart urged him to run into her waiting arms.

It was only five months since they left Connecticut. Margaret was blossoming in that environment. Martino had been back twice since, just to check on her. *Don't leave her behind*, Deanna had asked of him in their final moments alone together. Those moments that he preferred to leave forgotten. But it proved impossible. He could picture the wave in her hair as she tilted her head to kiss him for the final time. The feel of her skin as she held his hand while he professed his love. The smell of her body as she pressed against him as she lay dying. It was all too vivid in his memory.

Following the spell, Jacenta locked herself away for a week. She didn't wish to see or speak to anyone – not even Gabriel. And after she emerged it was Gail's lead she followed. They prepared the body to be transported back to Mount Orion for burial and then everyone was free to go their separate ways.

Back at Mount Orion, Bith had gone on her own journey to find Aaron. She had recruited Richard and Phillipe to go along. Chelsea waited until Sari returned and they were off to California as planned over two months ago. Eric went along begrudgingly, making plans to meet up with Sabina in Hawaii in the spring.

Trevor came and went – bringing Thor and Attila with him each visit. He was watching them to be kind, he said, but Martino knew that Trevor had become quite attached to the dogs and was more than willing to care for them while Richard followed Bith on her foolish quest to find the impossible.

Sitting at Jordan's desk, in the study that was forbidden except now that he was alone and no one could stop him, Martino stared at two letters in his hands. The first, in a stark white envelope with a *forever* stamp of hearts in the top right corner, was addressed to Blair and Robert Belamy at 245 Elmwood Avenue, Torry, NJ.

It wasn't sealed when Deanna gave it to him, making him promise to mail it after everything was over and done.

"What does it say?" he had asked.

"Everything. Whether they believe me or not, it doesn't matter, but I think they deserve to know the truth about their daughter. Hey, it's too late to put me in the looney bin. Can't hurt now." She laughed sadly like she regretted having been a part of their lives. "Promise me you'll mail it."

He did.

The second was in a pink envelope and stamped with a Disney *forever* stamp. It was addressed to Robert and Margaret Belamy, 52 Howe Avenue, Apt 2A, Torry, NJ. It was larger and felt like a card.

"Baby brother got married without me." There were tears in her eyes as she handed him the second letter. "That one just tells him I love him and wish him and Maggie all the best. Sari said she was pregnant. I don't know how she knows, but whatever. I miss my brother, a lot. I've never been a twin before – this was a good life."

This was a good life, Martino thought. Did she mean this life as Deanna Belamy or the six centuries of lifetimes that added up to her whole life? She never said but he was glad to be a brief part of two of her lives.

With the letters in hand, he walked outside using the basement door. The air was cool on his face and he pulled his jacket close to his body just for comfort. The sky was clear and filled with stars; no more snow for a while. The tombstone stood on the top of the hill covered in snow. He walked the distance easily even in the deep snow with only sneakers on his feet.

"Going to mail your letters like I promised," he said.

Eight stones filled the small enclosure under the large tree near the abandoned cottage. Just to the left of Deanna, Elizabeth had been laid to rest years earlier. The weeds were cleared from each of the seven graves when Deanna's hole was dug. Gail cleaned the area and placed fresh flowers on each grave. Martino picked up the frozen, snow-covered dead bouquets from the ground. He tossed them into the brush down the hill. He would put fresh flowers in their place when he returned. Maybe even a grave blanket for Deanna's plot.

She would like that as well. A wreath intertwined with Christmas foliage and ribbons. It would make her happy – wherever she was.

He looked up to the abandoned cottage. The feeling that he wasn't alone was strong. The stone front was frosted with snow like a holiday gingerbread house, but the uncut grass surrounding the porch gave it an air of the witch's house in Hansel and Gretel. He walked up the front steps and paused. His imagination was running wild, especially now that he had spent so many weeks alone. He could have sworn he saw movement in the frosted windows around the front door.

Maybe a candle flicker or a flashlight's glow, some light was extinguished as soon as his foot touched the porch steps.

"Hello?" He sounded unsure of himself. Being alone had filled his head with fanciful ideas and frankly, he was scared most of the time. He forced himself to knock on the heavy deeply carved door. "Is anyone there?"

There was no answer, but he still had the feeling of not being alone. He listened for noises. Creaking in the floorboards, rustling of papers, shuffling of feet on the hardwood floors. There was nothing. His imagination had created someone that was not real to deal with his loneliness and guilt.

As he turned away from the door, something caught his eye running behind the cottage. He ran to follow it, but it was gone. There were no tracks coming to or from the house in the snow. His imagination again? Could his imagination conjure up the blonde hair that he saw flying as whatever it was ran from him?

Could Nadia be awake?

In the distance he heard a dog barking and knew Trevor had returned. Martino felt the uneasiness melt away. He was thankful for some company. He looked down at the two letters he promised he would mail. His final promise. He had to keep it. Nadia could wait. He needed to fulfill his last promise to Deanna and then maybe he could move on. He looked again in the direction that she had run.

Town first, mail the letters, get fresh flowers, and then find Nadia.

A soft laughter seemed to accompany his last thought. The trees seemed to sway with it. A melodious yet contemptuous laughter that he knew meant she had read his thoughts.

"Wait here for me, Nadia. I will be right back."

The laughter followed him down the hill to his car. As he turned the key, he looked back to the cottage on the hill and saw the shadow of a girl staring down at him. Just like in his fantasies of Deanna, she stood, hair flowing in the wind, and she raised her hand to him. She wasn't beckoning him with her hand; maybe it was a greeting? He didn't know. It didn't matter. Nothing mattered until he mailed his last connection to Deanna.

He paused for only a moment longer and then put the car in drive and turned toward the road. The shadow on the hill remained as he passed the lake and pulled out on the road. And then it was gone.

ACKNOWLEDGMENTS

The adventure of writing this book has been the most exciting and stressful time of my life. There have been many ups and downs, many excuses I've created to avoid getting it into your hands. But it's out there now, in your hands, being read with your eyes. I want to thank you, dear reader, for giving me this chance. Whether you love it or hate it, I am excited that someone else got to know Deanna and Gail and everyone else in my Mount Orion universe.

Special thanks goes out to my husband, Randy and my daughter, Gail. I love you. Thank you for putting up with me hidden away in my fortress of solitude for hours on end, always yelling if someone disturbed me.

Thank you, Mom, Dad and Vincent. Even when you hadn't yet read the stories I created, you knew I could do it and your encouragement has meant everything to me.

Made in the USA
Middletown, DE
09 August 2021